The Best American Mystery Stories 2009

GUEST EDITORS OF
THE BEST AMERICAN MYSTERY STORIES

The Best American Mystery Stories™ 2009

Edited and with an Introduction
by **Jeffery Deaver**

Otto Penzler, *Series Editor*

A MARINER ORIGINAL
HOUGHTON MIFFLIN HARCOURT
BOSTON · NEW YORK   2009

www.hmhbooks.com

ISSN 1094-8384

ISBN 978-0-547-23750-3

Printed in the United States of America

DOC 10 9 8 7 6 5 4 3 2 1

Contents

Foreword

AS I SIT DOWN to write this, it is the early part of 2009, and Alvin Toffler's 1970 bestseller, *Future Shock,* comes to mind. This preternaturally prescient book accurately reflected the fact that we were being bombarded by information at an increasingly accelerating rate, with the result that we would be less and less able to absorb it all. In short, as we were provided with ever greater amounts of data, we would understand less of it, leaving us confused and exhausted.

We have all become inured to watching news shows on television, hoping to understand the arcana of the so-called stimulus package, say, or the ramifications of an election in some country in the Mideast, while a crawl at the bottom of the screen reports on an entirely different story. Add to the same screen a flashing "breaking news" banner, the latest stock market numbers, and the network logo, and we have passed information saturation and progressed to overload.

Along with more information, I'd like to note, there are more *things* with which to deal. The world changes so quickly, and so dramatically, that it is impossible for some of us to cope. Telephones became cell phones, which became cameras capable of taking snapshots, which became movie cameras, and, for all I know, will soon become television sets (if they haven't already; I don't keep up). This weighs on my mind as I am aware of the recent invention and virtually overnight success of things like the Sony Reader and the Kindle. If you are a Luddite like me, you may not know that these are little plastic boxes on which books may now be read. They can hold (I'm told) as many as twenty books at a time. They are about the size and weight of a single book, which means you can carry what was once a suitcase full of books and have it weigh a pound or two. Many people see them as a spectacular advancement in the disbursement of literature. I see them as the further diminishment of civilization, as well as another nail in the coffin of bookshops.

Pretty much all elements of the book world are suffering. Publishers have merged and eliminated some imprints, resulting in serious staff reductions. Nearly two thirds of independent book stores in America have closed their doors in the past two decades. As young people have gravitated to the mind-numbing joys of video games (an entertainment industry whose annual revenue has surpassed that of motion pictures), they have forgone the mind-expanding joys of the written word, resulting in the shrinkage of book sales. With fewer books being sold, authors necessarily suffer, too.

A well-stocked library, whether a single bookcase or a whole room, lovingly filled with favorite books, was once regarded as de rigueur for an educated and cultured person. Those same shelves are now increasingly filled, I guess, with boxes of *X-Men* or *Grand Theft Auto,* and maybe a Kindle, just as record collections morphed into rows of CDs and, now, an iPod — another little plastic device, this one with earplugs.

Admittedly, these are the lamentations of what used to be called an old fogy. A life that has been largely devoted to the wonderful world of books appears to be in jeopardy, which fills me with sadness and fear. I think the world is a better place with books, lots of them, and I worry for a country that appears to value them less each year.

Perhaps this would be a good time to leave Pity City and note that *you* are not the problem. You have had the good sense and impeccable taste, for example, to pick up this book, the thirteenth in the series, for which you should be applauded (and thanked). As seems to me to be true on an annual basis, this is a superb collection of original fiction about extremes of human behavior caused by despair, hate, greed, fear, envy, insanity, or love — sometimes in combination. Desperate people may be prone to desperate acts, a fertile ground for poor choices. Many of the authors in this cornucopia of crime have described how aberrant solutions to difficult situations may occur and why perpetrators felt that their violent responses to conflicts seemed appropriate to them. The psychology of crime has become the dominant form of mystery fiction in recent years, while the classic tale of observation and deduction has faded further into the background. Those tales of pure deduction may be the most difficult mystery stories to write, as it has become increasingly difficult to find original motivations for murder, or a new murder method, or an original way to hide a vital clue until the detective unearths it. The working definition of a mystery story for this series is any work of fiction in which a crime, or the threat of a crime, is central to the theme or the plot. The detective story is merely one subgenre in the literary form known as the mystery, just as are romantic suspense, espionage, legal legerdemain, medical thriller, political duplicity, and those told from the point of view of the villain.

To find the best of these stories is a year-long quest, largely enabled by my invaluable colleague, Michele Slung, who culls the mystery magazines, both printed and electronic, for suitable stories, just as she does short story collections (works by a single author) and anthologies (works by a variety of authors), popular magazines, and, perhaps the richest trove to be mined, literary journals. As the fastest and smartest reader I have ever known, she looks at about three thousand stories a year, largely to determine if they are mysteries (you can't tell a story by its title) and then to determine if they are worth serious consideration. I then read the harvested crop, passing along the best fifty (or at least those I liked best) to the guest editor, who selects the twenty that are then reprinted, with the other thirty being listed in an honor roll as "Other Distinguished Mystery Stories."

The guest editor this year is the outstanding author of the Lincoln Rhyme series, among much else, Jeffery Deaver. His nearly two dozen novels have been translated into twenty-five languages, and he has proven to be a master of the short story as well. He has been nominated for six Edgar Awards and three times won the Ellery Queen Mystery Magazine Reader's Choice Award for the best short story of the year. The first Rhyme novel, *The Bone Collector,* was filmed in 1999, starring Denzel Washington and Angelina Jolie.

This is an appropriate time (well, yes, it's *always* an appropriate time) to thank the previous guest editors, who have done so much to make this prestigious series such a resounding success: Robert B. Parker, Sue Grafton, Ed McBain, Donald E. Westlake, Lawrence Block, James Ellroy, Michael Connelly, Nelson DeMille, Joyce Carol Oates, Scott Turow, Carl Hiaasen, and George Pelecanos.

While I engage in a relentless quest to locate and read every mystery/crime/suspense story published, I live in terror that I will miss a worthy story, so if you are an author, editor, or publisher, or care about one, please feel free to send a book, magazine, or tear sheet to me c/o The Mysterious Bookshop, 58 Warren Street, New York, NY 10007. If it first appeared electronically, you must submit a hard copy. It is vital to include the author's contact information. No unpublished material will be considered, for what should be obvious reasons. No material will be returned. If you distrust the postal service, enclose a self-addressed, stamped post card.

To be eligible, a story must have been written by an American or Canadian and first published in an American or Canadian publication in the calendar year 2009. The earlier in the year I receive the story, the more fondly I regard it. For reasons known only to the nitwits who wait until Christmas week to submit a story published the previous spring, holding eligible stories for months before submitting them occurs every year, causing much gnashing of teeth while I read a stack of stories as my wife and friends are trimming the Christmas tree or otherwise celebrating the holiday season. It had better be a damned good story if you do this. Because of the very tight production schedule for this book, the absolute firm deadline is December 31. If the story arrives one day later, it will not be read. Sorry.

O. P.

Introduction

QUIT YER WHINING.

Sorry. I'm not speaking to you. Only to myself.

I just realized I was about to give the obligatory gripe required by the Anthology Introducers Union: do you know how difficult it was to pick these few tales from the final shortlist, which had in turn represented an excruciating culling from the slightly less short list, which in turn . . . well, you get the idea.

But then I had to put myself in time-out, as reality struck: what a wonderful thing this agony is.

The fact that the task of selecting twenty stories from a sea of submissions was so hard means that there are hundreds of talented writers producing superb short fiction nowadays and that the genre is thriving as never before, even if, as of this writing, the rest of the world is in meltdown. (Attention, future readers who aren't familiar with the economy and politics of 2009: if computers and electricity still exist, please Google "auto industry," "Wall Street," "banking," "Fanny Mae," "subprime," "chaos," "war," "disaster.")

In considering how I might introduce this anthology, I decided I'd play professor and gin together some scholarly remarks, perhaps on the history of the short story (it goes back a couple of hundred years but, I concluded, who cares?). Or I'd compile a list of thematic or stylistic characteristics unique to the form. Sadly, there's not much meat for a doctoral thesis there either. I came up only with this: the one thing short stories have in common is that they're . . . short.

Edgar Allan Poe, in his essay "The Philosophy of Composition," said that one should be able to read any piece of literature in one sitting. Now, as somebody who makes his living writing novels that average 130,000 words, I'm thankful that not everyone agrees with the bard from Baltimore. But as someone who also gets a huge kick out of reading and writing short fiction, I agree completely with what he's getting at: the intensity of emotional experience when reading a good short story can transcend the payoff from the more leisurely involvement with a novel.

Once we've agreed on this rather obvious requirement regarding word count, anything goes. As you'll see from the works represented in this astonishingly diverse collection, short stories can be about any subject, incorporate any structure, take any point of view, fall into any literary genre, use any grammatical or syntactical form (even paragraphs are optional; see Joyce Carol Oates's contribution herein).

Which is not to say that common themes didn't emerge. I found that the selections, while they align in many different ways, seemed to coagulate into certain categories naturally, and using these as a framework, I'd like to give you a preview of what's to come.

Police work has always been a popular theme for short fiction. One of the more interesting cop stories I've read in a while is "Rust," by N. J. Ayres. Since we could also put this in the "surprise, surprise" category below, I want to avoid tipping the author's hand and will say no more other than note the skill with which Ayres manages to keep us wholly involved with what is both a compelling crime story and a sharp take on the psychology of those who ply the very difficult job of being a law enforcer.

Police procedurals represent a challenge for those working in the short story form, since the author must present a lot of details — investigation, evidence, witnesses — in a limited number of pages while keeping the momentum of the story going. Alafair Burke's "Winning," both clever and moving, is a variation on this classic genre, what I've dubbed a reverse procedural. In the last few pages you'll realize what I mean.

Many of these stories could be placed in the noir category. But I'm taking the liberty of singling out two that feature a traditional noir scenario: the working-class Joe who runs into trouble.

What would any crime anthology be without a sexy dame and a guy who falls hard for her? Filling his story with dialogue that pops like a Sig Sauer 9mm and with characters witty and wry, Rob Kantner has delivered a real treat with "Down Home Blues," a story that, notably nowadays, revolves around residential real estate (Googled "subprime" yet?).

Jonathan Tel's "Bola de la Fortuna" unfolds not through a rigorously outlined plot but rather in a series of set pieces that take place over a period of time, revealing more and more about our character, a truck driver who becomes a poster boy for being in the wrong place at the wrong time. The subtlety of the story's flow and the insights into the people who populate Tel's world give it a literary aura. I was not surprised it was originally published in *The Yale Review*, one of the oldest literary journals in America.

I've selected several romans à clef for the anthology — stories that might be subtitled "inspired by true events."

Prolific Joyce Carol Oates brings to mind the anecdote about Alfred Hitchcock's phone call to the French writer Georges Simenon, who penned hundreds of mysteries in his lifetime. His wife answered the phone and told Hitchcock that her husband was unavailable; he'd just started work on a new book. Hitchcock replied, "That's all right, madame. I'll stay on hold until he's finished." Oates's chilling story in this volume, "Dear Husband," takes the form of a lengthy letter, which echoes a recent real crime in Houston, familiar to most readers. Her wrenching insights into the mind of the tormented perpetrator transcend even the best factual crime reporting. There are no twists here; the horrific outcome is well known early on. But I guarantee you will race through her story breathlessly, watching your views of right and wrong, blame and sympathy, flipping like the head and tail of a coin tossed into the air.

A very different take on fiction springing from truth is Kristine Kathryn Rusch's "G-Men." If you liked E. L. Doctorow's *Ragtime* or the writing of Caleb Carr (*The Alienist*), you'll enjoy this tale, one of our two period pieces. Part procedural, part political thriller, this clever tale features real-life characters — among them, J. Edgar Hoover and Attorney General Robert Kennedy — interacting with fictional ones. My only hope is that after government agencies note that the story appeared in an anthology I edited, I won't be spirited off to a secret prison somewhere. (I'm taking a moment to Google "extraordinary rendition" and "waterboarding.")

Let's get to the question, is it art or is it entertainment? A valid inquiry, but most who ask it do so by way of casting a value judgment — which I find decidedly *invalid,* if not intellectually lame. Answer this: which is better — tournedos stuffed with mousse and topped with demi-glace or a bowl of Special K topped with bananas? Neither, of course. Each is appropriate for the particular meal the diner desires.

So it is with writing. My point is that some of these stories, though dealing with crime, lean toward art more than entertainment, by which I mean simply that the writer's goal is not to amuse or divert but to rearrange perceptions, make readers think, make them question.

One of these stories, which would seem not to have literary aspirations, is Tom Bissell's "My Interview with the Avenger," in which a journalist has a secretive meeting with a superhero. Don't look for exploding cars, laser beams, or the leaping of tall buildings; expect rather to keep mulling over the questions Bissell raises — about heroism, the media, apathy, and responsibility — long after you've finished the story.

Alice Munro, the Canadian writer famous for her short stories, has been called our era's Chekhov because of her nuanced studies of human relationships. While she is not generally known for elaborate plotting, her story here, "Free Radicals," which first appeared in *The New Yorker,* is a bit of a departure. Meditations on love, marriage, and widowhood are shattered by the intrusion of a killer, who forces his way into our protagonist's life. The ensuing encounter, as harrowing as any scene in thriller fiction, expands well beyond the quiet kitchen where it takes place and forces us to reassess our own views on good and evil.

In a different era, had somebody submitted a Raymond Chandler story for my consideration in a similar anthology, I would undoubtedly have put it in this category — literature — since I have always felt his stories were more psychological examinations of humans in conflict than entertainments about crime. I was reminded of Chandler by Vu Tran's "This or Any Desert." Apparently about the breakup of a cop's marriage, the story soon broadens surprisingly into a perceptive look at the dark side of love and how obsession manifests itself across cultures.

Speaking of which, there was a time when writing a "foreign" crime story meant setting it in Kansas or Utah — anywhere outside of New York, L.A., or Florida. It's a different world now, so to speak, and several of our stories, though published in the United States, occur in whole or in part in other countries.

Ron Carlson's "Beanball," one of the longer pieces in this anthology, is a well-crafted tale about a baseball scout's trips to Central America to find players for pro teams in the United States and the consequences that result from his missions. Filled with punchy detail about the sports business and equatorial life, the story unfolds slowly but manages to keep us riveted on every page with a plot that spans two hemispheres and offers up some knuckle-ball twists.

The first decade of this century has focused on the Middle East perhaps more than on any other region of the world (future readers, no need to Google anything, I assume), and so I was pleased to select a story set in the United Arab Emirates, that small federation of states on the Persian Gulf, Garry Craig Powell's "Kamila and the King of Kandy." The title should not discourage you (the reference isn't to Hershey bars, believe me); this is a tough story about courage and determination in the aftermath of a terrible crime. It offers a searing look at a world that CNN and MSNBC cannot begin to make real for us.

"Manila Burning," by Clark Howard, plunges us into Graham Greene–like intrigue in a steaming setting half a world away. I found myself sweating right along with the characters on every page — and not just from the heat. The story also happens to feature one of the most curious urban attractions on earth, which, by the way, really exists. (Try Google Earth for this one.)

Several of these stories explore that perennial theme in fiction: families. . . . Yeah, lousy verb in that sentence. It belongs in a sociology paper, I know, but I couldn't think of a single word that means "stuns readers with a sharp, raw, and uncompromising look at." Which is just what the following three stories do.

Robert McClure's story, "My Son," starts out fast, flinging us onto a psychological roller coaster as we watch an impossibly tense reunion between father, a released convict, and son, a cop. How's that for a setup? Expect the unexpected — and possibly the welling of a tear or two when you get to the last page.

Michael Connelly's story, "Father's Day," features, I'm delighted to report, our old friend Harry Bosch. Nobody writes police fiction better than Connelly, as we know from his novels, and it's clear upon reading this contribution that he does cop short as well as he does cop long. Hold on tight as you read the interview room scene. I wouldn't be surprised if you'll find yourself reaching for Kleenex toward the end of this one, too.

You'll be equally moved by the mother-child story "Pretty Little Parasite," though David Corbett's tale slugs as well as tugs. A great stylist and a social observer (he's gifted with a particularly keen eye for Vegas), the author doesn't try for any strong-arm Scorsese riffs or casino capers, but rather has written a complex story about a very real woman trapped on the Strip and trying to turn her life around.

Short stories and twists go together like hedge funds and Ponzi schemes (Google alert). Sometimes the surprises are zingers that pull the rug out from underneath you — Damn, got me that time! — and in other instances they subtly rearrange our assumptions of what's been going on and reveal an unexpected story within a story. A perfect example of the latter type is Chuck Hogan's "Two Thousand Volts," about the night of a prison execution. You won't feel the same about death row — or last meals — after reading this fine piece.

M.M.M. Hayes's "Meantime, Quentin Ghlee" falls into the first, the zinger, category. The tale is about a man coming to terms with aging and the changing times, which he observes from a beloved outpost in the wilderness out West. I must comment, too, on Hayes's fine writing style. Here's one example: "Well warmed and lubricated, he sat and watched the night sky take over. The icy gleam of the stars blanketed him with indifference, the coyotes laughed in the hills." Superb command of the language.

Randy Rohn's "The Man Who Fell in Love with the Stump of a Tree" tells a quirky story well suited to its location, a small town in Indiana. Crime and humor are not incompatible, as anybody who's followed Illinois politics can tell you (future readers: this search engine assignment is "Gov. Blagojevich"). The dialogue is witty and the characters wry and appealing. I found myself smiling often as the story meandered along its Roy Blount Jr. path, even laughing out loud at points.

And then came the end. Phew.

I wasn't sure whether to group Nic Pizzolatto's great "Wanted Man" with the family stories, where it would certainly fit, or to single it out as our prime example of southern gothic. I decided on the latter. The story, about the intersecting and unraveling of lives in a small town in Louisiana, has echoes of Tennessee Williams and Faulkner, but Pizzolatto's voice is unique. He has a fine ear for talk and a keen eye for the hopes and hopelessness of people who inhabit a place where generations will forever talk about "the day the refinery exploded."

I'm pleased to report that this anthology includes a representative of one of the most important genres in all of thriller fiction: James Lee Burke. His "Big Midnight Special," set in the 1960s, is pure pleasure. A number of our stories have a southern flair, but nobody does Below the Mason-Dixon Line like Burke. He nails the region, the talk, and the spirit perfectly and with a poet's touch. If you love the blues, if you love prison stories, or if you love a left-hook, right-jab approach to storytelling, you'll love this contribution. . . . Oh, hell, it's James Lee Burke. You'd love it anyway.

All right, enough of the trailers; time for the feature presentation. I think you'll agree that, whatever else is going on in the world, this collection proves that the short story form is clearly experiencing a strong bull market. Enjoy what follows. As for me, I'm going to Google "recovery programs for those in codependent relationships with metaphors."

JEFFERY DEAVER

N . J . A Y R E S

Rust

FROM *At the Scene of the Crime*

TROOPER ERIN FLANNERY, out of Bethlehem, Pennsylvania:
Five-six. One-twelve, brown over brown. Red-brown over brown.
Over hazel, make it, a kind of green. At her funeral, speakers said
she was a loyal friend, good at her job, full of zip, had a beautiful
smile. Everyone loved her, they said.

When she came aboard Troop M, even I thought of asking her
out. But dating people from work — no good. The day our commander, Paul Ooten, told us a female was joining us, he warned not
to engage in excessive swearing and crude remarks to see how
she'd take it or to show she was one of the boys. He'd seen it before,
and it was comical and juvenile and nothing more than bias in the
guise of jokes. He reminded us of the word "respect" used in the
state police motto and that our training includes the concept of
military courtesy applied to civilians, peers, and superiors, whatever the gender. Unless some miscreant pissed us off while breaking the law, and then you can beat the shit out of him, he said. We
laughed. Commander Paul Ooten. A lot like my dad. Upright, ethi-
cal, fair. Firm, yet fun when the time called for it. He also reminded
me of my dad in the way he talked and in some of his mannerisms,
like swiping a knuckle under his nose after he delivered a punch
line. My father died when I was twelve. Heart attack in his police
cruiser.

Everything changed.

My mother was okay for a while. Then she slowly took to drinking.
By the time I was fourteen, she was into it full throttle. She dated,

and each time it hardened me more. The idea of her wanting anyone but Dad sickened me.

It wasn't like she brought guys home, but she might as well have.

As soon as I was out of school and found someone to share rent with, I moved out, enrolled in community college, and later, with my AA degree in hand, applied to the Pennsylvania State Police Academy. What I really wanted was to go to Missoula, where my uncle lived, study writing and film, and then wind up in California or New York, doing that scene. But I needed money from a job. I more than satisfied the physical training, aced the written and orals. Bingo, I are a cop.

Within seven years I earned a couple of medals for distinction in service. The last recognition was from the community, the "DUI Top Gun Award" for nailing forty-nine intelligent people who got behind the wheel while drunk.

Once, when I was ten, I alerted some neighbors across the street that their house was on fire. They called me a hero. I wasn't a hero. I was an ordinary kid who knew enough to realize a ton of smoke was not coming from a leaf pile in the backyard. My dad was the hero. He ran to the house with a ladder to get Mrs. Salvatore from the second floor.

I'm twenty-eight today. Today, like when you go to the doctor and the assistants ask and even the doctor asks how old are you today? Uh, yesterday I was twenty-eight, and today I'm twenty-eight also, thank you. And I'm single after a two-year marriage to a girl who couldn't dig someone who always thought he was right. I tried, really did, to see more gray instead of black and white. The marriage just wasn't meant to be. She went back to Alabama, teaches elementary school there. I wonder how she'd view me now.

How old are you today? A hundred inside.

When Officer Flannery transferred over, she was required to put in her time on reception. Nobody likes that duty, but there aren't enough civilians for it, even though our governor is high on recruiting them. Right away the guys started testing her, seeing how available she might be. Married, unmarried, didn't matter. It's a thing guys do. I should say here I never saw our commander flirt or kid in any way that made it seem Erin was anything but another trooper.

Commander Paul Ooten's a real family man. That's what I heard all the time. I'd seen him with his family at a state patrol picnic once. Pretty wife. Two kids, about eight, ten.

And I saw him one night, behind a motel near Tannersville, coming down the stairs from the second floor, Trooper Flannery in front of him.

I had just gotten in my car after coming out of a restaurant. Parked perpendicular to the restaurant, nose in to the motel, I went to wipe moisture off the side mirror and then looked up. At first I thought my eyes were playing tricks on me. The light over the staircase and landing was fuzzy from moist air. The couple had long coats on. I watched them walk over patchy snow to her car. She got in, and a different light, coming from the motel sign near the street, hit her face, brighter, paler. Paul shut her door. She rolled down the window, and he leaned over and kissed her, then stood watching as she pulled away.

The next day I had a hard time looking at him.

A couple of weeks later, I was at my desk on a weekend. I had off, but my review was coming up and I had to get some overdue paperwork in. Ooten's door was open. Half of him was visible through the doorway, cut vertically, or I'd see him when he'd get up to go to his file cabinet.

Bill Buttons was in, too. He's a kiss-up. Buttons thinks he's Bruce Willis. Shaves his head, swaggers around, crinks his mouth to smile. Sometimes when Ooten is around, Buttons makes like Bruce Willis making like John Wayne, saying, Wal, pardner, let's get 'er done. The effect: ridiculous.

That day Paul Ooten came out of his office a couple of times, said something to Buttons, something to me. I tried forcing my feelings, tried to look at him the way I did before the night outside the motel with Erin. But I kept picturing him on her, her doing stuff to him.

When Buttons left for lunch, Paul — it's hard to call him Commander Ooten anymore — came into Room 5, where there are mail slots against the wall, a supply cabinet, a small refrigerator, the coffee machine. I was pouring coffee for myself. Ooten put a memo in a slot and then took some time to mention the weather, the Eagles game, and how he'd been thinking of taking a course in Excel. I couldn't hide my lack of interest, but I guess because I had recently lost my mother to cancer, he said, "If you need to talk about it, Justin, my door's always open."

I said something like, Thanks, I'm fine. His manner, the kindness behind it, touched me. And I resolved to put what I saw at the motel out of my mind.

What's bitter is that Erin Flannery didn't die from a car accident or a long-hidden disease. She died from brain trauma in her own home.

Detectives interviewed the civilians in her life: family, friends, neighbors. They interviewed us at Troop M, too, in due time. I wondered what Paul Ooten had told them. I wondered if the strained expression I saw each day was worry about his secret being outed, or if the tightness in his face was the shame he knew he brought to the badge. I'll say this: for some guys, if they learned the commander was boning Erin, he'd only be more of a hero in their eyes.

No boyfriend turned up in the investigation. Bill Buttons said, That's sure hard to believe, a piece like that.

A crime of opportunity, we concluded. It happens. Even to cops.

Kleinsfeldt said he overheard there was something odd about the evidence in her case, he didn't know what. We asked who he heard it from. He wouldn't say.

I reminded the guys that Flannery had been an LEO, a liquor enforcement officer, up in Harrisburg. It sounds like soft duty, but not necessarily. You go undercover to nab idiots who sell to minors. You look for cheats who avoid taxes by importing liquor from other states. You bust speakeasies. Yes, they still call them that, those enterprises too unenterprising to get a liquor license. The Bureau of Liquor Control Enforcement also goes after illegal video gambling machines, looking for operations suspected as hooked to corrupt organizations. Maybe she found one and was afraid she'd get cashed out because of it. Patrol sees our fair share of action, I don't mean we don't. It's more than spotting violations of the ve-

hicle code. When your number's up, you can get killed responding to a disturbance call as well as by some desperate speakeasy
owner.

One time Erin found a note on the seat of her desk chair. It said
he wished he were her seat cushion. She told me about it only because I was walking through the lobby and saw the look of disgust
on her face as she studied the paper still in her hands. "Some jerk,"
she said. Said it quietly, almost with sadness. I don't know why that
particular note would bother someone so much, but then I've
never been a woman. I told her maybe it could be the computer
guy, Steve Gress. He was in every week, supposedly upgrading our
systems, which only created more problems. I'd noticed the way he
looked at her.

Carl Carolla had a thing for Erin, too. I could tell because of his
talk around her. He'd roll out some cockamamie story about which
creep he had to deal with that day, what some wiseass said. He said,
"Joker like that, what you do, you rack up more offenses. Keep the
dumb-ass violator from his appointed rounds, and hit him hard in
the pocket." Carolla could be a suspect, maybe like if Erin told him
to get lost after a clumsy pass.

Another cop, Rich Kleinsfeldt, resented her. Claimed women
cops are a danger to everybody. Some dingbat can grab hold of
their hair and then lift their sidearm, he said. Women's hair, according to dress code, has to be above the uniform collar points.
Even so, it could be used for a handle, especially if it was in a braid.
Another species, they are, says R. K. I'll agree that women offenders are the worst, you go to arrest them. They'll bite, yank, spit,
what have you. "She's skeeter skinny anyway," Rich said. "You want
that for your back?"

Something funny about the crime scene. Is that what Kleinsfeldt
said? I knew one technician at the crime lab in Lancaster I could
check with, but it would look odd, my poking around when the
case wasn't mine. I let that idea drop.

Before what happened to Erin, I'd be on my runs, doing my job,
and find myself thinking about Erin and Ooten. Ooten and Erin.
The ring to it. Her power to lure him. I could understand it, yet
not. I was just so disappointed in him. Hurt, you might say, though

I cannot exactly say why. Ooten has awards of valor himself, the fact known by reputation and not by paper plastered on his office walls. From his example I did not display mine.

While Erin was at the front desk one morning and no public was in, I was getting pencils — pencils, by the way, not pencil. My seventeenth summer I worked at a dollar store. The boss was training me for assistant manager, said I could take college classes at night, couldn't I, so I'd be free to do a full eight hours? In his instructions, he told me to keep an eye out for what the other employees might be up to. "If they aren't stealing a little, they're stealing a lot," he said. Those words came to mind as I grabbed my second and third pencil for home. I did it right in front of Buttons, whose arm was in the cabinet, too, taking a stapler. He already had one on his desk. What did he need two for? I almost think I did it to show him I wasn't such an uptight asshole after all. But I did razz him about it. He razzed me back about my three pencils.

On my way back to my desk, I heard Erin say on the phone she was letting her hair grow out. Who was she talking to? Her lover? I couldn't help but glance out the window to see if Ooten's car was in the lot. It wasn't. Every action or nonaction of Ooten's I couldn't help but attach to her.

My review was scheduled for the last day of the month. You always get a little anxious at that time. No one zips through with zero criticism. The review was the same week Erin was to complete her probationary period at the same time, a thing she had to go through even though she was a transfer-in and not a cadet. We're a paramilitary organization, the state police, why we're called troopers. "Soldiers of the law," we are, and we suck it up when we get assignments we don't want or when we get treated like newbies. Erin said she was content here for the time being, mentioned how good everyone was to her, how terrific Commander Ooten was.

Did she linger on his name? How would the others feel if they got wind of her seeing him on the side? There are more minorities on the force than women. Women, in other words, still stand out. Her misbehavior would come to tarnish all other females entering the force and could severely damage Commander Ooten.

And so it was that I asked if she'd like to have coffee sometime, after shift. In my own way, maybe I was trying to be a decoy. Protect her and the commander both. I was a little surprised that she took me up on the invitation. Not that I look like something a dog won't eat. It's just that if she had Paul Ooten, why me? Maybe she saw me as an opportunity for a decoy, too.

I suggested a seat near the window at a diner down the street, where we could watch the lazy snowflakes fall, the size of quarters that day. Erin's eyes showed her delight in it. She informed me that snowflakes fall at about the rate of a mile an hour, unless icy droplets form on them to increase their weight. How'd she know that? I asked. "Before I joined the Bureau of Liquor Enforcement, I thought of teaching biology. I'm a science junkie. Then I got out of BLE because the captain, a micromanager anyway, insisted on messing with a restaurant owner who allowed a singer to come in two nights a week."

"Say again?"

"The owner was licensed to sell liquor, could even allow people to dance in the aisles to the jukebox or to live music if he wanted. His mistake? He paid a band that had a vocalist. That heinous deed made him in violation of Liquor Law Section Four-Nine-Three-Point-Ten, 'Entertainment on a licensed premise without an Amusement Permit.'"

"You're kidding," I said. "Still, if it's on the books . . ."

"It's a stupid law."

"We're not paid to write the laws."

"Ah, but there was something else. The restaurant owner was an old high school enemy of the captain. So it was personal. It's not the only reason I left, just the last one. And, unfortunately, my judgment may have faltered when I wrote a letter to the editor about police harassment of small businesses. I disguised my identity, of course. But they were suspicious because of the way I'd been fuming about it. I got congratulations from the guys and glares from the brass."

"Ouch."

"Well, you learn to pick your battles. A lesson."

"I thought you were happy about the change."

"I am. But now I have to start over again."

She didn't get much of a chance to do that. Some evil character hit the delete key on her life.

*

Forget about the old days when people said tough guys don't eat quiche. Tough guys don't ever say the word "depressed." I'll say it here so that maybe my actions could be understood, if ever they can.

After Erin died, on duty I'd sit off Interstate 80 and watch violators speed by. And one day, while off the rolls, I spotted a shoplifter out back of Sear's in Stroudsburg look three ways and then languidly wheel a barbecue away and load it in the back of his SUV. Yesterday I saw that Gress guy, the computer jock, fudge his timecard, look at me, drop it in the bin, and walk away like saying, Challenge me, Muskrat, what you got in your den? And how did I know he stole time? The look. If he hadn't been smug, I wouldn't have gone to the bin and picked up the card. But he was right: I didn't challenge him. Something else was on my mind.

A few days after the coffee with Erin, I asked her out again, for a Saturday afternoon movie. We went to see *Jarhead*. Arrived in different cars. Paid our own tickets in. "You understand this is not a real date," she said. "You understand this is not real popcorn," I said. "It's packing foam." Afterward, we stood on the sidewalk outside the mall, discussing the movie. She saw stuff in it I didn't. In the chilly sunlight, talking about things outside of copdom, she was flat-out beautiful.

In the walk to our cars, I finally couldn't keep the question away. "Want to make it official sometime? A genuine date?"

"Probably not a good idea."

"Yeah," I said. "Peace."

"Peace."

We went our separate ways.

I consider myself a balanced man, don't go off halfcocked. What my nature allows, my training reinforces. So I do not tell the rest of this lightly. It's not that hard to understand the primitives who believe in demons entering a person's skin. I say this because I don't know what came over me in the case of Trooper Erin Flannery and Paul Ooten: I became a spy. I felt righteous, principled, and therefore gave myself permissions I would never give someone else. It was the mystery of her drawing power I couldn't get out of my head, that force that makes a man like Commander Ooten forsake his marriage vows and teeter on the verge of disgracing his profession.

I took to rolling through Nazareth some weekends to see if I could spot her. I knew that's where she lived, but not precisely. Nazareth isn't that big a town: six thousand people. It's about ten miles from troop headquarters and under nine from where I live in Bethlehem — Steel City, a name that fit before Bethlehem Steel and its support businesses fell victim to the Japanese business onslaught.

Driving down Center Street one day, I saw Trooper Flannery coming out of a dry cleaners with her bagged uniforms. I am ashamed to say I followed her to see the apartment complex in which she lived.

And later, on occasion I would go off my route to drift down her street and see if I could catch sight of the commander's car, see it in the apartment parking lot. Sneering at my own bad behavior, I called it "volunteer surveillance." I hated what I was doing yet could not keep from the patrol. We were on extra alert because of a terroristic threat. Watch for violations on small refrigerator vehicles, the bulletin said. Stop and search if indicated. Drive by Erin Flannery's residence to see if Paul Ooten's car was there. Other guys were out at bars, cracking wise and watching games. I was stuck on one note, and it was sour. Tomorrow I would shed this thing.

Don't ask me how a reporter for the *Allentown Morning Call* got it, but it happens sometimes. His piece told the basics of Pennsylvania State Police Trooper Erin Anne Flannery's demise. The state police spokesman was reserving comment on manner of death. I should think the public reader would conclude, as would any cop, that homicide was on the minds of investigators. I spent a restless night. The next day State Commissioner Corporal Robert Metcalfe announced before TV cameramen that Trooper Flannery's case was under investigation as murder, and he was sorry, but he could not release any details.

"Honor, service, integrity, respect, trust, courage, and duty." Our motto. I am familiar with courage as it pertains to rescue or in the midst of violent disputes, even in the frequent chaos of felony arrests. I've not only witnessed it but, if you'll excuse me for saying so, performed within its lighted shaft. But could it be that those were times not of action but reaction, mindless as a ball springing off the floor of a gym? Moral courage, there's the mark, and a harder one to hit.

It's clear that lying violates integrity. But does silence? We're not talking the silence of the citizens of Germany in World War II. Not that kind. In Erin's case, nothing will pull her up from the endless recycle machine, not even if I told I was there at the time of her death.

It broke. Mrs. Paul Ooten, given name Mallory, was a person of interest in Homicide Incident Number M1-645-whatever. Mrs. Paul Ooten! Our troop was on fire with speculation, with rethinking impressions of her. And then, of course, there was the terrible distance, disappointment, and suspicion toward the commander himself. I must admit I was halfway pleased there was no gloating, as I might have expected.

The commander was put on administrative leave. It wasn't the first scandal or the first capital case to stain the state police. But it was here, now, among us at Troop M, a mortal wound, it seemed to me. My fellow troopers talked themselves raw. Then steel bands slowly tightened on our hearts. We grew silent, more involved in what we were trained to do: to be soldiers of the law. We got back to business.

There was a message slip on my desk when I came in one morning two weeks later. It called me to a meeting at Bethlehem headquarters. I brought along my personal write-up detailing my performance accomplishments this year, as we are told to do at review time. I wondered who would be giving my review now that Ooten was out.

Whatever I can say about him, I'll say I have no doubt the commander would have given me a good one. The only thing he ever admonished me about was failure to properly orient a diagram sketch of an accident scene. For all my driving about, I'd put down *north* for a street that actually ran northeast, and he caught it.

As I approached the conference room, I saw an officer's winter coat draped on a chair. Two rank rings decorated the coat sleeve, signifying the coat belonged to a major. When I entered the

room, there sat the major at the end of the table, Commander
Ooten to his right. I looked from one to the other until Ooten
spoke. "Good morning, Justin." Motioning, he introduced Major
Bryan Manning.

"Have a seat, Trooper Eberhardt," the major said.

My heart was pounding. What kind of promotion could I be in
for?

The major began by apologizing for not making it out to Troop
M barracks before. "Been busy as a bartender on payday," he said.
Intended to put me at ease. I'm afraid I didn't laugh. After more
chat about nothing, he said, "Tell me, trooper, what do you recall
about your CPR training?"

Confused, I stumbled through a reply, first repeating, "Two
hands, two inches, three compressions in two seconds. Fifteen
pushes, then two ventilation breaths."

"And what is the distance of travel for compressions, trooper?"

"Two inches, as I said, sir."

"A third the depth of the chest," the major said.

"Yes sir."

"Makes a body tired, right, trooper?" the major asked with a
smile.

Ooten pitched in: "It can be brutal."

"Sure enough I busted a sweat first time I did it," Major Manning
said. "Was a big guy, close to three hundred pounds. I was drippin'
sweat on him."

You do the polite thing in a situation like this. Nod, chuckle. But
what the hell was this, a grilling on rescue efforts you'd give a cadet? My woolly-pully was on under my uniform shirt. It felt like
ninety degrees in there.

Commander Ooten sprang the next question. "You were pretty
tight with Trooper Flannery, weren't you, Justin?"

"Friends. I didn't know her well. I mean, we didn't have that
much time to get to know each other." I met his eyes, guessing if
the probe was meant to inquire if I had slept with her. Slept with
the woman Commander Ooten was cheating with. Her lunch hour
went long, people said. Dentist, doctor appointments, flat tire,
things like that, she would claim.

"She wasn't here but three months, sir." All along I'd considered
how quickly she and Ooten hooked up.

How can I describe the look in his eyes? Seeing me, not seeing me. Assessing, reflecting. The oil of the present saturating the rust of the past.

He said, "Carl Carolla observed you tagging after Trooper Flannery, Justin, and not once but twice. Carl thought that was odd. What can you tell us about that?"

"I . . . I wouldn't know. He's mistaken." I said nothing more. Silence is a tool in interviews. And even in sales. My uncle told me that. When he'd go to close a deal, he put a pencil to his lips to signal he was through talking. "He who speaks first loses," is what he said. I recognized the tool's use now with the commander and the major, the three of us soundless while the room temp climbed, even as I saw through the slats of the blinds behind the commander snow riding slanted chutes of wind.

At last Major Manning said, "Are you up to date on your CPR certification, trooper?"

"I'd have to check the date, sir. I think I might be due."

"You've rendered CPR before, right, Justin?" Manning asked.

"No sir."

Why did I lie? I did start CPR on a victim once. It was part of an action that won me a commendation medal, but in the write-up it was not mentioned, nor should it have been. Emergency techs had arrived at the scene seconds after I'd started, so I didn't consider it as actually "performed."

The major sat back, arms outstretched on the table, and looked at Paul, who asked me, "You usually wear a ring, don't you, guy?" Friendly, casual.

"A school ring, yes," I said, and shrugged. I hadn't put it on that day. I glanced at the commander's left hand as he toyed with a collector's pen our troop gave him last Christmas. His wedding ring was still on. I pictured his wife, Mallory, how she must look today, turmoil in her face, heartache visible in her robot motions, her walk, her interactions with her children. Commander Ooten sat there interviewing me about Erin Flannery while his family was torn apart because of his unstoppable urges toward a woman who wound up dead on the floor of her home.

No doubt his wife would be quickly cleared in Erin's case. Ridiculous, when you think about it, how she got tied to it at all. Who in this world would figure that she and Erin had in common a love of the oboe, I kid you not, a love of the oboe, which found the two of them in weekly classes at community college. Mrs. Ooten had lent Erin an old instrument her father gave her as an eleven-year-old, the name *Mallory Parsons* engraved on a gold plate on the case. The very fact that Mallory Ooten was innocently in the home of her husband's lover gave me a pang, my sympathy for her as tender as my own scoured nerves.

What I did not tell my superiors is that the night of Erin's injury she had consumed too much plum wine, and I had been the one to buy it. "I've been a little stressed out," she said. "Things."

"It can get that way."

"You know what? You're way easier to be around than I would've guessed."

"Thanks, I guess."

"It's just that on the job you're so serious."

"Is that bad or good?"

"It is what it is. Could go either way." Her hair looked like shined copper.

This was a couple of weeks after *Jarhead*. Ooten was out of town at a confab in Pittsburgh. Maybe that's why Erin weakened when I asked her out. I felt low about my reasons and almost sorry she accepted. Here she was already involved in deceit with Ooten, and now she was deceiving him with me. Of course, it wouldn't go so far as to be labeled true betrayal, I wouldn't let it go that far. But even if it did, at least the two of us were single.

We met at a Japanese restaurant, a new place I said I wanted to try near the Bethlehem Brew Works. Erin insisted on separate cars again, saying she had things to do that would put her in the vicinity anyway. We sat at one of the table-sized, stainless steel grills where the food is prepared before our eyes teppanyaki style. The flames flew high on the volcano of onions the chef built. We marveled at his antics with thrown eggs and knives and, with others, applauded each performance.

In between I looked for a way to caution Erin about her activities with Commander Ooten. I wanted to ask her what in the world did she think she was doing. Ask in a nice way but one that left no doubt that her new friend, myself, was there to help set her straight.

While waiting for the check, I said, "I'm going to tell you something."

She tilted her head, a smile on her lips. "Okay."

"Don't take this wrong."

"Oh boy," she said. She peered into her wineglass, refilled once already, and lifted my sake cup to drain the last few sips. Then she went for the pitcher. "Guess I'll have to do without," she said, shaking it as if more would loosen and come free. "How bad is it, what you're going to tell me?"

"You can handle it."

"Ah, thank God."

"You're a mystery to me, is all."

"Come again?"

"I can't quite figure you out."

She winked at me and reached for her puffy pink jacket from the back of the chair, saying, "Have you figured out I'm a little wasted? If I had any more I couldn't drive. You'd have to arrest me." The way she said it, like a flirtation.

We stood in the parking lot by her car, talking, and then she said, "Ugh. You know, I'm really feeling sick. I don't think I can make it home without urping." She hunched in, and I stood by her and put my arm around her. This could be the most unusual of come-ons, perhaps the same as she used on the commander to get him to take her home.

"It must be the food. It couldn't be the wine and sake. A certain person kept me from that," she said, looking at me sideways, a pixie tease in her smile.

Icy mud sprayed us as a car sped by faster than the driver should have in the lot. The snow was about three inches deep, the woods woven with chalky fog ahead of us.

"Come on," I said. "I'll take you home. In the morning I'll pick you up at your apartment and we can go get your car."

When she quickly met my eyes, I realized she hadn't mentioned whether she lived in an apartment, a house, or a boxcar.

She lived just a few miles away, near a Moravian cemetery. "I go there sometimes and just wander down the lanes. All the headstones lie flat to show that everyone is equal in the sight of God. Rich next to poor, whites next to blacks next to Mohican Indians."

"I didn't know that," I said. "I'm from Montana. We stuff 'em and put 'em in museums." She gave a soft laugh. Her eyes were closed and her head was back on the seat as I'd instructed. It's where my own should have been. I could feel the hot drink still in my veins, the sweet burn that beckons so many, the frayed ends strangely comforting.

"All but the women," Erin said. "The women are buried in their own section. Separate. Inside the church, too."

Her lips shone pink in the boomeranged light. I wanted to kiss her there, then. Instead, I turned the key in the ignition and pulled out onto the road, driving well within the speed limit, sight often flicking to the mirrors. I disdained the fact that Trooper Flannery would let herself get blotto even off duty, but the truth was I also knew in saner times I would not get behind the wheel either. She did it again, that woman. Getting men to tread over boundaries.

She seemed to feel better, once inside. "I guess it was the wine after all," she said. "I didn't eat lunch today. Hey, want some ice water? Or coffee? I'll be glad to make some." I said yes to the coffee.

That's when she got up from the couch we were sitting on. Perhaps I was sitting a little too close for comfort. I shifted to be farther away when she returned, but then I stood up and went into the kitchen with her. She faltered as she took a step, galumphing forward off the rug and slapping soles onto the tile. Laughing, she said, "Holy shit. I really am drunk . . . or something. You know what? I'm sorry, but I think I should just go on up to bed."

Sure, sure, I told her, meaning it.

"Just help me get upstairs and I'll be fine. Thank you, Justin. Thank you, really."

Was it this way with Ooten? But then she also seemed really embarrassed. Who was she? How could one woman do this to two men?

With my help she managed to mount four of the stairs. "Just flip the lock on the way out, will you, Justin? I can make it the rest of the way."

She smiled and thanked me again. I started to go down but then reached the next step up before she did, hardly aware of my action. I brought her around and pulled her to me and sank into her lips. "No," she said . . . and let me kiss her again.

What I wanted to do . . . what I intended to do . . . was scoop her up like Clark Gable did Scarlett O'Hara in *Gone With the Wind*, but it didn't turn out that way, oh no, it didn't. She jerked back and then . . . as I try to recall this, I am not sure just what happened. All I know is I tried to grab her to keep her from falling. Instead, as she sank she twisted, and my fist connected to the left jaw. In her dive down, her head shot against the square platform of the end stair rod, and then she flipped and her head went *smack!* on the tile, a gray tile with tan swirls in it until joined with the brightest of red.

Even as early as then I wondered if I'd let her fall. If I'd caused her to fall. My reactions are supposed to be quick. How could I let her slip by?

She was on the floor with her eyes rolled partway up. I began CPR.

You might suppose it crossed my mind to eat the hornet. Oh, I practiced caressing my weapon the way I'd seen it done in movies. And I drew other dramatic scenarios in my mind. My illicit favorite: death by scumbag. I would insert myself into a bad street scene and, while making like a hero, arrange for my own end.

I even imagined a sequence where my body would be found among the homeless at the Bethlehem mill. Once, on a perimeter canvass after a series of home break-ins, I went in at a downed section of fencing near the rear of Blast Furnace Row. Inside the steel skeleton, crows flutter. Cat eyes gleam in the alcoves. Scruffy-looking souls, both men and women, cook their meals over fifty-five-gallon drums, glance at you with little interest, as though even in uniform you're just another wanderer there. That is where I belonged. Now I lay me down to sleep . . . forever. But to involve them in my final act would be to pile wrong upon wrong.

Again I was summoned to headquarters. It was a whole month after the first interview with Major Manning and the commander. This time it was two sergeants from the homicide unit.

I won't drag it out. What they laid on me I knew was coming; knew it yet pretended it wasn't imminent, that each day I awakened would be like any other before the incident.

At the autopsy for Erin Flannery, it was discovered that her sternum and two ribs were cracked from the compressions I had rendered. When I first began, I did not want to remove her bra. To do so would seem a trespass of its own variety. Because I didn't remove it, the first several thrusts downward scored the flesh over her sternum. In due time I also heard a crackling, like the sound of a cereal bag being pinched tight, but I thought it was interference from the bra. With clumsy fingers, I unhinged the plastic hook in front and just kept on pumping, calling her name before I put my mouth to hers to force in another breath.

It must have gone on for thirty minutes, or so it seemed. And then, when I had no positive response, no reaction at all, curse me, I looked around trying to think of anything I'd touched, and then I fled.

The medical examiner, upon noting those injuries to the chest, instructed her assistant to swab around the mouth and to perform another separate swab on the lips of the deceased. Even this action, through DNA testing, would not have implicated me, save for the fact I volunteered a sample in one of the extra criminal investigation classes I took after joining the force. The sample was sent to the state laboratory as though it were any other, not a student's. It would be held as an unidentified profile. These are kept in the database in the hope that someday they will "hit" in another case that had other trace evidence with which to bust a suspect. Like Mrs. Ooten's fingerprint on the oboe case, my identity would not be known from that saliva sample — except that eventually my superiors pressed for a new sample to be taken. And of course I complied.

There was the ring the commander asked about — the twist in the garrote, you might say. Nothing at the scene of Erin's death would have pointed my way. I left no fingerprints. I had not touched a glass, nor the banister. I did open the door with Erin's key, but I had on gloves, as I did when I left. Even while rendering CPR, I avoided the blood on the floor. But the ring . . .

The sergeant who studied the evidence seized on a peculiar mark on Erin's jaw, a curved flame shape with a slight space below, and beneath that a kind of pear shape, a teardrop with a touch of high waist. Two of each shape. Sergeant Geerd Scranton showed me a photo of it. "What does that look like to you, son?"

"I don't know, crooked carrots? With a blotch below?"

"I took up an interest in Indians when I was a boy."

"Did you," I said. Where was this going?

"My name," he said, "means 'spear brave' in Dutch. Piscataway Indians used spears. They'd hunt fish and bear with them."

"Are you onto something, sergeant?" I asked, feigning only an intellectual interest in the case.

"It's part of a bear print. The nails, the pads. See? Perfect in the photo." He turned the photo my way.

"You could be right."

"I'm told you wear a ring with a bear print on it, Justin. Trooper Buttons says you always have it on."

"Hah. I do. Or almost always. I guess I left it on the sink this morning." I smiled. "I spent some time in Montana with my dad and uncle. God, what beautiful country. Have you ever . . . ? The grizzly is the state mascot. Lots of people wear it on jewelry," I said.

He nodded, waited a few beats, or maybe it was minutes, or maybe it was an hour, before he said, "Why don't you just tell me about what happened, Justin? It must be very uncomfortable for you. Sergeant Kunkle, myself, Major Manning—we know there must have been some pretty powerful extenuating circumstances or you would have done the right thing. Isn't that so, son? Look, we know that sometimes we get pushed to extremes. Maybe you tried to romance her? Maybe you had a little too much to drink?"

I sat looking at him, stunned he would suggest such things but not arguing, because arguing would only deepen what he already believed.

Again he went on like that, and I shook my head as if I just couldn't believe what test they were putting me through now. I did say I was clueless as to what response they wanted.

And then he used the tool of silence. Crows could have been squalling in the steel mill shadows. The wails of warning cats went chasing their own echoes around. The hollow laughter of the homeless kept piercing my ears.

There is a certain terror in the veins of those who would do right always. I am the junior to the senior, our standards so high there is no true escape.

Perhaps my father knew that, and maybe that's part of why he left us, his daily companions a fifth of whiskey, a bottle of bennies, and tricked-up tubing duct-taped to the exhaust pipe of his cruiser, snaked into his window on the passenger side as it sat hub-deep in mud on the side of a cornfield, a stand of trees blocking the scene from the main road, no reason known, no final written note to tell us why.

As a child, nights, I'd be in bed listening to my parents argue, my mother's voice loud and clear, my father only sometimes shouting back. After his death I tried recalling what-all they argued about. I couldn't then, but today I remember a woman's name. An odd name to me, even then: Clarabelle. I remember my mother calling her "whore" and my not knowing what the word meant but that it had an awful sound, the way a roar issues deep from within a throat. Perhaps I should have known, but I was a quiet child and did not hang with any special friends.

It wasn't until I was twenty and spent a final summer with my uncle outside of Butte that I learned the real story of my father's death. Until that time, and even after, I kept hearing what a good man he was. How positive. How good, how perfect. A model of a man. My image of him was forever ruined by what my uncle revealed and, later, by other things I came to know. I longed to be better than Enoch "Eddie" Eberhardt and determined to shape my longing into action to become, if it is possible in this world, the truly moral man.

Commander Ooten became my model. I would learn to be like him. Anything or anyone that got in the way to diminish the image I had must only be possessed of a fierce and terrible magic. In my obsession to know what the power was that did trip him up, I laid out a woman who in no way deserved an early end, whose only fault was to be a friend to a family and to a lonely madman.

To this day I do not know if I deliberately put my fist to her jaw. But does it even matter? I either committed or omitted, failed to do what I should have, and encouraged what I should not.

It may be two years now that I've lived on the banks of the Pocono River, there until weather drives me and my fellow campers to find a collapsed barn, a forgotten shed, a building in wait for a bulldozer. Days, we hook fish and toss whatever's left to forever-hungry cats skulking in the bushes. We keep watch on our meager holdings and quickly drive out any offenders. Draw straws to see who will go buy the wine. Days are good. Blackbirds chain-saw the nights. I tell those of you who would listen that even the strongest of girders rust. We are all just wanderers here.

TOM BISSELL

My Interview with the Avenger

FROM *The Virginia Quarterly Review*

THIS IS A STORY about heroes. Yes, it is also a profile of a famous man, a "celebrity," I suppose, but it is first and foremost a story about heroes, what they mean, and the draperies of significance with which we decorate them. The hero in question came to us as unexpectedly as a micrometeorite, and little has been the same since his impact. Of course, nearly everyone remembers how and when the man now known as the Avenger first made his existence public. Most origin stories are cumbrous with mythic overlay. But the Avenger arrived in twinkly, almost pointillistic detail. There was nothing to add to the story to make it better; it defeated augmentation.

New York City, 2005. A night in late January. A pair of muggers approach two Japanese tourists unwise enough to have wandered too deep into the swards of Central Park at too late an hour. Moments after the muggers assault the tourists, who do not resist them, a fifth party rushes into the fray. "We don't know what happened," one of the tourists tells the police afterward. "It happened so fast." One of the muggers, speaking to the police later that night from his hospital bed — his colleague's broken, wired-shut jaw rules out any statement — is slightly more descriptive: "He came out of nowhere, sprayed us with some shit, hit us a bunch of times, cuffed us to each other, and then he was, like . . . *gone.*" The mugger's statement is leaked to the press. The *Post*'s headline: "HE CAME OUT OF NOWHERE": GOOD SAMARITAN FOILS PARK THUGS. The *Times* strikes a less populist, more skeptical note: NYPD GRATEFUL FOR, CONCERNED BY ACTIONS OF PARK VIGILANTE. No follow-up, no one comes forward — just one of those uniquely weird New York stories of a person stepping out of the potential everythingness of the city and then retreating anonymously back into it.

Then, three days later, and once again in Central Park, a purse-snatching teenager from the Bronx is chased down shortly before midnight by a man he later describes as "the fastest white dude ever." The man, wearing "a black ski mask," and, evocatively, "motherfucking Batman's utility belt," extracts the purse from its captor with minimal force, but extends to him some friendly advice that will, of course, later become legendary: "If you plan to continue this line of work, may I suggest a better cardiovascular routine?" The next evening the crime's victim receives her purse, by courier, at her Upper West Side home. The sender of the purse lists a nonexistent Manhattan post office box under an equally nonexistent name, but he does include a typed note: "I believe you lost this last night. May I suggest you consider wearing your purse strap across your body?" The note is signed in all caps (THE AVENGER), but this small pertinence does not fully register for weeks.

The Avenger has been with us for so long now that those first few months when no one was quite sure what to call him are recalled through the same murky veil as the pre–September 11 skyline. The "Central Park Vigilante" was the NYPD's preferred cognomen. The *Times* opted for "New York City's Unknown Self-Appointed Guardian," but sometimes, and grudgingly, resorted to "the so-called Avenger."

In the beginning, though, he is for most of us not a person. He is rather a question: *Did you hear about that guy?*

Then, two weeks later, shortly after the purse snatcher (who was never charged) had come forward to the press, and immediately after the purse's owner had been photographed smiling while holding up her mysterious note for the cover of the *Times*'s City section, two burglars are found beaten and hogtied on the floor of a Chelsea brownstone. Their situation is brought to the police's attention by an anonymous pay-phone 911 call believed to have been made by That Guy Himself. The *Post*'s simple headline, in letters half a foot high, tells us all we need to know: HE'S BACK! Our news cycles will have a different algorithm now, synced to the actions of a man no one can find, no one knows, and whose actions no one can predict.

One thing was clear: New York City had an entirely new kind of inhabitant. Was he a polite Bernhard Goetz? A human Superman? A witty sociopath? A professional headline seeker? A nut? A saint? Yet few of us back then were asking, *Who is he?* The cookie containing that particular fortune seemed bound to crack open at any moment. This was what we were asking: *Why is he? And why now?* Months, and then years, later, no one was any closer to being able to answer either question.

Six months ago I wrote an essay for this magazine ("The Avenger Dies for Our Sins," September 2007) about why I believed the Avenger's actions were, from a legal and civic point of view, dangerous. I had not, of course, interviewed the Avenger for my essay. He had, famously, given only one interview, by phone, to Larry King, shortly after coming to terms with the New York City Police Department, and being granted, in absentia, by the mayor, the dubious and unprecedented legal status of "an honorary constabulary deputy of the greatest city on earth." The Avenger tried to explain to King what, legally, this meant, but even he was not sure. The interview, the third most downloaded clip in YouTube history, is famously unhinged: the man whom in our sacred unease we fantasized as a harsh sentinel, an incorruptible guardian, sounded more like a slurring crackpot taking a momentary break from a barbiturate triathlon. (Only later did we learn that the Avenger was nursing a concussion after falling off a fire escape, as he explained in the second of the three letters he is known to have sent to the *Times.*) But because he was finally being allowed to continue his mission as the city's protector without any more interference from authorities that once vowed to see him behind bars — though he must, at all times, report his planned whereabouts, via a secret text-message code that goes directly to the mayor and his police commissioner — the Avenger had finally elected to speak directly to the people. And despite his evasions ("I am not able at this time to tell you why I'm doing this"), his chilly bravado ("I am a most unique man"), and his stilted sloganeering ("I am the force that will make civilization civil once again"), we responded. We wanted him. We *needed* him.

We also hounded him, occasionally tried to capture him ourselves, and pointed an unending series of fingers at those we believed *were* him. This is why I wrote my article. This is why I believed the Avenger was doing more harm than good. Hardly any of the criminals he has stopped, and often beaten, have been convicted. There was, and remains, no legal precedent for what the Avenger is doing. By working in secrecy, by rejecting the elaborate and, yes, sometimes frustrating evidential byways upon which American society has settled when dealing with those who break its laws, the Avenger, I wrote, was a *negation* of American justice, not its embodiment. Viewed bloodlessly, and unsentimentally, he was, in fact, probably a criminal himself.

The thing about my essay was, I knew I was right, and I knew I was wrong. I was right because — more than any other event, and more than any other person — the Avenger captured the terminal nature of a culture that could not change even if it wanted to, even if it *had* to. We have always sought arbiters of fate that exist beyond the taxable realm of legality, and the Avenger had simply made actual the vigilante fantasy that had hitherto existed only in make-believe's less exalted basements. I was wrong because the Avenger changed things in ways no one could have predicted. He did not rise up out of a time of untrammeled crime. He was not the voice of the people. He was, instead, the first person in our national public life to suggest that virtue and not fame could come first, that one was not a prerequisite of the other, that they could exist alongside each other *accidentally*. As time went on, as he evaded capture, and as he refused to disclose his identity, it became clear that the Avenger *really did not want the attention* — at least, not per se. He *actually believed in what he was doing*. And he always, as I conceded in my article, seemed paranormally aware of exactly how much damage to deal out to those whose crimes he stopped. He has never killed anyone. In fact, he did not even seem all that vindictive. He seemed, rather, *professional*. Many of the criminals he has disarmed, coldcocked, limb-snapped, and leg-swept today profess their admiration for him, and a few credit him with the back they have shown their former lives of crime. Yes, some have sued, but this has gone nowhere. The Avenger was something entirely, paradigm-shiftingly new, and it was impossible to be entirely wrong or entirely right about a man we did not yet have the vocabulary to describe.

Days after my article appeared on newsstands, I received a letter from the Avenger. It had been postmarked in New York City. Strangely, and somewhat menacingly, it was addressed to my unlisted home address. The return address was that of this magazine, with a simply typed *A.* above it. My article had obviously riled and angered him, as part of me certainly hoped it would. The Avenger's tone was curt, and I have agreed not to quote his letter here, but he invited me, at a time and place of his choosing, to meet with him. I heard nothing else for weeks. Then he wrote again. I was to journey by train outside the city to the Goldens Bridge stop, wait forty-five minutes, and then follow precisely detailed directions into the nearby woodlands. I was to come alone. He wrote that he would know if I was being followed and if so, this and any future meeting would be impossible. I believed him. The man had evaded one of the biggest manhunts in New York City history for many months, all the while continuing to foil petty criminals, and in the meantime somehow become the single most famous human being in the country. Since his honorary constabulary deputization, I had felt very alone in my opposition to this man. I told no one but my editor of my plans to meet him. My editor asked, only half-jokingly, if I planned on bringing a weapon. I had not even considered this until my editor mentioned it. I then wished he hadn't.

Forty-five minutes, when you are waiting to meet the Avenger, is a long time, and while standing on the train platform at Goldens Bridge, I thought about the reading I had done about this peculiar species of costumed vigilantism. Others before the Avenger had taken to the streets, of course. There is Terrifica, a self-styled Valkyrie who patrols New York City bars to prevent predatory men from taking advantage of drunken women; Captain Jackson of Jackson, Michigan, "an officially sanctioned independent crime fighter," whose group, the Crimefighter Corps, works Jackson's troublous streets to little or no effect; Mr. Silent of Indianapolis; Ferox of Salt Lake City; Polarman of the Canadian Arctic. There are more. A website called the World Superhero Registry exists to keep track of these people. Look it up, and marvel at human aspiration at its most quietly noble and definitively unfounded. One other thing you will note is that the Avenger is not found on this site. Many of the registered superheroes I contacted for comment on the Avenger refused to say a word on the record about him. Off the record, the dissertations began. To the man — that is, to the *super*man (or -woman) — they regard him as a glory hound and a menace. They work *with* the system, they say, while the Avenger works at odds with the system. It seemed clear to me, at least, that a more green-eyed emotion was clouding these heroes' consideration.

The men and women listed on the World Superhero Registry are without exception grass-roots, community- and niche-based operators whose Lycra often poorly contains their girth. They are, in effect, noble clowns. But a few have tried to follow the Avenger's more dangerous, socially outlying path, the results of which have been vaguely comic, utterly tragic, and nothing else. In Los Angeles a hopeful who strapped two Tasers to his wrists and called himself Taserman accidentally zapped himself during an unsuccessful prevention of a carjacking. The Boomerang Kid was shot by unimpressed gangbangers in Las Vegas. Miami's Sunstroke was arrested for assault after being heckled by one of his fellow citizens. Chicago's Wolfreign was arrested for solicitation. These are (and, in the Boomerang Kid's case, were) not people like you or me, and further investigation of these "heroes" often revealed long histories of psychiatric inpatient care and Homeric rap sheets. No. They were not like you or me. But nor were they anything like the Avenger. They had made the mistake of blending the example of comic books with the inspiration of perhaps the single most peerless human being on this planet, which was rather like building a bomb from a design by Wile E. Coyote. The Avenger, as he admitted to Larry King with a chuckle, has no superpowers ("Not yet, at least"), but that did not mean the man was without some exquisite gifts. He is thought to be a fine, and perhaps even gifted, martial artist, and his bravery and physical strength are, by now, well established. The existence of his utility belt has been confirmed, as has been its assortment of nonlethal instruments: pellets of tear gas, smoke bombs, bolts of nylon cord, a supply of plastic handcuffs. At least a dozen of his prey reported catching eyefuls of Mace before being beaten senseless. The claim by one thug that he twice shot the Avenger in the chest to little ado seems to validate rumors of some kind of specially thin, easy-to-maneuver-in Kevlar vest.

Even after all this time, and all that has been written about him, I thought on the Goldens Bridge platform, *there was still so much about him we did not know.* There was no other famous person of whom this could be said — and I had spent a good portion of my career writing about, and contemplating, the famous. I looked off into the bran-colored brush thickets and up the hilly copse of leafless trees in which I knew he waited. My watch's alarm sounded. I had set it because I wanted to be exact, as exact as the man I was about to meet. The longest and shortest forty-five minutes of my life were up. I walked off to meet the Avenger.

I did not have to go far — perhaps a five-minute walk from the platform. The Avenger was sitting in a lotus position on a thronelike rock halfway up a hill. The sky, fittingly but discomfortingly, had gone as dark as a mud puddle, and the wind shook the stripped trees around us as though in indistinct warning; their trunks and branches groaned. But here he was. I lifted my hand in greeting.

Now, there is a question people ask when they learn you have met the Avenger. It is not about what he was wearing (a black ski mask — his one attempt at wardrobe iconography — and a plain gray hoodless sweatshirt; loose black pants with many marsupial pouches; black Puma running shoes; and his belt, also black, which was smaller than I had imagined but bulged with many little snap-shut pockets and holsters and plastic protuberances yet remained as essentially proletarian as that of a cable repairman), and it is not what his in-person voice sounds like (quiet, confident, accentless, a guy's and not a man's voice, somehow, all its energy and vitality at the edges rather than its center), and it is not whether he is friendly (read on). It is this: Is he funny? Because this is the rap on the Avenger, the attribute earned by all those suspiciously rehearsed and prefab comments he has made over the years to those he has stopped and those he has saved. The answer is that he is funny. He does not smile or make jokes, but then a fire does not need to blaze to give off heat. In fact, the very first thing the Avenger said to me, while certainly not hilarious, was funny, or at least mordantly engaged with the situation:

"Tell me. What sins of yours do I have to die for?"

I was still walking toward him, hummingbird-hearted. His voice so startled me I momentarily forget the title of my own anti-Avenger essay. I stopped. "Excuse me?"

With a grand little flourish he extended his hand. Given the darkness of his garb, his hand's flesh was so contrastingly white it seemed to glow. His only other bits of visible flesh were the twinned circles held within the eyelets of his ski mask and the oblong rectangular cutout around his mouth. His free hand, which remained on his knee, was gloved. "'The Avenger Dies for Our Sins.' The reason I'm sitting here and the reason you're looking at me."

Now we really *were* looking at each other, rather than working out wary approach vectors in anticipation of what we might first say. "I guess," I told him, "that I meant it as more of a metaphor."

He nodded. The nod of a ski-masked man is a strangely terrifying one — one imagines other, more frightening things that such a nod might result in — and then he un- and refolded his legs. His eyes, if I had to guess, were brown. "Metaphor? Okay. But kind of a shitty one. In my opinion."

"You have an interest in metaphor?" A stupid thing to say, perhaps, but conversations delimited by their own lack of precedent tend to result in circular restatement rather than interesting lunges.

He sat there and said nothing. I sensed that I had already disappointed him.

I asked him, "How do you know no one is going to walk along this path?"

Instantly he held up a device that looked like a cell phone. "I've placed a tiny wire across the trail fifty yards behind me. If someone trips it, this will vibrate. I can see behind you for another fifty yards. Don't worry. If anyone happens along, I'll be out of sight in twenty seconds, give or take. And you won't be able to follow me."

I motioned around at the surrounding forest, thinly treed suburban wilds through which a small recreational vehicle could have easily slalomed. "What about the rest of these woods?"

"I'll take my chances. People stick to paths, at any rate. It's one of the things that makes criminals so easy to anticipate. Most of us operate along a quantitatively smaller spectrum of choice than we realize."

"But not you."

"If I weren't a victim of the same coded inhibitions, I wouldn't be very good at predicting the behavior of others, would I? No, I'm the same. The only difference is that I am aware that when most people appear to have five or six choices, they really only have two." His chin lifted. "If that."

I pulled out my notepad. I held it up to him, I later realized, with the same hand, and with the same self-proud showmanship, that he had used to hold up his trip-wire-vibro box for me. "Do you mind?"

A small, annoyed, almost teenagery shrug. "Feel free." Two words into my first question, though, he interrupted me: "Why don't you write short stories anymore?"

At this I could do little but laugh. I had published a book of short stories more than a decade ago. It had received a small amount of acclaim and then quickly withdrew from the world of print. The praise was enough to attract a few editors' interest, and within months of the book's publication I began writing magazine journalism, which seemed to provide my talent a better, less frustrated outlet and my temperament a quicker, more active engagement. "You read my stories," I said. Once again he did not move. A few reluctant raindrops fell from the sky and pattered onto the scatter of autumnally crunchy leaves at my feet. I spoke again, this time with the proper inquisitive inflection. "You read my stories?"

"I've read everything you've written. Everything I could find, at least. I'm nothing if not thorough."

I looked at him, and he at me. I could not say I was surprised. I had come here expecting to be outwitted at every turn, but perhaps not so soon, or so intimately. I attempted a graceless flanking move. "Very interesting, Avenger. Why that name, anyway? Is that some reference to the Avengers?"

"What are the Avengers?"

"A comic book. A group of superheroes that operates out of a New York mansion. Captain America. Thor. Iron Man. Did you have a favorite? My boss wanted me to ask you that." My boss had wanted no such thing.

"I don't read comic books and I never have. Don't ask stupid questions."

"I don't read comic books either. The only reason I know anything about that is because I started to research you."

The Avenger remained as statuesquely still as some idol carved from the world's biggest piece of onyx. "I'll be honest. I didn't care much for all your short stories, but I liked one in particular: the story about the young guy whose brother was killed. Which of course happened to you. Now, what's interesting to me, as a reader, is that you never wrote about your brother's death elsewhere. That story is probably the best thing you've written, wouldn't you say? A rich vein of material there, obviously — one you dealt with quite effectively, I thought. It moved me. And yet what do you do after writing this story? You spend the next decade cranking out profiles of Michael Stipe and Will Ferrell."

I looked away. When I was nineteen and my brother was twenty-five, he was shot and killed while trying to intervene in a mugging in Washington, D.C. His killer was never found. "I've written things besides profiles."

"You write the occasional attempt at cultural criticism, and sometimes you write about violent crime. A fascination of yours, it seems. But — and this is what I, personally, find amazing — you somehow never manage to disclose that your own brother died at the hands of violent crime."

My head swung back quickly to face him. "I've written about my brother." And I had. I had written about my brother for this magazine, three years ago — a long essay about families who had lost a member to an unsolved murder, and how, in virtually every case, those families had never recovered; the four horsemen of divorce, substance abuse, depression, and suicide stalked them from the day of the murder on, plucking away the remaining family members one by one. Writing the piece proved so personally harrowing I have never written a piece of long-form investigative journalism again.

"You mentioned your brother in two paragraphs in that essay. The only time you've ever faced up to what happened to your brother is in your story. Everything else is peripheral."

"I haven't read that story in years. I barely even remember it." Insofar as something could be both true and false, this was it.

The Avenger now opened his legs, which spread apart as purposefully and smoothly as scissors, and after a quick little seesaw motion slid off his throne. But he took no further step. "I'm not a writer, but if *I* had suffered what you and your family suffered, and if *I* were writing critically about vigilantism, I might let the reader know what, exactly, was informing my criticism."

"I had something in there about him, at an early point. But I took it out."

His head tilted at a canine angle. "And why did you do that?"

"Because I didn't trust the impulse that moved me to include that information."

"You write about celebrities. What impulses do you trust when you're writing about Angelina Jolie?"

I put my notebook back into my pocket. Curiously, it had not rained any more than those first few drops. "You asked me here. I didn't ask you. You asked me."

"What did you do after your brother died?"

"How do you dispense Mace? There have been reports that you squirt it from a device hidden somewhere on your wrist."

He extended his left arm and with his right hand pushed down on the top of his belt's most central and plumpest barnacle. What began at his wrist as a jet of liquid became within two feet of its launching point a fine mist. Within seconds the wind had blown the lightly Tabascoed air my way, and my eyes filled.

"You asked," he said.

I nodded and rubbed my shirt against my eyes. "Fair enough. And how about the Kevlar vest?"

He lifted up his sweatshirt to reveal a tight black vest that appeared as shiny, and roughly as bullet-stopping, as neoprene. "It doesn't look like much, but this will stop a knife and most small-caliber bullets. A shotgun if I'm far enough away. I've been tapped a few times. One asshole shot me and broke two ribs. People assume I'm indestructible, but I get hurt all the time. More than half of my teeth have been knocked out." His demonstrative smile, which revealed a full set of enviably white choppers, lasted no more than a second. "Mostly dentures. All of this is part of the reason I'm not able to patrol as aggressively as I'd like. You know, the press amuses me. They write all the time about what I'm planning, and even print up little city maps that are supposed to show my patterns. There are no patterns and there are no plans. I never plan. What they call 'planning' is usually me holding an ice pack to my head, pulling the stitches out of my arm, and taking the splint off my big toe."

"Your vest — you designed that yourself?"

He shook his head. "Uh, no. I'm not . . . Bruce Wayne. Right? I ordered it from a Dutch company that provides armor for security guards, Halliburton, journalists who work in war zones. It wasn't cheap."

"And how do you make your money?"

"I've invested wisely. It's not like the stuff I use costs all that much. You'd be surprised by what you can get, no questions asked, through mail order. Becoming the Avenger required a financial investment of no more than six or seven thousand dollars. Total."

"And do you —"

"My turn." He crossed his arms. "What did you do after your brother died?"

I thought about how to respond. I had been in loving relationships where it had taken me many months to talk about my brother, and yet this stranger was asking me to winch up buckets sloshing with emotions and memories drawn from my darkest and most secret well. But I knew my answer would determine how close to him he would allow me to get.

"I did a lot of things. I cried. I studied the martial arts for a while, then gave it up. I traveled. Finally I wrote. He was a writer, too, by the way. At least he wanted to be. You don't know that because I've never mentioned it. Not in print."

"The martial arts. That's in one of the stories, too."

"I was fairly serious about it. Then it just seemed stupid. I was never very good. I don't even like to fight."

"Then why —"

"I didn't like feeling weak. I wondered if that's what got my brother killed: his weakness. He had such a good heart, but he was weak. That's one of the reasons I wrote my essay about you. I worried you would inspire people to step into situations they have no business stepping into."

"That must have been one of the parts you cut out."

"Everything I wrote is, from a legal point of view, inarguable. Inarguable. And you know as well as I do that the only reason they stopped trying to catch you is because they knew they couldn't."

The Avenger walked toward me. When I drew back he stopped and put up his hands. Slowly he lowered them. "Tell me why you drew back."

"Because I was afraid."

"Afraid of what?"

"Of you."

"What do you think criminals are, now, when they see me?"

"They're afraid."

"Of course they are. Your brother died trying to do what I have pledged to do. Your brother died because he found himself unable to stand by while someone in a position of strength victimized someone in a position of weakness. But *criminals* are weak, even the ones who get out of Rikers after pumping Volkswagens for six years. That's why they're criminals, and that's why their strength is always that of position, of circumstance. The criminal impulse is one of weakness — abject, encircling weakness. The police do not understand this. A few academics who study crime do understand this, but they embalm their understanding with misplaced empathy. How do you oppose criminals? You change their positioning. Most people can't do this. Almost anyone who stands up to a criminal will get hurt. It's the first thing they tell you: give them your wallet. I'd even tell you that if you were being mugged, and you look like a fairly strong dude. Still, give it to him — and know that this is where I come in. I'm the agent of repositioning. Give him your wallet, and let me do my work. I'm the only one who can. Most people drawn to what I do are sadists, revenge addicts, morons, or insane. Like the Boomerang Kid or any of the other idiots."

"Do you feel responsible for those people?"

"Not in the least."

I shook my head. "You are a most unique man."

"I was concussed when I said that."

"But you don't dispute it."

"I wish I were more unique. There are any number of crimes in this city, in this country, that I can't do a thing about. And so I essentially terrorize poor kids who had shitty situations to begin with. Am I happy about that? I am not."

"That was the point I tried to make in my essay."

"I agree with you. And I disagree. Because you have to start somewhere."

"Why are you telling me this? Why not write another letter to the paper of record?"

For the first and only time that afternoon, the Avenger laughed. "What do you want me to say? 'I am but a shadowy reflection of you. It would take only a nudge to make you like me, to push you out of the light'? I have nothing like that to say. And I have no story to tell you. I asked you here for one reason." He looked down, then, at his gloved hand, and then back at me. "Which will have to wait, because someone is coming." With a quickness all the more startling for how fully it incinerated my expectation, the Avenger broke away and ran into the woods, changing direction by wrapping a hooked arm around a birch tree, the momentum of which launched him over a rotten log. He did not look back.

I was still standing in the middle of the path when the couple that tripped the Avenger's hidden wire came upon me. An older man and woman, arm in arm, plump with retirement, looking at me with cool, New Englandy eyes. Here is the moment where I allow the Avenger to make sense. This is the event I adumbrate into meaningful sense. Now is when I come around to the Avenger. But no. I have not heard from him again, and he has apparently not been active since I saw him, which, at the time of this writing, now ranks among his longest silences. Is he healing? Or did our encounter do something to him that it did not do to me? I cannot say I have missed the Avenger. But sometimes I allow myself to believe he will soon tell me why he contacted me and what he finally had to say to me that day.

The man and woman stopped talking as they neared me. The enforced, artificial nature of their hush, their wariness, moved me to say, in a bright, friendly voice, "Hello!" But they *were* afraid, and by greeting them I had only made their fear worse. They hurried past me, as closely and solidly bundled together as siblings unaware of their divisibility.

ALAFAIR BURKE

Winning

FROM *Blue Religion*

LET ME TELL HIM for you, Jenny. You stay here and rest. I'll bring Greg in after — when he's thought it over a bit."

Jenny didn't have the energy to tell her partner, Officer Wayne Harvey, that there was nothing restful about lying in a hospital bed ten minutes after the completion of a rape kit. Thirty minutes after ingesting the morning-after pill and an HIV postexposure prophylaxis. Sixty minutes since the arrest. Three hours since the rape. That was her best guess — three hours, since it started, at least.

Talking to Greg would help her stop feeling this way that she didn't want to feel anymore. Weak. Embarrassed. Broken. She was ready to feel like herself again. Until the DA needed her testimony, she was finished with her duties as a crime victim. If she talked to Greg, she might feel more like Jenny. She would be the arresting police officer, delivering the news as gently as possible to the victim's family. She would also be his wife.

"No, Wayne. Go on home to Marcy. Just tell the nurse to get Greg for me."

Through the open slats of the drawn blinds in her room, she saw Greg talking to a young woman with bright pink scrubs and a blond ponytail. She knew both this process and her husband well enough that she thought she could actually make out some of the words. *Your wife is ready for visitors now, Mr. Sutton.* Greg looking worried still. Asking her something. Something like, *What happened? Was there an accident?* The nurse looking down at her hands, wishing there was a chart or a clipboard — some prop there to employ as a distraction. *Your wife needs you now. There's nothing more I can say.*

Greg opened the door and closed it gently behind him.

"You okay, baby? They won't tell me what's going on. Something happened on the sting?"

Jenny was one of two female patrol officers under the age of thirty-five working for the Missoula County Sheriff's Department. Tonight she was the one tapped to work as a prostitution decoy at the truck stops along I-90. She loved the job but not this assignment. Half naked in the bitter wind, the cold, dry air freezing the insides of her nostrils while an unwashed trucker eyed her over so she could negotiate an agreement of sex for money. But once the nasty part was over, it was easy. It was supposed to be easy. *Drive around back, hon, and I'll meet you there.* Then the supporting officers would take him down. That's the way it was supposed to go.

She patted the edge of the sterile blanket covering the bed, and Greg sat next to her. She held his hand. "I'm okay. A hundred percent. You understand?"

Her husband nodded, and some of the tension fell from his face.

"A dark green Bronco pulled in, not a truck-driving kind of truck, you know, but a regular Bronco, so he could maneuver better in the lot. Wayne was watching me just fine, but I wound up at the passenger side instead of the driver's. I made the deal."

"What's up, sweet thang?" Just looking for a date. "How much will that run me?" Twenty for a suck. Forty for straight sex. Fifty gets you half-and-half. I'm worth every penny. "Well, all right, then. That last one should get us started." Just pull around back, and I'll meet you; sometimes the cops watch from the road.

"So I told him to drive around back. It happened fast, but he pulled me into the car. He took me to a house out by Nine Mile Road, not far from the highway. He . . . he assaulted me, Greg, but I got away. I arrested him. Wayne came out and made sure the guy got processed just right. No technicalities for the courts."

"What do you mean, he assaulted you? You mean he —"

She looked him straight in the eye. Not one tear. Not even a quiver. "It was a sexual assault." *He raped me, Greg. And despite that look on your face, it was far worse than what you're imagining. So bad, I got to figure out a way for you never to know the details.*

Greg stood, leaving Jenny on her own in the bed. "I don't understand. How could they let this happen to you? How'd he get you out of that parking lot?"

"He sped right on out to the road. By the time Wayne got to his car, I guess a truck pulled in. The other guys were around back. It wasn't anyone's fault. It happened real fast, Greg." *No, it didn't.* "I'm all right."

"Where was your gun?"

"I can't carry when I'm a decoy." Underneath the tight outfits she wore undercover, the bulge of Jenny's Glock was as prominent as a road sign. "I guess we'll have to rethink the clothing in the future."

"You think that's funny?"

"I'll take humor anywhere I can find it right now."

"You couldn't fight him off? You're a cop. I've seen how strong you are."

"He was the one with the gun. I was lucky to get it away from him when I did, but the point was to come out alive." *I got my chance when he reached for the Vaseline on his dresser. He told me he needed it to get his fist where it would hurt me most. He kept his left hand on me while he reached with his gun hand. That's how he lost his balance.* "All I was focused on was getting out alive and getting back to you."

Greg's face was angry and injured at once. He worked his hands into claws while he paced the small room. "Baby, I'm sorry this happened to you. I can work more hours at the mill —"

"You work plenty." Jenny took her husband's hand and smiled up at him, hoping he'd see her face past the bruises that were starting to color. "How many times have you heard me say I'd keep working even if we hit the lotto?"

Greg helped Jenny change into the fresh clothes he'd been told to bring to the hospital. He even thought to take along his fleece-lined corduroy rancher's jacket for her, the one she loved to wear. When the nurse insisted she be wheeled to the exit, he did the honors. He even kept her mind busy in the truck on the way home to Lolo, making the antics down at the pulp mill sound like slapstick, the way he always did.

In their bed at home, though, with the lights off and with his back to her, he asked the question she knew he'd been thinking all along: "Why didn't you kill him, Jenny? When you got the gun from him, why didn't you do it?"

She gave him the answer she'd been working on since the hospital. "It wouldn't have been right. And I would've known it. And so I wouldn't have been the same person ever again. All the rest of it, I can get past."

Greg didn't speak to her again that night. If he ever turned to face her, Jenny didn't notice. Instead, she slept clenching Sushi, the stuffed purple goldfish that Greg won for her throwing rings at their first county fair together, the summer before they got married. *I told you I'd never let you down.* That's what he said when he won Sushi for her.

The next day Greg called in sick so he could stay with Jenny. Everything might have been different if he'd gone to the mill. The phone rang around three in the afternoon. Jenny answered. It was Anne Lawson, one of the deputy county prosecutors. Jenny knew her pretty well from testifying in a few of her cases. She was tough but fair and always treated people with respect, even the defendants she imprisoned.

"You feeling a little better today, Jenny?"

"A hundred percent. Thanks." Greg walked past her and patted her arm. It was the first time she'd felt his skin against hers since he helped her from the truck last night.

"You did real good getting out of there alive. And it's a good case. We're gonna get him. No plea-bargaining, either. I'll carry the file myself through to trial."

"Thanks, Anne."

"Hey, you got a second?"

"Sure."

"We had the arraignment this morning in front of Judge Parker. And the bail hearing."

"Oh, yeah?" Greg was watching her now, concerned. She shouldn't have let the tone of her voice say so much.

"Yeah. He's got Rick Deaver representing him." Jenny knew him, too. He was a decent public defender, a straight shooter as far as those guys went. "Anyway, we went for a no-bail hold. We thought we had a good shot."

"Did Judge Parker know it was me?" Jenny had testified in his courtroom last year against a man who locked his wife in a closet for two days after she forgot to buy barbecue potato chips at the market. Parker said she did a good job getting the wife to cooperate with the sheriff's department. Jenny found out later that Parker told the prosecuting attorney the woman should have killed the SOB and called it a day.

"He said afterward to tell you he's sorry about what happened. But he also said there was more threat of witness intimidation with civilians. I pushed really hard, Jenny. I said your being a cop obviously didn't stop him from —"

"What'd it get set at?"

"Two hundred thousand."

"Does he own that place out near Nine Mile?"

"He inherited it from his aunt about eight years ago. It's not much to look at, but with all that land, and the way prices have gone up —"

"How long's something like that take? If he puts up the house?"

"He doesn't even have to use a bank. A bail bondsman will have him out in a few hours. I'm real sorry, Jenny."

"Not your fault. I appreciate the call."

The sound of glass shattering against the kitchen tile broke the silence that filled Jenny's head as she hung up the phone. She looked up to see Greg's juice glass scattered on the floor across the room, red V8 oozing into the grouted cracks.

"Am I supposed to clean that up?"

"Of course not." Greg began plucking at the shards of glass.

"Be careful with that." Jenny kneeled to help, but Greg pushed her hand away. "What exactly did I do wrong here? Why are you so angry at me?"

"I'm not angry at you," Greg insisted. "I'm angry at him. I'm angry at everything else. I'm angry because I'm a human being. What I can't figure out is you. How can you be so damn calm about all this?"

"You think I'm calm inside? You think my mind is peaceful today? You have no idea. It's because of what's inside me that I don't have the energy for outbursts. I don't have the luxury of a temper tantrum. What you're going through is natural, but it's not about me."

"Damn it, Jenny. Don't you see what's going on here? He's getting away with it. He did this to you, and nothing's happening. He's winning."

Jenny sat cross-legged on the floor beside her husband as he sopped up the remaining spill with a towel. "You and me, we've got different ideas about winning. You think the only way to walk out of a fight a winner is to beat the other man down. That's how men talk about fighting, right? Only a loser runs away. It's not like that for us. We win by getting away. We win by staying alive. This happened to me, Greg, and it's my right to say I won. I got away, and he didn't."

"I'm not stupid. I know why Anne called. He's getting bail."

"You know what? B . . . F . . . D. He buys himself a couple of months of freedom, but soon enough he'll be pulling a dime at Deer Lodge, and we're still us. In the meantime, you can bet that Wayne and the other boys will make sure that if he so much as jaywalks, his bail will get pulled."

She smiled at him, but Greg shook his head and walked to the sink. He wrung the towel beneath the faucet, watching a pink stream of water circle the drain. "It's not enough."

One week later Greg went back to the pulp mill. Jenny was still on leave and used the day to prepare Greg's favorite supper, grilled steak and fettuccine Alfredo. Three hours after Greg's shift ended, the steaks were dry black bricks in the oven, and the noodles were glued together in a clump. An hour after that, the phone rang. Jenny answered and heard her husband's heavy breaths in her ear.

"Greg? Greg, what happened?"

"Oh, Jesus. I . . . I don't know what to do. I . . . there's blood everywhere. It's all over my clothes. If I get in the truck —"

Jenny was already in the bedroom, opening the top drawer of her dresser. "My gun. My service weapon? The ballistics are on file. What did you do? What did you do?"

"I'm so sorry."

Jenny held the top of her head with her free hand, like that might literally help her collect her thoughts. "Are you cut? Did he touch you?"

"No. I didn't let him near me."

"So the blood's all his?"

"There's a lot of it. It sprayed or something."

"Have you stepped in it? Are there footprints?"

The pause felt like an eternity. "No. Some got on the tops of the boots, not the bottoms."

"All right. Keep it that way. Don't step in any blood. Your clothes.

There's an attached garage there, Greg. And a tarp. I saw a blue tarp on the ground for painting." Jenny peered through the bedroom curtains. It was still snowing. That was good. "Stand on the tarp and strip off anything that's got blood. Put the gun in there, too. Wrap it all up, and be careful. Wipe down anything you might have touched. Doorknobs, door frames, stairwells —"

"I wore gloves. I've still got gloves on."

"Okay. Good. How'd you get in the house?"

"I knocked. I told him I was an investigator with the PD's office, sent there by Rick Deaver. He opened the door for me."

"Good. Just make sure he didn't lock the door behind him." Jenny moved through the house, collecting the things she'd need. A spray bottle of bleach. A book of matches. "Leave it unlocked, you hear? And open the windows. Are you listening to me?"

"Why —"

"Just do it. Whatever room his body's in. Open all the windows so it gets good and cold. Do you know how many times you shot him?"

"Twice."

"You sure about that?"

"Yeah, I'm sure."

She took two cartridges from the top drawer. "What phone are you calling on?"

"Um . . . oh, my God."

"It's all right. We'll deal with it. Just don't get anything from his house or his body in your truck. Okay?" What else? One of the quick-burn logs near the fireplace. Lighter fluid, too. She checked the mudroom. Greg's corduroy coat was missing from its hook. That was good. She began feeding the uneaten dinner to the garbage disposal. "It's isolated out there, so you've got enough time to be careful. Don't miss anything. Wrap the tarp up tight and put it in the back of the truck. And don't forget the gun. And drive perfect. Don't get yourself pulled over in your boxer shorts."

By the time Greg pulled onto their road, Jenny had everything ready. She pulled her shivering husband inside and washed his shaking hands under hot water in the kitchen sink. If they analyzed for gunshot residue, Greg would not be the one to test positive.

She checked him over for any blood he might have missed on his shorts and T-shirt, on his skin, in his hair. She poured him three fingers of Bushmills, made sure he downed it, then poured him another. She undressed him and tucked him into their bed, resting the whiskey bottle on the nightstand beside him. He'd wake from nightmares and reach for it. She stroked his cold, damp hair until his breathing was steady. She picked up Sushi from her side of the bed and tucked the little fish beneath one arm of her husband's resting body, kissed his cheek, and told him she was going to be gone for a little while to get rid of the tarp of clothing. To be safe, she grabbed his T-shirt, boxers, and socks, along with the kit she'd put together. She didn't wear a coat.

She used the quick-burn log to start a fire at a campsite along I-90 near the Clark Fork River. She burned his clothes — everything but the coat — using the lighter fluid to make sure the flames consumed it all. As a precaution, she poured half the bottle of bleach on the pile of charred wood and ashes. She turned the coat inside out, rolled it into a ball, and placed it gently on her passenger seat. She sprayed the empty tarp with bleach, then folded it and tucked it into her trunk. Finally, she held her familiar pistol and added two cartridges to fill the magazine. She fired two shots into a nearby tree and tucked the gun snugly into her waistband at the small of her back.

The drive to Nine Mile wasn't easy. The snow was sticking heavily, and she made a point of taking her Escort instead of the truck that Greg drove to work. The bad memories of the last time up this road didn't help. Neither did the current situation. By the time she neared the house she never wanted to see again, whatever tracks had been made by her husband's tires had been smoothed over by a perfect layer of white. She parked her car in the driveway, took a deep breath, ran through the plan one more time, and exhaled. She was ready. She retrieved the corduroy coat and blue tarp and walked through the unlocked front door.

The house was cold from the opened windows, like Jenny wanted it. The man's body was splayed on his living room floor. Two shots, just like Greg said. One near the bottom of his gut. One in the neck. The neck shot must have hit an artery. That's what caused the splatter. The gut shot probably took him down all mangled on his side like that. Jenny was grateful her husband wasn't a better shot. With a cool head and a well-formed intention to kill, Jenny could easily plug a man squarely in the middle of the brain and heart from this range. These wayward shots would allow a different narrative.

She tiptoed over the body to pull the windows shut, making certain not to traipse through any of the blood. Within a few minutes she could feel the room temperature rising from the wood-burning stove in the corner. Then she stepped near the body again, this time placing her boots firmly in the puddle that had formed beneath the man's torso. She took a quick look. The chill had kept the body fresh enough. Time of death wouldn't pose a problem. She walked to the phone and dialed a cell phone number she knew by heart.

"Wayne Harvey."

"Wayne, it's Jenny. I need your help."

"Anything. You know that."

Then she told Wayne the story. The man called the house during dinner. He said vile things about what he'd done to her. He said he'd tell everyone in prison. Montana is small. Her days in law enforcement would be over. Greg started drinking. She was at the Nine Mile house now and needed his help. She needed Anne Lawson from the County Attorney's Office to come out, too.

Jenny hung up the phone and walked to the back of the house. It felt smaller now. Used. Threadbare. Diminished in ways that she could not quite explain to herself. She sat on the man's bed and looked into the mirror above the dresser. She remembered turning her head away from that mirror a week ago so she would not have to see her reflection. Now she did not have to look away. She touched a smear of lipstick on her mouth. It made her think of blood. For just a moment, only a moment, she felt her heart quicken with a strange sense of pleasure.

JAMES LEE BURKE

Big Midnight Special

FROM *Shenandoah*

You know how summertime is down South. It comes to you
in the smell of watermelons and distant rain and the smell of cotton poison and schools of catfish that have gotten dammed up in a
pond that's about to be drained. It comes to you in a lick of wet
light on razor wire at sunup. You try to hold on to the coolness of
the night, but by noon you'll be standing inside your own shadow,
hoeing out long rows of soybeans, a gunbull on horseback gazing
at you from behind his shades in the turnaround, his silhouette a
black cutout against the sun.

At night, way down inside my sleep, I dream of a white horse running in a field under a sky full of thunderheads. The tattoos
wrapped around my forearms like blue flags aren't there for orna-
mentation. That big white horse pounding across the field makes a
sound just like a heart pumping, one that's about to burst.

In the camp, the cleanup details work till noon, then the rest of
the weekend is free. The electric chair is in that flat-topped off-
white building down by the river. It's called the Red Hat House because during the 1930s troublemakers who were put on the levee
gang and forced to wear stripes and straw hats painted red got
thrown in there at night, most of them still stinking from a ten-
hour day pushing wheelbarrows loaded with dirt and broken bricks
double-time under a boiling sun. The boys who stacked their time
on the Red Hat gang went out Christians, that is, if they went out at
all, because a bunch of them are still under the levee.

The two iron sweatboxes set in concrete on Camp A were bull-
dozed out about ten years ago, around 1953. I knew a guy who

spent twenty-two days inside one of them, standing up, in the middle of summer, his knees and tailbone jammed up against the sides whenever he collapsed. They say his body was molded to the box when the prison doctor made the hacks take him out.

Leadbelly was in Camp A. That's where prison legend says he busted that big Stella twelve-string over a guy's head. But I never believed that story. Not many people here understood Leadbelly, and some of them made up stories about him that would make him understandable, like them — predictable and uncomfortable with their secret knowledge about themselves when they looked in the mirror.

Wiley Boone walks out of the haze on the yard, his skin running with sweat, his shirt wadded up and hanging out of his back pocket, the weight sets and high fence and silvery rolls of razor wire at his back. He has a perfect body, hard all over, his chest flat-plated, his green pinstriped britches hanging so low they expose his pubic hair.

"You still trying to pick 'The Wild Side of Life'?" he asks.

"Working on it," I say.

"It's only taken you, what, ten goddamn years?"

"More like twelve," I say, smiling up at him from the steps to my "dorm," resting my big-belly J-50 across my thigh.

"Jody wants to match the two of us in the three-rounders up in the block."

I lean sideways so I can see past Wiley to the group out by the weight sets. There's only one chair on the yard, and Jody Prejean is sitting in it, cleaning his nails with a toothpick, blowing the detritus off the tips of his fingers. Jody has the natural good looks of an attractive woman but should not be confused with one. I mean he's no queer himself. Actually he has the lean face and deep-set dark eyes of a poet or a visionary or a man who can read your thoughts. Jody is a man of all seasons.

"Tell Jody I'm too old. Tell him I'm on my third jolt. Tell him I didn't come back here to take dives or beat up on tomato cans." I say all this with a smile on my face, squinting up at Wiley against the glare.

"You calling me a tomato can?"

"A bleeder is a bleeder. Don't take it personal. I had over fifty stitches put in my eyebrows. That's how come my eyes look like a Chinaman's."

"I'll do you a favor, Arlen. I'll tell Jody you'll be over to talk with him. I'll tell him you weren't a smart-ass. I'll tell him you appreciate somebody looking out for your interests."

I form an E chord at the top of the Gibson's neck and start back in on "The Wild Side of Life," running the opening notes up the treble strings.

When I look back up, Wiley is still standing there. There are a series of dates tattooed along each of his lats. No one knows what they represent. Wiley is doing back-to-back nickels for assault and battery and breaking and entering.

"Jimmy Heap cut the original song. Nobody knows that. Most people only know the Hank Thompson version," I say.

Wiley stares down at me, his hands opening and closing by his sides, unsure if he's being insulted again. "Version of what?"

"The Wild Side of Life," you moron, I think, but I keep my silence. Saying my thoughts out loud is a disease I've got and no amount of grief or twelve-step meetings seems to cure it.

"Wiley?"

"What?" he says.

"Chugging pud for Jody will either put you on the stroll or in a grave at Point Lookout. Jody goes through his own crew like potato chips. Ask for lockup if you got to. Just get away from him."

"One of the colored boys ladling peas owes me a big favor. Don't be surprised if you get something extra in your food tonight," he says. He walks back to the weight sets, pulling his shirt loose from his back pocket, popping the dust and sweat off his back with it. There's already a swish to his hips, double nickels or not.

The boys with serious problems are called big stripes. They stay up in the block, in twenty-three-hour lockdown, along with the snitches who are in there for their own protection. Jody Prejean doesn't qualify as a big stripe. He's intelligent and has the manners of a dapper businessman, the kind of guy who runs a beer distributorship or a vending machine company. His clothes are pressed by his favorite punk; another punk shampoos and clips his hair once a week. His cowboy boots get picked up at his bunk every night. Before sunup they're back under his bunk, their tips spit-shined into mirrors.

His two-deck bunk is in a board-plank alcove, down by the cage wire that separates us from the night screw who reads paperback westerns at a table under a naked light bulb until sunup. On the wall above Jody's bunk is a hand-brocaded tapestry that reads: *Every knee to me shall bend.*

I lean against Jody's doorjamb and look at nothing in particular. Jody is sitting on the edge of his bunk, playing chess with a stack of bread dough from Shreveport named Butterbean Simmons. Butterbean talks with a lisp and is always powdered with sunburn. He has spent most of his life in children's shelters and reformatories. When he was nineteen, his grandmother tried to whip him with a switch. Butterbean threw a refrigerator on top of her, then tossed her and the refrigerator down a staircase.

It takes Jody a long time to look up from his game. His dark hair is sun-bleached on the tips and wet-combed on his neck. His cheeks are slightly sunken, his skin as pale as a consumptive's. "Want something, Arlen?" he says.

How do you survive in jail? You don't show fear, but you don't ever pretend you're something you're not. "I do my own time, Jody. I don't spit in anybody's soup."

"Know what Arlen is talking about?" Jody asks Butterbean.

Butterbean grins good-naturedly, his eyes disappearing into slits. "I think so," he replies.

"So tell me," Jody says.

"I ain't sure," Butterbean says.

Jody laughs under his breath, his eyes on me, like only he and I are on the same intellectual plane. "Sit down. Here, next to me. Come on, I won't hurt you," he says. "You were a club fighter, Arlen. You'll add a lot of class to the card."

"No thanks."

"I can sweeten the pot. A touch of China white, maybe. I can make it happen."

"I'm staying clean this time."

"We're all pulling for you on that. Where's your guitar?"

"In the cage."

"A Gibson, that's one of them good ones, isn't it?"

"Don't mess with me, Jody."

"Wouldn't dream of it. Your move, Butterbean," he says.

I butcher chickens and livestock with a colored half-trusty by the name of Hogman. He has bristles on his head instead of hair, and

eyes like lumps of coal. They contain neither heat nor joy and have
the lifeless quality of fuel that's been used up in a fire. His forearms are scrolled with scars like flattened gray worms from old
knife beefs. He owns a mariachi twelve-string guitar and wraps
banjo strings on the treble pegs because he says they give his music
"shine." Some days he works in the kitchen and delivers rice and
red beans and water cans to the crews in the fields. While we're
chopping up meat on a big wood block that provides the only color
inside the gloom where we work, he sings a song he wrote on the
backs of his eyelids when he was still a young stiff and did three
days in the sweatbox for sassing a hack:

> My Bayou Caney woman run off wit' a downtown man,
> She left my heart in a paper bag at the bottom of our garbage can.
> But I ain't grieving 'cause she headed down the road,
> I just don't understand why she had to take my V-8 Ford.

"You're a jewel, Hogman," I say.

"Lot of womens tell me that," he replies. "Was you really at Gua-
dalcanal?"

"Yeah, I was sixteen. I was at Iwo in 'forty-five."

"You got wounded in the war?"

"Not a scratch."

"Then how come you put junk in your arm?"

"It's medicine, no different than people going to a drugstore." I
try to hold my eyes on his, but I can't do it. Like many lifers,
Hogman enjoys a strange kind of freedom; he's already lost everything he ever had, so no one has power over him. That means he
doesn't have to be polite when somebody tries to jerk his crank and
sell the kind of doodah in here that passes for philosophy.

"You was struck by lightning, though? That's how you got that
white streak in your hair and the quiver in your voice."

"That's what my folks said. I don't remember much of it. I was
playing baseball, with spikes on, and the grass was wet from the
rain. Everything lit up, then I was on the ground and my spikes
were blown off my feet, and my socks were smoking."

"Know what you are, Arlen? A purist. That's another word for
hardhead. You t'ink you can go your own way, wrap yourself in your
own space, listen to your own riffs. Jody Prejean has got your name
on the corkboard for the t'ree-rounders."

"Run that by me again?"

"Jody put your name up there on the fight card. You going against Wiley Boone. You cain't tell a man like Jody to kiss your ass and just walk away."

"Jody is a gasbag," I say, feeling the words clot in my windpipe.

"He'll break your thumbs. He'll get somebody to pour Drano down your t'roat. You can ax for segregation up in the block, but he's got two guys over there can race by your cell and light you up. Jody can walk t'rew walls."

"So screw him," I say.

"See, that make you be a purist. Playing the same songs over and over again. You got your own church and you the only cat in it. The world ain't got no place for people like you, Arlen. Not even in here. Your kind is out yonder, under the levee, their mout's stopped with dirt."

Hogman slams his cleaver down on a slab of pig meat, cracking through bone and sinew, covering us both with a viscous pink mist.

For supper this evening we had rice and greens and fried fish. The warden's wife is a Christian woman and teaches Bible lessons up in the block and oversees the kitchens throughout the prison farm. Sometimes through my window I see her walking on the levee with other women. Their dresses are like gossamer, and the shapes of their bodies are backlit against a red sun. The grass on the levee is deep green and ankle-high, and the wind blowing off the Mississippi channels through it at sunset. The sky is piled with yellow and purple clouds, like great curds of smoke rising from a chemical fire. Far across the water are flooded gum and willow trees, bending in the wind, small waves capping against their trunks, marking the place where the world of free people begins. The ladies sometimes clasp hands and study the sunset. I suspect they're praying or performing a benediction of some kind. I wonder if in their innocence they ever think of the rib cages and skulls buried beneath their feet.

My J-50 Gibson has a mahogany back and sides and a spruce soundboard. The bass notes rumble through the soundboard like apples tumbling down a chute, and at the same time you can hear every touch of the plectrum on the treble strings. The older the J-50 gets, the deeper its resonance. Floyd Tillman signed my soundboard in a Beaumont beer joint. Brownie McGhee and Furry Lewis and Ike Turner signed it in Memphis. Texas Ruby and Curly Fox signed it at Cook's Hoedown in Houston. Leon McAuliffe signed it under the stars at an outdoor dance on the Indian reservation in the Winding Stair Mountains of east Oklahoma. My only problem is it takes me ten years minimum to get a piece down right. I started working on Hank Snow's "I'm Movin' On" in 1950. Eleven years later I saw him play. Know how he created that special sound and rhythm that nobody can imitate? His rhythm guitarist used conventional tuning and stayed in C sharp. But Hank tuned his strings way down, then put a capo on the first fret and did all his runs in D sharp. Is that weird or what? What the rest of the band was playing in was beyond me. The point is Hank broke all the rules and, like the guy who wrote "The Wild Side of Life," created one of the greatest country songs ever written.

My bunk is military tuck, my snacks or "scarf" and my cigarette papers and my can of Bugler tobacco and my cigarette-rolling machine and my magazines all squared away on my shelf. The big window fan at the end of the building keeps our dorm cool until morning. After a shower and supper and a change into clean state blues, I like to sit on my bunk and play my Gibson. Nobody bothers me, except maybe to ask for a particular song. If you're a "solid" con, nobody usually bothers your stuff. But a musical instrument in here can be a temptation. Just before lights go out at nine o'clock, I always give my Gibson to the night screw, who locks it in the cage with him, along with the soda pop and candy bars and potato chips and Fritos for the canteen.

Tonight is different.

"Cain't do it no more, Arlen," he says. He has a narrow face and sun-browned arms that are pocked with cancerous skin tissue. One of his eyes is slightly lower than the other, which makes you think you're looking at separate people.

"That kind of jams me up, boss," I say.

"It ain't coincidence you're down on the 'bitch, boy. If you followed a few rules, maybe that wouldn't be the case."

"Don't do this to me, Cap."

"Don't degrade yourself. You're con-wise and a smart man, Arlen. Adjust, that's the key. You hearing me on this?"

"Yes, sir."

Jody got to you, you lying bastard, a voice inside me says.

"What'd you say?"

"Not a thing, boss," I reply, lowering my eyes, folding my arms across my chest.

"By the way, you're not working in the slaughterhouse no more. At bell count tomorrow morning, you're on the truck."

At sunrise I wrap my Gibson in a blanket, fold down the ends along the back and the soundboard, and tie twine around the nut, the base of the neck, and across the sound hole. I put my Gibson under my bunk and look at it for a long time, then go in for breakfast. We have grits, sausage, white bread, and black coffee, but it's hard for me to eat. Just before bell count on the yard, I look at my Gibson one more time. The morning is already hot, the wind down, clouds of gnats and mosquitoes rising from the willow trees along the river. Three U.S. Army surplus trucks clang across a cattle guard and turn into the yard. In the distance I can see the mounted gunbulls in the corn and soybean and sweet potato fields waiting on our arrival, the water cans set in the shadows of the gum trees, the sun coming up hard, like a molten ball lifted with tongs from a furnace. Some of the gunbulls are actually trusty inmates. They have to serve the time of any guy who escapes while under their charge.

At noon I see Butterbean Simmons hoeing in the row next to me, eyeballing me sideways, his long-sleeve shirt buttoned at the wrists and throat, his armpits looped with sweat. "The money is on Wiley in the three-rounder," he says. "I'm betting on you, though. You'll rip him up."

The soil is loamy, cinnamon-colored, and smells of pesticide and night damp. "Tell Jody he touches my box, we take everything to a higher level," I reply, my hoe rising and falling in front of me, notching weeds out of the row.

"Man, I'm trying to be your friend."

My oldest enemy is my anger. It seems to have no origins and blooms in my chest and sends a rush of bile into my throat. "Lose the guise, 'Bean, and while you're at it, get the fuck away from me."

The night screw had said I went down on the 'bitch, as in "habitual," as in three jolts in the same state. When you carry the 'bitch with you into a parole hearing, there's a good chance you're not even going out max time; there's a good chance you're going to stack eternity in the inmate cemetery at Point Lookout. Why am I working on my third jolt? I'd like to say it's scag. But my dreams aren't just about white horses pounding across a field under a blue-black sky forked with lightning. My dreams tell me about the other people who live inside my skin, people who have done things that don't seem connected to the man I think I am.

By quitting time, I'm wired to the eyes. After we offload from the trucks, everyone bursts into the dorm, kicking off work shoes, stripping off their clothes, heading for the shower with towels and bars of soap. I head for my bunk.

My Gibson is still there, but not under it, *on* it, like a wrapped mummy stretched out on the sheet. I put it back under my bunk, undress, and go into the shower. Wiley Boone stands under one of the pipes, a stream of cold water dividing on his scalp, his body running with soap, braiding in a stream off his phallus.

"Who moved my box, Wiley?" I ask.

"Guys cleaning up? The count screw?" he replies. "Maybe it was an earthquake. Yeah, that's probably it."

"You're planning to lay down in the three-rounder, aren't you?"

"I'm gonna hand you your ass is what I'm gonna do," he says.

"Wrong. I'm going to hold you up. And while I'm holding you up, I'm going to cut you to pieces. Then I'm going to foul you. In the balls, so hard your eyes are going to pop out. So you're going to lose every way possible, Wiley. When you figure all that out, go tell it to Jody."

"You got swastika tats on your arms, Arlen. Hope nobody wants their ink back. You ever have to give your ink back? Thinking about it makes my pecker shrivel up."

The night screw said I was con-wise and smart. After trying to bluff Jody by going at him through Wiley, I had to conclude that the IQ standards in here are pretty low.

But I'd screwed up. When you're inside, you never let other people know what you're thinking. You don't argue, you don't contend, you don't let your body language show you're on to another guy's schemes. You wrap yourself in a tight ball and do your time. I'd been a club fighter. Our owner took us from town to town and told us when to stand up and when to lie down. That's how it works, no different than professional wrestling. I'd shot off my mouth to Wiley and tipped him to what I'll do if Jody tries to make me fight by stealing my guitar. That was dumb.

Just before lights out, I go into Jody's alcove. He's wearing pajamas instead of skivvies, eating a bowl of blackberry pie and cream with a spoon.

"You won't have any trouble with me. I'll be on the card and I'll make it come out any way you want," I say. My eyes seem to go in and out of focus when I hear my words outside of myself.

"I'll give it some thought," Jody says. "A man disrespects me, he puts me in an embarrassing position, even guys I admire, guys such as yourself."

"Yeah?" I say.

"Wish you hadn't created this problem for us. You told Wiley I was gonna put him on the stroll? Why'd you do that, Arlen?"

"What do you want from me?"

He glances up at the tapestry on the wall, the one that says *Every knee to me shall bend.*

Tuesday the sun is a yellow flame inside the bright sheen of humidity that glistens on the fields and trees. The gunbulls try to find shade for themselves and their horses under the water oaks, but there is precious little of it when the sun climbs straight up in the sky. The air is breathless, and blowflies and gnats torment their horses' eyes and legs. A white guy nicknamed Toad because of the moles on his face collapses at the end of my row and lies in a heap between the soybean plants. It's the second time he has fallen out. A gunbull tells three colored guys to pick Toad up and lay him on a red-ant hill out in the gum trees. Toad is either a good actor or he's had sunstroke, because he lies there five minutes before the captain tells the colored guys to put him in the back of the truck.

I hear Butterbean thudding his hoe in the row next to me, his breath wheezing in his chest, sweat dripping off the end of his nose. He wears a straw hat with the brim slanted downward to create shade on his face and neck. "I didn't have nothing to do with it, Arlen," he says.

"With what?" I say.

"*It.*"

Then I know the price I'm about to pay for going against Jody. In

my mind's eye I see a trusty from the kitchen walking through the
unlocked door of the night screw's cage, the dorm empty, his flat-
soled, copper-eyelet prison work shoes echoing down the two rows
of bunk beds. I feel the sun boring through the top of my head, my
ears filling with the sound of wind inside a conch shell, my lips
forming an unspoken word, like a wet bubble on my lips.

I feel the hoe handle slip from my palms, as though the force of
gravity has suddenly become stronger than my hands. I hear the
creak of leather behind me, a mounted hack straightening himself
in the saddle, pushing himself up in the stirrups. "You gonna fall
out on me, Arlen?" he says.

"No sir, boss."

"Then what the hell is wrong with you?"

"Got to go to the dorm."

"You sick?"

"Got to protect my box, boss."

"Pick up your tool, boy. Don't hurt yourself worse 'n you already
have."

When I drop off the back of the truck that evening, I watch everyone else rush inside for showers and supper. I walk up the wood
steps into the building and cross through the night screw's cage,
wiping the sweat and dirt off my chest with my balled-up shirt. The
dorm is almost totally quiet, everybody's eyes sliding off my face as I
walk toward my bunk. One guy coughs; a couple of other guys head
for the showers, walking naked past me, their eyes averted, flip-
flops slapping the floor.

I get down on one knee and pull my guitar from under my bunk.
It's still wrapped in the blanket I tied around its neck and belly, but
the twine sags and the lines and shape of the blanket are no longer
taut. Inside, I can hear the rattle of wood. The contours of my Gibson now feel like the broken body of a child. I untie the twine from
the nut and the bottom of the neck and the belly and peel back the
folds of the blanket. The mahogany back and sides and the spruce
soundboard have been splintered into kindling; the bridge has
torn loose from the soundboard, and the strings are coiled up on
themselves and look like a rat's nest. The neck is broken; the exposed wood, framed by the dark exterior finish, makes me think of
bone that has turned yellow inside the earth.

I sit on the side of my bunk and take my Bugler tobacco can and my cigarette papers and my rolling machine off my shelf and start building a cigarette. No one in the dorm speaks. Gradually they file into the shower, some of them looking back at me, the night screw watching them, then shifting his eyes in my direction. "Better eat up, boy," he says.

"Give mine to the cat, boss," I reply.

"Say that again."

"Don't pay me no mind, Cap. I ain't no trouble," I say.

A few decks of Camels or Red Dots (Lucky Strikes) will buy you any kind of shank you want: a pie wedge of tin or a long shard of window glass wired and taped tightly inside a chunk of broom handle, a toothbrush heated by a cigarette lighter and reshaped around a razor blade, a sharpened nail or the guts of a ballpoint pen mounted on a shoe-polish applicator. Cell house shakedowns probably don't discover a third of the inventory.

Molotov cocktails are a different matter. The ingredients are harder to get, and gasoline smells like gasoline, no matter where you hide it. But a guy up in the block who works in the heavy equipment shed knows how to stash his product where his customer can find it and the hacks can't. It's a package deal and his product never fails: a Mason jar of gas, Tide detergent, and paraffin shaved into crumbs on a carrot grater. He even tapes a cotton ignition pad on the cap so all you have to do is wet it down, touch a flame to it, and heave it at your target. There's no way to get the detergent and the hot paraffin off the skin. I don't like to think about it. Ever hear the sound of somebody who's been caught inside a flamethrower? It's just like a mewing kitten's. They don't scream; they just mew inside the heat. You hear it for a long time in your sleep. You hear it sometimes when you're awake, too.

Jody comes to my bunk after supper. Some of his crew trail in after him, lighting smokes, staring around the dorm like they're not part of the conversation but lapping it up like dogs licking a blood spore. "You're starting to get a little rank, Arlen. You're not gonna take a shower?" Jody says.

"I'll get to it directly. Maybe in the next few days," I reply.

"Some of the guys think you ought to do it now."

"I think you're probably right. Thanks for bringing it to my attention."

I stub out my cigarette in my butt can and blow the smoke

straight out in front of me, not looking at him, the pieces of my destroyed Gibson folded next to me inside my blanket. I pull the corners of the blanket together and tie them in a knot, creating a large sack. I can hear the strings and the broken wood clatter together when I lift the sack and slide it under my bunk.

"My box is still with me, Jody," I say. "So is the music of all the people who signed their names on it. Busting it up doesn't change anything."

"You're as piss-poor at lying as you are at playing the guitar, Arlen."

"I was at Iwo," I say, grinning up at him.

"So what?" he says.

Truth is, I don't rightly know myself. I strip naked in front of Jody and his crew and watch them step back from my stink. Then I walk into the shower, turn on the cold water full blast, and lean my forehead against the cinder blocks, my eyes tightly shut.

Weasel Combs is a runner and jigger, or lookout man, for a guy up in the block who takes grapevine orders and provides free home delivery. Our crew is working a soybean field up by the front of the farm, not far from the main gate and the adjacent compound where the free people live. At noon the flatbed truck from the kitchen arrives, and Hogman and Weasel drop off the bed onto the ground and uncap the stainless steel cauldron that contains our red beans and rice. A dented water can full of Kool-Aid sits next to it. Weasel is an alcoholic check writer who always has a startled look on his face, like somebody just slammed a door on his head.

"How about an extra piece of cornbread, Arlen?" he says.

"I wouldn't mind," I say.

"I got that magazine you wanted. It's in the cab. I'll bring it to you when I get finished here." His eyes stare brightly into mine. His denim shirt is unbuttoned all the way down his chest. His ribs are stenciled against his skin, his waist so narrow his pants are falling off. A big square of salve-stained gauze is taped over an infected burn on his stomach.

"I could use some reading material. Thanks for bringing that, Weasel," I reply.

We eat in a grove of gum and persimmon trees, the sky growing black overhead. Down below the road that traverses the prison farm I can see the clapboard, tin-roofed houses of the free people inside the fence, clothes popping on the wash lines, a colored in-mate breaking corn in a washtub for the wife of the head gunbull, kids playing on a swing set, no different than a back-of-town poor-white neighborhood anywhere in the South. The irony is that free people do almost the same kind of time we do, marked by the farm in ways they don't recognize in themselves.

The hack at the gate sits in a wicker-bottom chair inside a square of hot shade provided by the shack where he has a desk and a tele-phone. He's over seventy and has been riding herd on convicts since he was a teenager. Legend has it that during the 1930s he and his brother would get drunk on corn liquor in the middle of the af-ternoon, take a nap, then pick out a colored inmate and tell him to start running. People would hear a couple of shots inside the wind, and another sack of fertilizer would go into the levee. His teeth are gone and his skin is dotted with liver spots. There's not a town in Mississippi or Louisiana he can retire to, lest one of his old charges finds him and does things to him no one does to an elderly man.

I can hear thunder in the south. The wind comes up and trowels great clouds of dust out of the fields, and I feel a solitary raindrop sting my face. Weasel squats down in front of me, his mouth twisted like a knife wound. A copy of *Sports Illustrated* is rolled in his palm. "There's a real interesting article here you ought to read," he says, peeling back the pages with his thumb. "'Bout boxing and all and some of the shitheads who have spoiled the game." He slips a beau-tifully fashioned wood-handled shank out of his bandage and folds the magazine pages around it. He lowers his voice. "It's hooked on the tip. You want to hear that punk squeal, put it into his guts three times, then bust it off inside. He'll drown in his own blood."

When the truck drives off, Hogman is looking at me from the back of the flatbed, his legs hanging in the dust, his eyes filled with a sad knowledge about the world that is of no value to him and that no one else cares to hear about.

The wind keeps gusting hard all afternoon, and lightning ripples silently through the thunderheads, sometimes making a creaking sound, like the sky cannot support its own weight. The air is cool and smells of fish roe and wet leaves and freshly plowed earth and swamp water so netted with algae it is seldom exposed to full light. The air smells of a tropical jungle on a Pacific island and a foxhole you chop from volcanic soil with an entrenching tool. It smells of the fecund darkness that lies under the grass and mushrooms that can bloom overnight on a freshly dug grave. Again I feel the gravitational pull of the earth under me, and I have no doubt the voices that whisper in the grass are whispering to me.

I sit on the front steps of our dorm and stare through the wire at the wide rent-dented expanse of the Mississippi River. Inside the flooded gum trees on the far side, a bolt of lightning strikes the earth and quivers like a hot wire against the sky. I think about the day I was struck by lightning and how I awoke later and discovered there was a quiver in my voice, one that made me sound like a boy who was perpetually afraid. But my voice and my deeds did not go with one another. The Japanese learned that, and so did my adversaries in New Orleans, Birmingham, Miami, Houston, and Memphis, or wherever I carried the sickness that lived inside me.

"A hurricane is blowing up on the Texas coast. It may be headed right up the pike," the night screw says.

"Why didn't you protect my box, boss? It's not right what y'all did," I say, my arms propped on my knees, my face lowered.

"Your problem is with Jody Prejean, boy. You best not be trying to leave it on other people's doorstep," he replies.

I raise my head and grin at him. "I'll never learn how to pick 'The Wild Side of Life.' It's not right, boss. It's got to be in the Constitution somewhere. A man has got a right to pick his guitar and play 'The Wild Side of Life.'"

His face clouds with his inability to understand what I'm saying, or whether I'm mocking him or myself. "Your problem is with Jody. You hearing me? Now, you watch your goddamn mouth, boy," he says.

For sassing him I should be on my way to segregation. But I'm not. Then I realize how blind and foolish I have been.

That night, as the rain drums on the roof, I catch Jody in the latrine. He's wearing flip-flops and skivvies, his skin as pale as alabaster, his dark hair freshly clipped. "The hacks are setting you up," I say.

"Really?" he says, urinating into a toilet bowl without raising the seat, cupping his phallus with his entire palm.

"Wake up, Jody. They've made me the hitter."

"This is all gonna play out only one way, Arlen. You're gonna be my head bitch. You're gonna collect the stroll money and keep the books and be available if and when I need you. You're gonna be my all-purpose boy. I'll rent you out if I have a mind, or I'll keep you for my own. It will all depend on my mood."

As I watch him I think of the shank I got from Weasel, the piece of glazed ceramic honed on an emery wheel, dancing with light, the tip incised with a barb that will tear out flesh and veins when the blade is pulled from the wound. I want to plunge it into Jody's throat.

"Why you looking at me like that?" he says.

"Because you're stupid. Because you're a tool. Because you're too dumb to know you're a punch for the system."

He shakes off his penis and pushes at the handle on the toilet with his thumb. He wipes his thumb on his skivvies. "It's just a matter of time. Everybody gets down on his knees eventually. You didn't go to Sunday school?"

The rain quits at sunrise, at least long enough for us to get into the fields. Perhaps fifty of us are strung out in the soybeans, then the wind drops and the sky becomes sealed with a black lid from one horizon to the next. Seagulls are tormenting the air as though they have no place to land. In the distance, a tornado falls from a cloud like a giant spring and twists its way across the land. A bunch of trucks arrive, and the gunbulls herd us to the levee and we start offloading bags of sand and dropping them along the river's edge.

The river is swollen and yellow, and the willow trees along the banks make me think of a mermaid's green hair undulating inside a wave.

More guys are brought up from the block, snitches and even big stripes from lockdown and malingerers from the infirmary, even Jody Prejean and his head punk, Wiley Boone, and Hogman and Weasel, anybody who can heft sixty-pound sacks and carry them up a forty-degree incline and stack them in a wall to stop the river from breaching the levee.

I think about all the dead guys buried in the levee, and I think about the hacks who set me up to kill Jody Prejean. I think about the Japs I potted with my M-1 when I was sixteen, some of it just for kicks. I think about what I did to a dealer in the French Quarter who tried to sell me powdered milk when I was jonesing and couldn't stop shaking long enough to heat a spoon over a candle flame. I think about what happened to a Mexican in San Antonio who tried to jackroll me for my Gibson. I remember the look in the eyes of every person I have hurt or killed, and I want to scrub my soul clean of my misspent life and to rinse the blood of my victims from my dreams.

I want to pick "The Wild Side of Life" the way Jimmy Heap used to do it. I drop the sandbag I'm carrying onto the levee.

"Where you going, Arlen?" Butterbean says.

"Stay off those pork chops, 'Bean," I reply.

I walk down the levee into the shallows, my hands open to the sky. The wind is whipping through the willow trees, stripping leaves off the branches, scudding the river's surface into froth along the shoals. I feel small waves slide over my pant cuffs and the tops of my work boots.

"You lost your mind, boy?" a gunbull hollers.

I wade deeper into the river, its warmth rising through my clothes, raindrops striking my scalp and shoulders as hard as marbles. The surface of the river is dancing with yellow light, strings of Japanese hyacinths clinging to my hips, clouds of dark sediment swelling up around me. Far beyond the opposite shore, the thunderheads look like an ancient mountain piled against the sky. I hear the pop of a shotgun in the wind, and a cluster of double-aught bucks flies past me and patterns on the water. The river is high on my chest now and my arms are straight out as I work my way deeper into the current, like a man balancing himself on a tightrope. A floating island of uprooted trees bounces off me, cracking something in my shoulder, turning me in a circle, so for just a moment I have to look back at the prison farm. All of the inmates are on their knees or crouched down in fear of what is happening around them. I see the night screw pull a shotgun from the hands of a gunbull on horseback and come hard down the levee, digging his boots into the sod.

Just as he fires, I smile at him and at the wide panorama of his fellow guards and their saddled horses and the convicts who seem to dot the levee like spectators at a ball game. In my mind's eye the twelve-gauge pumpkin ball flies from the muzzle of his gun as quickly as a bird and touches my forehead and freeze-frames the levee and the people on it and the flooded willows and the river chained with rain rings and the trees of lightning bursting across the sky.

One of my sleeves catches on the island of storm trash, and as I float southward with it, my eyelids stitched to my forehead, I think I see a mountain looming massive and scorched beyond the opposite shore, one I saw many years ago through a pair of binoculars when six of my fellow countrymen labored to plant an American flag on the peak.

RON CARLSON

Beanball

FROM *One Story*

OH, THIS WAS VERY GOOD: the road had become stiff ruts now, dried mud tracks that pulled Driscoll's Volkswagen right and left, and he grabbed the wheel with both hands, not slowing down as he was jolted around, a grin, almost the old grin, on his face. The bladed road simply ceased, and now he was getting close. That there were still these places revived Driscoll, rinsed the eight hundred miles from Houston from his view, and sat him forward. Then, still traveling at twenty miles per hour, his wheels took different tracks, and the little car crabbed sideways, jolted suddenly up, and into the bush. Driscoll himself swung and rapped his forehead against the top of the windshield, as he had done a dozen times in the four years he'd been in Central America, and sat back, stopped. He turned off the motor and got out. He already knew the damage: front bumper, trunk lid, compressed suitcase. He'd stopped carrying any of the equipment in the front after his first dirt road in southern Mexico. Now it was full of his personal gear and paperwork. The trunk latch had been gone for over two years, replaced by a wire loop of his own making. He had the laptop, the video camera, and the speed gun in the back seat in an old baseball duffel.

He stepped out of the little car one leg at a time. It was just a bush, some sweet, effulgent tropical plant, into which he had driven, and it was time for a break. Driscoll set his two large hands open on the car roof and leaned against it to stretch the backs of his legs and the old injury in his left shoulder. Carefully he placed his hand on the side of his head. He waited to see if his vision would waver, but it held. This was fun. The kid, whoever he was, would be thrilled to see him, to play catch and then to throw for the gun. Driscoll would leave two dozen baseballs in the village and write his little one-page report. One in twenty of the young men would get a trip north. Two of Driscoll's discoveries were playing in the American League now and would be for a long time. This kid was the first Guatemalan he'd scouted. Alberto Molinas, nineteen. Driscoll would probably stay with the family; he liked that, being part of a few good days in these people's lives. His Spanish was sketchy, and he met their effusive hospitality with frank realism. No conseguir tus esperanzas para arriba. It was stupid, because their hopes were already up. But he contended with that fairly. He was kind, and he always sent things back: team jackets, cartons of baseballs, and a letter. "It was an honor meeting you and staying in your wonderful home. I regret that I am unable to offer you a chance to try out for our team at the present time. As you remember from our talk, our pitching staff is now full. I send my best wishes for your future playing baseball in your country. I still think it is the finest game in the world. God bless you, G. Driscoll." The funny thing was, though the letter was nearly always something like that, Driscoll meant every word, every time.

Suddenly a noise set up in the jungle, a hissing that sounded at first like a leak in one of his tires. Then the friction jumped a notch and began to increase, until he could feel it in the ground — approaching vehicles. Driscoll stood behind his little car and waited. Sixty yards ahead of him, a convoy burst from the tree line, traveling at almost fifty miles an hour on what must have been an improved road that he hadn't seen. It certainly wasn't on his map. There were almost two dozen vehicles, jeeps and patchwork Suburbans and a ratty troop truck. The sight stunned him and he ducked. A movement in the brush ahead of him became two shirtless boys, who stood as the last jeep passed and threw rocks at it. Two little outfielders throwing for the plate. For a moment after the convoy passed it was quiet in the jungle, and then the birds began again, crying in the trees.

"Yo," Driscoll called to the two kids, their brown backs twisting in alarm. He waved his baseball cap. And thus he was delivered to the village of Rio Pallisades and the little house of Alberto Molinas.

*

Driscoll had never been in a smaller town. The equatorial jungle grew right up to whitewashed buildings that lined the little packed road. There was a shallow fountain in what served as an open public square, and the sky was crisscrossed with hundreds of jury-rigged electrical wires. Driscoll could hear the generators working off in the bush as he followed the two boys, Ernesto and Larry, to Casa Molinas after parking his car in front of the one-story taverna. He was not surprised to see a satellite dish on the roof. One world. The two boys struggled as they carried Driscoll's duffel to the end of the village and then down a one-rut lane two hundred yards to a cluster of little cottages, each with a garden. The shirtless young man on the small shady side of one of the little houses wearing fatigue pants and combat boots and reading — in English — a paper copy of *The Book of Lists* was Alberto Molinas.

Molinas threw with Driscoll for an hour. There were few things he loved more than playing catch; it was so clear that man was designed to throw a ball. Driscoll's arm felt good, and the throwing cleared his head from his three-day trip. They didn't talk, they just threw. He found that the speed gun was broken, and so Driscoll improvised some things, and after he'd seen what he'd needed to see, Driscoll took three of the four baseballs they'd been using and lobbed them to the small gaggle of boys who had stood at the perimeter of the yard. After their catch, Driscoll walked around the square until his cell phone registered, and he left a message for the owner, Morgan Winchester: I'm bringing someone up for a look.

Dinner that evening at the Molinases' was an event: two chickens and bottles of Moza on ice. Alberto's mother and sister saw to the table: platters of tortillas and dishes of salsa and plates of avocados and tomatoes and a big black pan of frijoles borrachos and a large ceramic bowl of rice and the two chickens, browned and simmering on a platter. At the table were Alberto's grandmother, his parents, and his older sister, Lucinda. Alberto's parents were Gloria and Juvenal, and when Driscoll was introduced to him, he told the older man in his shaky Spanish, "Your father must have been a scholar to name you after the Roman leader."

Juvenal smiled. "My father was a teacher, but he was funny about it. When I asked about the Roman, he said that he'd seen the name in a book once when he was in Havana, and it was good enough for whom it was for." Driscoll laughed. The dinner had begun.

Throughout the meal, he could tell they were watching him for a sign, but carefully. Alberto had said only one thing and in English. When they'd finished throwing, Alberto had said, "I want so much to play in the American leagues." And now, despite their sharp hopes, everyone was being discreet, warm, familiar. The food platters surrounded his plate, and seconds were pressed upon him. Finally the sister was unable to stand it any longer and said, "We saw you play baseball, Mr. Driscoll."

"Yes?" Driscoll said.

"You are very fine."

"I loved to play." They all heard the tone of this response, and in the silence he added, "You saw my injury?"

"We did," the father said.

"You are strong now," Lucinda said.

"I'm strong," Driscoll said, and again something in his tone changed the room, so that Lucinda reached from where she sat next to him and touched his face.

"Pero no sonríes?"

"Not quite," he said, turning to her and adjusting his face into the expression which, since his injury, would have been a smile. "But I can chew." And he lifted his fork again.

"You were very skilled," Juvenal said. "It is a shame that your life in baseball was . . ." And here he paused for a word and said, "Abbreviated."

"I'm fine," Driscoll said, speaking slowly. "I am still able to meet so many fine young players."

"Where do you go from here?" Juvenal asked him.

Alberto's grandmother put her hands flat on the table and looked directly across at Driscoll. Her chin was elevated, and her Spanish was slow and careful. Juvenal responded to her somewhat sharply, and the sister said the old woman's name, Grandmama, as a kind of objection.

"Would you like some coffee, Mr. Driscoll?" Juvenal asked him, and his wife rose.

The grandmother spoke again, softly to Driscoll. Her eyes were wet, and she was smiling bravely. Juvenal began to object again when Driscoll cut in, reaching across the table and putting his fingers on the top of her wrist. "Alberto is a very fine baseball player. He is a good pitcher."

"You are not telling me," she said.

"Let me be specific," Driscoll said. "Alberto will hear from me again, though it may come to nothing. Do you understand?"

"We are realistic," she said.

"He is a strong young right-hander with an unusual accuracy and very significant speed. He throws the ball harder than anyone I've caught. This is true."

"And you are an expert in such matters," the old woman said as a fact.

"I am an expert." He smiled. "But even so, there are so many variables." Driscoll turned to Juvenal and then to Alberto. "I am going to arrange a tryout," he said. "Can you come north in two weeks?"

"Todos nosotros?" the grandmother said.

"No," Driscoll said to her. "Just Alberto. To throw for the coaches. I'll arrange the travel."

"I will come," the young man said.

"And this may come to nothing, except a trip and a few hours in the ballpark throwing as you did today."

The three women were crying and hugging each other and laughing and hiding their faces.

Juvenal said, "We understand."

Driscoll looked at him and waited. "This may come to nothing."

"Usted fue golpeado en la cabeza," the grandmother said, now putting her hand on top of his, "Pero usted es sabio."

In the morning, the bird cries woke Driscoll, and the air was sweet with the humid perfume of the jungle and the smell of baking bread. He found his car had been washed in the night and someone had pounded out the largest two dents in the hood. It was over a bowl of coffee that he felt his vision start to go. Alberto's mother saw his face and said, "It is your injury?"

He had his pills out and took four, and he said, "Yes, I hit my head yesterday in the car. I may lie down for a moment."

He was there two more nights, the crushing pressure in his temple and his sight gone. Dark clouds rode in thick circles around the edge of his eyes. He rested, no longer ringing with the terror that lived in him when he first recovered. If he was blind, so be it. He was still a young man, and his greatest pleasure was to go to Boston or Kansas City and see some kid he'd met in Texas or Cuba throw six innings. He would listen to the games on the radio. He'd never find another talent, but he could follow baseball.

When he woke, Lucinda was sitting beside his bed. They looked at each other for a moment, and he understood she had been studying his face when he'd been sleeping. She called out and the grandmother came in, eyes wide, and her face lit and she bent and kissed Driscoll on the cheek, and he knew his head was clear.

"It's Thursday," Lucinda said.

"Is there any more of that coffee?" he asked her.

The grandmother lifted her hand and nodded, turning from the room. Lucinda perched on her stool. "I'm glad you're feeling better," she said. Her wonderful black hair was all caught back in a comb, and she folded her arms. "We were dreadfully upset."

"I'm all right."

"I know you are," Lucinda said. "Did you know, Mr. Driscoll, that girls play baseball, too?"

He smiled and he felt the bones in his face, but there was no constriction.

"What position are you?" he asked the young woman.

Her grandmother came in with a thick slice of toast and a bowl of creamy coffee. She set it all down, and they helped him sit up, giving him another pillow, and Lucinda's hands on his shoulders and then one on his forehead humbled him again.

"Are these your father's pajamas?"

She handed him the coffee, and her face in the gray aura of his vision was like a blessing.

"Sí," the grandmother offered. "They are. If you feel better, you can shower, and my son said he will drive with you as far as Riadma, where the highway joins. It will be safe from the Guard."

Lucinda said, "Grandmama, por favor, we were talking." She turned back to Driscoll. "I bat right and throw right, and I am best at second base."

Driscoll had been Rookie of the Year, a catcher who could throw a rope to second base from a knee and who hit .325. When he was drafted for the majors, he came with a good signing bonus and another pleasure: he found his old coach from Saint State was the new battery coach. "You're golden," Red Rawlins said that first day in the bullpen. "You are the golden boy." It was what he'd said all four years at State. "I've come out of retirement, just for this." His grin was one of Driscoll's favorite things. Rawlins had played favorites at school and had that reputation, but Driscoll had been one of his favorites, and he thrived.

He was starting catcher and hitting .340 his second season in the majors when Duke Hullinger, a thirty-six-year-old right-hander who still had some smoke, let a brushback pitch get away, and the ninety-four-mile-per-hour fastball took Driscoll in the face. It had been thrown behind him, and he ducked into it and went down, and he never got up. Hullinger ran up, scared; everybody ran over scared. When you meant to hit someone, you threw behind them. Hullinger was ejected, but not before he showed where his third finger was freshly cut and bleeding, the reason for the accident, a blister or a tear.

Driscoll died on the operating table, his head in pieces, and was revived. After the surgeries he was in a coma for sixty-one days. The blow destroyed his left eye socket, which was rebuilt, and the temporal bone was shattered and two slivers went into his brain. There were pilgrimages, and his hospital room was full of flowers and then plants and photographs. Morgan Winchester, owner of the team, had left the picture of Driscoll at the White House awards ceremony from last winter. They all had flown to the District of Columbia for the afternoon, and in the old rooms of the famous house they had their pictures taken, boys in sport coats.

One afternoon Driscoll woke and looked at the array. The next day his teammates started coming by, and it got noisy; it was all about when he'd be back and they were waiting, and there were some jokes, and sometimes one of them would retell yesterday's game, blow by blow. Driscoll couldn't talk. He knew he was wasted. In the hospital the pain was nothing but a knife in his face until the tenth day (he kept track of the days with tape on the bedrail) of his waking, when the pain shifted, like a needle withdrawing, and then he felt it fly away slowly, like a giant bird that had had his head in its hot claw for too long.

He lost weight, became drawn and serious. He couldn't smile, but it was more than that. He had been broken and they'd put him back together, but now he knew. He'd been in his last chapter as a boy when his face was broken, and now he was a man, a serious man who took his major joy from working with the young players. It took him five weeks to get over flinching when the ball was thrown to him, but he did it. He could catch, and he had a Gold Glove to prove it.

His life, which had been beginning, fell apart until there was only baseball. He was silent with his girlfriend, Jessica, and he knew it wasn't fair, but he couldn't bring himself back to her. After some weeks, when she asked, he simply said it was better to let it go.

Alberto Molinas came north a month later, and Driscoll met him at customs, and they did the paperwork. It was amazing what baseball could do for a young Guatemalan who had five hundred words of English and one change of clothes, not counting his baseball glove. Driscoll lived for this moment, walking into the empty ballpark with a new kid, some pitcher who statistically represented one in the almost three hundred whom Driscoll had seen throw in the last few months. It was a Monday and the pitching coach, Red Rawlins, was waiting. Driscoll watched Alberto take in the area, turning a big walking circle, looking at the sixty thousand red and blue seats. A crew was fixing a row of chairs in the left-field stands. Driscoll felt it, too. Raymond Dodge, the rookie who came up with Driscoll, always said, "It's worse than being in church." Worse or better, it was something.

Red came out of the bullpen and said, "Get changed and let's throw a little."

Alberto nodded. He was scared.

Red said to Driscoll, "Maybe he'd rather throw out here, use the real mound. We can; they're doing the field at four."

Alberto turned to walk to the infield, but Driscoll took his arm. "Let's play baseball," he said.

Red Rawlins stood in with a bat, and Alberto threw as Driscoll had told him to, very deliberately. Plenty of time between pitches and every time a full wind-up and then a half, full and then half. He gave the boy four signals: fastball, curve, slider, drop. Alberto could put the ball in any quadrant of the strike zone, and he demonstrated up and down the inside corner and then the outside corner. His breaking balls all moved late and were deceptive. After half an hour Red threw down the bat he'd been holding and went behind Driscoll and observed as an umpire.

"It's good," he told Driscoll. "How did you find him?"

"One thing leads to another," Driscoll said. "I met a coach in Costa Rica who couldn't get him to come and play for nothing. It was forty miles one way. Those were the tricky forty miles."

"Did you use the gun?"

"It's in for repair."

Red got the speed gun, and Alberto threw a while longer. Ninety-seven, one hundred one, ninety-nine.

"Nice work, Driscoll," Red said finally, taking the ball and waving the kid over. "He's golden."

Alberto's success was immediate. Like any new player who can cope, he was called a phenomenon, and Driscoll smiled reading Andy Masters's column twice a week in the papers. Andy had twenty phrases he recycled through the years, and he pulled them all out for Alberto Molinas. "This powerful right-hander is rewriting the book on the strike zone; you can hear the roar of his fastball from the upper deck. He's a phenomenon that's going to create more K's than the printing press." Once a week Masters mentioned control as being an issue, which just showed that Masters wasn't coming to all the games and that he had too many column inches to fill to stick to the truth.

Two months later Driscoll was in Kobe, Japan, catching batting practice. Seventeen pitchers had come out for the call, and he kept two for the following morning. The first day had been comical. He'd used his old alphabet for scouting, giving every pitcher an index card with a letter and then calling them in turn by holding up the lettered poster boards, one by one. He had no Japanese, and the translators were always cumbersome. It was a good system, but every time he'd call out a new letter, all the players who were strung out around the pretty ballpark would fish out their cards and turn them upside down. "G!" Driscoll would say, and everyone would stand up and read until there was a match. The two players he called back the next day were D and M, which is what he called them through the second morning. They were both muscular guys who had huge hands and who could each move the ball four inches, in, out, or down. No fire, but wide sliders with no tells. Keepers. When he went back to the hotel after bowing to the young players, his knees hurt in the old way, hard and good, but it was in his room that he heard of the accident. His BlackBerry just said,

Trouble w/Albert. Get back here. It was from Winchester. Driscoll spent the night calling Red Rawlins and Alberto, but no one picked up.

It was in the *Mainichi Daily News* at the airport. Alberto had killed a man. A terrible accident: he had struck the Orioles centerfielder with a high slider. The kid was a rookie out of Arizona State. Driscoll knew of him. The flight was endless, and Driscoll let go of the two days he'd scheduled for rest in Oahu to fly straight through.

Back in the city with jet lag at his head in a friction, he went to the ballpark and found Winchester in his funky little office high above third base. Winchester kept another office, a corporate showplace way up back of the plate, a carpeted palace full of all the framed goods and memorabilia. Driscoll had never been in there when it wasn't catered and full of suits. But Winchester did the business of the team from an old school desk by the window in this cell. Today he looked wrecked. He looked like Driscoll felt. They had coffee and Driscoll sat on a cane chair, afraid that the couch would take him right to sleep.

"You look like hell," Winchester said.

"Everybody does. What happened?" Driscoll asked.

"He put him down." Winchester waited and then looked Driscoll square. "It was the worst I've seen. I knew Ellington was dead."

"Where's Alberto?"

"He's at his condo. He may talk to you. He may not. I'm afraid we've lost him."

"Where's Red?"

"He's crashed, too."

"Who talked to the papers?"

"Me. All day and all night. Goddamn it, Driscoll. Go see him. I want him to be okay. I want him back, but I want him to be okay." Winchester took a cassette out of the television and handed it to Driscoll. "Here's the tape. How was Japan?"

"Full of ballplayers." Driscoll stood. "You're going to get a look at two fine right-handers, one named D and one named M. I'll be in touch."

Alberto's condominium was on the tenth floor overlooking the river, and it was all carpet and no furniture. Driscoll forced the doorman to take him up — an emergency, he said, and he would not be dissuaded. They were at the big modern door for five minutes. Driscoll called and called, and finally the door opened all the way and there was Alberto, his face gray.

Driscoll embraced his friend, holding him up, and then, after looking around, he called the American Grill, down two blocks, for breakfast delivery, the works. Alberto had lost weight and his face was altered, swollen and older.

"I was in Japan," Driscoll said. "There are some guys who can break a curve a foot at ninety miles an hour. Have you seen the doctor?" Driscoll said. "Talk to me."

Alberto shook his head. Driscoll stood the boy up and walked him through the huge master bedroom and into the bath. He took his shirt. "Shower, right now. Then we'll eat. I'm starving. And then we'll have the doctor come up."

When Alberto came out in his big plaid robe, Driscoll had moved the table by the window and was setting out the breakfast, fried eggs and pancakes and two small steaks and juice and more coffee. The young man's eyes were different; there was more than hurt there. There was blame.

Driscoll watched him, glad to see Alberto eat. "Did you talk to Red?"

Alberto nodded.

"What did he say?"

Alberto kept his eyes down, eating.

"Did you talk to your family?"

"Quiéro irme a casa," Alberto whispered.

"Good," Driscoll said. "We can go home. But, Alberto, what happened?"

The young man looked across the table at his friend. His voice was strange when he said the next thing. "You know what happened," he said. "I was instructed to brush him back, but I threw too hard and I lost it."

"Had this ever happened before?"

"No." Alberto pushed his plate away. "And now a man is dead. I'm going home. Will you help me?"

The team doctor, Ned Wilson, arrived and checked Alberto out, his blood pressure, his eyes. He pushed the young man's hair back and looked at the scar there. "It's old," Alberto said in English. "I was a kid."

"You're still a kid," Wilson said. "And you're in good health."

"He needs to sleep," Driscoll said. To Alberto he said, "I'll arrange our travel. But tomorrow you have to help me with something. Can you do that?"

"I will," Alberto said.

Wilson laid out two medicines on the kitchen counter. "One each at bedtime."

"One each," Alberto said. "Gracias."

Back at his hotel, Driscoll's eyes were dimming, but he cleaned up and took a cab in the low gray overcast of the June day out to Red Rawlins's house. It was a little place in a working-class neighborhood, and when Driscoll got out of his car, two dogs quickly frisked him and continued cruising down the street. The little lawn needed mowing, but nobody had bothered this week. Driscoll saw the door open, and Red stepped onto the tiny porch looking ruined, shrunken and old. "Come on," the coach said. "At least there's coffee." Red had lived alone forever, a wife in his past long gone somehow. He never spoke of it. And there were no photographs in his house of anything but his ballplayers. He'd converted the garage into a carpeted sun porch where he had his television and recliner, and the two men took their mugs of coffee out there and sat while the Brewers played the Padres with the sound off. As they sat, Driscoll pointed at the Padres pitcher, a kid named DeReneau whom Driscoll had found outside Las Vegas. He'd made him finish high school and then brought him up. They watched his sprawling wind-up and pitch.

"Too much with the leg," Red Rawlins said. "He's tipping the cart."

"Call him up. Call the coach."

"Pat Daniels. Pat knows. But it's trouble trimming a pitcher back. He thinks he's getting ten miles per hour by throwing his leg at the plate. He doesn't want to lose that. Oh hell, they'll be okay."

"Will we?" Driscoll asked him. "Are you okay?"

"I don't know, son. I'm home on a game day; I should be in Chicago, and frankly, I don't know that I'll even go tomorrow." Rawlins looked into his coffee. "It was awful. I'm glad you weren't there. I keep seeing it. Alberto lost it from his fingertips, and it was the hardest pitch I've seen in thirty years. There was one guy, Parry

Cleary, who played at State for about a month when I was a rookie, for chrissakes, and he could throw ten pitches in a row right at a hundred, and that was it. He didn't have the control or staying power, but he had the leverage for a few minutes every other day. Alberto threw the ball harder than that."

"Did he trip?"

"No, he came off straight and just threw it at Ellington's head."

Driscoll sat quietly. His fatigue was overwhelming. His eyes burned.

"Did you go see him?"

"Yeah," Driscoll said. "He wants to go home."

"So do I," Red Rawlins said. "Maybe he should. There's talent and youth and strength, and then there's nerve. If they lose the nerve, you let them go home."

"You still got your nerve?"

"Oh shit, kid, we'll see."

"I'm taking him home day after tomorrow," Driscoll said. He closed his eyes and knew he was going to pass out. He needed to sleep. His head was hot, and he could feel again how it was put together, lines of pressure played above his ear and over his forehead. He stood up. "After we have a catch."

The next day in a light rain, Driscoll sent a car for Alberto and met the young man under the famous blue awning of the players' entrance of the greatest baseball park in the world. Driscoll shook his keys out and let them in.

"Thanks for coming," he said to his friend. "How do you feel?"

"What are we doing here?" Alberto said. "I don't want to be here."

"You're on the team. We've got a day." Driscoll turned on the stadium lights. "We're going to have a catch."

They dressed in sweats and went out into the empty arena. The rain was a periodic mist in the deep gray day, which looked like a downpour as it exploded past the lights, and Driscoll covered the bucket of baseballs with a towel. They threw in the outfield, slowly, not talking. God, Driscoll loved to see this kid throw. Alberto had it all: the roll, the shoulder, and at the end his strong wrists worked the ball as if made for it. You could tell the kids who grow up throwing from two years old. You could see in the way they walked up to you and shook hands. In the cathedral-like silence of the morning, Alberto was not himself. He tossed the ball to Driscoll, and there was nothing on it or in it. "Let it rip," Driscoll said, after a while. "We're warm."

Alberto would not.

Driscoll upped the ante, firing the ball back to the pitcher. It felt good in the moist air to snap his wrist. "No pensar! Lanze la pe-lota." Driscoll threw harder. "We're going to throw until you throw," Driscoll called. "I've got the day."

Alberto put something on it then, and Driscoll was braced. He looked up above third and saw Winchester at the window. He lived there.

After a few minutes, Driscoll waved his glove and they stopped. "Now a few off the mound," he said. They went to the infield. The batting cage was up behind the plate, and Driscoll crouched as Alberto wound up and threw strike after strike. It was like last spring: pure pitching. Curve, slider, fastball down, fastball up. In a rhythm back and forth, the pitching was a kind of music, the sharp pop of the ball into Driscoll's catching mitt and the little snap when Alberto caught the return, every beat like the tempo in the heavy day. Driscoll saw Alberto's face become his face again, as the boy just pitched, blowing a breath with every downbeat.

But when Driscoll dragged the bucket of balls out to the mound and stood at the plate with the bat, Alberto wouldn't throw it near him. Couldn't. He was outside two feet. "Throw slower," Driscoll said. They went through the bucket and picked up all the baseballs once again. As he toweled them and dropped them in the bucket, Driscoll told Alberto, "Slow it down until you can bring it in." But Alberto could not.

Finally Driscoll put down the bat and told Alberto to toss it to him so he could catch it barehanded. "Slower. Closer." Driscoll stood back in with the bat. They went through the bucket again. "Think of it this way," Driscoll said. "Just let me hit one and we'll get out of the weather."

Alberto was like a man made of stone. He could not throw it near the batter. He finally threw one of the last balls in the third bucket close, and Driscoll stepped across the plate and lined it into left field, the ball skipping in the wet outfield like a flat stone on a lake: one, two, three. Driscoll walked out to the mound. Alberto stood with his arms folded in the rain, which was now real rain, light and steady. "It took me two months," Driscoll said. "I couldn't even catch the ball. You've got what I've got." He knew it was true when he said it. "We can work this out."

"Soy quiéren irse a casa," Alberto said. Water dripped from the brim of his cap.

"We're going tomorrow."

Alberto shook his head gravely. "You are not going."

"I want to see the kids in town, and I want to see your grandmama, your family."

"No."

"Alberto."

"No. They don't want to see you."

"I'm coming with. It's what I do."

Alberto stepped down the wet clay mound toward Driscoll and pushed him backward.

"What are you going to do, Alberto, hit me?"

Driscoll could see that he wanted to; a hatred swam through his eyes. Then Alberto turned and walked toward the locker room. This was all broken now. Driscoll's head pulsed, and he put his hand on the side of his face. *You've got what I've got.* The baseballs glistened wet and white in the noonday rain, and he moved with the bucket, picking them from the field.

In the morning Alberto was gone. Driscoll went to the condo and then back to the ballpark. He packed a trunk of gear, bats and bases and cases of baseballs and ten fielder's gloves. He grabbed the videotapes of Alberto's games. He found four umpire counters. He threw in two rosin bags. He couldn't fix this any other way.

In the capital of Guatemala, he hired a van, and when the driver heard where they were going, out by the border, he charged Driscoll double and made him pay up front. As they got in the old Explorer, the driver handed him a dirty automatic pistol in an old shoebox and told him to put it under the seat. "It's loaded," he told Driscoll. "Mine's here, too." He lifted another gun from the door sleeve. "Did they teach you how to shoot in the army?" the man asked.

"I'm not in the army," Driscoll said.

"Yes you are." He pointed at the trunk. "Or you wouldn't go this far north."

On the six-hour drive they encountered every kind of road that has ever been: the rippled city pavements, the short new highway, unlined, the hundred miles of bladed gravel that broke every windshield in the country sooner or later and that soon became a corridor of dust, the three-rut clay roads as the jungle commenced, branches brooming the side of the vehicle, and finally the potted trails leading to Alberto's village.

Driscoll cranked the smeared window down and smelled the oiled clay and orchids in the warm air. There was never any baseball weather when he grew up in Laramie. The days got longer and it should have been spring, but the wind blew every minute, and there were a dozen times when games were snowed out. Driscoll got the nickname Sleeve because he always wore three sweatshirts, each with the left arm cut off, so his mitt hand was free and his throwing arm was warm. Even so, his arm was sore in that weather for years, but he tended it.

Driscoll's life had changed one Sunday in March when he was eleven. He was in the basement throwing his old tennis balls across the furnace room at a square he'd chalked on the cement wall, and he heard his father on the stair. His father had been busy, preoccupied as the manager of a fleet of equipment trucks for a small drilling company during the oil boom, but now the man came down the wooden steps, and instead of telling Driscoll to stop, he said, "Get your glove."

They drove to the shop in the periodic sleet, and his father turned on the overhead lights and backed all eight trucks outside into the ice storm. Inside, the man spray-painted a home plate in one corner and stepped off the distance to second base across the room. "Throw low, son," his father had said, putting on his fielder's glove. "Let's not break any of the lights."

They started short, and his father backed up, step by step, through the day. They caught like that three times a week after dinner, and Driscoll learned how to work a manual transmission and move the vehicles back and forth. The eight-bay shop was the cornerstone of Driscoll's career as a catcher. The first raw spring in high school he showed up able to throw to second from a knee, from both knees, and he started every game there and in college.

The driver became silent as they drove through the thick brush, and in the little plaza of the village he hurried and pulled the trunk from the back of the car. Driscoll stopped the man and gave him four twenties and put the pistol in his own pack. "Sold," the man said. "Tenga cuidado." He got in and did an easy U-turn, and disappeared.

Driscoll slid the trunk into the doorway of the taverna and gave the barman a ten-dollar bill to watch it. He walked out to Alberto's family's house and was surprised at the bright new metal fence around the perimeter. The gate was locked. The cement around the postholes was new, and the drive winding back toward the house in the trees was run with new gravel.

When he returned to the village and went into the taverna, he found the two ten-year-olds, Ernesto and Larry, sitting on his trunk.

"Estos dos hombres son demasiado jóvenes para beber," he said to the owner.

"I do not drink," Ernesto said in English. "I am a baseball."

"Do you want something?" the owner said to Driscoll.

"Tres limonadas," he said.

The boys were kicking their heels softly against the side of the big black box. "What is in the trunk?" they asked him. The barman brought over three bottles with straws.

"I can throw with either hand," Larry said.

"Can you catch with either hand?" Driscoll asked the boy. Both children sipped their lemonade very slowly.

"I can catch everything," he said. "I have nine years."

"Is it something for us?" Ernesto said. He plucked at the little lock in the latch.

"Where is your team?"

"Sleeping," Ernesto said. "School is expended."

"Let's wake them up," Driscoll said. "And practice."

The boys ran off, and the owner of the taverna came over. "Is there more trouble?" he asked.

"No," Driscoll said. "Some baseball and no more trouble. What happened here?"

"I can't say, because I don't know."

Driscoll had upended the trunk, and the barman brought over his beer cart, sliding it under an end. He whispered, "Alberto's sister was taken and then returned."

"When?" Driscoll asked the man.

There was a screaming of old brakes, and dust ballooned through the open doorway. When Driscoll turned, the owner was again behind the bar, and he shook his head at Driscoll as four soldiers came into the taverna. They were dressed in camouflage trousers and black T-shirts.

"A tourist," one said to Driscoll. "Welcome to paradise."

"Gracias," Driscoll said, and he wheeled his cargo into the humid sunshine.

Halfway to the clearing, Driscoll had plenty of help. The dolly had been taken from him by two boys and a girl, and two other boys walked with their hands on the trunk to the clearing. It was as before: the base paths were clear, but weeds grew generally and rocks littered the ground.

There were seven kids; the tallest came to Driscoll's shoulder, and one of the boys was very young. "Eduardo has six years," Larry said.

"Let us warm up by pitching rocks," Driscoll told the group. He lined them up midfield, a column straight out to center field, and they stepped as a group, picking the round rocks, all the size of soup cans, and lobbed them to the edge of the space. Then they went the other way. The late afternoon cloud cover thickened over the jungle.

Larry and the girl ran to the trunk when they were finished making two rock piles at each side of the field, and the girl called, "I'm warmed up. Play ball."

Driscoll gathered the kids again and had them say their names: Eduardo, Michael, Inez, Larry, Ernesto, George, and Juan Paul, who had been named after the pope. Driscoll unlocked the trunk, and the children beheld the treasure. George reached in and took the big white padded base, and he turned and ran for the trees.

"George!" Ernesto called. "Come back here!"

"What is it?" asked Juan Paul. "What has he taken?"

They all watched him run into the trees and disappear.

"These are the bases," Driscoll said, throwing the pads out onto the ground.

"My Lord," Inez said. "They are gigantic."

"These are major league bases," Larry said. He stood on one. "I can see everything from here."

The rest tested all their belief. He gave them the gloves. Michael was a leftie, and Driscoll had a glove for him. Driscoll sat on the ground and pulled out his marker and wrote their names large on the thumb of each mitt. The kids had their faces in the leather smell of the pocket, and they wanted Driscoll to read all of the information on the heel and the fingers, and they wanted to know the histories of each person whose signature was embossed in the palm. The baseballs were astonishing. He paired them up for catch, but they were afraid to throw the balls. "Don't drop it," Larry called to Ernesto as they began, and when someone missed a catch, they reacted as if there had been an accident. The wind came up now, preceding the rain. A moment later George came walking back, both arms around his base, and traded it for a glove.

While they all played catch, four or five young mothers came down the dirt street to the field, one with a baby, and they watched the assembly. Driscoll spoke to them. "Is it all right to coach these children for a few days?" he asked the oldest woman. She was maybe thirty.

"It's fine," she said in English. "We know who you are. I will ask my husband."

"This is what I do in many places," Driscoll told her. "I mean it to help. Baseball can help."

"Eduardo is my son," the woman said. "He has six years."

Driscoll looked at the group, the tiny Eduardo and the girl Inez, and he was taken at how they could all throw, how they used their whole bodies to step and roll, one fluid piece, and send the ball out. Dust gusted in pockets now, and they heard the first friction of the rain on the trees.

"All in," Driscoll called. "Let us meet tomorrow and we will do some hitting."

Larry came up to Driscoll, all business, and said, "I have an understanding of the strike zone."

Driscoll held the trunk open, and the children put the bases inside. There was a moment of quiet panic. "Do we give the gloves back to you?" Inez said.

"No," he said. "Take your glove and a ball." He snugged a baseball into each outstretched glove. "I'll see you tomorrow." Before he had finished speaking, two of the boys had stuffed their mitts under their shirts against the rain and were running for home.

The rain only had one speed: full. Driscoll was wet by the time he ducked into the taverna and found Alberto's father, Juvenal, sitting at a table in the empty room. He didn't speak or stand, but he nod-

ded at a chair, and Driscoll sat with him. The owner appeared in a
minute and stood beside them. "Coffee?" Juvenal said.

"Yes, please."

The afternoon was a glowing darkness under the equatorial
downpour. The silver cascade filled the doorway, the street a sheet
of water.

"How are you?" Driscoll said.

"I have come to arrange your travel."

"Tell me what has happened."

"I have a reliable car now," Juvenal said. "And I can get you back
to the capital."

The two small cups of coffee were placed on the wooden table.

"I need to see Alberto. I want to help. I was traveling when the accident happened."

"You cannot."

"Juvenal," Driscoll said. He leaned onto the table over the cup
and saucer. "What has happened here?"

"You have betrayed us," Juvenal said. "And now you will go back."

"I am speaking truthfully," Driscoll said quietly. "I have been part
of something I do not understand."

Juvenal raised his eyes to Driscoll's face.

Driscoll said, "Tell me the story."

Then, without a sound, two soldiers entered the room, and then
three more. Driscoll recognized some of them from midday. They
shook their camouflage caps and stamped their boots on the floor
as they went to the bar. Juvenal watched them and sipped his coffee.

"Can you do that for me, Juvenal?"

The older man looked weary now. "Come with me," he said, and
he put ten pesos on the table.

Juvenal told Driscoll the story after dinner. The warm covered platters had been set out, and they had eaten alone. Driscoll had seen
none of the family since being brought back to the house. The
week before, Lucinda had not come home from the school where
she taught. When they'd looked for her, the commander of the
band of soldiers told the family she was being detained. She was
safe, but she had been detained. "They kept her two nights," Juvenal told Driscoll.

"Last week," Driscoll said.

"Thursday. The second day they cut off her finger."

Driscoll was quiet. They were sitting in large canvas chairs on the veranda in the first dark, the eaves still dripping from the day's rain. "Who did it?"

"The commander. His name is Herrera. He's a Mexican in Guatemala."

"Tell me everything," Driscoll said.

"They cut off part of her finger and made her call Alberto."

As the rain subsided, the birds began to sing and answer, great cries near and distant, and there was steady rustling in the broadleafed thicket.

"Friday morning."

"He was in his apartment before the game."

"What did they have her say?"

"The commander spoke to my son, and then she told him they had removed her finger."

"Did the commander tell Alberto to do what he did?"

"You know this already."

"Juvenal. I don't. I swear on my mother's grave and my father's grave, I do not."

"The commander said for Alberto to follow orders."

"Did he give the orders?"

"No, Mr. Driscoll. They came from your man in New York."

"Who?"

"You may know better than I, despite all your swearing." Two foxes came into the grassy clearing behind the house and ran as one under the veranda.

"Did Alberto know the person?"

"He's a Guatemalan who lives in the metropolis," a voice said. It was Alberto, coming out onto the covered deck. In the evening light, he loomed over them. Alberto looked rested, and again Driscoll noted his powerful shoulders. "His name is Calloz."

Alberto's mother followed him and lit the glassed candles on every table. Driscoll stood and greeted her. She lit the candles one by one, and when she lit the one on his table, she said, "Me alegro de verle otra vez."

"Gracias," Juvenal said to the woman, excusing her.

When she had gone back inside, Alberto said, "The man is from the capital, but he lives now in the United States."

"What did he say, Alberto?"

The young pitcher moved a candle and sat on the rattan coffee table before the two men. "He was in the players' lot before the game. He was waiting in a dark suit and a white shirt, and he asked me if I received a call from my sister. He said that I was to hit Ellington in the head with a fastball when he came to bat. I need to hit him in the head or they would kill Lucinda." Alberto leaned forward, his elbows on his knees. "I don't know who he was or how he came to be there." Alberto fixed on Driscoll's eyes. "I knew he was telling the truth. Then I went out and did what I did. Do you know the man?"

"I don't, Alberto. But I will find him."

Voices came from inside, and Alberto stood and went in.

"Who is the constable in your village?" Driscoll asked Juvenal.

"There is none, not for almost two years."

"Who are these guards? It is the army?"

"Not the army proper. These are thugs. They haven't bothered us until now." Alberto came back onto the veranda with a bottle of mescal and two glasses. "Good," Juvenal said. "Consiga un cristál, el hijo." Alberto smiled and pulled a glass from his pocket. Juvenal opened the bottle and poured them each a dram.

"I don't understand this terrible violence," Juvenal said. "But, Mr. Driscoll, you are among us again."

Driscoll slept on a hammock on the lower terrace, and he woke in the dawn with a hand on his forehead. In the rare light, her face glowed. Lucinda's hand was a white gauze mitt, and again she brushed his head and stepped back. "Is it too early for coffee?" There was a bowl of milky coffee on the table. The straws of sunlight pierced the space, and the air was tangibly sweet and moist.

"No. It is not too early. Thank you." They sat not talking, and then he asked her, "Are you all right?"

"I am all right. The fear is now gone."

"Are you feverish from the injury?"

"I have the same headache you do. That's all. The doctor has been here."

Driscoll lifted her bandaged hand carefully, and then her other hand was in his and he touched each finger. He tried to speak without this new anger. "Was it the commander?"

"It was the young commander. He did it."

"Did he say anything?"

"He said it was political. Did you see Alberto hurt the batter?"

"I was in Japan. I should have been there; I could have changed things."

"Maybe not."

The grandmother came onto the sleeping porch. "We were told the wise man was here again," she said in Spanish.

"I'm not wise."

The old woman sat in the big wicker chair, the lines of sunlight like strings on her lap. "Do you know what I am this morning?"

"Is it a riddle?" Driscoll said.

"I am the attendee for young ladies." She smiled. Lucinda blushed and stood up and withdrew.

"The chaperone," Driscoll said. "And it is so early in the day for such duty." He gave her his smile and raised his chin. "You are mischief," Driscoll told her.

"Muchas gracias, señor. You are so kind to say so." She put her hands over her smile. "And wise."

The cadre of renegade soldiers had set up quarters in the old free dental clinic that American volunteers had erected in the seventies. It was a ruined low cinder-block structure near the mission school at the edge of the village. Driscoll walked toward the building in the steamy morning, but before he arrived he heard calling and saw the soldiers on the weedy field, throwing baseballs back and forth. Now he walked to the end of the street and saw there were six men, two of them in an argument because one had made a bad throw and tipped over a bottle of beer. Beer bottles stood upright in the grass. Driscoll's trunk was splintered and sprung, and the men wore new baseball gloves. Baseballs were scattered around, and now a large young man was pitching to the young commander, who stood apart with one of the bright new bats. The big guy was sweating and throwing the ball all over the place, and the commander was swearing at him. A catcher stood well behind the batter, and he retrieved the wild pitches and hurled them back.

"You said you could pitch, Roberto. Get away. Somebody else come throw, so I can swing this bat."

The struggling pitcher pointed at Driscoll. "The American."

The commander saluted awkwardly with the bright new bat. "It is the former major league catcher. Good morning. We are enacting the World Series here. Perhaps you'd like to take one of us north to the great fields of money."

Driscoll walked over to the man and noted he was short and young and his English was fairly good. "Are you the leader of these men?"

On the belt of his camouflage pants, the man had a pistol and a cell phone. The black leather holster was not the proper one for the pistol, and the handle barely protruded from the large sleeve. The arms had been cut from his white T-shirt, and the word "TEXAS" was tattooed in an arc on his brown shoulder. "I am Colonel Herrera. These are my men."

"Colonel of what?"

"Of all you see."

"Where do you report?"

"I cannot tell you that."

Driscoll was on the edge of his temper, and he backed from it. "I want to talk to you."

"We can talk." The man was smiling. "But we are in recreation. Will you pitch?"

The men were sitting in the outfield, and he called for them to get up. He pounded the base before him and cocked into his stance. Driscoll could see the man had played ball, but not for a long time. He had the bat held way back dramatically. He fouled off the first pitches, missing every third one. He slashed at each pitch, trying to kill it. Driscoll was lobbing strikes, and the leader finally popped a few up, and after two dozen pitches he swung and missed and threw the bat and hit the old damaged trunk.

"You can't pitch," he said to Driscoll. "It is no wonder you were fired."

"I want to talk to you," Driscoll said. He was sweating now in the humidity.

"Maybe you'll show us how to hit," the man said. He had straightened his belt and stepped through the weeds to where Driscoll stood among the baseballs.

"I need to speak with you. Colonel."

"You shouldn't be here," the man said. "This is no place for you. You started all of it. You took Alberto north, and now he is home. You go home."

"I only need a minute," Driscoll said.

"After you hit for us. We are your fans." The man grinned and waved his hands, indicating the cadre of young soldiers.

Driscoll retrieved the bat. He'd brought kids' gear, and it was a 32-inch and felt like a toy in his hands. He stood and waited for the pitch. The leader looked at him and then rocked into a full wind-up and threw the ball behind Driscoll. He threw as hard as he could, the balls spraying around, nothing to hit. After he'd thrown all the balls and was waiting for the catcher to retrieve them, the young colonel dropped his mitt and shook out a cigarette and lit it. "Leandro," he called. "Give the American scout a few pitches." A tall kid jogged in from the perimeter. He was a leftie with long arms, and Driscoll could see by his shoulders that he had thrown before. The first pitch was straight, high and outside, and Driscoll tapped it to right. Driscoll hit four or five line drives around the outfield, and the men shuffled to get the balls.

"Hit one!" the leader called from behind the pitcher. He conferred with Leandro for a moment, his back to Driscoll, and when Leandro turned again, Driscoll knew he was going to throw at him. Now Leandro wound up and threw a sidearm pitch that Driscoll could not avoid. It hit him in the top of the thigh, an unmistakable pitch. The kid threw hard and was ready again.

"Put it over the plate," Driscoll said.

"Hit the ball, you all-star," the leader said.

The next pitch came at his head, and he dropped to a knee. The catcher was way back against the bushes, thirty yards.

"Strike two!" the leader said.

Driscoll was a little dizzy. The last time he'd tried to duck like that, he hadn't gotten up. He could feel the blood beating in his temples. Without considering any other options, he stood again. He was angry, and he knew if he could keep it from coming out, he would need it. Leandro made no pretense of where he was throwing, and he stepped at Driscoll and threw a low sidearm fastball that came at Driscoll's heart. There was no time for anything but to stride into the pitch swinging, and Driscoll got it all in the fat of the bat, and the struck ball assumed a racing arc way left, still ascending as it crossed the tree line.

Without stopping, Driscoll took the bat and walked toward where Leandro stood, not fast, just coming, and the young man backed into the weedy lot and turned and jogged out to where the others stood in the field looking where the ball had disappeared. The leader barked orders, which Driscoll could not follow.

"I need a few minutes of your time," Driscoll said. "Now that we have had our recreation."

The young colonel drained his beer and threw the bottle into the effulgent weeds. "You want a beer?" he asked Driscoll.

"No. Just a talk. Then I'll be on my way."

The old dental clinic made a squalid garrison. The anteroom was full of boxes and laundry and porn magazines. Driscoll waited while the man unlocked the other room. His pack was heavy with the revolver. The colonel's office was dark, and litter filled the corners. There was a gash in the floor where the dental chair had been torn out, but the overhead elbow light was still there, folded against the ceiling. The old steel desk was piled with papers and a wooden fruit crate full of grimy rotary telephones. The young man sat behind the desk in a huge black office chair, and Driscoll sat across on the cracked vinyl bench seat from some vehicle.

"What time do you leave?" the young colonel asked.

"Right away. We will talk, and you will never see me again."

"Very good."

"What has happened here?" Driscoll asked.

"Nothing."

"Where are you from?" Driscoll asked the man.

"The south. I prefer it here."

"Your English is good. Were you in school in the U.S.?"

"I was in Texas for one year of high school."

"Did you take the girl?"

"The girl was with us, yes."

"Why?"

"Not your affair. Politics."

"Money."

The colonel smiled. "More money than you'd guess."

Driscoll erased his face and waited. He knew the man would tell him.

"Ten thousand dollars." There was glee in his voice. "For part of one finger."

"Did you do it?" Driscoll pressed. He was on a conveyance now he could not arrest. "Did you cut her and call your associate in the United States?"

The colonel tossed his open hand. "Of course I did. It's my money."

Driscoll heard the outer door and the men come into the building. The fat kid who had been pitching at first came into the room.

"Es todo okay?" he asked.

"Yes," the commander said.

"Do you have English?" Driscoll asked the man.

"A little."

"A question or two?" Driscoll asked the leader.

"What are they?"

Driscoll turned to the big man in the doorway. "Is this your commander?"

"Sí."

"Does he issue all the orders?"

"Sí."

"Do you ever give orders?"

The man laughed. "No, no. I do not."

Driscoll felt himself stand and shake the man's hand. "Bién. Gracias." The man nodded and withdrew, closing the door.

When Driscoll turned he asked the colonel, "Where?" Now the room felt filthy and small.

"Where?" The man laughed. "Right here. Politics." He swept away the papers from the front corner of the desk, and there was a smear of blood in the dirt that was dark and dry even onto the side of the table.

Driscoll opened his cell phone and stepped forward quickly and took the man's picture.

"Oh, no." The colonel stood. "You must not. Give me that." He was at his oversized holster, trying to extract his pistol, when Driscoll bent without hesitation and withdrew the pistol from his own kit, and he leaned forward and shot the man under the chin, which sent him back through his chair, bubbling blood into the trash on the floor. Driscoll stood poised, ready to fire again. He stepped around the desk, and the colonel was twisted back and dead. He knelt and took another picture and snapped his phone shut. Driscoll pulled the man's cell phone from his belt.

Outside there was shouting and he heard car doors slam, and the gray entrance winged open and the huge young man came in. Driscoll yelled at him, "Do you realize how much trouble you are in?" He held the gun down at his side. "The army is coming, and they will hunt you down."

The man stared at the bloody body of the commander. "What have you done?"

"My orders." Driscoll was still speaking loudly. He reached into his kit and pulled out the photograph of himself with the president in the Rose Garden. He held it up. "This is serious. They will hunt you down. You must fly."

The man turned and went out to where the others had brought up their dented Suburban. Driscoll followed. He didn't care if he was shot now, and he expected it. "Stop." He pointed with the gun. "Take him."

The tall left-hander, Leandro, and two others dragged the body from the trashed room and laid him in the back of the vehicle. The driver was gunning the engine, and none of the men would look at Driscoll. "Go, go," he said. "Váyanse."

And the truck was gone. For a minute Driscoll's head roared, and then he felt the blood go out of his legs and he sat on the high step with his feet in the street. The shadow of the building was like a pool of quiet in the dirt, rippling with his heartbeat. The village was empty, and there were no birds calling. He rode out his heart and felt the place on his thigh where the southpaw had drilled him with that pitch. He went back into the ruined building and retrieved his pack, stuffing the photograph and the cell phones into it, and he saw again the pornographic place on the desk where Lucinda's finger had been severed. When he came out of the building, Driscoll met Juvenal in the street. "I need to depart," he told the older man.

"What is it?" Juvenal asked, pointing at the pistol still in Driscoll's hand.

Driscoll went back inside and returned, wrapping the pistol in newspaper. He handed it to Juvenal. "Throw this in the river. The criminals are fled. I don't think they will return. Now, I must go. Don't be seen talking to me."

"Nonsense, my friend. Come home. We'll get the driver." He hefted the newspaper package. "Which river?" he said. "As you know, there are three."

*

At the Molinases' Driscoll packed. The grandmother brought him a large burrito full of shredded beef and goat cheese and an enamel cup of iced tea. She set it on the tray table by his hammock. "I do not want to go north," she said. "Everyone goes to the United States. It must be crowded by now."

"I'm sorry for the trouble that has followed me," he told the old woman.

"You will get ahead of it," she told him. "A man like you will stay afloat."

Alberto came down and asked, "You are going?"

When the grandmother had withdrawn, Driscoll told the young pitcher, "I killed the gang leader. I shot him and he is dead. Now I am going back to find out where this begins." He took Alberto's elbow. "Don't come until you are ready. If you do not wish to return, advise me of that, and I will see to your contracts. I will see to all of it."

"The man who cut Lucinda."

"Alberto, I shot him." Driscoll stood still. "The men are scattered. I will call the police from the capital."

"Don't," Alberto said. "Just go and do what you need to do. The capital is too far to want our stories."

Now Lucinda came in. "Is your vacation in the jungle at an end?"

"What is it, Lucinda?" Alberto said.

"I know what you are doing. There will be trouble."

"Yes," Driscoll said.

"They took my finger," Lucinda said. She touched his wrist. "You will come back. Am I correct?"

"Yes," Driscoll said. "You are correct." He put his hand on her shoulder and spoke in front of Juvenal. "I am coming back."

Driscoll arrived in the city the afternoon the two Japanese pitchers were having their first workout. He went by the ballpark and watched the men and their translators talk to the press. The team was in California for a six-day road trip. Driscoll went by Winchester's office and found the owner standing at his window.

"Hey, scout," he greeted the young catcher. "That's baseball," he said, pointing down to the cluster of people near the mound. "You don't need English; you need the sign for fastball and breaking ball."

"These guys have got ten pitches. Twelve. The catcher's going to
be using both hands. Will you keep them?"

"Oh yes. They're great." He came across and embraced Driscoll.
"You're great. But I'll have to hide them for the rest of the season
in Dubuque."

"That's a good league. You're all set."

Winchester walked back to the window. "It's fun, isn't it. These
kids."

"Baseball," Driscoll said. "It's fun." It hurt him to say. He was
churning, but he worked for the best owner in the league.

"Is our boy coming back from South America?"

"Guatemala. And not yet."

"It's a shame," Winchester said.

Driscoll watched the older man, his face for any shadow, and
there was none.

"It is a shame."

"You going to go down and greet these new American heroes?"

"It'll wait," Driscoll said. "I'm going to take some time and re-
group. There's a lot of unfinished business in this city."

"We're back here against the Pirates Sunday," Winchester said.
"Come by and we'll watch the game." He looked up from the score-
book. "What is it?"

"When I got hit, W?"

"Yeah?"

"Was anything funny about it, something smell wrong?"

"This thing with Alberto woke it all up for you. I can understand
that. And yes, the whole fucking thing was on wrong. You were dying, Driscoll, and everybody else went nuts. It cost Hullinger his career, and he was lucky to get out of town without Red and Raymond
Dodge putting him in the river. They talked some nasty stuff, accident or no. Go find him and kick his ass good. Nobody had seen a
pitch like that. Crazy days. Listen to me, son: you didn't look so
good. Your fucking head was this big." Winchester looked at the
ceiling. "And Jessica fell apart, and truth be told, I think you did
the right thing by letting her go." Now the older man shook his
head slowly. "Did she ever marry Courtland?"

"I don't know. I didn't get invited if they did."

"He was a nice guy, but not much. You can't play third with a
dozen errors a season and break through."

"He could bunt."

"Oh he was a standup, utility guy, but no magic. He's gone now or coaching out west. How you feeling?"

"I'm strong," Driscoll said. "I hit an inside pitch the other day."

Morgan Winchester sat up. "You had a bat in your hand?"

"I stood in and hit a few."

"You want to talk?"

"I'm a long way from a comeback, Morgan."

"I'm not going anywhere. It's a good game, and they tell me it can be enjoyable to play."

"Have you still got a number for Jessica?"

"She was in Boston last year, some graduate program."

"Just a number would be fine."

Driscoll went to the window and put his fingertips on the glass. D and M were still talking to the reporters through their interpreters. The afternoon had fallen apart, and the field was one shadow. Driscoll could see from the way the two interpreters held themselves that they'd played ball. He knew for a fact that in a month one of them would be throwing batting practice in Iowa. You stood around with your mitt in your off hand until they invited you to throw a while.

He drove to Boston that night and saw the Red Sox beat the Orioles in extra innings. Seven home runs. There were always seven home runs these days. The game had changed. In the morning he called Jessica and met her at her flat by the river. Meeting her, as always, was a charge. She answered her door and they looked without speaking. She'd cut her hair off and nodded that he should enter. She was barefoot in Levi's and a blue tattersall shirt rolled to the elbows. Her apartment was modern, and anybody else would have arranged the place to look out the windows onto the Charles, but Jessica had the place in corridors of files and stacks of books. There was an OfficeMax folding table set with her computer square in the middle of the room. They stood like that, not speaking, their faint smiles registering the years between. Finally she said, "You look good. You look well. Sit."

"Thanks, you look the same, Jess." He sat on a wooden church pew against one wall.

"No, I don't. I look like a woman who will be a lawyer in a year."

"Congratulations."

"Careful with that. You want some coffee?"

"Sure. That would be perfect."

They set up the coffee and talked in the kitchen, where there was a short wall of books along the perimeter of the table. "It's good to see you," he said.

"You mean it is strange to see me. Because, my dear, it is strange to see you."

"I guess," he said. "There is a lot of strangeness right now."

"I read about your pitcher. It's horrible and I'm sorry."

"Jess, when I got hit, was there anything funny about it? Anything you saw out of line?"

"No, D. You got hurt. That's all. I was there, and when you went down, I knew that I would never see you again. I thought you were dead."

"I don't remember even going to the ballpark that day."

"You survived. But when you went down, it changed everybody's life. I prayed for you."

"I know you did. What happened with Court?"

"Billy Courtland is a good guy, and he was good to me after you made your decision. But you know how it is for ballplayers. He never broke through, and he didn't want to coach. He came up here with me for a year, and then we both saw the truth."

"What?"

She looked him in the eye. "He wasn't you, D."

"Nobody was me. I wasn't me."

"Are you now?"

"I don't know. There are days."

Jessica poured the coffee and held the creamer. "Same?"

"Same."

She poured cream into his cup.

"What are you studying?"

"Public policy. I came up into the MBA program and a year later got tired of everything being about money. Then I worked for the state and I saw that everything is about money. So I'll be okay. My eyes are open. And you, my dear, are all torn up. Is it this new accident?"

"It's not an accident, Jess."

She looked at him. "Oh, D, be careful."

"It's okay. I just wanted to talk to you for a minute. My memory of the time is all shot." He sipped his coffee and said, "I like your hair."

"No you don't. But it's okay. It was a nightmare, D. Still is. I'm so sorry. I remember Red being out of his skin. I mean real crazy. He was everywhere, always talking, such a shame, over and over, such a shame, like you were his."

"I guess I was."

"No, he was odd. And the pitcher disappeared. Hullinger. Last I heard he was living in the Berkshires; I was friendly with his wife. Do you want their number?"

"You know it?"

Jessica had pulled a file from a box, and Driscoll could see it was full of old newspaper clippings. "I kept some of the stuff."

"Then yes," he said. "I do. Thanks." Driscoll looked at her among her books, her face remembered as if from a dream, her smile easy and warm and sad.

"You were my prince," she said. She put her hand over his.

"I guess I knew that."

"We were kids." She stood up and walked back into the living room. "Do what I said," she said. "Be careful."

Driscoll drove his rental car out of Central Square, and he could sense the tangled village lost in the city and the traffic and the heat. He'd called Hullinger's house in Pittsfield, and his wife said to come ahead. Duke was not around, but he should come out anyway; she'd talk to him. Once she understood who was calling, she said, "Come on; I want to meet you."

The Massachusetts Turnpike was a ribbon in the billowing green of the season, trees in their glory to every horizon. In western Massachusetts, he followed her directions and met her in the small parking lot of Herman Melville's house. Rebecca Hullinger waved her cell phone and pulled off her sunglasses as she walked up to shake his hand. "Well, Mr. Driscoll," she said. "You look just fine." She gestured at her car. "Get in. If you're here this evening we can get dinner, but now we're going off to sell a house. It is strange to meet you, I'll admit."

"Strange?" he said.

"I've only heard your name a thousand times in these years. Duke used to say it in his sleep. Think of that. And here you are. I'm glad you're okay. You are okay, right? You look absolutely normal. I mean that in a good way." The hills she drove through were choked with green, the thick trees growing right up to the road's edge. She turned at the ornate colonial sign for Berkshire West Estates.

"How is Duke?"

"Oh," she said. "I wondered when you called. I was hoping you'd know." Now along the pavement were great gray stone Tudors with little spruces newly staked in the big new lawns. She wheeled the car slowly onto the paving stones of the circular drive. "Duke's gone. He's been gone three years. He called once in the winter after the accident. He was in Greece. So, I'm sorry, Mr. Driscoll, but I guess he's in Greece." She pursed her keys and opened the car. "Come on. You want to see the newest house in western Massachusetts?" She unlocked the huge paneled entry doors and left them open, enough to drive a boat through. She carried a bottle of champagne. The floors were faux stone and the ceilings were twenty feet. "These are easy to sell because the people don't live here four weeks a year, August or October. Nobody's home in this country, you notice that? I don't even have to put any potpourri on the stove. You're a quiet one, hey? What do you need from Duke?" She opened the French doors onto the backyard, which gave way to trees. It was like a park. "Can I ask you: Is this something with your doctor? Closure or something like that?"

"No, I don't know. Sort of. I can't remember much of it, and I thought he might be able to tell me part of the story."

"You're normal, right? This isn't revenge or bullshit like that, is it?"

"Oh no. I'm glad you met me. I'm confused is all, and I'm talking to a few people."

"Well," she said, opening and closing the huge stainless steel fridge and laying the bottle of champagne with a red bow in the empty lighted space. "Here's what I know. Duke cracked. He hit you and that was the end of him." She fished a tissue from her bag. "I mean he stopped talking to me or the kids. He didn't go crazy drinking or anything like that, but he clamped up and his therapist couldn't open him and he wouldn't go to church and he stopped sleeping as far as I could tell. He made a lot of lists. You ever do that, sit and fill a notebook up with lists?"

"What were they?"

"I have no idea. He carried them with him and never showed me.

I hoped for a while that it was the way he was going to climb out of it, but no. They must have been his travel plans or something. In February, three and a half years ago, he disappeared. One phone call a month later. He left some money, which is in the bank for college, and I have a financial manager and a trust at the bank for the long term. I don't think he took much at all."

She was crying silently, and she stopped and washed her face in the kitchen sink, wiping up with paper towels for a minute. "Now I show houses to folks who don't need them. And I don't even need makeup on to do it." She smiled and blew her nose. "I'm not helping, am I? I want you to know that I'm so pleased you're here. You seem okay. If I ever talk to Duke again, I'll tell him. It would change things for him, I think. He had wicked nightmares. He certainly said your name a lot, and he talked to himself days. I mean, I knew he was hurting, but I couldn't help. No way. He loved baseball and was happy at it. He was a good pitcher."

"He was," Driscoll said. "He was a pro."

"Even your guy tried."

"My guy?"

"The guy from your team, the coach."

"Winchester, the owner?"

"No, your coach. I forget his name."

"Red Rawlins."

"Right. That guy. Red Rawlins. He came up a couple times."

Suddenly the light changed in the house, and a shiny black Escalade pulled along the front of the open castle doors. Mrs. Hullinger waved two sheets of paper at him. "I'm about to make thirty-seven thousand dollars. Want to watch?"

He smiled at her. "Thanks, but I'll wait in the car."

He passed the handsome couple on his way out, nodding at them, and as they passed, the man said, "You're Driscoll."

He had to turn. "I am."

"God, are we bidding against you for this place?"

"No, I'm in the city. I'm a perpetual renter."

The man took his hand and shook it. "Are you back? Are you playing this year?"

"I might be back," Driscoll heard himself say. "But not this year."

Then they turned their attention to their waiting realtor, and the woman said to him, "Good luck."

*

When Driscoll left Massachusetts, he was broken. He begged off dinner with Mrs. Hullinger, thanking her for her time, and he motored through the town and the woods to the Taconic Parkway. He knew what to do next, but he had nothing left. He was exhausted. The New England twilight collapsed to green, and then he exited the highway and took a meandering road, village to village. Deer grazed under the heavy trees between the clusters of buildings in each town: the closed auto body, the windows of the inns lit with candles, and the taverns with their neon signs advertising beer. After half an hour he stopped at a roadside motel. He pocketed the room key and smiled. He didn't have any kind of kit, but he couldn't go back home tonight. He didn't even have a toothbrush. He walked next door to the village store, and from the front of that small all-purpose mercantile he could see field lights just beyond and hear the voices from the game. When he came out, he took his new toothbrush and walked around until the Little League game was revealed to him. They'd tucked the ball field against the grassy bank of the railroad trestle. He walked up to the third base side and leaned on the rail fence there. It was an impressive and dramatic display: two uniformed teams and a night game. Clouds of insects worked around each of the clusters of lights. Driscoll smiled to watch the little third baseman. He moved in a synchronicity that wasn't teachable, posting left or right or drifting forward with each pitch. He looked to be eleven. In the game, strikes were rare, and the cries of the parents made a sad noise. There was now a small pressure in Driscoll's head, which felt almost good, and then it was like a hand on his throat and he was crying. What the hell. The third baseman would smack his glove twice before each pitch and then he'd lean in. He wanted so much to dive for the line shot in the gap; he wanted the bunt, the pop foul. Tears dropped onto Driscoll's sleeves. His throat was now closed, and he stood invisible in the night at the dark edge of the beautiful game.

The next noon in the city, Driscoll removed the adaptor from the Guatemalan commander's cell phone. It had been dead, and now with it charged, Driscoll scrolled through the numbers on the little screen one by one. He had done this the day he'd returned, but he needed to see it again. There were only two numbers in the phone, and one was a number that Driscoll knew. He looked at it again, then dialed from his own phone.

Red Rawlins's voice raised in the kind of goodwill he'd always used to greet Driscoll. "Are you back?"

"Red, I'm back and I need to talk to you."

"Wonderful."

"I'm coming over, Red."

"What is it, kid?"

"I need you to tell me a story."

"Kid. I'm not so sure."

"I'm coming over."

"Driscoll. Don't do it." There was a long pause. "Oh, kid."

Driscoll stood in his little kitchen in the first apartment he'd taken when he came to the city. It was empty almost a year after his injury, and now, in the few years since, he was home once a month to change clothes and go to Puerto Rico or Vancouver and scout the leagues. The place had never felt so hollow, a nowhere station in Driscoll's old life. He dropped his chin to his chest and said, "Coach."

In the early afternoon he sat in the gloomy carport of Red Rawlins's house. The television was off, and Red was drinking Wild Turkey out of a small jelly jar. He looked ghostly in his old recliner, and he sat without moving. He spoke softly. "I'm sorry, kid. I heard about your trip south." He finished his glass of whiskey. "I think you know the story."

"Why, coach?"

"Kid, if I talk about it, I won't see the morning."

Driscoll looked at his old friend. "Do this," he said. He crossed the room and knelt and put Red's hand on the side of his head.

"Oh, kid."

This is where Driscoll stalled. Red's hand felt like a memory. "I need you to, Red. Tell me."

Red took his hand back and lifted his jelly jar. "You want a glass?"

"No."

"Then pour this." Driscoll filled the jar and sat on the floor beside Red Rawlins. They were silent ten minutes.

"Let me just say it. I did it. I didn't know what it would all be. I didn't know it would be as bad as it's been. I was something, something I hate now." He sighed and was silent again. "I did it for the money."

"Money?"

"I had the paperwork, and I insured your contract. Driscoll, it was all me." The words ground out of Red's mouth as if he was pushing them. "If you didn't finish the season, the team still had to pay you. I insured that."

"With Winchester?"

"No, he didn't know a thing. There were two sets of papers."

"A million?"

"A little over."

"You paid Hullinger?"

"I did, but it was the end. It crushed him. He was bitter about not ever breaking through, but after he hit you he cracked."

"What about you, Coach?"

"I cracked, too. I'm no good." He held out the glass again, and Driscoll poured. "Look, kid, I see now that I've been waiting for this visit. I'm sorry, son. I'm just sorry, and I've been sorry every minute since. I must have been a sorry soul beforehand. It doesn't matter. I'm glad you're okay, but I'm not okay, and this little talk won't fix that either. I was crazy on the other side of this, wanting my share of the money. There's a half-billion dollars in the air at any time for this team, and I was crazy with wanting some to come down on me. I didn't have a share. And then I did what I did to you, and the money came through, and Driscoll, you don't need to believe this, but it was like poison to me. It is now."

"What about Alberto?"

"That's another story. I had nothing to with that, kid. At all."

"Say it."

"Hullinger started talking."

"Where is he?"

"He's dead, but he was in Greece drinking himself to death, and he ran into the guy, Franco Calloz, and he told the story, how we did it. Calloz pried it out of him. I think he went over there to find out what we'd done, and he got it out of Duke."

"Is this Franco Calloz's number on the phone I've got?"

"It would be."

"He fixed it all?"

"He's a fixer. He's fixed some games. He wanted a big score after the authorities started watching his bets in Vegas. I did what I could to keep him away from the park, but not enough." He looked at Driscoll. "I was scared. Calloz has been waiting for a year for a kid like Alberto, a dead-red kid who had a family far, far away. He shopped around, and then Alberto dropped into his lap."

"Is he Guatemalan?"

"He's Mexican. In that mafia. He's a chief here."

Driscoll shook his head slowly.

"Driscoll, I watched Hullinger crack, and it was like looking in the mirror." He put his glass down and sat still. "Thanks for coming over. I'm sorry, but sorry can't matter. I'm done. I'm sorry, son."

Driscoll put his hands on the side of his head there on the floor. There had been times when he could press his head and go weak in the knees, but now it was something else. The place where he was broken had knit up now; it was not even warm. Now it just felt like his head in his hands.

The team came back to town the next day for an afternoon game. Driscoll dressed early and walked uptown and then across the long span bridge, miles, and walking helped. A slate of blue sky slid by in the thin overcast, and heavier clouds banked the horizon like a wall. The bass thunder was distant and periodic, sounding like someone beating a rug. In the old days, five years ago, he and Jessica would walk the city on off days. No destination except some late lunch in a café sixty blocks away, and then talking about every possible thing, her girlhood, her career in volleyball in high school, her poetry in college, and she'd say some, and he would say the parts of "The Cremation of Sam McGee" he remembered from Miss Cranley at Laramie Junior High, and he'd talk about Miss Cranley and how she said athletes should be literate and she gave him a hard ride with a gentle hand all through that year, setting him up for high school. Those walking days he'd be stopped three or four times by fans who would have seen him throw someone out at second the day before or the day before that, and he'd sign an autograph thinking nothing of it, thinking it would last and last. Today he wore his ball cap tilted low on his brow, and he walked through the city. They'd always said the reason for the city was a walk, block by block. There had been days the second year after his injury when the cap seemed to hold his head together. He'd always felt his heartbeat against it.

Driscoll stopped outside a cigar store and pulled the commander's cell phone out of his pocket, and he did what he'd been waiting to do for three days. He dialed the other number. It sounded, and then there was a short indecipherable message and the beep. Driscoll didn't bother trying to disguise his voice; he just spoke in Spanish: "Serious trouble. Meet me at the ballpark today right after the game."

There was a group of kids playing ball tag in the street, hiding behind cars and throwing two tennis balls back and forth across the street and taunting each other. It was a great drill for throwing in a hurry from the wrong foot. They all threw sidearm. One kid had mastered a lob, which he dropped on his opponents as a surprise; a changeup.

Driscoll had no plan, but the walk had helped. He went into the pawnshop on the corner and bought a pair of binoculars for twenty bucks. The woman in the shop cleaned them for him with her jeweler's cloth, and he called a cab.

At the park he didn't go down to the players' entrance but bought a stadium ticket and went in and got a coffee on the concourse, and he took a long time stirring in the cream. The field always called to him, and he hadn't had this view, two tiers above first base, for ten years. It was sweeter and more charged in the close cloud cover. How many times had he stood on the dugout steps with his catcher's mask in his hand? He'd had a coach as a kid in Laramie that always huddled the team for half a minute before the moment, and he'd said, "Boys, when you take the field, go ahead and take the field. Let's *just take it*. Now go." And the team would run out in a fan to their positions. From those early days Driscoll always ran to the plate, never walking. It was his favorite moment, waiting for the guys to fall into place and for the pitcher to stride out and throw warm-up.

Today the upper deck was half full, and Driscoll sat on a row with eight or nine folks who were celebrating one woman's birthday. Driscoll sipped his coffee and watched his team, his old team, the team he scouted for, as they took the field. He glassed the dugout and the bullpen and everything was in order. He could see Winchester at the window in his field office above third. He wouldn't miss a pitch. Driscoll didn't know what he was doing or what he was looking for or how he felt, but he was calm as the first pitch came in.

There was a wild play in the fourth inning, when the rookie center fielder overran the pitcher at third base. Wild to have a triple,

he hadn't watched the throw come in from right field but instead
put his head down and was almost to third when he looked up and
saw the pitcher standing there. Pure energy and no brains, Red
Rawlins always said at such times. The kid had to stand for the tag
like a pedestrian in the base path, and he trotted off under a scattering of risible catcalls.

Driscoll's seatmates wouldn't let a vendor pass without calling
out, "June wants one!" and the section was a festival of licorice
ropes and peanuts and beer. June herself was just happy about it
all, and a couple of times, as the giant cookies or cotton candy
came her way, she rolled her eyes at Driscoll. What are you going
to do?

Then his phones started ringing.

The first number was Franco Calloz, and he rolled out a great angry line of Spanish, which said something like *do not call* or *why are
you calling*, and then he said, "Dónde?"

Driscoll paused and then said, "Third base. Afterward."

He couldn't tell, because of all the noise around him, if the man
was at the ballpark or not.

Then his own phone rang, and it was Winchester. "Driscoll,
where are you?"

"What's going on?"

"Oh, Jesus."

Driscoll lifted the binoculars again and checked Winchester's
window, but it was empty. "What's the matter?"

"It's Red."

Driscoll's head closed. He watched a looping fly ball slice into
right, and the fielder moved underneath it and made the catch.

"Driscoll?"

"Was there a note?"

"You knew?"

"It's been coming."

"Where are you?"

"I'm here. I'll be in touch. Don't let anything get to the papers."
He folded the phone and put it in his pocket.

"Do you want some of this?" He turned. It was the birthday girl,
June, holding out three bags of peanuts. "They won't quit."

He smiled at her and took one of the bags. "I better."

"It's a ball game," she said.

"It is," he said. "Happy birthday."

He sat and ate peanuts. He thought, It's all coming down now.

He scanned the bullpen and the dugout wondering if Franco Calloz would come alone.

In the ninth, Ketchum put on the hit-and-run, and the batter swung and missed, but the catcher fumbled and the runners got second and third. Sometimes it was luck. After a walk, the catcher, Raymond Dodge, broke his bat on a Texas league single to center and won the game. The crowd around Driscoll stood from their litter and cheered. June pointed at him and said, "We won."

Now he glassed the third base seats and watched the crowd file up the steps. At the top, near the concourse gate, there he was. Dark slacks and an expensive brown plaid polo shirt. Black silk jacket. High-maintenance mustache. Driscoll stood up and started down.

The man was still there ten minutes later when Driscoll came up to him. "Hola, señor. Let us have a word." He said this without stopping and walked down the cement steps. Except for a handful of fans here and there, the place was empty. Beer cups and paper bags. Driscoll stepped down to the third row and sat down in one of the reserved seats. When Franco came down, he came carefully looking left and right. He sat down one seat away from Driscoll.

"So?"

"I want to show you something."

"I don't have any business with you."

"Just this," Driscoll said. He held the cell phone up, snapping it open. He punched up the photograph of the commander, dead on the floor.

"So." The man said. It wasn't a question.

"I'd like to take your picture."

Franco shifted and reached into his jacket pocket, extracting a beautiful pistol which he held in his lap. "So, you can see, Mr. Driscoll. We are done here."

"We are not even started. You're not going to shoot me in the box seats."

"Oh, my friend. You are incorrect." Calloz reached over the seat with his arm and clipped the shoulder of Driscoll's shirt in his fingers. "Walk away from this."

"I don't think so," Driscoll said. "You've made a big mistake, Mr. Calloz."

On hearing his name, the man's face rinsed with malice. Now he shifted, turning to Driscoll like a confidant, and he leaned across and pressed the pistol against Driscoll's lowest rib. The barrel there felt like a touch Driscoll had been waiting for. The man made a noise as if clearing his throat, and Driscoll saw his eyes narrow. Why am I not moving? Driscoll thought.

The stadium crew had started running their backpack blowers in the outfield seats, cleaning the place. This was a time, every third or fourth home game, that Driscoll used to come back out onto the field in the empty park with whoever the rookie pitcher was and let him throw from the mound for half an hour. He was always warmed up after the game and more ready than ever for a catch. He always had two games in him, extra innings, and he was best in the second of any double-header, though those were rare.

"You are at an end, señor," Driscoll said. "Finished." He didn't care about the gun now or the shot to come. Calloz would not get out of the ballpark.

"You have miscalculated, Mr. Driscoll. You have a broken head, and it cannot be trusted. You assaulted me here, and I defended myself. You mean nothing to me, less than nothing. Your body is already dead."

Then Driscoll heard his name called from below, and a head appeared above the dugout roof. It was Alberto, his cap off, his jersey unbuttoned. "Hey."

Now Franco stood, the gun in his hand, and what happened next seemed all part of one motion as Alberto stepped and threw and Franco Calloz coughed, but it was more than that, a deep gasp, as the baseball caught him in the neck and took him over the row of seats and his pistol flew back five rows. Driscoll stood and looked at the man where he lay twisted in the baseball litter. He had both hands over his windpipe. He was gray.

Alberto climbed into the section and Driscoll intercepted him, taking him by both arms. "We'll call the police, Alberto." Driscoll signaled two ushers and guided one until the kid found the gun.

Driscoll flew to Guatemala alone. At the airport he walked the line of variegated vehicles until he found his driver from the last trip. "You know where I'm going."

"Okay," the man said. "No trunk this time?"

"No, just me."

He'd spent three weeks putting Alberto back in place. They had thrown seven innings all alone in the ballpark every morning at dawn. The workouts were wooden, and then they became a joy. And Driscoll himself had taken some batting practice. They were good days, and he learned to stand in and assess the pitches. It all came back.

The driver took him all the way into the remote village. Driscoll asked him, "No gun this time?"

"Not now. You'll be okay."

The town square was quiet and empty, and the driver parked in front of the high curb at the taverna and got out with Driscoll. Juvenal was already out front, having heard the vehicle. "You made good time," the older man said, shaking his hand.

"Where is everybody?" Driscoll said. "Is it church?" He turned to the driver. "Is it Sunday or Monday?"

"Church is concluded," Juvenal said. He pointed down the street. "It is a Sunday tournament."

The driver had already walked ahead toward the open field, from which Driscoll could now hear the sounds of the game.

There was an assemblage of villagers along each foul line on benches and kitchen chairs and upturned buckets, many eating picnics as the game progressed. Driscoll could see Inez pounding her mitt at second base and calling at the batter. The base paths were well worn now and the infield weeds mowed. A three-panel backstop had been erected of a timber frame painted silver and stapled with chicken wire. The big bases were gray, and Eduardo stood with both feet on third, jumping up and down, impatient to be home. Juan Paul was pitching, and he leaned seriously toward the plate, the ball behind his back, studying the fidgeting catcher. He took his time. He shook off three pitches and then nodded. The kid is eleven — Driscoll smiled — and he already has four pitches. Some pitchers liked to have the catcher display the whole inventory on their fingers every time.

"He's too selective," Juvenal said. "You must talk to the boy about it."

Lucinda stood up from where she had been sitting with some of her students across the field and waved. Driscoll felt his face warm. He was taken by the sight and then thought to raise his hand, and he waved. Her bandage was smaller, and she indicated with both hands very clearly that when the inning was complete, she would cross over to him.

MICHAEL CONNELLY

Father's Day

FROM *Blue Religion*

THE VICTIM'S TINY BODY was left alone in the emergency room enclosure. The doctors, after halting their resuscitation efforts, had solemnly retreated and pulled the plastic curtains closed around the bed. The entire construction, management, and purpose of the hospital was to prevent death. When the effort failed, nobody wanted to see it.

The curtains were opaque. Harry Bosch looked like a ghost as he approached and then split them to enter. He stepped into the enclosure and stood somber and alone with the dead. The boy's body took up less than a quarter of the big metal bed. Bosch had worked thousands of cases, but nothing ever touched him like the sight of a young child's lifeless body. Fifteen months old. Cases in which the child's age was still counted in months were the most difficult of all. He knew that if he dwelled too long, he would start to question everything — from the meaning of life to his mission in it.

The boy looked like he was only asleep. Bosch made a quick study, looking for any bruising or sign of mishap. The child was naked and uncovered, his skin as pink as a newborn's. Bosch saw no sign of trauma except for an old scrape on the boy's forehead.

He pulled on gloves and very carefully moved the body to check it from all angles. His heart sank as he did this, but he saw nothing that was suspicious. When he was finished, he covered the body with the sheet — he wasn't sure why — and slipped back through the plastic curtains shrouding the bed.

The boy's father was in a private waiting room down the hall. Bosch would eventually get to him, but the paramedics who had transported the boy had agreed to stick around to be interviewed. Bosch looked for them first and found both men — one old, one young; one to mentor, one to learn — sitting in the crowded ER waiting room. He invited them outside so they could speak privately.

The dry summer heat hit them as soon as the glass doors parted. Like walking out of a casino in Vegas. They walked to the side so they would not be bothered, but stayed in the shade of the portico. He identified himself and told them he would need the written reports on their rescue effort as soon as they were completed.

"For now, tell me about the call."

The senior man did the talking. His name was Ticotin.

"The kid was already in full arrest when we got there," he began. "We did what we could, but the best thing was just to ice him and transport him — try to get him in here and see what the pros could do."

"Did you take a body-temperature reading at the scene?" Bosch asked.

"First thing," Ticotin said. "It was one oh six point eight. So you gotta figure the kid was up around one oh eight, one oh nine, before we got there. There was no way he was going to come back from that. Not a little baby like that."

Ticotin shook his head as though he were frustrated by having been sent to rescue someone who could not be rescued. Bosch nodded as he took out his notebook and wrote down the temperature reading.

"You know what time that was?" he asked.

"We arrived at twelve-seventeen, so I would say we took the BT no more than three minutes later. First thing you do. That's the protocol."

Bosch nodded again and wrote the time — 12:20 P.M. — next to the temperature reading. He looked up and tracked a car coming quickly into the ER lot. It parked, and his partner, Ignacio Ferras, got out. He had gone directly to the accident scene while Bosch had gone directly to the hospital. Bosch signaled him over. Ferras walked with anxious speed. Bosch knew he had something to report, but Bosch didn't want him to say it in front of the paramedics. He introduced him and then quickly got back to his questions.

"Where was the father when you got there?"

"They had the kid on the floor by the back door, where he had brought him in. The father was sort of collapsed on the floor next to him, screaming and crying like they do. Kicking the floor."

"Did he ever say anything?"

"Not right then."

"Then when?"

"When we made the decision to transport and work on the kid in the truck, he wanted to go. We told him he couldn't. We told him to get somebody from the office to drive him."

"What were his words?"

"He just said, 'I want to go with him. I want to be with my son,' stuff like that."

Ferras shook his head as if in pain.

"At any time did he talk about what had happened?" Bosch asked.

Ticotin checked his partner, who shook his head.

"No," Ticotin said. "He didn't."

"Then how were you informed of what had happened?"

"Well, initially we heard it from dispatch. Then one of the office workers, a lady, she told us when we got there. She led us to the back and told us along the way."

Bosch thought he had all he was going to get, but then thought of something else.

"You didn't happen to take an exterior-air-temperature reading for that spot, did you?"

The two paramedics looked at each other and then at Bosch.

"Didn't think to," Ticotin said. "But it's gotta be at least ninety-five, with the Santa Anas kicking up like this. I don't remember a June this hot."

Bosch remembered a June he had spent in a jungle, but wasn't going to get into it. He thanked the paramedics and let them get back to duty. He put his notebook away and looked at his partner.

"Okay, tell me about the scene," he said.

"We've got to charge this guy, Harry," Ferras said urgently.

"Why? What did you find?"

"It's not what I found. It's because it was just a kid, Harry. What kind of father would let this happen? How could he forget?"

Ferras had become a father for the first time six months earlier. Bosch knew this. The experience had made him a professional dad, and every Monday he came in to the squad with a new batch of photos. To Bosch the kid looked the same week to week, but not to Ferras. He was in love with being a father, with having a son.

"Ignacio, you've got to separate your own feelings about it from the facts and the evidence, okay? You know this. Calm down."

"I know, I know. It's just that, how could he forget, you know?"

"Yeah, I know, and we're going to keep that in mind. So tell me what you found out over there. Who'd you talk to?"

"The office manager."

"And what did he say?"

"It's a lady. She said that he came in through the back door shortly after ten. All the sales agents park in the back and use the back door — that's why nobody saw the kid. The father came in, talking on the cell phone. Then he got off and asked if he'd gotten a fax, but there was no fax. So he made another call, and she heard him ask where the fax was. Then he waited for the fax."

"How long did he wait?"

"She said not long, but the fax was an offer to buy. So he called the client, and that started a whole back-and-forth with calls and faxes, and he completely forgot about the kid. It was at least two hours, Harry. Two hours!"

Bosch could almost share his partner's anger, but he had been on the mission a couple of decades longer than Ferras and knew how to hold it in when he had to and when to let it go.

"Harry, something else, too."

"What?"

"The baby had something wrong with him."

"The manager saw the kid?"

"No, I mean, always. Since birth. She said it was a big tragedy. The kid was handicapped. Blind, deaf, a bunch of things wrong. Fifteen months old, and he couldn't walk or talk and never could even crawl. He just cried a lot."

Bosch nodded as he tried to plug this information into everything else he knew and had accumulated. Just then another car came speeding into the parking lot. It pulled into the ambulance chute in front of the ER doors. A woman leaped out and ran into the ER, leaving the car running and the door open.

"That's probably the mother," Bosch said. "We better get in there."

Bosch started trotting toward the ER doors, and Ferras followed. They went through the ER waiting room and down a hallway, where the father had been placed in a private room to wait.

As Bosch got close, he did not hear any screaming or crying or fists on flesh — things that wouldn't have surprised him. The door was open, and when he turned in, he saw the parents of the dead boy embracing each other, but not a tear lined any of their cheeks. Bosch's initial split-second reaction was that he was seeing relief in their young faces.

They separated when they saw Bosch enter, followed by Ferras.

"Mr. and Mrs. Helton?" he asked.

They nodded in unison. But the man corrected Bosch.

"I'm Stephen Helton, and this is my wife, Arlene Haddon."

"I'm Detective Bosch with the Los Angeles Police Department, and this is my partner, Detective Ferras. We are very sorry for the loss of your son. It is our job now to investigate William's death and to learn exactly what happened to him."

Helton nodded as his wife stepped close to him and put her face into his chest. Something silent was transmitted.

"Does this have to be done now?" Helton asked. "We've just lost our beautiful little —"

"Yes, sir, it has to be done now. This is a homicide investigation."

"It was an accident," Helton weakly protested. "It's all my fault, but it was an accident."

"It's still a homicide investigation. We would like to speak to you each privately, without the intrusions that will occur here. Do you mind coming down to the police station to be interviewed?"

"We'll leave him here?"

"The hospital is making arrangements for your son's body to be moved to the medical examiner's office."

"They're going to cut him open?" the mother asked in a near-hysterical voice.

"They will examine his body and then determine if an autopsy is necessary," Bosch said. "It is required by law that any untimely death fall under the jurisdiction of the medical examiner."

He waited to see if there was further protest. When there wasn't, he stepped back and gestured for them to leave the room.

"We'll drive you down to Parker Center, and I promise to make this as painless as possible."

*

They placed the grieving parents in separate interview rooms in the third-floor offices of Homicide Special. Because it was Sunday, the cafeteria was closed, and Bosch had to make do with the vending machines in the alcove by the elevators. He got a can of Coke and two packages of cheese crackers. He had not eaten breakfast before being called in on the case and was now famished.

He took his time while eating the crackers and talking things over with Ferras. He wanted both Helton and Haddon to believe that they were waiting while the other spouse was being interviewed. It was a trick of the trade, part of the strategy. Each would have to wonder what the other was saying.

"Okay," Bosch finally said. "I'm going to go in and take the husband. You can watch in the booth or you can take a run at the wife. Your choice."

It was a big moment. Bosch was more than twenty-five years ahead of Ferras on the job. He was the mentor, and Ferras was the student. So far in their fledgling partnership, Bosch had never let Ferras conduct a formal interview. He was allowing that now, and the look on Ferras's face showed that it was not lost on him.

"You're going to let me talk to her?"

"Sure, why not? You can handle it."

"All right if I get in the booth and watch you with him first? That way you can watch me."

"Whatever makes you comfortable."

"Thanks, Harry."

"Don't thank me, Ignacio. Thank yourself. You earned it."

Bosch dumped the empty cracker packages and the can in a trash bin near his desk.

"Do me a favor," he said. "Go on the Internet first and check the *L.A. Times* to see if they've had any stories lately about a case like this. You know, with a kid. I'd be curious, and if there are, we might be able to make a play with the story. Use it like a prop."

"I'm on it."

"I'll go set up the video in the booth."

Ten minutes later Bosch entered Interview Room Three, where Stephen Helton was waiting for him. Helton looked like he was not quite thirty years old. He was lean and tan and looked like the perfect real estate salesman. He looked like he had never spent even five minutes in a police station before.

Immediately he protested.

"What is taking so long? I've just lost my son, and you stick me in this room for an hour? Is that procedure?"

"It hasn't been that long, Stephen. But I am sorry you had to wait. We were talking to your wife, and that went longer than we thought it would."

"Why were you talking to her? Willy was with me the whole time."

"We talked to her for the same reason we're talking to you. I'm sorry for the delay."

Bosch pulled out the chair that was across the small table from Helton and sat down.

"First of all," he said, "thank you for coming in for the interview. You understand that you are not under arrest or anything like that. You are free to go if you wish. But by law we have to conduct an investigation of the death, and we appreciate your cooperation."

"I just want to get it over with so I can begin the process."

"What process is that?"

"I don't know. Whatever process you go through. Believe me, I'm new at this. You know, grief and guilt and mourning. Willy wasn't in our lives very long, but we loved him very much. This is just awful. I made a mistake, and I am going to pay for it for the rest of my life, Detective Bosch."

Bosch almost told him that his son paid for the mistake with the rest of *his* life but chose not to antagonize the man. Instead, he just nodded and noted that Helton had looked down at his lap when he had spoken most of his statement. Averting the eyes was a classic tell that indicated untruthfulness. Another tell was that Helton had his hands down in his lap and out of sight. The open and truthful person keeps his hands on the table and in sight.

"Why don't we start at the beginning?" Bosch said. "Tell me how the day started."

Helton nodded and began.

"Sunday's our busiest day. We're both in real estate. You may have seen the signs: HADDON AND HELTON. We're PPG's top-volume team. Today Arlene had an open house at noon and a couple of private showings before that. So Willy was going to be with me. We lost another nanny on Friday, and there was no one else to take him."

"How did you lose the nanny?"

"She quit. They all quit. Willy is a handful . . . because of his condition. I mean, why deal with a handicapped child if someone with a normal, healthy child will pay you the same thing? Subsequently, we go through a lot of nannies."

"So you were left to take care of the boy today while your wife had the property showings."

"It wasn't like I wasn't working, though. I was negotiating a sale that would have brought in a thirty-thousand-dollar commission. It was important."

"Is that why you went into the office?"

"Exactly. We got an offer sheet, and I was going to have to respond. So I got Willy ready and put him in the car and went in to work."

"What time was this?"

"About quarter to ten. I got the call from the other realtor at about nine-thirty. The buyer was playing hardball. The response time was going to be set at an hour. So I had to get my seller on standby, pack up Willy, and get in there to pick up the fax."

"Do you have a fax at home?"

"Yes, but if the deal went down, we'd have to get together in the office. We have a signing room, and all the forms are right there. My file on the property was in my office, too."

Bosch nodded. It sounded plausible, to a point.

"Okay, so you head off to the office . . ."

"Exactly. And two things happened . . ."

Helton brought his hands up into sight but only to hold them across his face to hide his eyes. A classic tell.

"What two things?"

"I got a call on my cell — from Arlene — and Willy fell asleep in his car seat. Do you understand?"

"Make me understand."

"I was distracted by the call, and I was no longer distracted by Willy. He had fallen asleep."

"Uh-huh."

"So I forgot he was there. Forgive me, God, but I forgot I had him with me!"

"I understand. What happened next?"

Helton dropped his hands out of sight again. He looked at Bosch briefly and then at the tabletop.

"I parked in my assigned space behind PPG, and I went in. I was still talking to Arlene. One of our buyers is trying to get out of a contract because he's found something he likes better. So we were talking about that, about how to finesse things with that, and I was on the phone when I went in."

"Okay, I see that. What happened when you went in?"

Helton didn't answer right away. He sat there looking at the table as if trying to remember so he could get the answer right.

"Stephen?" Bosch prompted. "What happened next?"

"I had told the buyer's agent to fax me the offer. But it wasn't there. So I got off the line from my wife and I called the agent. Then I waited around for the fax. Checked my slips and made a few callbacks while I was waiting."

"What are your slips?"

"Phone messages. People who see our signs on properties and call. I don't put my cell or home number on the signs."

"How many callbacks did you make?"

"I think just two. I got a message on one and spoke briefly to the other person. My fax came in, and that was what I was there for. I got off the line."

"Now, at this point it was what time?"

"I don't know, about ten after ten."

"Would you say that at this point you were still cognizant that your son was still in your car in the parking lot?"

Helton took time to think through an answer again but spoke before Bosch had to prompt him.

"No, because if I knew he was in the car, I would not have left him in the first place. I forgot about him while I was still in the car. You understand?"

Bosch leaned back in his seat. Whether he understood it or not, Helton had just dodged one legal bullet. If he had acknowledged that he had knowingly left the boy in the car — even if he planned to be back in a few minutes — that would have greatly supported a charge of negligent homicide. But Helton had maneuvered the question correctly, almost as if he had expected it.

"Okay," Bosch said. "What happened next?"

Helton shook his head wistfully and looked at the side wall as if gazing through a window toward the past he couldn't change.

"I, uh, got involved in the deal," he said. "The fax came in, I called my client, and I faxed back a counter. I also did a lot of talking to the other agent. By phone. We were trying to get the deal done, and we had to hand-hold both our clients through this."

"For two hours."

"Yes, it took that long."

"And when was it that you remembered that you had left William in the car out in the parking lot, where it was about ninety-five degrees?"

"I guess as soon — first of all, I didn't know what the temperature was. I object to that. I left that car at about ten, and it was not ninety-five degrees. Not even close. I hadn't even used the air conditioner on the way over."

There was a complete lack of remorse or guilt in Helton's demeanor. He wasn't even attempting to fake it anymore. Bosch had become convinced that this man had no love or affinity for his damaged and now lost child. William was simply a burden that had to be dealt with and therefore could easily be forgotten when things like business and selling houses and making money came up.

But where was the crime in all this? Bosch knew he could charge him with negligence, but the courts tend to view the loss of a child as enough punishment in these situations. Helton would go free with his wife as sympathetic figures, free to continue their lives while baby William moldered in his grave.

The tells always add up. Bosch instinctively believed Helton was a liar. And he began to believe that William's death was no accident. Unlike his partner, who had let the passions of his own fatherhood lead him down the path, Bosch had come to this point after careful observation and analysis. It was now time to press on, to bait Helton and see if he would make a mistake.

"Is there anything else you want to add at this point to the story?" he asked.

Helton let out a deep breath and slowly shook his head.

"That's the whole sad story," he said. "I wish to God it never happened. But it did."

He looked directly at Bosch for the first time during the entire interview. Bosch held his gaze and then asked a question.

"Do you have a good marriage, Stephen?"

Helton looked away and stared at the invisible window again.

"What do you mean?"

"I mean, do you have a good marriage? You can say yes or no if you want."

"Yes, I have a good marriage," Helton responded emphatically. "I don't know what my wife told you, but I think it is very solid. What are you trying to say?"

"All I'm saying is that sometimes, when there is a child with challenges, it strains the marriage. My partner just had a baby. The kid's healthy, but money's tight and his wife isn't back at work yet. You know the deal. It's tough. I can only imagine what the strain of having a child with William's difficulties would be like."

"Yeah, well, we made it by all right."

"The nannies quitting all the time . . ."

"It wasn't that hard. As soon as one quits, we put an ad on craigslist for another."

Bosch nodded and scratched the back of his head. While doing this, he waved a finger in a circular motion toward the camera that was in the air vent up on the wall behind him. Helton could not see him do this.

"When did you two get married?" he asked.

"Two and a half years ago. We met on a contract. She had the buyer, and I had the seller. We worked well together. We started talking about joining forces, and then we realized we were in love."

"Then William came."

"Yes, that's right."

"That must've changed things."

"It did."

"So when Arlene was pregnant, couldn't the doctors tell that he had these problems?"

"They could have if they had seen him. But Arlene's a workaholic. She was busy all the time. She missed some appointments and the ultrasounds. When they discovered there was a problem, it was too late."

"Do you blame your wife for that?"

Helton looked aghast.

"No, of course not. Look, what does this have to do with what happened today? I mean, why are you asking me all this?"

Bosch leaned across the table.

"It may have a lot to do with it, Stephen. I am trying to determine what happened today and why. The 'why' is the tough part."

"It was an accident! I *forgot* he was in the car, okay? I will go to my grave knowing that *my* mistake killed my own son. Isn't that enough for you?"

Bosch leaned back and said nothing. He hoped Helton would say more.

"Do you have a son, detective? Any children?"

"A daughter."

"Yeah, well then, happy Father's Day. I'm really glad for you. I hope you never have to go through what I'm going through right now. Believe me, it's not fun!"

Bosch had forgotten it was Father's Day. The realization knocked him off his rhythm, and his thoughts went to his daughter living eight thousand miles away. In her ten years, he had been with her on only one Father's Day. What did that say about him? Here he was, trying to get inside another father's actions and motivations, and he knew his own could not stand equal scrutiny.

The moment ended when there was a knock on the door and Ferras came in, carrying a file.

"Excuse me," he said. "I thought you might want to see this."

He handed the file to Bosch and left the room. Bosch turned the file on the table in front of them and opened it so that Helton would not be able to see its contents. Inside was a computer print-out and a handwritten note on a Post-it.

The note said, "No ad on craigslist."

The printout was of a story that ran in the *L.A. Times* ten months earlier. It was about the heat-stroke death of a child who had been left in a car in Lancaster while his mother ran into a store to buy milk. She ran into the middle of a robbery. She was tied up along with the store clerk and placed in a back room. The robbers ransacked the store and escaped. It was an hour before the victims were discovered and freed, but by then the child in the car had already succumbed to heat stroke. Bosch scanned the story quickly, then dropped the file closed. He looked at Helton without speaking.

"What?" Helton asked.

"Just some additional information and lab reports," he lied. "Do you get the *L.A. Times*, by the way?"

"Yes, why?"

"Just curious, that's all. Now, how many nannies do you think you've employed in the fifteen months that William was alive?"

Helton shook his head.

"I don't know. At least ten. They don't stay long. They can't take it."

"And then you go to craigslist to place an ad?"

"Yes."

"And you just lost a nanny on Friday?"

"Yes, I told you."

"She just walked out on you?"

"No, she got another job and told us she was leaving. She made up a lie about it being closer to home and with gas prices and all that. But we knew why she was leaving. She could not handle Willy."

"She told you this Friday?"

"No, when she gave notice."

"When was that?"

"She gave two weeks' notice, so it was two weeks back from Friday."

"And do you have a new nanny lined up?"

"No, not yet. We were still looking."

"But you put the feelers out and ran the ad again, that sort of thing?"

"Right, but listen, what does this have to —"

"Let me ask the questions, Stephen. Your wife told us that she worried about leaving William with you, that you couldn't handle the strain of it."

Helton looked shocked. The statement came from left field, as Bosch had wanted it.

"What? Why would she say that?"

"I don't know. Is it true?"

"No, it's not true."

"She told us she was worried that this wasn't an accident."

"That's absolutely crazy, and I doubt she said it. You are lying."

He turned in his seat, so that the front of his body faced the corner of the room and he would have to turn his face to look directly at Bosch. Another tell. Bosch knew he was zeroing in. He decided it was the right time to gamble.

"She mentioned a story you found in the *L.A. Times* that was about a kid left in a car up in Lancaster. The kid died of heat stroke. She was worried that it gave you the idea."

Helton swiveled in his seat and leaned forward to put his elbows on the table and run his hands through his hair.

"Oh, my God, I can't believe she . . ."

He didn't finish. Bosch knew his gamble had paid off. Helton's mind was racing along the edge. It was time to push him over.

"You didn't forget that William was in the car, did you, Stephen?"

Helton didn't answer. He buried his face in his hands again. Bosch leaned forward, so that he only had to whisper.

"You left him there, and you knew what was going to happen. You planned it. That's why you didn't bother running ads for a new nanny. You knew you weren't going to need one."

Helton remained silent and unmoving. Bosch kept working him, changing tacks and offering sympathy now.

"It's understandable," he said. "I mean, what kind of life would that kid have, anyway? Some might even call this a mercy killing. The kid falls asleep and never wakes up. I've worked these kinds of cases before, Stephen. It's actually not a bad way to go. It sounds bad, but it isn't. You just get tired and you go to sleep."

Helton kept his face in his hands, but he shook his head. Bosch didn't know if he was denying it still or shaking off something else. He waited, and the delay paid off.

"It was her idea," Helton said in a quiet voice. "She's the one who couldn't take it anymore."

In that moment Bosch knew he had him, but he showed nothing. He kept working it.

"Wait a minute," Bosch said. "She said she had nothing to do with it, that this was your idea and your plan and that when she called you, it was to talk you out of it."

Helton dropped his hands with a slap on the table.

"That's a lie! It was her! She was embarrassed that we had a kid like that! She couldn't take him anywhere, and we couldn't go anywhere! He was ruining our lives, and she told me I had to do something about it! She told me how to do something about it! She said I would be saving two lives while sacrificing only one."

Bosch pulled back across the table. It was done. It was over.

"Okay, Stephen, I think I understand. And I want to hear all about it. But at this point I need to inform you of your rights. After that, if you want to talk, we'll talk, and I'll listen."

When Bosch came out of the interview room, Ignacio Ferras was there, waiting for him in the hallway. His partner raised his fist, and Bosch tapped his knuckles with his own fist.

"That was beautiful," Ferras said. "You walked him right down the road."

"Thanks," Bosch said. "Let's hope the DA is impressed, too."

"I don't think we'll have to worry."

"Well, there will be no worries if you go into the other room and turn the wife now."

Ferras looked surprised.

"You still want me to take the wife?"

"She's yours. Let's walk them into the DA as bookends."

"I'll do my best."

"Good. Go check the equipment and make sure we're still recording in there. I've got to go make a quick call."

"You got it, Harry."

Bosch walked into the squad room and sat down at his desk. He pulled out his cell phone and sent a call across the Pacific.

His daughter answered with a cheerful hello. Bosch knew he wouldn't even have to say anything and he would feel fulfilled by just the sound of her voice saying the one word.

"Hey, baby, it's me," he said.

"Daddy!" she exclaimed. "Happy Father's Day!"

And Bosch realized in that moment that he was indeed a happy man.

DAVID CORBETT

Pretty Little Parasite

FROM *Las Vegas Noir*

ONE HAND ON HER HIP, the other lofting her cocktail tray, Sam Pitney scanned the gaming floor from the Roundup's mezzanine, dressed in her bright red cowgirl outfit and fresh from a bracing toot in the ladies'. Stream-of-nothingness mode, midshift, slow night, only the blow keeping her vertical — and she had this odd craving for some stir-fry — she stared out at the flagging crowd and maniacally finger-brushed the outcrop of blond bangs showing beneath her tipped-back hat.

Maybe it was seeing her own reflection fragmented in dozens of angled mirrors to the left and right and even overhead, or the sight of the usual trudge of losers wandering the noisy mazelike neon, clutching change buckets, chip trays, chain-smoking (still legal, this was the eighties), hoping for one good score to recoup a little dignity — whatever the reason, she found herself revisiting a TV program from a few nights back, about Auschwitz, Dachau, one of those places. Men and women and children and even poor helpless babies cradled by their mothers, stripped naked, then marched into giant shower rooms, only to notice too late — doors slamming, bolts thrown, gas soon hissing from the showerheads: a smell like almonds, the voice on the program said.

Sam found herself wondering — no particular reason — what it would be like if the doors to the casino suddenly rumbled shut, trapping everybody inside.

For a moment or two, she supposed, no one would even notice, gamblers being what they are. But soon enough word would ripple through the crowd, especially when the fire sprinklers in the ceiling started to mist. Even then people would be puzzled and vaguely put out but not frightened, not until somebody nearby started gagging, buckled over, a barking cough, the scalding phlegm, a slime of blood in the palm.

Then panic, the rush for the doors. Animal screams. Blind terror.

Sam wondered where she'd get found when they finally reopened the doors to deal with the dead. Would she be one of those with bloody nails or, worse, fingers worn down to raw gory bone, having tried to claw her way past so many others to sniff at an air vent, a door crack, ready to kill for just one more breath? Or would she be one of the others, one of those they found alone, having caught on quick and then surrendered, figuring she was screwed, knowing it in the pit of her soul, curled up on the floor, waiting for God or Mommy or Satan or who-the-fuck-ever to put an end to the tedious phony bullshit, the nerves and the worry and the always being tired, the lonely winner-takes-all, the grand American nothing . . .

"Could I possibly have another whiskey and ginger, luv?"

Sam snapped to, turning toward the voice — the accent crisply British once, now blurred by years among the Vegas gypsies. It came from a face of singular unlucky pallor: high brow with a sickly froth of chestnut hair, flat bloodless lips, no chin to speak of. The Roundup sat just east of Las Vegas Boulevard on Fremont, closer to the LVMPD tower than the tonier downtown houses — the Four Queens, the Golden Nugget — catering to whoever showed up first and stayed longest, cheap tourists mostly, dopes who'd just stumbled out of the drunk tank and felt lucky (figure that one out), or, most inexplicably, locals, the transplant kind especially, the ones who went on and on about old Las Vegas, which meant goofs like this bird. What was his name? Harvey, Harold, something with an *H*. He taught at UNLV, if she remembered right, came here three nights a week at least, often more, said it was for the nostalgia . . .

"You are on the clock, my dear, am I right?"

She gazed into his soupy green eyes. Centuries of inbreeding. Hail, Brittania.

"I'm pregnant," she said.

Come midnight she began looking for Mike, and found him off by himself in the dollar slots, an odd little nook where there were fewer mirrors and the eye in the sky had a less than perfect angle (he thought of these things). He wore white linen slacks, a pastel T, the sleeves of his sport jacket rolled up. All Sonny Crockett, the dick.

"Hey," she said, coming up.

He shot her a vaguely proprietary smile. His eyes looked wrecked, but his hair was flawless. He said, "The usual?"

"No, weekend coming up. Make it two."

The smile thawed, till it seemed almost friendly. "Double your pleasure."

She clipped off to the bar, ordered a Stoli rocks twist, discreetly assembling the twelve twenties on her tray in a tight thin stack. The casino's monotonous racket jangled all around, same at midnight as happy hour — the eternal now, she thought, Vegas time. Returning to where he was sitting, she bowed at the waist, so he could reach the tray. He carefully set down a five, under which he'd tucked two wax-paper bindles. Then he collected the twelve twenties off her tray, as though they were his change, and she remembered the last time they were together, in her bed, the faraway look he got afterward, not wanting to be touched, the kind of thing guys did when they'd had enough of you.

"Whoever you get this from," she said, "I want to meet him."

From the look on his face, you would've thought she'd asked for the money back. "Come again?"

"You heard me."

He cocked his head. The hair didn't budge. "I'm not sure I like your attitude."

She broke the news. In the span of only a second or so, his expression went from stunned to deflated to distinctly pissed, then: "You saying it's mine?"

She rolled her eyes. "No. An angel came to me."

"Don't get smart."

"Oh, smart's exactly what I'm going for, believe me."

"Okay then, take care of it."

With those few words, she got a picture of his ideal woman — a collie in heat, basically, but with fewer scruples. Lay out a few lines, bend her over the sofa, splay her ass — then, a few weeks later, tell her to *take care of it.*

"Sorry," she said. "Not gonna happen."

He chuckled acidly. "Since when are you maternal?"

"Don't think you know me. We fucked, that's it."

"You're shaking me down."

"I'm filling you in. But yeah, I could make this a problem. Instead, I'm trying to do the right thing. For everybody. But I'm not gonna be able to work here much longer, understand? This ain't about you, it's about money. Introduce me to your guy."

He thought about it, and as he did his lips curled into a grin. The eyes were still scared though. "Who says it's a guy?"

A twinge lit up her lower back. Get used to it, she thought. "Don't push me, Mike. I'm a woman scorned, with a muffin in the oven." She did a quick pivot and headed off. Over her shoulder, she added, "I'm off at two. Set it up."

It didn't happen that night, as it turned out, and that didn't surprise her. What did surprise her was that it happened only two nights later, and she didn't have to hound him half as bad as she'd expected — more surprising still, he hadn't been jiving: it really wasn't a guy.

Her name was Claudia, a Cuban, maybe fifty, could pass for forty, calm dark eyes that waxed and waned between cordial welcome and cold appraisal — a tiny woman, raven-black hair coiled tight into a long braid, body as sleek as a razor, sheathed in a simple black dress. She lived in one of the newer condos at the other end of Fremont, near Sahara, where it turned into Boulder Highway.

Claudia showed them in, dead-bolted the door, offered a cool muscular hand to Sam with a nod, then gestured everyone into the living room: suede furniture, Navajo rugs, ferns. Two fluffed and imperial Persian cats nestled near the window on matching cushions. Across the room, a mobile of tiny tin birds, dozens of them, all painted bright tropical colors, hung from the ceiling. Interesting, Sam thought, glancing up as she tucked her skirt against her thighs. Thing must torment the cats.

"Like I said before," Mike began, addressing Claudia, "I think this is a bad idea, but you said okay, so here we are."

Sam resisted an urge to storm over, take two fistfuls of that pampered hair, and rip it out by the roots. She turned to the woman. "Can we talk alone?"

"That doesn't work for me," Mike said.

With the grace of a model, Claudia slowly pivoted toward him. "I think it's for the best." For the sake of his pride, she added, "I'm sure I'll be fine."

That was that. He sulked off to the patio, the two women talked. It didn't take long for Sam to explain her situation, lay out her plan, make it clear she wasn't being flaky or impulsive. She'd thought it through — she didn't want to get even, pick off Mike's customers, nothing like that. "I don't want to hand my baby off to day care, some stranger. I want to be there. At home."

Claudia eyed her, saying nothing, for what seemed an eternity. Don't look away, Sam told herself. Accept the scrutiny, know your role. But don't act scared.

"There are those," Claudia said finally, "who would find what you just said very peculiar." Her smile seemed a kind of warning, and yet it wasn't without warmth. "I'm sure you realize that."

"I do. But I think you understand."

It turned out she understood only too well — she had a son, Marco, eleven years old, away at boarding school in Seville. "I miss him terribly." She made a sawing motion. "Like someone cut off my arm."

"Why don't you have him here, with you?"

For the first time, Claudia looked away. Her face darkened. "Mothers make sacrifices. It's not all about staying home with the baby."

Sam felt backward, foolish, hopelessly American. Behold the future, she thought, ten years down the road, doing this, and your kid is where? In the corner of her eye, she saw one of the cats rise sleepily and arch its back. Out on the patio, Mike sat in the moonlight, a sudden red glow as he dragged on his cigarette.

Claudia steered the conversation to terms: Sam would start off buying ounces at $2,000 each, which she would divide into grams and eightballs for sale. If things went well, she could move up to a QP — quarter pound — at $7,800, build her clientele. She might well plateau at that point, many did. If she was ambitious, though, she could move up to an elbow — for "lb," meaning a pound — with the tacit agreement she would not interfere with Claudia's wholesale trade.

"I want you to look me in the eye, Samantha. Good. Do not confuse my sympathy for weakness. I'm generous by nature. That doesn't mean I'm stupid. I have men who take care of certain matters for me, men not at all like our friend out there." She nodded toward Mike all alone on the moonlit patio. "These men, you will never meet them unless it comes to that. And if it does, the time will have passed for you to say or do anything to help yourself. I trust I'm clear."

The first and oddest thing? She lost five pounds. God, she thought, what have I done? She checked her sheets for blood, then ran to Valley Medical, no appointment, demanded to see her ob-gyn. The receptionist — sagging desert face, kinky gray perm — shot her one of those knowing, gallingly sympathetic looks you never really live down.

"Your body thinks you've got a parasite, dear," the woman said. "Just keep eating."

She did, and she stunned herself, how quickly her habits turned healthy. No more coke, ditto booze — instead a passion for bananas (craving potassium), an obsession with yogurt (good for bone mass, the immune system, the intestinal lining), a sudden interest in whole grains (to keep her regular), citrus (for iron absorption), even liver (prevent anemia). She took to grazing, little meals here and there, to keep the nausea at bay, and when her appetite craved more, she turned to her newfound favorite: stir-fry.

She continued working for three months, time enough to groom a clientele — fellow casino rats (her old quitting-time buddies, basically, and their buddies), a few select customers from the Roundup (including, strangely enough, Harry the homely Brit, who came from Manchester, she learned, taught mechanical engineering, vacationed in Cabo most winters, not half the schmuck she'd pegged him for), plus a few locals she decided to trust (the girls at Diva's Hair-and-Nail, the boys at Monte Carlo Tanning Salon, a locksmith named Nick Perino, had a shop just up Fremont Street, total card, used to host a midnight movie show in town) — all of this happening in the shadow of the police tower on Stewart Avenue, all those cops just four blocks away.

Business was brisk. She got current on her bills, socked away a few grand. At sixteen weeks her stomach popped out, like she'd suddenly inflated, and that was the end of cocktail shift. Sam bid it goodbye with no regrets, the red pleated dress, the cowboy hat, the tasseled boots. From that point forward, she conducted business where she pleased, permitting a trustworthy inner circle to come to her place; the others she met out and about, merrily invisible in her maternity clothes.

The birth was strangely easy, two-hour labor, a snap by most standards, and Sam shed twenty pounds before heading home. The best thing about seeing it go was no longer having to endure strangers — older women especially, riding with her in elevators or standing in line at the store — who would notice the tight globe of her late-term belly and instinctively reach out, stroke the shuddering roundness, cooing in a helpless, mysterious, covetous way that almost rekindled Sam's childhood fear of witches.

As for the last of the weight gain, it all seemed to settle in her chest — first time in her life, she had cleavage. This little girl's been good to you all over, Sam thought — her skin shone, her eyes glowed, she looked happy. Guys seemed to notice, clients especially, but she made sure to keep it all professional: so much as hint at sex with coke in the room, next thing you knew the guy'd be eyeing your muff like it was veal.

Besides, the interest on her end had vanished. Curiously, that didn't faze her. Whatever it was she'd once craved from her lovers she now got from Natalie, feeling it strongest when she nursed, enjoying something she'd secretly thought didn't exist — the kind of fierce unshakable oneness she'd always thought was just Hollywood. Now she knew better. The crimped pink face, the curled doughy hands, the wispy black strands of impossibly fine hair: "Look at you," she'd whisper, over and over and over.

By the end of two months, she'd pitched all her old clothes, not just the maternity duds. Some old bad habits got the heave-ho as well: the trashy attitude, slutty speech, negative turns of mind. Nor would the apartment do anymore — too dark, too small, too blah. The little one deserves better, she told herself, as does her mother. Besides, maybe someone had noticed all the in-and-out, the visitors night and day. Half paranoia, half healthy faith in who she'd become, she upscaled to a three-bedroom out on Boulder Highway, furnished it in suede, added ferns. She bought two cats.

Nick Perino sat alone in an interview room in the Stewart Avenue tower — dull yellow walls, scuffed black linoleum, humming fluorescent light — tapping his thumbs together and cracking his neck as he waited. Finally the door opened, and he tried to muster some advantage, assert control, by challenging the man who entered, blurting out, "I don't know you."

The newcomer ignored him, tossing a manila folder onto the table as he drew back his chair to sit. He was in his thirties, shaggy hair, wiry build, dressed in a Runnin' Rebels T-shirt and faded jeans. Something about him said one-time jock. Something else said unmitigated prick. Looking bored, he opened the file, began leafing through the pages, sipping from a paper cup of steaming black coffee so vile Nick could smell it across the table.

Nick said, "I'm used to dealing with Detective Naughton."

The guy sniffed, chuckling at something he read, suntanned laugh lines fanning out at his eyes. "Yeah, well, he's been rotated out to Traffic. You witness a nasty accident, Mike's your man. But that's not why you're here, is it, Mr. Perry?"

"Perino."

The cop glanced up finally. His eyes were scary blue and so bloodshot they looked on fire. Another sniff. "Right. Forgive me."

"Some kind of cold you got there. Must be the air conditioning."

"It's allergies, actually."

Nick chuckled. Allergic to sleep, maybe. "Speaking of names, you got one?"

"Thornton." He whipped back another page. "Chief calls me James, friends call me Jimmy. You can call me sir."

Nick stood up. He wasn't going to take this, not from some slacker narc half in the bag. "I came here to do you guys a favor."

Still picking through the file, Jimmy Thornton said, "Sit back down, Mr. Perry."

"Don't call me that."

"I said — sit down."

"You think you're talking to some fart-fuck asshole?"

Finally the cop closed the file. Removing a ballpoint pen from his hip pocket, he began thumbing the plunger maniacally. "I know who I'm talking to. Mike paints a pretty vivid picture." He nudged the folder across the table. "Want a peek?"

Despite himself, Nick recoiled a little. "Yeah. Maybe I'll do that."

Leaning back in his chair, still clicking the pen, Jimmy Thornton said, "You first blew into town, when was it, 'seventy-four? Nick Perry, *Chiller Theater*, Saturday midnight. Weaseled your way into the job, touting all this 'network experience' back East."

Nick shrugged. "Everybody lies on his resumé."

"Not everybody."

"My grandfather came over from Sicily, Perino was the family name. Ellis Island, he changed it to Perry. I just changed it back."

"Yeah, but not till you went to work for Johnny T."

Nick could feel the blood drain from his face. "What are you getting at?"

The cop's smile turned poisonous. "Know what Johnny said about you? You're the only guy in Vegas ever *added* a vowel to the end of his name. Him and his brother saw you coming at the San Genero Festival, they couldn't run the other way fast enough, even when you worked for them. Worst case of wanna-be-wiseguy they'd ever seen."

Finally Nick sat back down. "You heard this how? Johnny doesn't, like —"

"Know you were the snitch? Can't answer that. I mean, he probably suspects."

Nick had been a CI in a state case against the Tintoretto brothers for prostitution and drugs, all run through their massage parlor out on Flamingo. Nick remained unidentified during trial, the case made on wiretaps. It seemed a wise play at the time — get down first, tell the story his way, cut a deal before the roof caved in. He was working as the manager there, only job he could find in town after getting canned at the station — a nigger joke, pussy in the punch line, didn't know he was on the air.

"All the employees got a pass," Nick said, "not just me. Johnny couldn't know for sure unless you guys told him."

"Relax." Another punctuating sniff. "Nobody around here told him squat. We keep our promises, Mr. Perry."

Nick snorted. "Not from where I sit."

"Excuse me?" The guy leaned in. "Mike bent over backwards for you, pal. Set you up, perfect location, right downtown. Felons aren't supposed to be locksmiths."

"Most of that stuff on my sheet was out of state. And it got expunged."

A chuckle: "Now there's a word."

"Vacated, sealed, whatever."

"Because Mike took care of it. And how do you repay him?"

"I don't know what you're talking about."

"Every time business gets slow, you send that fat freak you call a nephew out to the apartments off Maryland Parkway — middle of the night, spray can of Super Glue, gum up a couple hundred locks. You can bank on at least a third of the calls, given your location — think we don't know this?"

"Who you talking to, Mike Lally over at All-Night Lock'n'Key? You wanna hammer a crook, there's your guy, not me."

"Doesn't have thirty-two grand in liens from the Tax Commission on his business, though, does he?"

Nick blanched. They already knew. They knew everything. "I got screwed by my bookkeeper. Look, I came here with information. You wanna hear it or not?"

"In exchange for getting the Tax Commission off your neck."

"Before they shut me down, yeah. That asking so much?"

Jimmy Thornton opened the manila folder to the last page, clicked his pen one final time, and prepared to write. "That depends."

Sam sat in the shade at the playground two blocks from her apartment, listening to Nick go on. He'd just put in new locks at her apartment — she changed them every few weeks now, just being careful — and, stopping here to drop off the new keys, he'd sat down on the bench beside her, launching in, some character named Jimmy.

"He's a standup guy," Nick said. "Looker, too. You'll like him."

"You pitching him as a customer or a date?"

Nick raised his hands, a coy smile. "All things are possible," inflecting the words with that paisano thing he fell into sometimes.

Natalie slept in her stroller, exhausted from an hour on the swings, the slide, the merry-go-round. Sam wondered about that, whether it was really good for kids to indulge that giddy instinct for dizziness. Where did it lead?

"Tell me again how you met this guy."

"He wanted a wall safe, I installed it for him."

She squinted in the sun, shaded her eyes. "What's he need a wall safe for?"

"That's not a question I ask. You want, I provide. That's business, as you well know."

She suffered him a thin smile. With the gradual expansion of her clientele — no one but referrals, but even so her base had almost doubled — she'd watched herself pulling back from people, even old friends, a protective, judicious remove. And that was lonely-making. Worse, she'd gotten used to it, and that seemed a kind of living death. The only grace was Natalie, but even there, the one-ness she'd felt those first incredible months, that had changed as well. She still adored the girl, loved her to pieces, that wasn't the issue. Little girls grow up, their mothers get lonely, where's the mystery? She just hadn't expected it to start so soon.

"He's a contractor," Nick went on, "works down in Henderson. I saw the blueprints and, you know, stuff in his place when I was there. Look, you don't need the trade, forget about it. But I thought, I dunno, maybe you'd like the guy."

"I don't need to like him."

"I meant 'like' as in 'do business.'"

Sam checked the stroller. Natalie had her thumb in her mouth, eyes closed, her free hand balled into a fist beneath her chin.

"You know how this works," Sam said. "He causes trouble, any-thing at all — I mean this, Nick — anything at all comes back at me, it's on you, not just him."

They met at the Elephant Walk, and it turned out Nick was right, the guy turned heads — an easy grace, cowboy shoulders, lady-killer smile. He ordered Johnnie Walker Black with a splash, and Sam remembered, from her days working cocktail, judging men by their drinks. He'd ordered wisely. And yet there were signs — a jit-ter in the hands, a slight head tic, the red in those killer blue eyes. Then again, if she worried that her customers looked like users, who would she sell to?

"Nick says you're a contractor."

He shook his head. "Project manager."

"There's a difference?"

"Sometimes. Not often enough." He laughed, and the laugh was self-effacing, one more winning trait. "I buy materials, hire the subs, make sure the bonds are current and we're all on time. But the contractor's the one with his license on the line."

"Sounds demanding."

"Everything's demanding. If it means anything."

She liked that answer. "And to relax, you . . . ?"

He shrugged. "I've got a bike, a Triumph, old Bandit 350, gathering dust in my garage." Another self-effacing smile. "Amazing how boring you can sound when stuff like that comes out."

Not boring, she thought. Just normal. "Ever been married?"

A fierce little jolt shot through him. "Once. Yeah. High school sweetheart kind of thing. Didn't work out."

She got the hint and steered the conversation off in a different direction. They talked about Nick, the stories they'd heard him tell about his TV days, wondering which ones to believe. Sam asked about how the two men had met, got the same story she'd heard from Nick, embellished a little, not too much. Things were, basically, checking out.

Sensing it was time, she signaled the bartender to settle up. "Well, it's been very nice meeting you, Jimmy. I have to get home. The sitter awaits, with the princess."

"Nick told me. Natalie, right? Have any pictures?"

She liked it when men asked to see pictures. It said something. She took out her wallet, opened it to the snapshots.

"How old?"

"Fifteen months. Just."

"She's got her mother's eyes."

"She's got more than that, sadly."

"No. Good for her." He returned her wallet, hand not trembling now. Maybe it was the Scotch, maybe the conversation. "She's a beauty. Changed your life, I'll bet."

Yes, Sam thought, that she has. Maybe we'll talk about that sometime. Next time. "Have kids?"

Very subtly, his eyes hazed. "Me? No. Didn't get that far, which is probably for the best. Got some nephews and nieces, that's it for now."

"Uncle Jimmy."

He rattled the ice in his glass, traveled somewhere with his thoughts. "I like kids. Want kids. My turn'll come." Then, brightening suddenly: "I'd be up for a play date sometime, with Natalie. I mean, if that doesn't sound too weird."

That's how it started, same playground near the apartment. And he hadn't lied, he hit it off with Natalie at first sight — stunning, really. He was a natural, carrying her on his shoulders to the park, guiding her up the stairs to the slide, taking it easy on the swing.

He had Sam cradle her in her lap on the merry-go-round, spun them both around in the sun-streaked shade. Natalie shrieked, Sam laughed; it was that kind of afternoon.

They brought Natalie home, put her down for her nap, then sat on the porch with drinks — the usual for him, Chablis for her. The sun beat down on the freshly watered lawn, a hot desert wind rustling the leaves of the imported elm trees.

Surveying the grounds, he said, "Nice place. Mind if I ask your monthly nut?"

"Frankly?"

He chuckled. "Sorry. Professional curiosity. I was just doing the math in my head, tallying costs, wondering what kind of return the developer's getting."

She smiled wanly. "I don't like to think about it." That seemed as good a way as any to change the subject. "So, Nick says you wanted to ask me something."

Suddenly he looked awkward, a hint of a blush. It suited him.

"Well, yeah. I suppose . . . You know. Sometimes . . ." He gestured vaguely.

She said, "Don't make me say it for you."

He cleared his throat. "I could maybe use an eightball. Sure."

There, she thought. Was that so hard? "Let's say a gram. I don't know you."

"How about two?"

It was still below the threshold for a special felony, which an eightball, at 3.5 grams, wasn't. "Two-forty, no credit."

"No friend-of-a-friend discount?"

"Nick told you there would be?"

"No, I just —"

"There isn't. There won't be."

He raised his hands, surrender. "Okay." He reached into his hip pocket for his wallet. "Mind if I take a shot while I'm here?"

She collected her glass, rose from her chair. "I'd prefer it, actually. Come on inside."

She gestured for him to have a seat on the couch, disappeared into her bedroom, and returned with the coke, delivering the two grams with a mirror, a razor blade, a straw. As always, a stranger in the house, one of the cats sat in the corner, blinking. The other hid. Sam watched as Jimmy chopped up the lines, an old hand. He hoovered the first, offered her the mirror. She declined. He leaned back down, finished up, tugged at his nose.

"That's nice," he said, collecting the last few grains on his finger, rubbing it into his gums. When his hand came away, it left a smile behind. "I'm guessing mannitol. I mean, you've got it around, right?"

Sam took a sip of her wine. He was referring to a baby laxative commonly used as a cutting agent. Coolly, she said, "Let a girl have her secrets."

He nodded. "Sorry. That was out of line."

"Don't worry about it." She toddled her glass. "So — will there be anything else?"

She didn't mean to sound coy, but even so she inwardly cringed as she heard the words out loud. The way he looked at her, it was clear he was trying to decipher the signal. And maybe, on some level, she really did mean something.

"No," he said. "I think that's it. Mind if I take one last look before I leave?"

And so that's how they wrapped it up, standing in the doorway to Natalie's room, watching her sleep.

"Such a pretty little creature," he whispered. "Gotta confess, I'm jealous."

Back in his car, Jimmy horned the rest of the first gram, then drove to the Roundup, a little recon, putting faces to names, customers of Sam's that Nick had told him about: card dealers, waitresses, a gambler named Harry Thune, homely Brit, the usual ghastly teeth. After that he drove to the strip mall on Charleston where the undercover unit had its off-site location, an anonymous set of offices with blinds drawn, a sign on the door reading HALLIWELL PARTNERS, LTD. He logged in, parked at his desk, and wrote up his report: the purchase of one gram Cocaine HCL, field-tested positive with Scott Reagent — blue, pink, then blue with pink separation in successive ampoules after agitation — said gram supplied by Samantha Pitney, White Female Adult. He invented an encounter far more fitting with department guidelines than the one that had taken place, wrote it out, signed it, then drove to the police tower, walked in the back entrance, and delivered the report to his sergeant, an old hand named Becker, who sent Jimmy on to log the gram into evidence. Jimmy said hey to the secretaries on his way through the building, went back to his car, moved $120 from his personal wallet to his buy wallet to cover the gram he'd pilfered, then planned his next step.

The following two buys were the same, two grams, and she seemed to grow more comfortable. He got bumped up to an eightball, and not long after that he rose to two. He always took a taste right there at the apartment, while they were talking, one of the perks of the job. Later he'd either log it in as-is, claiming the shortage had been used for field-testing, or he'd pocket the light one, chop it up into grams, then drive to Henderson — or, on weekends, all the way to Laughlin — work the bars, a little business for himself, cover his costs, a few like minds, deputies he knew.

He found himself oddly divided on Sam. You could see she'd tried to cultivate an aura: the wry feminine reserve, the earth tones, all the talk about yoga and studying for her real estate license. Maybe it was motherhood, all that scrubbed civility, trying to be somebody. Then again, maybe it was cokehead pretence. Regardless, little things tripped her up, those selfless moments, more and more frequent, when she let him see behind the mask. Trouble was, from what he could tell, the mask had more to offer.

He'd nailed a witness or two in his time, never a smooth move, but nothing compared to bedding a suspect. As fluid as things had become morally since he'd started working undercover, he'd never lost track of that particular red line. That didn't mean he didn't entertain the thought — throwing her over his shoulder, carrying her into her room, dropping her onto the bed, watching her hair unfurl from the soft thudding impact. Would she try to fight him off? No, that would just be part of the dance. Soon enough she'd draw him down, a winsome smile, hands clasped behind his neck, a few quick nibbles in her kiss, now and then a good firm bite. And was she one of those who showed you around the castle — how hard to pinch the nipples, how many fingers inside, the hand clasped across her mouth as she came — or would she want you to find all that out for yourself? Playing coy, demure, wanting you to take command, maybe even scare her. How deep would she like it, how slow, how rough? Would she come in rolling pulses or one big back-arching slam?

Then again, of course, there was Natalie. Truth be told, she was the one who'd stolen his heart. And it was clear her poor deluded mother loved her, but love's not enough — never is, never has been. He remembered Sam asking, in their first face-to-face, about his marriage, about kids. You're not a cop till your first divorce, he thought, go through the custody horseshit. Lose. Bobby was his name. Seven years old now. Somewhere.

When he found himself thinking like that, he also found himself developing a mean thirst. And when he drank, he liked a whiff, to steady the ride, ice it. And so soon he'd be back at Ms. Pitney's door, repeating the whole sad process, telling himself the same wrong stories, wanting everything he had no right to.

Six weeks into things, he asked, "What made you get into this business, anyway?"

She was sitting on the sofa, legs tucked beneath her, wearing a new perfume. From the look on her face, you would've thought he'd spat on the floor. "No offense, but that came out sounding ugly."

He razored away at three chalky lines. "Didn't mean it that way. Sorry."

She thought about it for a moment, searching the ceiling with her eyes. "The truth? I wanted to be a stay-at-home mom."

He had to check himself, to keep from laughing, and yet he could see it. So her, thinking that way. "Why not marry the father?"

Again she paused before answering, but this time she didn't scour the ceiling, she gazed into his face. Admittedly, he was a little ragged: his mouth was dry, his eyes were jigging up and down, his pupils were bloated. And his hands, yeah, a mild but noticeable case of the shakes.

"Some men are meant to be fathers," she said. "Some men aren't."

Sam let one of Claudia's Persians settle in her lap, pressing her skirt with its paws. The other cat lay in its usual spot, on the cushion by the window, lolling in the sun. Natalie sat in her stroller, gumming an apple slice, while Claudia attended her ferns, using a teakettle for a watering can.

"I usually charge thirty, which is already low, but I'd trim a little more, say twenty-eight." She was talking in thousands of dollars, the price for a pound — or an elbow, in the parlance.

"That's still a little steep for me."

"You could cut your visits here by half. More."

"Is that a problem?" Secretly, Sam loved coming here. She thought of it as Visiting Mother.

Over her shoulder, Claudia said, "You know what I mean."

"Maybe I'll ratchet up another QP. I don't want any more than that in the house."

Claudia bent to reach a pot on the floor. "The point is to get it *out* of the house."

Well, duh, Sam thought, feeling judged, a headache looming like a thunderhead just behind her eyes. She was getting them more and more. "There's something else I'd like to talk over, actually. It's about Natalie."

Claudia stopped short. "Is something wrong?"

"No. Not yet. I mean, there's nothing to worry about. But if anything ever happened to me, I don't know who would take care of her."

A disagreeable expression crossed Claudia's face, part disdain, part calculation, part suspicion. "You have family."

"Not local. And not that I trust, frankly."

"What exactly are you asking?"

"I was wondering if she could stay with you. If anything ever happened, I mean."

Claudia put the teakettle down and came over to a nearby chair, crossing her legs as she sat. "Have you noticed any cars following you lately?"

"It's not like that."

"Any new neighbors?"

"That wasn't what I meant. I meant if I got sick or was in a car accident." She glanced over at Natalie. The apple slice was nubby and brown, and both it and her fingers were glazed with saliva.

Claudia said, "I couldn't just walk in, take your child. Good Lord." Her voice rippled, a blast of heat.

Sam said, "I'm sorry, I didn't mean —"

"A dozen agencies would be involved, imagine the questions." She rose from her chair, straightened her skirt, shot a toxic glance at Natalie that said, *Your mother can't protect you.* "Now what quantity are you here for? I have things to do."

Sergeant Becker called Jimmy in, told him to close the door. He was a big man, the kind who could lord over you even sitting down.

"This Pitney thing, I've gone over the reports." He picked up a pencil, drummed it against his blotter. "Your buys are light."

He stared into Jimmy's whirling eyes. Jimmy did his best to stare right back.

"I'm a gentleman. I always offer the lady a taste."

"She needs to sample her own coke?"

"Not sampling, indulging. And there's always some lost in the field test."

"Think a jury will buy that? Think I buy that?"

"You want me to piss in a cup?"

Becker pretended to think about that, then leaned forward, lowering his voice. "No. That's what I most definitely do not want you to do. Look, I'll stand up for you, but it's time you cleaned house. You need some time, we'll work it out. There's a program, six weeks, over in Bullhead City, you can use an assumed name. It's the best deal you're gonna get. In the meantime, wrap this up. You've got your case, close it out."

Jimmy felt a surge of bile boiling in his stomach — at the thought of rehab, sure, the shame of it, the tedium, but not just that. "Like when?"

"Like now." Becker's whole face said, *Look at yourself.* "Why wait?"

Jimmy pictured Sam in her sundress, face raised to the light, hand in her hair. Moisture pooling in the hollow of her throat. Lipstick glistening in the heat.

He said, "There's a kid involved."

Becker stood up behind his desk. They were done. "Get CPS involved, that's what they're there for. Make the calls, do the paperwork, get it over with."

"For chrissake, don't overthink it. Sounds like the last nice guy in Vegas."

It was Mandy talking, Sam's old best friend at the Roundup. She'd stopped by on her way to work, a gram for the shift, and now was lingering, shoes off, stocking feet on the coffee table, toes jigging in their sheer cocoon. They were watching Natalie play, noticing how her focus lasered from her ball to her bear, back to the ball, moving on to her always mysterious foot, then a housefly buzzing at the sliding glass door.

"Dating the clientele," Sam said, "is such a chump move."

"Rules have exceptions. Otherwise, they wouldn't be rules."

Natalie hefted herself onto her feet, staggered to the sliding glass door, reached for the fly — awestruck, gentle.

"He's got a bit of a problem." Sam tapped the side of her nose.

"You can clean him up. Woman's work."

"I don't need that kind of project."

"If you don't mind my asking, how long's it been since you got laid?"

Admittedly, sometimes when Jimmy was there, Sam felt the old urge uncoiling inside her, slithering around. "To be honest, I do mind you asking."

They weren't close anymore, just one of those things. To hide her disappointment, Mandy softly clapped her hands at Natalie. "Hey, sweetheart, come on over. Sit with Auntie Man a little while." The little girl ignored her, still enchanted by the fly. It careened about the room — ceiling, lampshade, end table — then whirled back to the sliding glass door, a glossy green speck in a flaring pool of sunlight.

"She doesn't like me."

"She can be persnickety." Sam glanced at the clock. "Don't take it personally."

"You think if you let this guy know you were interested, he'd respond?"

Sam felt another headache coming on. Each one seemed worse than the last now. "It's not an issue."

"You're the one playing hard to get, not him."

Jimmy's last visit, Sam had almost thrown herself across his lap, wanting to feel his arms around her. Just that. But that was everything, could be everything. "I've given him a few openings. Nothing obvious, but since when do you need to be obvious with men?"

Mandy crossed her arms across her midriff, as though suddenly chilled. "Maybe he's queer."

Once Mandy was gone, Sam tucked Natalie in for the midday nap with her blue plush piglet, brushing the hair from the little girl's face to plant a kiss on her brow. Leaving the bedroom door slightly ajar — Natalie would never drop off otherwise — Sam fled to her own room and took a Demerol. The pain was flashing through her sinuses now, even pulsing into her spine. Noticing the time, she changed into a cinched sleeveless dress, freshened her lipstick, her eyeliner. Jimmy had said he'd stop by, and she still couldn't quite decide whether to push the ball into his end of the court or abide by her own better instincts and let it go. Running a mental inventory of his pros and cons, she admitted he was a joy to look at, had a soldier's good manners, adored Natalie. He was also a flaming cokehead, with the predictable sidekick, a blind thirst. Those things trended downward in her experience, not a ride she wanted to share. Loneliness is the price you pay for keeping things uncomplicated, she thought, pressing a tissue between her lips.

She heard a shuffle of steps on the walkway out front, but instead of ringing the bell, whoever it was pounded at the door. A voice she didn't recognize called out her name, then: "Police! Open the door." To her shame, she froze. Out of the corner of her eye she saw three men cluster on the patio — shirtsleeves, sunglasses, protective vests — and her mouth turned to dust. The front door crashed in, brutal shouts of "On the floor!" and shortly she was face-down, being handcuffed, feeling guilty and terrified and stupid and numb while cops thrashed everywhere, asserting claim to every room.

When they pulled her to her feet, it was Jimmy who was standing there, wearing a vest like the others, his police card hanging around his neck. The Demerol not having yet kicked in, her head crackled and throbbed with a new burst of pain, and she feared she might hurl right there on the floor.

"Tell us where everything is, and we won't take the place apart," he said, regarding her with a look of such contemptuous loathing she actually thought he might spit in her face. And I deserve it, she told herself, how stupid I've been, at the same time thinking, Now who's the creature? She could smell the Scotch on his breath, masked with spearmint. So that's what it was, she thought, all that time, the drink, the coke. Mr. Sensitive drowning his guilt. Or was even his guilt phony?

She said, "What about Natalie?" In her room, the little girl was mewling, confused, scared.

Jimmy glanced off toward the sound, eyes dull as lead. "She's a ward of the court now. They'll farm her out, foster home —"

Sam felt the room close in, a sickly shade of white. "Why are you doing this?"

Almost imperceptibly, he stiffened. A weak smile. "*I'm* doing this?"

"Why are you being such a prick about it?"

He leaned in. His eyes were electric. "You're a mother."

You miserable hypocrite, she thought, trying to muster some disgust of her own, but instead her knees turned liquid. He caught her before she fell, duck-walked her toward the sofa, let her drop — at which point a woman with short sandy hair came out of Natalie's bedroom, carrying the little girl. Her eyes were puffy with sleep, but she was squirming, head swiveling this way and that. She began to cry. Sam shook off her daze, turned to hide the handcuffs, calling out, "Just do what the lady says, baby. I'll come get you as soon as I can," but the girl started shrieking, kicking — and then was gone.

"Get a good look?" Jimmy said. "Because that's the last you'll see of her."

He was performing for the other cops, the coward. "You can't do that."

"No? Consider it done."

Sam struggled to her feet. "You can't . . . No . . . ."

He nudged her back down. She tried to kick him, but he pushed her legs aside. Crouching down, he locked them against his body with one arm, his free hand gripping her chin. Voice lowered, eyes fixed on hers — and, finally, she thought she saw something hovering behind the savage bloodshot blue, something other than the arrogance and hate, something haunted, like pity, even love — he whispered, "Listen to me, Sam. I want to help you. But you've gotta help me. Understand? Give me a name. It's that simple. A name, and we work this out. I'll do everything I can, that's a promise, for you, for Natalie — everything. But you've gotta hold up your end. Otherwise . . ."

He let his voice trail away into the nothingness he was offering. For Sam knew where this led, she remembered the words exactly: *I have men who take care of certain matters . . . The time will have passed for you to say or do anything to help yourself . . .*

And there it was: her daughter or her life, she couldn't save both. Maybe not today or tomorrow but someday soon, Claudia's threat would materialize, assuming a face and form but no name — the police would promise protection, but the desert was littered with their failures — and Sam would realize this is it, that pitiless point in time when she would finally know: Which was she? One of those who tried to kick and claw and scream her way out, even though it was hopeless? Or one of those who, seeing there was no escape, calmly said, *I'm ready. I've been ready for a long, long while.*

M . M . M .   H A Y E S

Meantime, Quentin Ghlee

FROM *The Kenyon Review*

QUENTIN GHLEE HAD COMMANDEERED a nineteenth-century one-room schoolhouse abandoned out on the Mhuirich ranch, and the following summers he built on a lean-to with storage beneath it for mining tools, an underground compartment weighted closed by a massive chair. Every winter, hunters or snowmobilers, parties foraging in the wilderness area, even Forest Service or BLM officials had been known to break into buildings uninhabited during the heavy snows. Household utensils, appliances, or fixtures would disappear, even old phones or picture frames if they might be antique. But summers? Ah. Then Ghlee would return with the swallows, unearth what bare essentials he needed for shack existence, and work all day dynamiting and breaking rock in his mine. Finally, tired, dirty, and satisfied with his progress along a gold-bearing outcrop of quartz, he would set himself down in a well-worn folding chair and drink down the evening sun.

Sunset was a moment that always surprised him and never repeated itself. This evening's sun spreading shifting dunes of melon-gold clouds, films of it settling over the ragged horizon of the Rough Hills, turning the slopes fiery, then golden, then oyster blue, the peaks diamond-pointed with the last slant rays of light, canyons and gullies already dark and secret, returned to themselves. An endless show, every night, the silent guardian Venus edging in, impatient for the night to begin. He never tired of it. Sprawled under his makeshift canopy, drink in hand, he slipped warmly into the cold mountain night.

He had arrived back in high country from Salt Lake City three days ago, had taken stock of what work his diggings needed this year, and totted up a list of things to buy in Elko — mostly dynamite and sour mash. Stocked with a Jeep-full of canned baked beans that he'd brought from Utah, he had borrowed back his goat from Mhuirich's ranch, which he passed on the way. Today he'd noticed a slow leak in one leg of his WW II surplus Jeep and decided to stop by Barnabus Mhuirich's toolshed to get a patch and fix his tire before he set out again on the two-hundred-mile round trek to Elko. Might even stop by Barnabus's toolshed tonight, start for Elko tomorrow. Play it by ear.

It was good to be back. Good to be back. He missed the quiet up here, missed the loneliness, the heat and itch of grasshoppers rasping in the afternoon, the proximity of the sky and clouds so low their shadows moved like a giant blight over the sage and hollows and foothills ascending out of the valley. Ten-thirty every morning, like a church bell, the jets from Mountain Home Air Base broke the sound barrier. Ghlee still hired on as a mining engineer, even though he'd retired five years ago when he turned fifty-five, but these days Salt Lake City tightened around him — more traffic, more anger, more people moving in from the East and telling all the westerners how to live, even though they'd fled what they were trying to duplicate. And it changed the *weather!* Smog, body heat, elbows. Lifelong neighbors and business associates squeezed you now, turned on a man. Ghlee's own wife, Ellie, actually shot him — well, to be fair, he'd shot her first, during a late-night descent into a discussion about President Bush. The woman kept at him and wouldn't listen either, just wouldn't shut up and listen, which drove him nuts. She still did. He shouldn't have shot her, of course, no, not good, but it was late and they'd both been drinking, and to tell the truth, he couldn't remember doing it anyway, the shooting that is. But he'd apologized, damn it, and the woman, with malicious aforethought, had waited a whole year to waylay him up here, in the same spot, with the same gun, the old warhorse. A survivor, he had to give her that.

He carried the face wound permanently, a mangled left cheek that looked like the black lava spilled across southern Idaho. Ghlee had been forced, what choice did he have, to quit inviting Ellie to come to Nevada with him. Fine with her, she said, but even without Ellie there was no end of evil afoot. Ghlee preferred spending some of each Utah winter in the Southern Hemisphere, and last year his own brother had jumped uranium claims Ghlee had staked in Patagonia. No one could be trusted. People might not know what they wanted, but they wouldn't keep their misery to themselves.

Too many people on the planet, if anyone asked him, which no one had, but that's what he thought anyway. The whole globe was proving the trapped-rat thesis, so that you got yourself out to what was supposed to be the middle of nowhere — Elko, say — and you find gamblers, prostitutes, hippies, gunrunners, and lately gangs of Mexicans marrying Indian girls and using them to deal meth, all the way up in Idaho, he'd heard. Old and new people coming up out of the sewers, although Elko didn't need sewers, there was so little rain. Just let 'er run off.

Out here, working on abandoned mines under a metal-blue sky, no one could get to him. Oh, they would, sooner or later — he'd heard motorcycles up on the county road this afternoon. Sooner or later the overflow would stumble across the corkscrew entry into this maze of mountain valleys, but for the moment this was that one lost corner of the planet, roads impassable nine months of the year, which not too many folks had found. A place where a man could finish a thought.

Well warmed and lubricated, he sat and watched the night sky take over. The icy gleam of stars blanketed him with indifference, the coyotes laughed in the hills. On his own, Ghlee slipped quietly into the land, the air, the warmth of sour mash, and a welcome consciousness that old Ghlee himself was headed for that great dust migration. Still, in the meantime — *in* the meantime.

He may have dozed. Yes, he definitely dozed, but the cold woke him, and he pushed himself up out of the saggy yellow-and-lime-striped folding chair and pocketed a square bottle for companionship. He shuffled off for his Jeep, which was also for the junk heap soon, the two of them on last legs, but tough old legs. They'd do another 300,000 miles together, he'd warrant, both of them too ornery to go down easy.

Late now, but a good time to stop by Barnabus Mhuirich's toolshed, so Ghlee drove the Jeep up the dusty spur to the county road, without lights because he liked moving in moonlight, after thirty summers up here knowing this road as well as his own fingernails.

Yep, he'd knock off as many jackrabbits as he could, catching them from behind in the dark. Collect 'em on the way home, skin 'em tonight, and fry up rabbit for breakfast. Ghlee liked to look out from the inside of the night.

What he saw tonight, up the road a good ways, were silhouettes, two of them, just past Barnabus's house and walking south down the road. They carried bags, or maybe blankets. He couldn't tell in moonlight, so he pulled to the side of the road, well north of Barnabus's. The two lurching shadows, heavy-footed walkers, looked to be men. After a while they sat and shook loose whatever it was and covered themselves.

Ghlee pulled out his bottle and calculated. These wouldn't be ranchers, not with nothing better to do than sneak along a dark road well past the middle of the night. Ranchers'd be sleeping fast, with chores waiting at dawn, and that was only an hour or two away. No ranch hands either, not traveling these roads on their *feet. Ha!* Ghlee laughed at his own pun, had some more companionship, and leaned back, shoulders melting into his seat.

Pretty soon the shadows rose and rocked away, one charging, one limping and falling behind. Interesting, the lameness, the weak one who couldn't keep up. Ghlee heard them yelling, although not what they said. It didn't make much sense, and he consulted his bottle and listened to the percussive arrhythmia of their shouting, the fricatives of what sounded like swearing and obscenities.

The straggler sat again, but the second silhouette walked ahead. After about ten minutes, Ghlee concluded that what he'd found were little blobs of trouble bubbling up from places Ghlee had escaped. Here were your basic rats, moving in and digging into the alkali to reconnoiter these pristine mountains. Already they were turning on each other. Ha! Hadn't he said as much?

He stirred his Jeep awake, thought to get his pistol from the seat, but decided his hands, molded by pickax handles, were weapons enough. He pottered forward in the Jeep to the sitter, who had become a dark spot, barely visible on the side of the road with the hill of sage behind him. Ghlee kept his window open to hear any more sounds of what had seemed a pretty fair facsimile of a fight. He rolled to a stop and leaned out the window. "You in trouble there?" he croaked, slurring to disguise his curiosity.

The figure struggled upright. "Sure am." A boy, teenager perhaps, stood and limped to Ghlee's window. A slight kid, not much mass to him, with his head shaved bald and earrings up and down both ears. Ghlee never could remember in which ear jewelry signaled strange music, but both ears cinched it. Certified strange. The boy poked his noggin in the Jeep window, blond stubble now visible, and with him came a stink that immediately put Ghlee in mind of garbage. The voice even cracked, started high and finished low and hoarse: "There any way we could get a ride to Elko? Or anywhere we could get some gas?" He peered inside the Jeep, the passenger side and then in the back, and Ghlee chuckled, thinking the kid — he was a kid — probably thought he could handle this old guy. The boy came closer, his voice stronger and deeper. "We had a motorcycle accident, up to the pass. My bike slid off this wall of snow, and then we didn't know — a rancher down here told us — there's a town, t'other side of the pass? Instead we walked all day to get back to that paved road from Elko. I smashed my leg going over the cliff, and it hurts like hell. I need a doctor."

Ghlee pursed his mouth and noticed the boy flinch at the mangled right side of his face, Ellie's brand. Ghlee couldn't even grow beard to cover it, although tiny whiskers did grow out of crevices. The boy stepped away. "It's okay," said Quentin, used to the reaction. He touched his face. "I had a little accident myself. But get in. Get in. I'll take a look at the leg."

"You a doctor?" Suspicion, tinged with challenge.

Ghlee loved it. "Nope." He leaned back and squeezed the wheel. "No doctors up here, so we learn to do for ourselves. But I can patch up a leg and get it so's you can walk on it, and maybe we can find you a good knot of wood to use as a walking stick."

"I got a friend. In Elko. He might could come get me."

"Sure. We'll call your friend."

"Call? I thought you were headin' towards town. Why aren't your lights on?"

"Don't need 'em. Saves gas. And hell no, I'm not going to town in the middle of the night, not about to. But you can make a call from my place. I'm just back up the road some."

"I . . . I'm with a friend, too. Just went round the corner." The boy pointed, his voice turning whiny. They both looked at the swath of gravel disappearing around a hill of high sage.

"Where?" said Ghlee. "Don't see nobody."

"Well, he's up there. Could we pick him up, too?"

"Don't see a thing."

"He's there. You can't see him around that next turn, not in the dark."

Can't see around the corner in the light either, thought Ghlee, but he said, "He can't be too worried about you then. That blood on your leg? Cougar probably out stalking your scent right now."

"Cougar!"

"You bet, cougar. Where'd you think they lived?"

The kid made a funny gurgling sound. "But on the road? They come down here?"

"Never noticed cougar paying much attention to traffic signs, if that's what you mean."

"No. No. But — if we could just find Dewayne —"

"Dewayne? He Indian?"

"Part. Why?"

"Well then. Indian set loose in sagebrush, he'll be fine. Like Br'er Rabbit. We'll fix that leg a yours and put you back here. He'll be around somewhere. But it's late. I got to get home and go to bed. I've a big day ahead of me. And I don't think you'll find many other offers tonight."

"But" — and the boy looked behind the Jeep — "you some kind of sheriff or something? Where you comin' from?"

"What difference does that make? And hell no, I'm no sheriff, just . . . your basic . . . knight-errant, roaming the land to right all wrongs, stamp out discord, find folks . . . in distress." Ghlee laughed at himself. "Found you, didn't I?"

The boy moved back another step. "Oh, fuck." He rolled his eyes. "Well, okay. I'm in distress. What's your name?"

"Cain!" Ghlee lied, then suddenly sensed discovery and, excited by its danger, upped the stakes. He added his real last name. "Cain Ghlee."

"Glee? You're kidding. Like in *wheeeee?*"

"Sometimes." Kid's a loudmouth. Which warmed Ghlee's heart. Warmed his heart. Made him . . . gleeful.

"Where's your place?"

"Oh, c'mon, get in. Or . . . get lost! I'll help, but I want to get going." And he did.

The boy wavered, his nose twitching.

Ghlee felt the moment stop, as if neither of them were breathing. The boy lifted his hand and let it drop, looked at the corner ahead, and Ghlee felt a wave of heat begin, blood rising in his head, the familiar warm tingle through his thighs. Here, surfacing right beneath Quentin's feet, came your classic rat, nose twitching as it emerged from the warrens of gambling and prostitution in Elko, and here he crept in, thinking he'd discovered these clean-smelling mountains. Ghlee felt a pulse in his chest and solid forearms.

Then the surrender: a final look up the disappearing road, a shaky sigh, and the youngster limped around to the passenger door. Settled in the seat beside Ghlee, he slammed the door, and already Ghlee caught the scent. Putrefaction. The old man felt his body click into place, poised to erupt.

Plan your work and work your plan, his father always said when Ghlee screwed up and needed to be taught a lesson. Ghlee turned the Jeep around and headed back to his cabin. This half-grown rodent would return, to show his friends the valley. Ghlee could imagine them on their motorcycles, raising dust devils all the way up the road to the pass. That's what would happen, if he let it. Once people saw what they could get away with, they poured through the holes, the law of the bad example. That was the way the world worked, and it was this world Ghlee calibrated, measured, and put in motion. If there was another world, another time, fine, he'd be some part of that, too, but here and now he was one of the forces that operated according to a system of physical laws, same as the stars circulated according to a pattern beyond their own control. What did it tell him, this oily urchin stumbling into his private territory? He felt the quick flick of something unseen, heard a discordant hiss in the sounds of the night, and shuddered, chilled even as he sped toward the incandescent moment of tying the boy to the chair in the shed.

CHUCK HOGAN

Two Thousand Volts

FROM *Ellery Queen's Mystery Magazine*

IT WAS A DINER off the interstate exit, pushed back from the
road to make room for a truck turnaround.

The customer with the handgun inside his jacket sat on the first
red-padded stool at the front counter, the seat closest to the takeout register. He had come in alone, ordered a Coke. Other than
turning to watch every car pulling in, he sat there as patiently as
night waiting for day.

Sam, the grill man, worked out in front. He lifted off two half-
pounders of cooked patty meat and tucked them into prepared
rolls, wrapped them up tight in a square of wax paper, and then
dropped them into a yellow Best Burger To-Go sack. He thumbed
three or four yellow Best Burger napkins off the top of the stack
next to the register and stuffed them into the sack before folding and curling down the top. The moves were routine, automatic,
normally requiring no thought — except that Sam could feel the
counter customer eyeing him. The woman he was serving paid and
thanked him and carried her burgers out the door.

The counter stool croaked, metal grating against metal, and Sam
thought the customer was turning to watch the woman leave. She
wasn't much to look at from behind, but she was a woman.

A green sedan came rolling up outside, tires popping gravel. The
young driver took off his sunglasses and carefully laid them upside
down on the dash before getting out. Sam saw that the customer
was still turned toward the front windows.

Sam knew then that the customer wasn't watching the woman.

This sudden feeling made him turn away. He went to scrape the grill top clean, watching the counter customer out of the corner of his eye. Sam tensed as he saw the man reach over near the register — only to pull a yellow Best Burger napkin down off the stack.

The customer clicked the top of a ballpoint pen and scratched down something on the napkin quick, no more than a word or two or three. Sam had to look away then or else be caught snooping.

When he casually turned back toward the counter, the pen was gone. The napkin, too, almost as though he had replaced it on the stack. The customer's hands rested still and empty on the chrome-edged Formica.

The bell jingled over the door, and the young man walked inside. He blinked a bit and glanced around — his first time here — then nodded to Sam and stepped to the takeout counter. "How's it going?" he said.

Up close the man was not as young as he had appeared. He wore a light black jacket over a blue shirt and khaki pants. Someone, probably a girlfriend, had taken care to snip his hair short and tight so that it stood up on his skull in pinched clumps like little black flames.

The customer seated at the counter didn't look up.

"What can I getcha?" said Sam, working his hands into the towel that hung from his belt.

The man went rummaging through his pockets, finding a torn slip of paper. "Uh — a Double-wide Best Burger, rare, extra mayo, hold the pickles, hold the cheese."

"Sandwich or meal?" said Sam. "Meal comes with fries and slaw."

"Meal, I guess."

"For a dollar more, you get two half-pounders. Today's special. Comes with a side order of Lipitor and a chair to nap in."

The man smiled and gave what amounted to a courtesy laugh. "No — just the one, thanks."

"One Double, still mooing, mayo, no picks, no cheese."

Sam turned to the grill and was reaching for the plump patties in the grill-side cooler when the counter customer said, "I'll have the same."

Sam stopped and looked back at him. The takeout man looked, too, for the first time, Sam expecting an electric moment of recognition on his face. But there was nothing. Just an amiable nod from the takeout man to the customer on the stool next to him, stranger to stranger. The counter customer nodded back and looked at the grill.

Sam took up two cool patties and played them down side by side, hitting the cooking surface with an immediate crackle of meat on heat. Sam didn't like what he was feeling. He had seen the customer's gun tucked under his arm when he'd first sat down. He'd seen his eyes, which looked prepossessed and somehow — almost — familiar. Sam decided to forget about him, or else try. He focused on the takeout guy.

"First time here?" Sam said, turning back.

"First time, yeah."

"Best burger in seventeen counties."

"So I've heard, so I've heard." The man drummed his fingers on the glass over the display counter showing mugs and T-shirts featuring the Best Burger logo: a friendly hamburger with arched eyebrows and stick-thin arms holding up a sign that read, EAT ME.

Sam said, "You work at the pen?"

The man stopped drumming. He looked down, checking himself, wondering where upon him it was written.

"Your car," said Sam. "The blue state tags. We get a lot of guards loading up before and after shifts."

The man nodded, relieved. "I'm not a guard, though," he said.

"I know. Your shoes."

The man looked down at them. "You're pretty good," he said.

Sam gave him a friendly shrug before checking on the burgers. The coolness had run out of them, and he flattened each with the spatula, spilling juice for them to simmer in. *Rare,* he remembered, plucking up two pairs of buns and going at them with mayo from the tub. "Another busy one up there tonight, huh?"

"You could say."

"About how many votes they run through them?" When Sam said "volts," it came out sounding like "votes."

"I don't know exactly. I think two thousand's the number."

He laid the buns out on the stainless ledge in front of the grill and said, "That'd be enough." Execution nights were generally slow. A feeling of unease settled over the entire region, like the threat of bad weather. "Which one is it tonight?"

"Uh — Mossman? Sonny Mossman."

"Mossman. Oh, yeah. I remember. The little girl, wasn't it?"

"A couple of girls, I think. And two grown women. But they got him for the girl."

Sam nodded. "They came round here afterward. That's how I remember. Asking questions." Sam flipped the burgers as he spoke, the patties hissing in protest as they were turned. "He'd been in here that night."

"Here?" said the man, with more surprise and unease than Sam expected. Almost with concern.

"The very same night." Sam laid up the spatula over the front lip of the grill and leaned back against the serving ledge. "How'd they get him? Fingerprints, wasn't it?"

"One fingerprint. In the trunk of his car. And, like, two strands of her hair."

"Didn't he confess, though?"

"At first. Then he recanted. They couldn't use it — I forget why."

"Reading him his rights, maybe."

"I don't know. They never found the murder weapon either. Dredged three lakes around here, trying to turn it up."

"Right, right. Didn't make any friends of the fishermen that week. What was it?"

The man squinted in confusion. "What was what?"

"The weapon."

The man shrugged. "Got me there."

They both kind of nodded quietly, ready to quit the topic for something more agreeable like the weather or sports.

"A claw hammer," said the customer at the counter.

The man turned to him. He stared, and Sam stared. "You said . . . ?" said the takeout man — not because he hadn't understood him, but because he never expected it. Because he knew more was coming.

"It was a claw hammer."

It was quiet then except for the sizzle. Sam put things together, first slowly, then all at once. The shoulder holster, the eyes.

"I remember you," Sam said. "You were heavier then." Words escaped before he had time to properly consider them. "You had pictures for us. Asked me where he sat . . ." His voice tailed off, the memory returning full-bloom.

"He sat right here," said the detective. "Right in this seat." He laid his palms flat against the countertop and looked around the diner. "This place was one of his compulsions. He said he could never pass by without stopping in. Best Burger was his favorite food."

He said this last part looking at the takeout man from the penitentiary, who appeared stricken. He hadn't moved.

"He stopped here that night. Parked right outside and sat down here and ordered himself a Double-wide. He ate his burger and drank a large Coke. The girl he'd snatched, her name was Kelly-Louise Traynor. Six years old. She was still out in his trunk. Still alive."

Ice shifted in his glass. Otherwise nothing moved.

Sam said, "You were the one who caught him?"

The detective squinted, having gone off thinking about something else.

"He had hidden his car somewheres," said Sam, more and more coming back to him now. "Tried to clean it. Finding it is what did him in."

"Fourth finger, right hand." The detective showed them, rubbing his with the pad of his thumb. "On a fire extinguisher Mossman kept in the trunk. Two blond hair strands in the carpet."

"Two thin strands," said Sam. "The difference between him being up there . . . or being out here."

"Being right here," said the detective, occupying the killer's seat in front of him.

Sam didn't like him having to say that. He couldn't see how this involved him.

"You're heading up to watch?" asked Sam. "You on your way up there now?"

"Me?" said the detective. He shook his head. "I'm on my way home." He looked past Sam to the grill. "Just stopped off here for a bite to eat."

Sam went silent then. After a moment he returned to the grill and the cooking meat. He pressed down with the spatula, bleeding off juice, before remembering he had done that already.

The burgers were ready. He lifted off the sizzling patties, one at a time, laying them onto the waiting buns. The clock on the wall said a little before six. Sam, who could normally juggle seven separate orders in his head, was having trouble focusing and had to look back at the takeout man. "That was — no cheese?"

The man went back into his jacket pocket for the slip of paper, found it, unfolded it, turned it right side up. He cleared his throat before speaking. "No cheese. No pickles."

Sam focused on the torn paper in the man's hand. "It's not for you?"

"No," answered the man. He tried to look casual.

Sam swallowed. He looked over near the detective. "And yours?"

"No cheese. No pickles. Exact same."

Sam turned back to the open-faced burgers. He covered up the patties with the mayonnaise-slathered buns. He had the feeling he was being made part of something he wanted no part of.

He prepped two meal orders of fries and slaw, one going into a plastic serving basket lined with paper, the other into a Best Burger To-Go sack. He brought the two burgers around, side by side, not knowing what to do. He set them down before the two customers.

Sam said, "Which one do you . . . ?"

The takeout man said nothing.

The detective told Sam, "You choose."

Sam hated him for saying that. He looked at the takeout man, who wouldn't meet his eye. Then he wrapped one burger and dropped it into the sack, laying the other down in the basket of fries. He set the basket meal in front of the detective. The takeout man paid cash and asked for a receipt.

"Don't forget napkins," said the detective.

Sam, rushing now, thumbed six or seven yellow Best Burger napkins off the top of the stack and stuffed them into the bag and rolled the top shut. He wanted the takeout man to leave now.

The takeout man did leave. The detective didn't turn to watch him go. He waited until the bell over the door stopped ringing and the engine started up and the tires rolled back, popping over the gravel. Then he took the sandwich into his hands. Sam saw it still steaming, saw the bottom of the bun already sagging with grease. He watched the detective bite in deep and felt a tang in the back of his own throat, almost sick-making. He saw grease and juice run down over the man's fingers, dripping into the basket, and then he had to look away.

Cooper drove the Ford sedan up the interstate back toward the penitentiary. He hadn't cared at all for that cop in the diner.

Trying to make him feel bad. Cooper's job sucked, no question. He worked at the pen because it was a night job and they reimbursed half his tuition. But as to job satisfaction, there was zero. Cooper wasn't out catching killers. He did what he was told. They sent him out to pick up a sandwich — and he was happy to do it. Happy to get away from there, even just for thirty minutes. Drudgery pervaded the pen like a factory choking on its own pollution. So what did he have to apologize for? That he wasn't rich? That he had to work to make a better life for himself?

A claw hammer.

He was angry. He'd had to put the sack into the trunk, which was the last thing he'd wanted to do after listening to that cop — open a car trunk — but it was his boss's order. Cooper would be passing protesters on the way back inside, and they weren't to see the food or anything else that might set them off.

He almost regretted stealing those few fries out of the bag — at the same time wishing he had some more. The Coke was handy, stuck into the cup holder at his side, so he righted the steering wheel with his knees and popped the clear plastic top off the cup and took a few sweet sips. He was returning it and trying to squeeze the cover back on when he thought he heard a thumping inside the trunk. It stopped his heart for a second. Like that feeling that someone is hiding behind you in the car.

For a moment he imagined he was Mossman, driving into the woods with someone bound and gagged in his trunk, knowing what he was going to do to them . . .

The penitentiary exit surprised him, and he looked down and saw that he was doing eighty-one. The wheels squealed as he took it too fast.

Early protesters were indeed assembling with their signs and bullhorns and candles — ready to make a night of it. How good it must feel to stand for something, he thought. To commit oneself to a lost cause. To gather with other like-minded souls and lock arms and sing songs under the stars. Wallowing in futility. Championing it, actually. How wonderful it must be to fight only losing battles. How safe and how comfortable. To posit yourself squarely on the side of peace and good. How brave the sand on an eroding beach.

They stared through his windshield as he slowed near the front gates. Cooper was nobody to them, but the sedan was a prison vehicle, and so one of them — a woman wearing a black robe, her hair drawn back fiercely into a long white-gray whip — pounded once on the roof over his head, so startling Cooper that his foot hit the gas pedal, jerking the vehicle forward, almost running over three people.

They scattered out of his way pretty fast after that. He thought about stopping and walking back to confront them. Not with cant, but with food. Passing around the bag of French fries, one to each. And then asking them, Is this really whose last supper you want to be at?

He parked inside the safety perimeter and stood before the trunk with keys in hand before opening it and finding the food sack tipped over onto its side. Grease soaked the side of the bag, leaving a dark oily stain on the carpet lining the trunk, and Cooper erupted suddenly, unleashing a string of bitter curses into the prison night, even though it wasn't his fault and it wasn't even his car.

Sonny Mossman looked up from where he sat on the slab bed of his special holding cell. They had just shaved his head and one leg. A Restraint Team guard entered in full kit — riot helmet, spit shield, lineman's gloves, breastplate, jump boots — with two others backing him, their steel batons extended. The Restraint Team ran the Death Tank because some cons lose it at the end. They go screaming like a virgin to the flaming stake. But not Sonny.

The lead guard brought him a familiar yellow paper sack all grease-soaked on the bottom and one side. He set it on the shelf with the Coke and then stood there a moment looking at Sonny through his goggles. They think it's their job to eye-rape you. They backed out and closed the tank door, and Sonny stood and went to the bag.

His mouth was already filling up with saliva. He'd been looking forward to this for a long time now. The only thing he *had* to look forward to. If they really wanted to hurt him, they would have brought this in and showed it to him, pushed it into his face, then taken it away. Left his stomach jumping like a stuck puppy.

Sonny opened the sack and quickly unwrapped the big, soggy burger. He took it in his thick fingers and bit in quick — and the taste exploded in his mouth. It was perfect, made just the way he

liked it. He chewed through half of it before realizing that this was
it, there wasn't any more, and maybe he should slow down.

He lifted out the fries and napkins and set aside the coleslaw. He
smiled at the cartoon burger with the EAT ME sign on the napkin.
It put him right back inside Best Burger: the front counter with the
busted stools and the meat cooked in front of you by the grill man
with fast, mechanical hands.

Sonny opened a napkin to tuck into his collar, the way his grandmother taught him. He saw the wet wrinkle first and realized that
this was a used napkin. Somebody had already swiped their dirty
mouth on it. Then, unfolding the napkin further, he saw the writing.

He recognized the penmanship right off. He knew it from the
court papers. Sonny read the girl's name, and then his eyes lost
focus.

Everything went bland as he wondered how that goddamn cop
got to his food. The rumbling in his stomach continued, but the
wanting was like a distant thunder now. He had cotton all wadded
up in his mouth. His eyes were wide and blank as he faced the
green-painted wall, on the other side of which was the last room he
would ever see.

The detective drove home, his gut full, the rare meat roiling. A
wave of nausea raised a sheen of sweat over his skin like condensa-
tion forming on glass. He kept swallowing to put out the fire. He
would keep the burger down. He had to.

Prostate cancer had turned him into a vegetarian. Nuts and
grains and kale and okra. Three-plus years without red meat, until
today. Three-plus years cancer-free.

The meal burned like a cancer in his belly. It bloated him, his
stomach acids hitting it with everything they'd got. Turmoil and
torment: his gut the final circle of hell.

Tomorrow he would deliver it where it belonged and be done.

He went into a sort of trance as he drove. Something like a fever
dream — only it was real. A memory. One he returned to willingly
now.

He was inside the girl's bedroom again. The mother had left it
untouched, as grieving mothers do. He asked for a minute alone.
She went out without questioning it, and he gently closed the door.

He pulled on his gloves and looked around. Everything was in pink and yellow — a dead girl's room decorated in fringe and frill. He scrutinized every windowpane. He breathed on the mirror glass, raising prints, none of them pristine. He had to be very careful now. He had just found Mossman's abandoned car in the woods. Nobody else knew yet. He stood underneath the still ceiling fan, full to bursting with this knowledge, eyeing the soft toys, the dolls, the figurines. He needed a surface that was flat and hard and smooth. He found a china tea set on the top shelf of her bookcase and pulled it down. Tiny little finger cups done in a fine, glassy finish. Using a prepared strip of tape, he lifted one perfect print. He held it to the sunlight. Graceful hairpin whorls, unbroken by crease of injury or wrinkle of age. It would transfer faintly yet true. He then selected a hair bow from a drawer full of ribbons and clips and used tweezers to unwind from it two strands of fair hair. He slipped them into a manila coin envelope, which he then slipped inside his jacket pocket. He did this lovingly. He made the case. He did his job.

Sam, the grill man, lay on his side on the back-room cot, listening to Conway Twitty on the clock radio. His shift had ended at ten, but the diner stayed open all night, the grill never going cold. Sam was back on the clock at six A.M., and it was easier just to crash there than drive all the way home and back.

He felt weird about the detective. That was what had him still awake near midnight — that and his empty stomach, for which the smell of the burgers cooking suggested no cure. He couldn't get it out of his mind. Did the detective blame Sam for having served somebody he didn't know was a killer? Sam didn't feel real good about having fed a guy who had a little girl locked up in the trunk of his car — but then, who knew what the detective had locked up in his? Who knows what anybody has locked away?

Okay — tonight he knew. He had figured out what that takeout burger was, who it was for. He supposed he could've spit on it. Would that have made the detective like him better? He could've not finished cooking it. Thrown it into the trash — made a great big show.

But he did cook it. He wrapped it up and sold it to the man from the prison. He put the money in his cash register.

And he served the detective his. Grilled it for him and served it up like his own enemy's heart.

A killer would die tonight with one of Sam's burgers in his belly. Be buried with it in the morning. Packed up together with his earthly remains in a to-go pine box.

Sam rolled onto his back. He pictured the detective finishing his burger, wiping the juice off his empty hands. Sitting still awhile at the counter, disappearing into himself. Then standing, laying money next to the empty Coke, heading home. The bell jingling on his way out the door.

The radio cut out first, before anything else. Going to static — a disruption over the airwaves.

Then the lights flickered. The rattling air-conditioner unit outside the back door clicked off, shutting down.

Lights dimmed, surging off and on for ten seconds . . . fifteen seconds . . . twenty seconds. A deep draw on the grid. Sam imagined an aerial view, lights dimming all across the county in one long, complicit blink.

They flickered once more, then came back on. The air conditioner kick-started again, whirring back to life, and the static cleared and the radio music resumed playing, the same song, the glowing red digits of the clock now blinking 12:00 like a sign urgently advertising midnight.

Two thousand volts.

Sam rolled over and hoped his appetite would return in the morning.

CLARK HOWARD

Manila Burning

FROM *Ellery Queen's Mystery Magazine*

DANIEL CARGO SAT on the back of a flatbed truck as it rumbled and rattled along a grossly rutted dirt road on its way from the outback of the Palayan Penal Farm to the farm's main administration building. The truck, which was a decade or more old, was painted bright yellow. Across its two side-cabin doors was lettered, in red, PHILIPPINE NATIONAL PRISONS. There were four other men on the flatbed with Daniel Cargo, all of them dressed in loose prison garb identical in yellow color to the truck.

When the vehicle reached the administration building, it parked at a rear dock and a corrections officer motioned the men off. The guard was unarmed and the five men were not cuffed or shackled. There was no need for security, since the prisoners were not escape risks; they were being released from prison that day.

Once inside the building, the men sat in a line on a wooden bench outside an office on the door of which was painted DIS-CHARGES. One by one, the men were summoned into the office. When it was Daniel Cargo's turn, he stood in front of a desk at which sat a Filipino prison department official dressed in a spotless white uniform, shiny black hair slicked back, thin mustache perfectly trimmed, with a fragrance of cologne emanating from him. When he spoke, his words were practiced and precise.

"Inmate Daniel James Cargo, number 1172307, having successfully completed your one-year sentence for illegally trading in fossil stone without a license, you are hereby discharged from the Philippine National Prison System. Since you are a foreigner, I am returning herewith your passport, which was issued by the government of the United States of America. Sign this form to acknowledge receipt of the passport."

Cargo leaned over the desk and signed the form.

"In addition," the official continued, "you are being given the legally prescribed prisoner discharge money in the sum of two thousand three hundred Filipino pesos. Sign here to acknowledge receipt of this money."

Hardly worth signing for, Cargo thought as he signed a second form. Twenty-three hundred Filipino pesos was less than fifty U.S. dollars.

"It is also my duty," the officer concluded, "to advise you that as a convicted felon without Philippine citizenship, you are no longer welcome in this country. Therefore, your passport has been stamped with a seven-day visa, requiring you to leave within that period. That visa must be validated at an airport or seaport point of exit within that period or a warrant will be issued for your arrest, and you will be required to serve an additional one year in custody." The official nodded curtly. "Dismissed."

Money and passport in hand, Cargo joined the other four men as they were led to a clothing-issue room, where they exchanged their yellow prison garb for identical white shirts and trousers. They were allowed to keep their flip-flop sandals, which were of hard black rubber made from recycled truck tires. Afterward, they were herded into a yellow prison van to be driven into Manila.

It was a two-hour drive south to Manila, and because the city was situated at sea level and the prison camp had been about one thousand feet higher, Cargo could look down and see their destination when they were still half an hour away. From the road above, Manila looked like a pristine crescent of white block buildings surrounded by greenery on the eastern edge of Manila Bay, connected to a series of bridges leading across the Pasig River, which flowed around it, all of it backdropped by the South China Sea and its constant water traffic. On the page of a four-color travel brochure, it could be described as scenic, picturesque, resplendent. But that was only from the road above.

As the prison van descended and left the deceptions of altitude behind, the real Manila began to emerge. The first sign that the city was imminent was the landmark familiar to all of them: an infa-

mous disgrace known as Smoky Mountain. A huge tower of garbage infested with rats and maggots, the enormous dump derived
its name from a gray-green methane mist that hovered over it. As
the van neared the dump, what might have been mistaken for animals swarming all over it became, on closer observation, young
children, adolescents, old people, all of them scavenging over the
enormous mass of garbage steaming and stinking in the moist tropical heat.

"Roll up the windows," the driver of the van ordered. "I don't
want that stench in here when I drive back."

The five passengers obeyed at once; they did not want to smell
Smoky Mountain either. But they could not make themselves look
away; it was like witnessing a car accident or a building on fire or a
homeless person dying in the gutter. The scene was ugly but its observation somehow imperative, mesmerizing.

When the van reached the Manila City Jail parking lot, the driver
cut the engine and rose from behind the wheel. "Okay, you're free
to go," he said.

Incongruously, the Manila City Jail was not situated in some remote, outlying area; it was squarely in the midst of central Manila,
surrounded by shopping malls, lines of small stores, bus stops, commercial buildings, and all other manner of bustling city life. The
five released men exited the van directly into society and went their
separate ways.

As Daniel Cargo walked off the parking lot, he was immediately
approached by a smiling street girl in hot pants and a skimpy top.
"Hey, goo'-lookin', how long you no have girl, huh? Me treat you
super fine."

"No money," Cargo said, without stopping.

"Bullshit!" she snapped, her smile fading to a glower. "I know you
get two thousand pesos discharge money! You think I stupid? You
lie, son of bitch!"

Someone else fell in beside him, prettier than the first. "Hey, guy,
you like it jail kind? I give you jail kind pretty good." One glance
and Cargo knew it was a ladyboy: a male made up to look like a
street girl.

As Cargo stepped around him, a boy who looked like a boy
joined him. "You want some *shabu*, man? Good stuff. Cheap." Cargo
shook his head. *Shabu* was Filipino methamphetamine. What Cargo

could have used at the moment was a bottle of gin and a bucket of ice.

To get away from the jailhouse street hustlers, Cargo cut his way against traffic across the busy street, and on the other side melded into the pedestrian flow. As he walked, Cargo thought about Carli. Carlotta Gomez, a nurse at St. Luke's Hospital in nearby Quezon City. Cargo had met her while being treated in the hospital's emergency room for a broken thumb. He told the hospital admissions clerk that the injury occurred while helping a friend move a heavy bookcase. Actually it had happened when he and another man were loading slabs of fossil stone onto the back of a pickup. The two men had bought the fossil stone on the black market to sell at a profit to a freighter captain on the docks, who would then transport it to Hawaii to be used as tabletops for very expensive furniture. The activity was illegal, since fossil stone could only be found on the Philippine island of Mindanao, and its mining, processing, and distribution were strictly controlled by the Philippine government.

When Daniel Cargo and Carlotta Gomez met in the hospital emergency room, there was an immediate attraction between them. Carlotta was one of those subtly sultry young Filipina women with flawless caramel skin, naturally florid lips that never required cosmetic enhancement, and eyes dark as a raven's. Cargo, who was nothing if not direct, had asked what time her shift ended. And Carlotta, just as directly, had replied, midnight. When they met outside the hospital that night, they kissed as if it was the most natural thing in the world to do, as if they had known each other and been kissing for a lifetime.

Cargo and Carlotta lived together for eighteen months. Then one night the Philippine National Police ambushed a pickup truck loaded with fossil stone just outside Rutulo. The driver, Danny Cargo, was caught. The other man escaped in the darkness. A month later, Danny Cargo was sentenced to prison for a year.

Down a little alleyway off Roxas Boulevard, Cargo found a second-hand clothing store and went in to buy a pair of worn khakis and a cheap black pullover shirt. Those and a pair of decent cloth deck shoes cost him 480 of the 2,300 pesos he had, but it was worth it to Danny Cargo. He did not want to go see Carlotta wearing prison-issue release clothes, which he left for the merchant to sell to some-one else.

Back on the boulevard, Cargo boarded the first bus with a desti-nation sign for Quezon City. When he tried to pay his fare, the bus driver stopped him for more money. The fare had increased. The driver looked at him as if he might be trying to cheat the bus com-pany.

In Quezon City an hour later, Cargo got off at Rodriguez Avenue and walked several blocks to St. Luke's Hospital. At the informa-tion desk, he inquired whether Carlotta Gomez was on the day shift. A young volunteer intern checked her computer, frowned, and said, "She no longer works here, sir."

Cargo went to the personnel office. A clerk there said, "Miss Gomez left our employ six months ago. I believe she took a job at Makati Medical Center up in Manila."

Back on another bus, now knowing what fare to pay, Cargo re-turned to Manila. Not being a Philippine citizen, while in prison he had no civil rights, no visiting privileges, and could not send or re-ceive mail. Still, it had not once occurred to him that he might lose track of Carlotta. For some reason — wishful thinking, perhaps — he had simply assumed that when he was released, Carlotta would be right where he had left her. Now that he had learned to the con-trary, he began to worry about not being able to find her.

The bus driver gave him directions to Armosola Street, where he found the Makati Medical Center. There he received similar news.

"Carlotta Gomez left our employ three months ago. She was only with us a short time. Someone said that she went to work for a free health clinic somewhere."

As he was being told this, another clerk came up. "Are you a friend of Carli's?"

"Yes. I used to work with her down at St. Luke's in Quezon City," Cargo lied easily. "I just got back from an overseas job in Borneo and wanted to say hello."

The clerk who had asked the question studied Cargo for a thoughtful moment, then said, "I think you'll find her at the Mary Magdalene Orphanage Clinic over in the Tondo district. It's near Smoky Mountain."

"Thanks. Which bus line goes there, do you know?"

"None. The government stopped bus service to Tondo. Too

much trouble over there: robbery, drugs, prostitutes, everything bad. You'll have to use a jeepney to get there."

Thanking her again, Cargo went outside to look for a jeepney. Cheap, unauthorized public transportation, the jeepney was a contraption built from used Isuzu engines, reconditioned Toyota transmissions, and retreaded tires attached to a metal-pipe frame with a stretched metal-plate floor that had two facing wooden benches bolted to it. Passengers got on and off at will, usually for a fare of three pesos, about seven cents in U.S. money.

Cargo flagged down five jeepneys before agreeing to pay ten pesos to a pockmarked teenage driver willing to make a run to Tondo. The trip, through increasing late afternoon traffic, took more than an hour, with a dozen riders getting on and off along the way. The closer the jeepney got to the Tondo district, the more poverty Cargo saw. Shantytowns began to crop up here and there, until eventually there was nothing else: only thrown-together shacks or cardboard hovels, people living under bridges, along abandoned railroad embankments, in makeshift family camps among burned-out buildings. The sewage system was a ditch that was a median down the center of the street.

And in the middle of it all Smoky Mountain, its greenish gray haze rising up and wafting out to hover over the destitution like lingering death.

Cargo began to feel slightly nauseated. Part of it was because of the stench starting to reach the jeepney from Smoky Mountain, part because since early that morning he had been riding, riding, riding, and he had eaten nothing except the rice, black beans, and moldy bread fed to the prisoners in the penal camp at daybreak, before they went into the bean fields to work. Several times he thought about getting something to eat at one of the dozens of kiosks along the way, whenever the jeepney was stuck in traffic, but he knew the driver would leave him if he did not get back on in time, and he did not want to try looking for another one. If Carlotta was working a day shift, he might miss her. And he wanted desperately to see her.

The Mary Magdalene Orphanage was in a very old white brick building in a cul-de-sac down a side street. Only three stories tall, it nevertheless seemed to soar over the landlocked impoverishment that surrounded it. A single-story wing jutted out from one side of the building like a skillet handle, ending in double doors over which a large red cross was painted. Inside that wing, Cargo found a medical receiving room filled to capacity with young mothers and children waiting to be seen by a doctor or nurse. All of the children, he noted dismally, had cleft palates or harelips.

At a sign-in desk, Cargo said to a very young woman wearing a white summer nun's habit, "Excuse me, sister, is Carlotta Gomez on shift, do you know?"

"Gee, no, you just missed her." She smiled up at him. "But you can probably catch her down the street at Rose's. It's a bar where a lot of staff hang out."

Slightly taken aback by her candor, he said, "Ah, okay, sister, thank you."

The young woman blushed slightly. "I'm not really a sister yet. Just a novitiate."

"Oh." Cargo hesitated, not knowing what else to say. Finally he managed, "Well, good luck. And thanks anyway." Quickly he left.

He found Rose's Bar and Grill in a surprisingly well preserved storefront building between an open vegetable market and a bicycle repair shop. Inside, the bar was semicooled by four ceiling fans that circulated over half a dozen small tables on one side, a bar and bar stools on the other, and an unwalled, open kitchen in the rear. Cargo saw Carlotta at once, sitting at the bar with another woman. He went over to them. Carlotta was raising her glass to drink when he said, "Hello, Carli."

Unnerved at seeing him, she spilled a little of the drink on her hand. "Danny — my God —"

"Sorry, I didn't mean to startle you —"

"No, no, it's all right," she said, taking a paper napkin handed to her by the woman sitting with her. "It's just such a surprise — my God — when did you, ah —"

"This morning." He smiled at her. "You're a hard lady to find these days."

Carlotta laughed, a little nervously. "I have moved around a bit in the last year. Oh, Danny, this is my friend Angie O'Brien. She runs the clinic pharmacy. Angie, Danny Cargo. I've told you about him."

Cargo shook hands with a slim, red-haired Anglo woman in khaki slacks and blouse that looked almost military next to Carli's light blue scrubs. After they exchanged greetings, Angie immediately finished her drink and slid off the barstool.

"If it's been a year, you two must have a lot of catching up to do, so I'll run along —"

"Oh, Angie, no, you don't have to leave —"

"I've got some things to do anyway. I'll call you later. Nice to meet you, Danny."

Cargo took Angie's seat at the bar. He and Carlotta awkwardly got through a long moment of silence.

"You look good, Carli," he finally said.

"You don't," Carli replied. "You look — I don't know, Danny — *tired*. Almost gaunt."

He shrugged. "A year in the bean fields up in Palayan will do that." He took a sip of her drink. Carli held up two fingers for the bartender to bring two fresh ones. "I missed you, Carli," he said, his voice catching a little. "I missed you a lot."

Reaching out, she put a hand on his. "I tried to visit you, to write you, but —"

"I know. I was a foreign prisoner: no privileges." He covered her hand with his. "I thought about you every day, every night —"

"Danny, before you say anything else, I have to tell you something." She glanced down. "I'm with someone else now."

"Oh." He forced a spiritless smile. Swallowing, he cleared his throat. "Sorry, I, ah . . . wasn't prepared for that."

Their drinks were served and their hands parted.

"I didn't mean to hurt you, Danny."

"No, no, it's okay," he was quick to assure her. Now he managed a more sincere smile. "I don't know why I'm even surprised. Greatlooking gal like you can't be expected to stay unattached too long. You, uh — you happy?"

"Very."

Cargo raised his glass. "I'm glad for you, Carli. Cheers."

They toasted.

"Do you have any plans?" she asked.

"Most of my plans," he told her, laughing softly, "involved you. I've got a week to get out of the Philippines or go back to jail for another year. I was hoping to hide out with you until I could get something going and maybe bribe somebody to get the exit visa lifted. I guess my best bet now is to find a way to get out. Trouble is, I've only got about fifty bucks U.S." Embarrassed, he looked away before asking, "How would you feel about lending an ex-boyfriend some money?"

"I'd do it in a heartbeat, Danny — if I had any to lend."

"But you're still working as a nurse, aren't you? Making good money?"

She shook her head. "The place I work now is a charity clinic, Danny. I get room, board, uniforms, and forty-five U.S. dollars a week. I haven't got a cent in the bank."

Cargo shook his head in dismay. "I don't understand, Carli. How'd you end up in a job like that?"

"I didn't exactly 'end up' here," she replied, her tone stiffening a little. "I made a conscious decision to come to Mary Magdalene." Carli took a sip of her drink. "Let me tell you a story. When I was at Makati Medical Center, a little girl, probably not even a week old, was left in a dumpster behind the hospital kitchen. A cook found her. She had a cleft palate, so severe that it was almost impossible to feed her; we had to use an eyedropper, and it took two hours. The clinic had no facilities to keep her, so they called the offices of several social services. Every place they called referred them to someplace else. No one wanted to accept the responsibility of taking care of a baby girl with a grotesquely deformed face. Finally the clinic's Catholic chaplain called the mother superior of Mary Magdalene Orphanage. She told him to send the child to her. I was the nurse selected to take the baby there. The center provided an ambulance. What I saw when I got there . . ."

Carli's voice broke. Pausing, she took another swallow of her drink. Exhaling deeply, she then continued.

"What I saw when I got there was an orphanage full of children of all ages, from toddlers to teenagers, all with harelips and cleft palates of one sort or another. Some had already undergone surgery and were in the healing stage; others were waiting their turn. There is a cadre of corrective surgeons all over the Pacific Rim who volunteer their services and come to Manila to operate on children like these. It's a fairly simple procedure, actually; most operations take only thirty or forty minutes.

"While I was there delivering the baby, the mother superior asked if I knew of any nurses who might, or if I myself might, consider volunteering a few hours a week in the orphanage's clinic. I told her I would ask around. That night I was unable to sleep at all. I kept seeing images of children with horribly deformed mouths, lips, and noses. I was haunted by those images. The next day I left my well-paying job at the clinic and went to work full-time at Mary Magdalene. I've been here ever since. And I intend to stay here."

Carli fell silent, and neither she nor Cargo spoke for what seemed like a long time. Each of them sipped from their glasses. They exchanged constrained glances.

"I suppose you think I'm a fool," Carli said at last. "Giving up a well-paying job and a far more comfortable life —"

"I don't think that at all," Cargo interrupted. Now it was he who touched her hand. "As a matter of fact, I'm proud of you, Carli."

"Really, Danny?" Her dark eyes glistened.

"Really."

"Even though it means I can't help you with any money?"

"Hell, don't worry about that, honey," he said dismissively. "You know me. I'll come up with something." Patting her hand, he withdrew his own, already beginning to worry about what his next step would be.

"Do you have a place to stay tonight?" she asked.

"Not yet." Cargo shook his head.

"Well, there's a cheap little hotel just outside the cul-de-sac called the Rittz, with a double *t*. It's owned by a German national named Manfred Haas; everybody calls him Freddy. It's a dump — hardly anyone ever stays there. Rumors are that it's just a front for something — stolen goods, pearl smuggling, who knows what. Anyway, when the beds in our clinic are full, he lets the mother superior put patients in his hotel rooms on a temporary basis — always with a couple of nuns to stay overnight as chaperones."

"Isn't that kind of odd?" Cargo asked. "An arrangement like that between a mother superior and the type of guy you say this Haas is?"

"Perhaps it is kind of odd," Carli acknowledged, her tone once again tightening, "but we're all dedicated to the orphanage and the clinic and what we're doing for these unfortunate children, so sometimes we make our own rules."

"Hey, Carli, I understand," Cargo said quickly. "I wasn't being critical — not with my background."

"Okay," she said, more softly. "What I was getting at is that I can

probably persuade Freddy to let you bunk at his place for a couple
of nights, if you want me to."

"Sure, great. Listen, thanks." He leaned over and kissed her
lightly on the cheek. He was already wondering if this Haas
could put him onto something so that he could manage to stay in
Manila.

And maybe get Carli back again.

A little while later, Carli walked him out of Rose's Bar and around a
corner to the Rittz Hotel, a shabby, ramshackle, two-story wooden
building in front of which two teenage meth addicts were leaning
shoulder to shoulder staring into space. Inside, at a scarred roll-top
desk, wearing shorts and a sweaty undershirt, was a squat, muscular,
completely bald man whom Carlotta introduced as Freddy Haas.
There was a suspicious cheerfulness about him, and it irritated
Cargo that he hugged Carli with such familiarity.

"Sure, sure, of course, Carli, anything for you," he agreed at once
when Carli asked about a room for Cargo, and he shook Cargo's
hand with a powerful grip. "Happy to help your friend out, my
pleasure."

As Carli thanked him and took her leave, Cargo noticed that the
bulldog German's eyes swept over her lush young body until she
was all the way out the door.

"So," he then asked Cargo, "how close were you to Carli?"

"Just good friends," Cargo lied.

"Ever get her in bed?"

Cargo kept his growing irritation in check and shook his head.
"Like I said, just friends."

"I've been trying to get her in bed ever since she came to work at
the clinic," Haas said candidly, "but no luck. Yet, anyway."

"I got the impression she was involved with someone," Cargo
said, trying to sound casual.

"What the hell difference does that make?" Haas growled. "I
don't want to marry her, I just want to screw her." Opening a
drawer in the roll-top, he took out a key. "Come on, I'll show you
your room."

A while later, ravenous by then, Cargo left the hotel and walked
around until he found a reasonably clean café and had a double
order of *adabo* and *sinigang*, which he washed down with four bot-

tles of San Miguel, the Filipino national beer. The *adabo,* which was shredded pork stewed in soy sauce and peppercorns, and the *sinigang,* soup made from guava, tamarind, and tomatoes, then poured over steamed rice, tasted like a feast to Cargo, who in the penal camp had subsisted for a year on beans and plain steamed rice, with an occasional hunk of undercooked chicken or pork.

Walking back to the Rittz, he began to feel the results of the earlier drink with Carli, now boosted by the four bottles of beer. Several young Filipino street hoodlums took note of his slightly faltering gait with more than passing interest, but he managed to make it back to the hotel unmolested.

Freddy Haas was nowhere to be seen when Cargo got there, which was a relief. He instinctively disliked the German and wanted to have as little to do with him as possible, so he hurried directly upstairs.

Once in the room, Cargo undressed and lay down on the lumpy cot mattress in his underwear. There was a single light bulb dangling from the ceiling, but he did not bother to turn it on. One small window, with no shade or shutters, he left open in case a rogue breeze happened to penetrate the steamy night heat. But nothing came in except the mixed noises of the slum around him: a baby crying, a woman screaming angrily at someone, laughter now and again about God knew what, music from ghetto blasters, people's names being called out, children screeching in the streets — all of it blended into a raw symphony of people trying to get through the night and probably dreading the day to come.

Closing his eyes, Danny Cargo thought about all the nights he had gone to sleep on his straw mat at the penal farm. That had been the only pleasant part of the endless days, resting in the coolness of that higher altitude, listening to the soothing sounds of night herons.

Odd, he thought as he began to drift off into an alcoholic buzz of sleep, that he should miss anything at all about the penal farm . . .

Early the next morning, Cargo was awakened by someone gently shaking his shoulder. Opening his eyes, he saw that Carli, in a fresh nurse's uniform, was sitting on the side of his bed holding a container of steaming coffee for him.

"My God, Danny, you're covered with mosquito bites!" she scolded him. "Why didn't you close the window?"

"I guess I didn't think to," he said sleepily. "We didn't have mosquitoes up at Palayan. Too high." He accepted the coffee. "I didn't expect room service in this trap," he quipped. Carli was not amused; her pretty face was fixed in a serious expression.

"Listen, I want you to get up and come with me. I think I may have found a way for you to get enough money to get out of the country before your visa expires."

"How?" he asked, coming wide awake with interest.

"Get out of bed, wash up, and come with me. Then you'll find out."

At a grimy, brown-stained sink in one corner of the room, Cargo washed as best he could without the benefit of soap, slicked his hair back wet, and dried off with his undershirt, which he left on the bed. Getting into his shirt and trousers, he was conscious of Carli scrutinizing his haggard body and, embarrassed, turned away as he dressed.

Managing to burn his mouth with several sips of the coffee she had brought him, he also began to perspire with the first muggy heat of the day, which made his mosquito bites begin to itch.

"Don't scratch those!" Carli snapped. "When's the last time you had a malaria shot?"

"Hell, Carli, I don't know!" he snapped back, beginning to get irritated now. "Two, three years, I guess."

"We'll stop at the clinic on our way," she decided.

"On our way where?"

"You'll see. Come on, hurry."

It was a short walk to the clinic, but on the way they saw scores of people — old, young, feeble, addicted, desperate — hurrying along the street toward Smoky Mountain to be there when the overnight garbage trucks arrived to dump new loads onto the massive pile, which had already begun to emit its methane haze as the tropical sun heated it up. Neither Carli nor Danny Cargo said anything about it. There was nothing *to* say.

At the clinic, Carli gave him a malaria shot and handed him two pills.

"Chloroquine and Fansidar," she said. "Drink this full glass of water with them."

"Yes, nurse."

She also gave him a small bottle of oily liquid. "Carry this with you. It's tea-tree oil for the itching. And *don't* scratch those bites."

"Yes, nurse," he repeated.

From the clinic, Carli led him to Rose's Bar. "We're meeting Angie, my friend that you met yesterday."

"The pharmacist."

"Yes."

At Rose's they went directly through the bar, which even that early had several customers, and past the open kitchen to a small office in the rear. Angie O'Brien was there, sitting at a rusting metal desk. Exchanging greetings, she explained to Cargo, "Rose, the owner, is letting us borrow her office." When Carli and Cargo were seated in front of her, she said to him, "Obviously you're wondering what this is all about."

"Obviously," Cargo agreed.

"As Carli told you yesterday, I run the pharmacy at the orphanage clinic. And as I'm sure you are able to guess by now, the clinic, as well as the orphanage, is being run on severely limited resources. That's why people work there for practically nothing. And that's why the mother superior has arrangements with people like Freddy Haas, as Carli also told you, to obtain extra bed space. She has arrangements with others also, to obtain everything from food to cleaning supplies to clothes for the children. A regular group of very proficient thieves sell to us every day at extremely reasonable prices. We wouldn't be able to exist without them."

"But what about the church?" Cargo asked. "It's a Catholic orphanage, isn't it? Don't you receive funds from the church?"

"A limited amount," said Angie. "The problem is that we have expanded far beyond our original charter, because of an ever-increasing number of patients. You see, Danny, the Philippines, even though one of the smallest countries in the world, has now risen to fifth in the world in the number of cleft-palate births. And that is due to one simple reason: the lack of folic acid. Do you know what that is?"

Cargo shook his head. "No."

"It's a B vitamin, usually derived from a healthy diet of fresh fruits, vegetables, and enriched cereal and grain products. Even a quick look around the Tondo district will tell you that healthy diets of such foods are the exception, not the rule." Angie leaned forward and clasped her hands together on an unrusted space on the desktop. "Folic acid, Danny, significantly reduces the incidence of cleft-palate deformity in unborn children. What we desperately need in our medical operation here is a huge supply of folic acid supplement pills that we can distribute to every woman who becomes pregnant. But we haven't the funds to purchase those supplements in such quantity." She fixed Danny Cargo in an unblinking stare. "That's why we decided to meet with you. We want your help."

Cargo spread his hands in a helpless gesture. "I don't understand. How can I possibly be of any help?"

Angie held him in her stare. "By hijacking a truck full of pharmaceutical supplies."

"By *what?*" Cargo's mouth dropped open. "You want me to *hijack* a truck for you?"

"Yes. We have an informant on the docks who has told us when the next major shipment of pharmaceutical drugs arrives for the wholesale distributor in Manila. That shipment will be picked up by one of the distributor's trucks and taken to a warehouse where orders for various drugs are filled for pharmacies all over the city. We want the truck commandeered before it reaches the warehouse."

Cargo looked from Angie to Carli and back again, several times. "I don't believe this," he said incredulously. "You're talking about committing a serious crime, a major felony —"

Carli reached over and put a hand on his arm. "No, Danny, we're talking about preventing dozens, hundreds, perhaps even *thousands* of babies from being born with awful facial deformities."

"Okay, I understand that. I understand your purpose. But hijacking a truck loaded with drugs isn't like buying food and clothes from petty thieves. Hell, I wouldn't even begin to know how to go about it."

"The plan is already in place," Angie assured him. Rising, she came around the desk and knelt in front of him. "We have someone who has worked everything out. We know the exact place where the truck can be taken; we even know who the driver will be. We just need one more person to put the plan into effect." Angie touched his knees as if she were praying. "We need you, Danny. The unborn children need you."

For the first time, Cargo closely studied Angie O'Brien. Her eyes were tawny, her red hair cut short in a helter-skelter way, as if she had done it herself with dull scissors. Her lips, compared to the lushness of Carli's, had to be called thin, and curved down slightly at their corners. Overall, there was a certain something about her — a bearing, a presence, a quality — that, with the nearness of her, seemed to take Danny into its grip and hold him.

"Please, Danny," she pleaded, "just talk to the other person and have everything explained to you. You'll see how simple the whole plan is."

Cargo could not force his eyes away from her. He felt spellbound.

"All right," he said.

Angie rose and opened the office door. "Come in," she said.

Cargo looked around as someone entered. It was Manfred Haas.

Angie sat back down, and Haas hung a leg over the corner of the desk nearest to Cargo.

"So," he said, "you know what we are planning. Let me advise you that if you decide not to participate and you repeat anything you hear in this room, perhaps to get that visa of yours lifted, it will be most unhealthy for you." Haas raised one side of a tropical-flowered shirt he wore outside his trousers to show Cargo an automatic pistol stuck in his belt. "Most unhealthy," he repeated. "Do you take my meaning?"

"Yes."

"Good!" Haas smiled an artificially cheerful smile. "Now, here is the plan. I have already reconnoitered everything. The drug shipment arrives the day after tomorrow on the freighter *Vancouver* from Canada. The drugs will be offloaded onto Pier Nineteen, where longshoremen will then pack them into a large transport truck. The driver will be a Chinese named Heng, who is a longtime employee of DuPree Wholesale Drugs. He is grossly fat and lazy and has been making this run for so long he could probably do it with his eyes closed.

"Now then, the DuPree warehouse is north of the city in the Malolos district. From the docks, Heng drives directly to Independence Boulevard and travels north to Kasibu Street, where he makes a right turn toward an on-ramp of Highway One, which is four blocks away. Between Independence Boulevard and the on-ramp is Matalon Street, which has a stop sign. When Heng stops at the intersection of Kasibu and Matalon, we take him. This is a quiet residential area, where it is highly unlikely that we will be observed. I will approach on the passenger side with this" — Haas patted the pistol in his belt — "and order him to move over toward me. You get in on the driver's side and —" Haas suddenly frowned. "You do know how to drive, don't you?"

"Yes."

"We assumed so. Carli told us about your previous fossil-stone business. But I had to make sure. Anyway, we drive away with Heng between us. But instead of going north on Highway One, we go south, toward Quezon City. We leave the highway at Manolo Avenue and drive to the E-Z Storage facility, where I have rented a storage unit under an assumed name. We take Heng's cell phone away, tie him up, gag him, and leave him in the rented unit." Haas glanced at Carli, then Angie, with an ingratiating smile. "Later, of course, we'll telephone his employer and tell him where the driver is; we want no one hurt in this operation." Then, back to Cargo: "We drive the truck to a small warehouse I own back here in Tondo. There we sort out the various boxes of drugs —"

"What kind of drugs are we talking about?" Cargo asked bluntly. "I don't want to take a chance of being executed for moving street drugs."

Angie O'Brien shook her head. "No need to worry about that. These are pharmaceuticals only, drugs that physicians prescribe: for allergies, high blood pressure, diabetes, asthma, glaucoma — that sort of thing. And, of course, folic acid. But no drugs that are on the illegal controlled substances list." She nodded to Haas. "Go on, Freddy."

"Sure. Once in my warehouse, we will separate out all the cartons of folic acid and leave them there for later transfer to the orphanage clinic. The rest of the shipment we will drive to another warehouse, where we will meet an associate of mine. He will buy the load from us, truck and all, for twenty-five percent of the value stated on the import bill of lading, minus the folic acid amount. In turn, he will negotiate with DuPree to sell the shipment back to him, minus the folic acid, for fifty percent of the value." Haas paused to smile broadly. "The beauty of this is that *everybody* profits. The clinic gets its folic acid, you and I, my new friend, get our money, the middleman gets his, and even DuPree comes out ahead, because he gets most of his drug shipment *and* a payoff from the insurance company, which does not know the shipment has been returned. The plan is wonderful. Happiness will prevail for all!"

Cargo did not like the practiced smile that Freddy Haas flashed, and it rankled him that Haas had referred to Danny as his "new friend." But in his mind, Cargo had to admit to a certain genius in the plan. No violence. No one would get hurt. Everyone would get something out of it. And there seemed no way of anything going wrong. Could be, he decided, this would be his way either out of the country or being able to bribe away that exit visa.

And now, looking more closely at Angie O'Brien, imagining he could still feel the warmth of her hands on his knees, he found his interest in her growing. Next to Carli, she was no raving beauty, of course, but there was still that *something* about her . . .

"If I decide to come in," he said to Haas, "what's the split?"

"Seventy-thirty," said Haas. "I take an extra twenty percent for the planning and arranging the buyer."

"How much do you estimate the take will be?"

Shrugging, Haas deferred to Angie, who held her hands out, palms up in uncertainty.

"There can be no promises made, of course. A lot will depend on the types of drugs in the shipment and the quantity of each. But if I had to set a figure, strictly on speculation, but based on knowing which drugs are most popular in local hospitals and pharmacies, I would say" — she paused a beat, taking a deep breath — "ten million Philippine pesos."

Pursing his lips in thought, Cargo tried to quickly work the exchange figures in his head, but Freddy Haas was too fast for him. "Danny, my new friend, it comes to a little over two hundred thousand U.S., which means our share would be approximately fifty thousand. You can figure your end at about sixteen."

Danny made a quick decision. "I don't want a seventy-thirty split. Or any split. I want a flat guarantee of twenty thousand."

The answer from Haas was just as quick. "Done," he said with that smile.

There was a heavy silence in the room for a long moment, everyone's eyes darting from one to another. Finally Carli rose, took a deep breath, and said, "Well, now that things are settled, I have to get back to the clinic." She stepped over to Cargo and gave him a kiss on the cheek. "Thanks, Danny. This means a lot to me."

After she left, Haas said to Cargo, "I'll see you back at the hotel, my friend. I have a few things to go over with Angie."

Cargo rose. "Sure."

Cargo left the bar, but instead of going back to the hotel, he crossed the narrow street and stepped into a small open-air hut filled with stacks of stolen canned goods for sale. Since he had not eaten yet that day, he picked out a can of albacore and had the merchant open it for him. At the counter, he laced it with white mustard and took a plastic fork. Sitting down on an upturned wooden box, he ate while he watched the front door of Rose's Bar.

Haas and Angie came out a quarter-hour later. For a minute or so they stood together in conversation, then parted, Haas going in one direction, toward the Rittz, Angie in the opposite direction, toward the clinic. Cargo waited until they were far enough apart, then left the rest of his albacore on the box and hurried after Angie.

"Hey," he said, falling in beside her. "I was hoping to catch you alone. Are you in a hurry to get back?"

"What's on your mind, Danny?" she asked warily, even a little knowingly.

"I was wondering if maybe we could stop and have a cup of tea together."

Angie paused, studying him, and he knew she was weighing how critical he was to the hijack plan. "All right," she said finally. "Let's."

There was a tea shop nearby that Angie knew of, so they went there and ordered a pot of green tea.

"Well, we are having tea together, Danny," she said with an openness that he knew he should have expected. "What now?"

Danny shrugged. "I just hoped we could get to know each other, that's all."

"Are you sure you aren't just looking for a replacement for Carli?"

He felt himself blush. "I guess I might be," he admitted. "But not exactly in the way you might be thinking." He looked down at the green liquid circle in his cup. "Maybe I just need a friend."

"Why would you need a friend? You'll be gone from the Philippines in a few days."

"Maybe, maybe not. With part of my share of the money, I can probably bribe some official to cancel the visa. Then I could stay in Manila."

"Why would you want to stay in Manila?"

He wondered if she realized how difficult she was making it for him. "I don't really have a reason." He met her direct look with one of his own. "Yet," he added. Leaning forward on his elbows, he said, "Look, could we just lighten up this conversation a little?"

"All right." Angie sighed quietly and sipped a little tea.

"Where are you from, Angie?" he asked, looking for neutral ground.

"Chicago. You?"

"Houston."

She grunted softly, but with a slight smile. "A cowboy?"

"Kind of. Oil-rig cowboy." He liked the way her thin lips curved down at their corners even when she smiled. "How'd you end up in Manila?"

Now her smile morphed away. "Danny, let's not go there just yet."

"Go where?"

"The past."

He nodded understandingly. "Dark secrets?"

"A couple of secrets, yes. I don't know about dark."

"If I manage to stay in Manila, will you tell me about them?"

She gave him another of her long, contemplative stares before finally answering. "Yes, if you want me to." She leaned forward a little. "I want you to know something, Danny. Your helping us with what we're doing means an awful lot, not just to Carli and me, but to everybody involved in Mary Magdalene Orphanage and the clinic. The mother superior, the nuns, the nurses, all the children, their mothers: there are many, *many* people who would thank you if they knew. But they don't and never will. No one knows that anyone from the orphanage or the clinic is involved except the four of us, so you will never receive the gratitude you deserve —"

"Your gratitude is enough for me," Cargo interrupted. He took one of her hands across the little round table where they sat. Angie's eyes misted a little.

"Thank you, Danny." She withdrew her hand from his. "Now I really must go."

Outside the tea shop, as he watched her walk away, the morning sun making her short, tangled hair shine like copper, Cargo's expression became perplexed, because he could not resolve in his mind exactly what there was about Angie O'Brien that had reached out to him so quickly and grasped something inside him so completely. But with his perplexity there was also a very warm feeling, a flicker of something that made him make up his mind at that moment that he was somehow going to remain in Manila.

Two days later, Danny Cargo's whole world blew up in his face. Nothing went wrong with the job itself; the hijacking of the truck and its aftermath, right up to the time he and Freddy Haas returned to Freddy's warehouse in Tondo, went off like clockwork.

They had watched the shipment of pharmaceuticals being offloaded from the freighter *Vancouver* onto the DuPree truck parked on Pier 19. When the transfer was nearly complete, they had a waiting taxi take them to a corner a few blocks from where the hijacking was to take place. Some thirty minutes later, at the intersection of Kasibu and Matalon Streets, they successfully commandeered the DuPree truck with no resistance at all from Heng, the Chinese driver, who was clearly indifferent to what happened to the truck and its load as long as he himself was not hurt.

The trip from the hijack point to the rented unit at the E-Z Storage facility was made without incident, and once there Haas bound the driver's wrists and ankles with nylon cord under several layers of three-inch adhesive tape from the clinic. He also used that tape to securely gag the man.

"You no leave me here to die, you no do that — please!" Heng begged just before he was gagged.

"Don't worry," Haas assured him with one of his artificial smiles. "We are thieves, not murderers. You will be released in three or four hours."

After locking Heng in the rented storage unit, Cargo and Haas drove to the small warehouse that Haas owned in Tondo, where they spent the next two hours sorting through the cartons of pharmaceuticals and setting aside the folic acid boxes. The cartons were all stenciled in black letters with the name of their contents. In all, there ended up being thirty-two cartons of folic acid, each carton, according to the shipping invoice Haas had taken from the driver, containing two dozen bottles of the drug; 786 bottles, 250 tablets per bottle.

"Nearly two hundred thousand doses," Haas figured with his calculator-like mind. "That should make Carli and Angie very happy." He slapped Cargo on the back in another of his hollow gestures of camaraderie. "Come on, my friend, let's get the rest to my buyer and get our money."

They drove to another warehouse, in the Pulian district, this one bustling with activity, with a loading dock long enough to accommodate ten trucks at a time. Painted above the dock was FONG LEE FONG—RESHIPMENT CO. LTD.

As soon as Danny had backed the truck into an empty space, four husky dockworkers hauled a huge canvas tarpaulin onto its top and unrolled it down each side to conceal the DuPree Pharmaceuticals name and logo. At the same time, six others began unloading the truck at the rear.

"You can wait in the truck," Haas told Danny. "Since you are not in for a percentage, you don't need to be a party to the financial transaction. I'll be back in a while with your twenty thousand."

Danny did not like that arrangement, but he knew Haas was right; by his own choice, Danny was not a partner in the job, only a paid employee. Exiting the truck, Haas joined an Asian man of unclear origin holding a clipboard and checking off each carton as it was moved into the warehouse. When the truck was empty, Haas handed the man the packet with the shipment invoice and insurance documents taken from the hijacked driver. Together they went inside the warehouse.

Half an hour later, Haas returned to the loading dock carrying two canvas duffel bags and gestured for Danny to join him. Danny got out and hopped up onto the dock. Haas handed him one of the two bags.

"Four hundred and fifty thousand pesos, my friend. A trifle more than the twenty thousand U.S. you have coming, but I can't be bothered counting small bills. Shall we go?"

An air-conditioned taxi was waiting on the street to take them to the Tondo district. Neither spoke on the way there, for fear the driver understood English. At the edge of the Tondo district, the two men dismissed the taxi, slung on their duffel bags, and walked the mile or so to the warehouse Haas owned, where they had left the cartons of folic acid.

"How much did you get for the load?" Danny could not help asking on the way. Haas laughed gleefully.

"Ah, don't you wish you knew! Having second thoughts about taking a flat guarantee, Danny?"

"No, just curious."

"Well, don't be. What's the old American saying? Curiosity killed the cat?" The German's voice lost its jovial tone. "You don't want to be the cat that was too curious, do you, Danny?"

Remembering the automatic that Haas carried in his belt and deciding that those last words were clearly a warning, Danny replied, "No, Freddy, I don't."

At his warehouse, Haas said, "Danny, open a carton and pull out a bottle of that stuff, will you?" It was half request, half order.

Danny examined one of the cartons. It was securely sealed with filament tape. "I don't have anything to cut this tape," he said.

"You know, Danny," Haas smirked, "if you're going to be a successful criminal, you must learn to carry the tools of your trade. Here." He tossed Danny a six-inch Italian switchblade stiletto. While Danny began carefully slicing the fibers of the tape, Haas studied him thoughtfully. After seeming to ponder something, he said, "You're not a bad fellow, Danny. How would you like to work for me on a permanent basis?"

"As what, a bellman at the Rittz?"

Haas laughed. "Come now, I'm sure Carli or Angie must have at least suggested to you that my little hovel of a hotel is merely a legitimate front for my more, shall we say, covert business."

"Which is?" Danny asked.

"Sex, dear boy. To be exact, sex *slavery*. Naturally, no one at the orphanage or the clinic is aware of this." He chuckled. "If they were, they wouldn't spit on me, much less do business with me. You see, I deal in young girls — *very* young girls: eleven and twelve are the favorite ages. I snatch them off the streets of Tondo and other stinking slum areas and hold them captive in this very warehouse. After I collect half a dozen or so, I sell them to the captain of one of the foreign ships docked here — much as you previously did with your black-market fossil stone. Except that my product doesn't go to Honolulu to be used in furniture making; my product goes to places like Syria, Turkey, Pakistan, Algeria, to be used for . . . well, other purposes. How would you like to join me in that venture?"

"No, thanks," Cargo replied coldly. "That's not in my line."

"You'd make good money," Haas encouraged. "Right now I can

only manage, working alone, one sale of six units a month. But with the right assistant, I could probably triple that."

"I said no," Cargo repeated. "Forget it." He finished slicing the tape and put the stiletto aside. "When are we going to call DuPree to tell them where to find their driver?"

"We aren't," Haas replied matter-of-factly. "Don't ask foolish questions. Did you really think we were? The man has *seen* us, he can *identify* us." Haas chuckled again. "Besides, one Chink more or less won't matter to anyone."

"If we leave him there, he'll suffocate from the heat."

"Probably," Haas agreed absently. Coming over to the now open carton, he removed a bottle of folic acid pills and hefted it in one of his hamlike hands as if it were a trophy of some sort. "I'm going to show this," he said, a leer spreading over his face, "to sweet young Carli, and before agreeing to deliver the rest of the shipment extract from her a, ah, shall we say, little extra charge for my services. She's such a dedicated young woman, so devoted to those freakish children, I'm sure in order to get the rest of these, she'll do anything I ask of her."

As Haas turned away, Danny picked up the stiletto and buried its thin silver blade all the way into the side of the German's neck.

Gasping, throat throbbing in a panic reflex, esophagus shriveling inside him, blood spurting around the pearl handle of the knife sticking out of his neck, Haas reached for the pistol in his belt.

Danny Cargo was a split second faster and got to the gun first.

While Manfred Haas was thrashing and kicking on the floor, gurgling like a stuck hog, desperately trying not to die, Danny retrieved the DuPree truck driver's cell phone, scrolled the call menu, and telephoned the pharmaceutical company's number. To the woman who answered, he gave the name of E-Z Storage and the street he remembered it being on, so that their driver could be rescued.

Then Danny transferred the money from his duffel bag into the larger one that Haas had carried and tossed the extracted bottle of folic acid pills in with it. As soon as the German stopped writhing, Danny stripped him of his clothes, identification, and keys, pulled the knife from his neck, wiped up the blood, and rolled the cell

phone and everything else except the warehouse keys into a bundle. Taking that, he dragged Haas out a back door, eased his body
into a six-foot-deep open sewage trench, waited until it sank, then
tossed the bundle in after it and watched as the putrid brown sewage stream floated it slowly away.

"So long, Freddy," he said to himself.

It was late afternoon as Danny, the duffel bag slung on one shoulder, hiked deeper into the Tondo district to the Mary Magdalene
Orphanage clinic. Inside, he found the same young woman in
white novitiate habit that he had spoken to the day he was released.

"Hello." She smiled up at him. "I remember you. Looking for
Nurse Gomez again?"

"Actually, no." Danny smiled back. "I'm looking for Angie
O'Brien this time."

The young novitiate frowned. "I'm sorry, who did you say?"

"Angie O'Brien. She works in the pharmacy."

"Oh, you mean Sister Angela. Just a moment, please."

Sister Angela? The words stung him sharply.

Danny was only remotely aware of the young woman speaking
into the telephone on her reception desk. His brain was in a sudden turmoil, his thoughts a bedlam of disorder. For a brief, insane
moment, he felt as if he were the only person on the face of the
earth, all alone, with no idea what to do next.

Then he heard her voice.

"Hello, Danny."

She stood in a white summer nun's habit, a white cowl covering
her clipped red hair, those usually piercing dark eyes of hers seeming somehow softer, but not even the hint of a smile on her thin
lips.

"Shall we talk outside?" she said, taking his arm.

One side of the clinic wing was in shade, and they stood there to
talk.

"So this is the secret you said you had." Danny's voice was
strained.

"One of them, yes."

"Is there another?"

"Yes. The other is Carli."

As she spoke Carli's name, the young Filipina nurse came outside and joined them. Nurse and nun stood side by side, each reaching for the other's hand. Seeing that, Danny felt inert, as if some kind of narcosis had overcome him. Suddenly he was very tired, experiencing a fatigue that overcame the nervous tension of the long day of robbery and murder and now the astonishment of this crushing moment.

"We didn't want to hurt you, Danny," Sister Angela said quietly.

"No," Danny muttered, "I don't believe you did."

"We had to think of the children first."

"I know. I . . . understand." He looked at Carli. "I asked before if you were happy. You said you were."

"I am, Danny." She squeezed Sister Angela's hand. "I'm very happy."

"Okay, then." Danny unzipped the duffel bag and handed Carli the bottle of folic acid. "The rest is in Freddy's warehouse. Thirty-two cartons." He handed the keys to Sister Angela, their hands brushing briefly. "You know where the warehouse is?"

"Yes. Is Freddy there?"

"No."

"Where is he?"

"Gone," Danny said.

At the way he said it, the two women exchanged glances and asked nothing further.

Zipping the duffel back up, Danny slung it once more, threw the two women a sad wink, and silently walked away. Behind him, he heard their farewells.

"Take care, Danny," said Carli.

"God bless, Danny," Sister Angela added.

On his way out of Tondo, Danny had to walk past Smoky Mountain. As in the early morning, waiting for the night collection trucks, now in the early evening the people who scavenged the unspeakable filth were waiting once again, this time for the day collection trucks. Bent, toothless old people mingled with skinny, ragged children, twitching drug addicts with hungry young mothers and their babies, stray dogs with greasy rats.

Shouldering his way through the restless, anxious press of bodies, Danny's eyes scanned faces that reminded him of a documentary film he had once viewed about the Nazi concentration camps of World War II and how the survivors of those camps had looked.

But the people he saw here, he knew, were not prisoners of an in-humane society but rather of a modern government that chose to ignore them to death. Through poverty and indifferent neglect, their problem was left to solve itself by attrition. Danny thought of the penal camp at Palayan. Even the lowliest convict there was better off than those who fed off Smoky Mountain.

When he was almost past the huge dump, Danny abruptly turned back. Stepping across an open sewage trench, he began to wade up and through the swamp of rotting garbage, the stench as-saulting his nostrils, meth haze burning his eyes, shoes slogging as the mire became deeper. Breath laboring, nausea building, he finally trudged his way to the top. Below and all around him, the waiting people were chattering and pointing at him.

Unslinging and opening the duffel, Danny grabbed two hand-fuls of loose pesos and held them up high.

"Come and get it!" he yelled, and flung the money into the air.

The mass of people at the bottom rushed toward him like a tidal wave.

"Come on!" he yelled. "Come on! Come on!"

Grabbing more handfuls, he threw the currency as far as he could, in all directions. Again and again he reached into the duffel bag and scooped out money to throw, and he continued to yell.

"Come on! Come on!"

People surged around him like a raging fire, but no one came really close to him; they were fearful that he was a crazy man. Be-sides, no one wanted to interfere with the blizzard of money he was creating.

"Come on! Come on! Take it!"

Danny showered the impoverished of Tondo with money until the duffel was empty. Then, impoverished himself, he waded back down and out of Smoky Mountain.

He did not at all dread the thought of Palayan and the penal camp he was sure to be sent back to.

The air up there, after all, was clean and pure.

ROB KANTNER

Down Home Blues

FROM *robkantner.com*

"CAN'T HEAR YOU," I said into my cell phone. "Hold on a sec."
Threading my way through the clusters of chattering kinfolk and
such, I stepped out of the church's fellowship hall into the bright
sunshine. First I lit a short cork-tipped cigar, then I wedged the
phone back under my ear. Priorities. "Say again?"

"I asked where are you," Raeanne said.

"Oh. Georgia."

"Why there?"

"Funeral."

"Who died?"

"Great-aunt."

From the gravel parking lot of the Gethsemane Deliverance
Primitive Baptist Church, the Cohutta and Blue Ridge mountain
ranges ran into the misty distance, the rich green of the pine for-
ests contrasting with silvery mist puff-clouds and deep blue sky.

"Well, I'm sorry," Raeanne said.

"Thanks."

"Listen," she said briskly, "I've decided to go ahead and rent my
house out."

"I'll put Owney on it."

"And something else."

"Yeah?"

"My accountant says you haven't cashed my checks."

People were exiting the church now, Perkins, Humfreys, other
distant kin too plentiful to mention. Among these was Caroleen,
who waved when she saw me, then helped a nameless ancient step
gingerly down the wood staircase.

"Your 'accountant,'" I echoed. No reply. "I'll just, uh . . . we'll convene a meeting of my bookkeeper and comptroller and VP Finance."

"Ben —"

"My girl will get back to your girl. That work for you?"

Silence. "Do things always have to get pissy when we talk?"

"Hey. I'm not the one who left."

"Hey. I'm not the one who didn't come along."

"Gotta go," I said, flipping the phone shut as Caroleen reached me. My cigar, cold and dead, went into my jacket pocket. "All set?" I asked my cousin.

"Yessir." She was hefty and close to my height, like many women on my mother's side. Her face was round and cheery; her strawberry blond hair was short and wavy-thick. She wore a cream flowered dress that must have been warm on this early April afternoon. "Crisis call? You got that Perkins thunder-look."

"Who, me? Mister Blank Face over here?"

"You made me wanna duck, darlin'."

"Yeah, well. Just my ex."

"*Uh*-huh," she said diplomatically, and slid behind the wheel of her Ford Taurus. "I had a call, too. Tenant complaint."

I slammed my door shut as she fired up the engine. "Tenant?"

"Up at my rental cabin. Says the downstairs toilet gurgles."

"Better'n it overflooding."

She laughed, swinging the car onto the blacktop headed steep downhill. "There's an old boy in town tends to that stuff for me. But I can't get holt of him."

"How 'bout I sort it out."

She shot me a glance. Her eyes were Humfrey cornflower blue. "You do fix-up?"

"Been known to," I answered, thinking about my fifteen-year, and now ended, tenure at Norwegian Wood.

"Thought you were a private detective or some such."

"This and that," I said easily. "Here and there."

Being a Humfrey, and cross-related on the Perkins side also, Caroleen knew the code. "Well, if you could slap me a fix on that mess, I'd be obliged."

"Least I can do." I cracked my window; the early April sun was warming the car up quick. "You putting me up and feeding me and all?"

"That's the least *I* can do," she answered, laughing. "You come all the way down from De-troit to be here for Aunt Sarah."

I didn't bother to mention that the ends I was at these days were even looser than usual: unemployed and without a home of my own. A couple-day getaway from bitchy exes and money woes, clamoring clients and cranky creditors seemed like a swell idea. Kids get spring break. Why not me? North Georgia was no South Padre, but what the hell. "This tenant you got, he ain't some kind of window-smashin' psycho-screamin' problem child, is he?"

"Oh no." She laughed. "It's this darlin' couple. Rent the place this time each year, like clockwork. Lovely folks."

The drive back from Kilby Mill was sixty-odd miles of twisting, climbing, and plunging blacktop lined by pine forest interrupted at times by sleepy villages, ramshackle mobile homes, and granite rock walls spray-painted PREPARE TO MEET THY GOD. Caroleen and I chatted easily about the generations of Perkinses and Humfreys that had roamed these mountains, from the peaks and waterfalls and kudzu-choked hollows of Rabun County to the rolling hills and wooded crevasses west of Brasstown. Family legend had it that the earliest Perkinses washed ashore with the first wave of folks flushed out of British debtor prisons. Nothing that had happened since gave me any reason to doubt it. From what I'd heard, they'd scratched out a living doing crops here, pigs there, timber, poultry, and hey-boy, interrupted by a bit of soldiering during the Late Unpleasantness. Supplemented, no doubt, by the strictly secret production of a certain high-octane untaxed beverage.

Evening was hard on us by the time we reached Caroleen's snug log cabin along a chattering stream at the foot of Mount Bezetha. She handed me a kit of tools in an old tin tackle box and directions and keys to her rental cabin. In my rented Ford Fusion I navigated the rutted, red clay, and often treacherous two-track trails around the base of Mount Bezetha, then turned onto a narrow gravel lane that switchbacked up the side of the heavily forested mountain.

When not fighting to keep the car from veering over the lip of one cliff or another, I thought about Caroleen: second cousin thrice removed, or third cousin twice removed, take your pick. She was a warm-hearted gal of about my age, pretty in a well-seasoned way, with a musical laugh and a very direct way of looking at me. Her drawling mountain lilt reminded me of my long-gone parents.

Upon meeting that morning after my run up from Atlanta, we'd admitted to vague childhood memories of each other. Probably sprang from one of the several driving trips "down home" that my parents took Bill and Libby and me on, way back when. I gathered Caroleen was married to a long-haul trucker who was rarely home. She gathered that I was a dad, between (cough) careers, and seeing somebody, sorta. These disclosures took the tension out of the fact that we'd be sharing her cabin alone tonight.

Then tomorrow, of course, I'd head home to Detroit.

At least, that's what I thought.

Bear-y Loverly cabin was a brown-stained two-story frame structure with fake log siding, big windows, wraparound porch, brick chimney, and red tin roof. Set at the road's end near the crest of the mountain, it perched literally on the side of a terrifying steep slope. The view was stunning: blue-gray mountain vistas rippling out into the misty distance. The driveway, a gravel notch hacked out of the side of the red clay slope, was empty. Good. Maintenance is best done when the tenant is absent.

I let myself in and looked around. The inside was a bright shiny spectacle of notched beams and knotty pine siding, glossy wide-plank floors and a corner fieldstone fireplace. Some of the furniture was cabin-style: tables and chairs made of varnished tree limbs mortised and tenoned together. The rest of the place was plush to the point of luxury. Big flat-screen TV. Large soft sofas, chairs, and recliner. CD and DVD players. Well-equipped kitchen. On the deck out back sat a big humming hot tub, covered now. Evidence of occupancy included dirty dishes, a half-finished solitaire game on the table, open suitcases in the master bedroom, and a half-full wastebasket. And everywhere there were bears, of the stuffed variety: on the tables, the driftwood mantle, occupying the big recliner, and shinnying up the chimney. Cute.

Downstairs was a rec room with pool table, foosball, lounging area, and yet another flat-screen with DVD player. Off the lower bedroom I found the bathroom with the errant toilet. In short order it gurgled its last. Wandering back upstairs, I was struck by the vast silence of the place, way up here on the mountain. There wasn't another cabin within sight. From what Caroleen had said, most of these places were not occupied full-time. If you've got a lot of "it all" to get away from, I reflected, this is the place to do it.

The sofa facing the flat-screen TV had several pillows on it, a face-down Sara Paretsky paperback, and a blue woven throw. On the split-log coffee table beside it lay a thick ring-bound book, flopped open next to an uncapped ink pen. It was a guest book for the Bear-y Loverly cabin, each spread of pages filled out as a kind of diary. Today's entry, written in loopy female hand, read:

> Billy met me at the airport and drove us up here last night. This place is as awesome as Billy said it would be!!! So quiet and beautiful and views to die for! We're going to Helen and Amicalola today. But mainly we're going to :) kick back :) and do our thing :), all alone for days & days. Billy is so sweet. He can't bear to be apart from me. He even hid my cell phone to have me all to himself! LOL!

From outside came faint vehicle sounds. Replacing the book exactly as I'd found it, I went to the door to see a couple getting out of a big black boxy Lincoln Lexicon. The driver, an average-height dark-haired younger man wearing black T-shirt, blue jeans, and flip-flops, was on the porch by the time I opened the door. "Who are you?" he asked, tone and expression just this side of abrupt.

"Maintenance. Fixed the commode."

The man, whom I took to be Billy, walked in, passing me just a tad too close. He was good-looking enough, younger than me by a fistful of years, and athletic to the point of masochism. His eyes were close-set, his lips almost nonexistent. His curly black hair was cropped close and receding rapidly from his lined forehead. To make up for it, he had lots more everywhere else: arms, hands, even the tops of his flip-flopped feet. Glancing around the cabin's living room, as if taking inventory, he said, "Whyn't Caroleen send the billhilly?"

I couldn't place the accent. Southern somewhere, but not these parts. "Who?"

"The old guy she usually sends," he said, as if to a child. His companion, a long-legged gal with flowing auburn hair, came in, grocery bags in each arm, and stood next to Billy with a pleasant shy smile for me. Quite a contrast: Billy wore black, the woman wore all red, top and shorts. Billy had diamond ear studs, she did not. He was burnished to bone and gristle, she was all curvy/cuddly. Even in flat thin sandals, she was as tall as Billy, maybe a tad taller. Jostling her grocery bag, she extended a long hand. "I'm Wendee."

"None o' his bidness who you are," Billy cut in. "He's just the help. Now go get me a ice water. I'm dry as a popcorn fart."

She bobbed her head and, with a polite smile for me but no eye contact, headed into the kitchen area. The back of her red T-shirt said *Good Girls Are Soon Forgotten.* Billy eyed me. "Live in Blue Ridge?"

"Visiting."

"Us, too." He shrugged. "From where?"

"Detroit."

He brightened. "Home of the Final Four this year! Your timing sucks, Bub, picking this weekend to leave town."

"There's always TV."

Wendee brought a tumbler of ice water. Instead of taking it, he just stared at it. "What's wrong with this picture?"

"Uh . . . sorry?" she said, smiling a bit too brightly.

"You know I always like the glass as full of ice as possible," he said, tone measured, as if giving dictation. "Cram-full to the top. You *know* that."

"Sorrr-eee," she flustered, and went back into the kitchen.

Billy rolled his eyes at me, placing us both firmly in man-to-man country: *Why do we put up with these bitches?* I just stared back at him, then gave him a small lame salute. "I'm out of here. Take it easy."

"Take it any way I can get it, bub."

I backed my Ford Fusion carefully out of the driveway onto the gravel lane and bumped the car warily down the steep rutted lane. My business up here is done, I told myself. Yes, it is absolutely, positively done. Okay, all right: the man's an asshole. But that ain't against the law. Not in Georgia, not anywhere.

Supper was country ham with redeye gravy and cheese grits on the side. After making only token resistance to my offer to clean up, Caroleen retreated to the deck. Fifteen minutes later I went out there, to find the sun down, moon up, stars a-twinkling. Caroleen bobbed in the round redwood hot tub, up to her neck in steaming, burbling blue water.

"It's just delicious out here," she said, smiling at me, "evenings like this."

"Special," I agreed. Grabbing a chair, I sat near the opposite end of the deck and lit a short cork-tipped cigar. Pines towered over us.

A straw-strewn pathway meandered twenty feet to the brook, which ran in a fast silver torrent through a cluster of big rocks. Caroleen had draped a towel over a chair by the tub. "Nice private place," I said.

"Except for canoeists." She grinned. "Sometimes they paddle by when I'm in the tub. Crane their fool necks. Hoping for a thrill."

And do you oblige them? I thought unwillingly, reminded of biker rallies I'd been to: *Show us your tits!* "Thanks again for supper," I said. "That kind of cooking I don't get much these days." Except, I reflected, on the rare occasions when Bill and Marybeth invited me over.

"Well," Caroleen said, "thanks for fixing the busted toilet."

"Nothin' to it. Wiggle and a jiggle."

"Man like you, good with your hands, you could do right well in these parts."

What parts did she mean? "Kind of you," I said easily. Time for the topic. "Your renter and his gal, they're interesting."

"Good folks," she said, thinking she was agreeing. "Regular and reliable."

"Uh-huh." Beneath the towel, on the chair seat, I saw Caroleen's neatly folded jean shorts and blouse.

"Regulars is where it's at, with cabin rental," she was saying as she paddled around in the water, still invisible except for her head and an occasional glimpse of shoulder. In the pale moonlight her skin and blond hair were brilliantly white. "I can't live on one-shots. The big operations suck up most of that traffic. To survive, I need regulars, like Mr. Suttles."

"Yeah, every year he's here, you said."

She nodded. "They pay for two solid weeks, full freight. But they only stay for five, six days."

"Wow." Curious. Man had cash to burn, evidently. "Where they from?"

"Dallas area, I b'lieve."

"I reckon you checked him out every which-a-way."

She cut on the hot tub jets, sending up steamy bubbles and a low-throated drone from the tub. "Yeah, well. Let's just say, back when they first came, I was just starting out. I wan't as thorra as I am now."

"That so."

"Now I'm super-careful. Folks I don't know, they get a credit check, pay a whopping deposit, sign a ironclad contract. All kinds of rules. No pets. No smoking. Limit two adults."

"How come the limit?"

"One year, early on, an old boy and his wife showed up carrying half their high school graduating class with 'em. Cost me a thousand dollars to put right the mess they left."

"Wow. That had to suck."

"Yessir. Lesson learned."

In the silence, a bird cawed somewhere. I puffed the cigar. "So this Suttles guy, he's more or less grandfathered in?"

"Why, sure. They been coming six, seven years. I know 'em." She was facing me now. Against my will, I was actively wondering what she had on. If anything. "He's such a kindly man, too. One year his girlfriend got sick. He wouldn't settle for our clinic up here. He rushed her all the way down to Atlanta. Paid for the whole stay anyway."

That was curious — another big dot to connect — but I let it go for now. Silence fell. I finished my cigar and held it to go cold. The hot tub hummed, the stream chattered, some kind of critter howled in the distance. Caroleen paddled very slowly, backward, then forward. She seemed to be watching me. She seemed somehow expectant. Was there a glint of invitation in those big wide cornflower eyes? Was she in fact naked behind all those bubbles? I could resolve the question easily enough. Stand up and walk over and see.

But I stayed put. It sure was hard. Behaving, that is. And frustrating, too, just like this talk. I'd hoped that Caroleen could create some clarity. But all I'd learned was that she didn't know the Billy Suttles I had met. Still, there were no smoking guns, no red flags. Just that sick itch in the back of my brain. I've been around longer than a little bit. I knew the itch would not, all on its own, go away.

"Think I might stay over an extry day or two," I said. "Okay with you?"

"I'd enjoy that," she said brightly. I rose to go inside. The tub water, bubbling furiously and reflecting crazily from the tub light, masked her body. Just as well. "Care for a soak?" Caroleen asked. "It's snug, but there's room for two."

"Ah, no thanks," I replied. "I'm pretty much up to my quota of hot water."

She laughed briefly. Stared at me in silence. "You sure?" I didn't answer. Smile fading, she grabbed the tub edge with both hands and hoisted up to her full height. The bluish water steamed as it rolled over her bare shoulders and down her white low-cut one-piece swimsuit. She killed the jets. "I'll just shut her down then."

Over a hearty breakfast of coffee, sausage, and waffles drowned in gray mule, Caroleen said she'd be off working her bookstore job till midafternoon. I told her I'd fend for myself just fine, and was out the door by ten.

The mountain morning was crisp. The orange sun reached fingers of flame across the valleys and along the ridges and danced on the surface of the stream. I drove my Fusion the gingerly couple of miles up Mount Bezetha, through shadows and sunshine, to the rental cabin. During the night I'd woken up thinking about the place: things I'd seen and, most troubling, things expected but not seen. I tried to focus on facts, such as they were, and evidence, to the extent that there was any. I had nothing solid. But I just couldn't get past the unease I felt about the situation in Bear-y Loverly Cabin, miles of meandering, mostly unnamed mountain lanes away from anywhere.

The Lexicon was gone, the cabin deserted. I let myself in with the key I'd plumb forgot to return, moved quickly from room to room, scanning everything. Amid the gizmos and the knotty pine and the sleuth of stuffed bears, there was some everyday clutter, but nothing remarkable. No plates of rotting food, odd powders, pipe bombs in production, or puke puddles. Even the king bed had been crisply made, the country quilt tucked neatly at the corners. But the item I sought was not in there either.

Damn.

Keeping an ear cocked for noise on the lane, I went through the Delsey hard-side suitcase that was clearly Billy's. I found casual clothes — jeans and black shirts — all clean and well worn. There were also some large silk scarves, a surprisingly unmasculine touch. There was a hefty Sony camcorder in a black case and a zip pocket with several blank white DVD boxes. The disks inside were titleless. Interesting.

Wendee's soft-side roll bag was brand-new. So were its contents: jeans and such, dressier things, some unopened word-search books, and lots of Victoria's Secret silky satiny. Looked to me like she'd left home with nothing and bought all this on the way to the airport. Tucked into a side pocket was a small change purse. Inside was a thick wad of currency, a Saab car key, a Capital One card stamped WENDEE L. SAKSTRUP, and a gold wedding band with a triple-diamond engagement ring. Well, then.

Bathroom was a bore except for Wendee's hair and makeup accessories and supplies, dominating every inch of counter space. Stepping out, I was debating whether to risk viewing, or swiping, one of the DVDs when I heard gravel rustle in the driveway outside. In came the happy couple.

"You again!" greeted Billy. Not smiling, not scowling, just watchful. Again he wore flip-flops and jeans and black shirt, this one long-sleeve, snug to his honed athletic chest. His ear studs twinkled. "What up, bub?"

"Stopped by to make sure the plumbing stayed fixed."

He stopped, stood there, watched me. "Stopped by," he echoed.

"Little customer satisfaction thing we do," I said jauntily.

Wendee, wearing a maroon long-sleeve shirt with white tank top beneath and cargo Capris, went into the kitchen area. Billy suddenly beamed at me. "Plumbing's fine," he said. "Bring me a beer, Wen." He looked at me. "Want a beer?"

It wasn't even noon yet. Not that it matters, usually, but for the drive back down the mountain a clear head seemed like a good idea. "Thanks anyhow. Y'all got big plans today?"

"Kick back," he answered, and grinned. "Final Four starts tonight."

"Uh-huh."

"State's gonna whup 'em some lame Yankee-boy ass." Wendee handed him a tall glass of beer. He screwed up his dark face in distaste and glared at her. "Too much head, girl. I'm shocked. Usually you don't give enough."

"Need more practice," she said archly, and went to the big sofa.

He took a big long drink, blinked rapidly, looked at me. "I might watch the game tonight," he said. "But maybe not." He winked at me and raised his voice. "I might have better things to do! Ain't that right, Blowjob. Wendee, I mean."

"Bill-eee!" she tittered. "Jeez Louise!" Flopping back on the sofa, she picked up her book.

"I *said* I was kidding," Billy said jauntily, giving me a wink. He finished the beer with another long draft, set the damp glass down, and went over to her. Wordlessly they kissed, long and deep, her arms caressing his broad back. I edged over toward the door. Billy came up for air. "Stand by, Bub," he ordered. Kissing Wendee again, he murmured, "You be good now."

"I'm always good," she cooed, "except when I'm with you."

"My naughty dirty girl," he growled, nuzzling her neck.

I wanted to tell them to get a room. But this *was* the room.

"I wish you wouldn't go," she pouted.

"I *told* you, I got errands." Straightening, he smacked her shoulder. "Don't start without me."

Outside he faced me, jingling his car keys, squinting into the sun. "This 'customer satisfaction' thing? Hang it up for the rest of the weekend. 'Kay, Bub? We're plenty satisfied."

"You got it."

"G'wan." He gestured me toward my Fusion. "I'll follow you out."

He did, too. Crowded my bumper on the steep winding clay-gravel trail, all the way down the mountain. Only at the bottom, where I swung right, did I lose him. And then, as the wilderness swallowed up the Lexicon in my rearview mirror, the thought hit me. Something Wendee had written about Billy in the guest book: *He can't bear to be apart from me.*

So where was he headed, all by his lonesome?

Swinging the Fusion into a disused farm lane, I backed out and barreled the other way. Didn't dare run up on Billy quick, but didn't dare lose him, either. I flew by a poultry farm and a series of kudzu-collapsed barns. Just past a one-lane wood bridge, the two-track dead-ended at a blacktop road. No sign of Billy. I knew the highway was to the right. To the left was God knew what. I turned right.

Just past the hamlet of Tippy Ditch, I saw the big chrome ass end of the Lexicon rounding a curve up ahead. I settled back and kept my distance, sighting him only occasionally as allowed by hills and curves. Obviously, he knew my car. But he had no reason to watch for a tail. I could stay on him if I was careful.

Be quite the hoot if all I was doing was following him to the Piggly Wiggly in Blue Ridge to buy chips and salsa for the big game. But no. When he reached the highway, he turned south. I waited a bit and followed suit. This was easier. The road was a divided four-lane, very busy, moving fast. I kept a half mile and at least two vehi-

cles between me and him. Rolled along, at five over the limit, mile
after mile. Where the *hell* was he going? A hundred miles on was Atlanta. All kinds of other places were in between. Whatever he could
possibly need, there were plenty of options in Blue Ridge. So whatever this was, it was no shopping trip . . .

My phone hummed. Mary Kate. "Yo."

Pause. "I thought you'd be on the plane by now."

Then why did you call? "Nah, something came up. Won't be back
for a couple more days prob'ly."

Silence. "Oh. I *wish* I'd come along."

Signs blipped by announcing the approach of Ellijay. "Well, you
had to work."

"But my place is with you at a time like this."

"It's all right. Really." The subject needed serious changing.
"What're you up to?"

"Oh," she said, sounding excited, "I'm meeting an old girlfriend
tonight at Miller's. Haven't seen her since we were little kids in
Redford."

The speed limit dropped. "Redford? Or Old Redford?"

"Old. Why?"

"I lived there, too," I said, thinking, *Small world.* "Bennett Street."

"Wow. Not that far," she said. The Lexicon's right blinker came
on. "We lived on —"

"Gotta let you go," I cut in. "See ya, bye."

"Call me!"

I let a big braying log hauler get between me and the Lexicon in
the right turn lane as we approached a red light. Traffic was thick
here, it being a big commercial sprawl at a major intersection. Presently the Lexicon made his right and then swung left into a shopping center. I inched along behind the log hauler, watching the
Lexicon, and chose the second driveway for myself. Staying in the
distant, almost empty part of the sprawling lot, Billy made a sweeping U-turn and halted beside a long, midnight-blue Buick Park Avenue.

I slotted my Fusion between two minivans, facing downhill, with
a clear view of the action. Billy dropped out of the Lexicon to greet
the two men emerging from the Buick. They had that upper-thir-
ties look and wore flip-flops, baggy shorts, and T-shirts commemo-
rating Southeast Conference schools. The driver was a wiry little

guy with a hatchet face, shaved head, and a ball cap with *#3* embla-
zoned above the bill — making him, I guessed, a fan of the late
Intimidator. His pal was oversized, with a shiny bowling-ball head,
bowling-ball belly, and a stooped way of walking. After handshakes
and backslaps, the two new guys transferred overnight bags from
the Buick into the Lexicon. And then they rolled out.

After giving them a minute to clear, I cruised by the back of the
Buick. Georgia tag and, on the side window, a rental company
decal.

The drive north lacked the suspense of the southbound. The
Lexicon led me into Blue Ridge, where they stopped at, you
guessed it, Piggly Wiggly. The trio came out swinging cases of beer
and bulging sacks, swaggering, bantering, braying laughter, hog-
ging the walkways, forcing others to give way. Lots of testosterone
on the hoof, I thought. It was either the casual male playfulness of
three old friends catching up or something less pleasant.

Beat shit out of me.

On my way back to Caroleen's, a voice mail dropped in from
Joann Sturtevant with an investigation job lead for me. I made a
note, then called T. Tommy Fledderjohn in Detroit. If there was
anyone who knew all there was to know about the Final Four, it was
T. Tommy.

Caroleen was sitting at her round wood table when I came in, a
sack in each arm. She was barefoot, wearing a snug white tank top
and blue-jean shorts, and she had glasses pushed back atop her
blond head. "Chow for tonight," I announced. "Pulled pork, baked
beans, fried okra, and all the fixings. My treat."

"Right kind of you," she murmured. "Just put it up, we'll deal
with it later."

"Yes, ma'am." I put the containers away. "Sweet tea?"

"I'm fine," she said faintly behind me. "Help yourself, though."

"Thanks." I poured myself a big tumbler of tea and turned to
face her. I'd planned to launch right in, but the sight of her
stopped me short. Her smile reached no further than her generous
mouth. Her cornflower eyes were dark and troubled, and there was
obvious tension in the set of her shoulders and the tilt of her head.
The table was covered with envelopes, papers, and a calculator.
More papers were spiked on a thin steel spindle.

"Bills, huh," I said.

Shaking her head, she closed her eyes briefly. "Train wreck, more like," she breathed.

"I can relate."

Humfreys don't cry. Perkinses neither. But Caroleen was close. "I just don't know what to do." She took off her glasses and kind of flipped them onto the table. "We're behind on a bunch, maxed out on the rest. And our mortgages just reset."

I didn't have to ask which direction. "Ouch."

She was really getting wound up now. "And Dees, I gotta say, he's no help a-tall."

"Dees?"

"My husband. Short for Diesel," she hurtled on. "Shows up once't every couple weeks. Brings home loads of excuses, a little lovin', and zero cash."

"That's too bad. I'm really sorry." She just looked away, shook her head. "Married long?" I asked.

"Two years. Craigslist." Her quick smile was rueful. "I know. Stupid."

"Hey hey," I said gently.

Long silence. Outside, a vehicle passed by on the lane. I drank some sweet tea. It was, as my daddy would say, peppy. Gradually Caroleen's scowl softened. "So cards on the table, Ben. Why'd you ask to stay over? Really?"

"Well . . ."

"I know it wan't about me."

She sounded casual enough, any hurt well hidden. "Well," I fumbled, "yeah, there's another situation needs seen to. I think."

"Which is what?"

First things first. "That guest book you have, at the cabin?"

"What about it?"

"You save the ones for the previous years?"

An hour later she came out on the deck and sat down at the picnic table across from me. "You got that thunder-look again, darlin'."

I set down the last of the six guest books. "Well, ma'am."

"What?" She eyed me intently. "Something wrong at my cabin?"

"Could be nothin'," I lied. "But let me run this by you."

She took a deep breath, seeming to brace herself. I told her about tailing Billy Suttles down to Ellijay earlier. "I drove by the cabin again," I said, "just before coming back here. His vehicle is there. My guess is they're all inside, Billy and his buddies. Plus Wendee, the girlfriend."

Her jaw was set, but she worked at staying casual. "So he broke the rules, not registering those boys. I'm sure all kinds of rules get broke, when my back's turned."

"Uh-huh," I said patiently. "But I read what Wendee wrote in the guest book on Friday. She expected her and Billy to be alone. Nothing about these boys joining them."

"Spur-of-the-moment thing, maybe."

"On top of that," I pressed, "the way Billy's friends arrived seems fishy. They have a rental car. Could've drove all the way to the cabin. Instead they park in Ellijay for Billy to pick them up. Why do that?"

"Afraid of getting lost? The roads is tricky around here."

"Why not meet in Blue Ridge, then? Closer by. Easier for everyone, seems like."

"Well, why do *you* think?" she asked, edge in her voice now.

"I don't know. Just seems sneaky. I just don't like it."

She nodded, mouth fixed. "You just got a suspicious mind, Benjy."

"That I do. And I notice things."

Silence, broken only by the hot tub hum and the chattering brook. "Meaning?" Caroleen said.

"Wendee ain't some longtime girlfriend like you thought. She's never been up here before."

"How do you know?"

"What she wrote in the guest book. Plus," I said, "I looked in the older books for Billy's earlier visits. Each time it's a different handwriting."

"But how do you know 'zactly when he's been here?"

"Final Four weekend, every year," I answered. "I got the dates from a friend of mine up in Detroit."

"Okay," she said after a pause, looking thoughtful. "So I was wrong about the girlfriend. So each time he brangs someone different. You been six years with the same woman?"

"Not hardly," I admitted. "But take a look at this." I opened the guest book for 2006 and showed her the block-printed entry for Sunday, April 2:

I hate to leave early, but I really have to go. The cabin is very nice but this
is not at all what I expected. As soon as it gets light, I'll

Caroleen looked up at me. "That's curious."

"Yeah. Like, why didn't she finish?"

"Could be anything," Caroleen said, without conviction.

"What year was it, the girlfriend got sick?"

"Don't remember," she said fretfully.

"Don't matter. Point is, it's another thing that happened."

She said nothing. I opened the book for the following year.
"Check this out. We have March thirty-first," I said, showing her the
page. "And we have April second," I went on, showing her the next
one, which was blank. "So where's the page for April first?" I slid
the open book over to Caroleen and pointed to the gutter. "Cut
right out, that's where. Prob'ly with a razor."

"Yup," she said grimly, straightening. "Wonder why."

"Me too. And I wonder about something else yet. Cabin's got a
landline phone, doesn't it?"

"Course it does."

"Well, I looked, and there ain't a phone to be found in there."

She stared at me. "Sure there is. Kitchen and bedroom, both."

"Not now." I leaned back, fetched a cigar from my shirt pocket.
"Wendee wrote that Billy confiscated her cell phone," I reminded
her. "No cell phone. No landline. He's cut her off."

Caroleen rose abruptly and walked over to the hot tub, clenching both fists in front of her. "Mister Suttles is the best customer
I've got," she muttered.

I just sat there, waited, watched her percolate.

"Could still all be a great big nothin'," she declared, still not
looking at me.

I stuck the cigar in my teeth, lit it up, puffed it hot, closed and
stacked the guest books.

"Don't tell me, let me guess," she said softly, turning to face me.
"You got a plan."

West of Mount Bezetha, a narrow two-track dead-ended at a small
brushy clearing, deserted this Saturday evening. I wedged the
rental car against a cluster of pines and got out. Sure enough, even
in the fading evening light I could see, meandering into the forest,

the Cohutta Panther Creek Trail, as promised by Caroleen's hand-sketched map.

Which was about all I got from her. At my request for a gun, Caroleen just snorted. Confederate gene pool has thinned out something awful, I thought as I started the trek along the narrow winding trail. Those old gals sent their boys into harm's way well fed, fired up, and armed to the teeth. Caroleen shooed me off with a map, a penlight smaller than my dick, and dark warnings about brambles, breaking my fool neck, and bears.

Her real worry, of course, was that I'd interrupt a session of "Kumbaya" around the fire pit.

The trail was uneven and winding, with jinks this way and that, dodging big rock outcrops and enormous fallen trees. Evening light faded gradually as I hoofed along. Though the moon was high and about three-quarters full, its pale silvery light dimmed in the deeper places where the pine canopy thickened. I heard occasional animal cries and rustling movements in the thick underbrush. The crisp mountain air was befogged for a bit by the stench of rotting meat. I felt my heart start to pound as I moved deeper and deeper into the woods. I'm a street guy, an urban Detroit alley rat. I may have the mountains in my DNA, but I never spent more than a few weeks at a time around these kinds of woods. And I sure as hell never went banging around in them after dark. So — yeah — I was tense.

I was just starting to fret that I'd miss the landmark when, just to my right, there it was. Silhouetted by moonlight, it looked like a Ford. The Mainline Tudor, probably a 'fifty-four; who could tell. And who knew how it ended up here, miles from any road, crumpled up and wedged against a tree, with another, newer tree fallen down over it.

It was really dark now. Stars blanketed the deep black sky, more than I'd ever seen at one time except maybe at that party Raeanne took me to in Nashville. I flicked the penlight on briefly to locate the new trail. And I found it. But this little rocky hen-scratch made the Cohutta Panther Trail seem like the Edsel Ford Freeway.

Twisting and turning, threading among rocks and trees and along cliff lips, the trail snaked this way and that but mostly uphill — sometimes straight up the slope. I learned three things. My running shoes were entirely wrong for this. Years of cigar smoking had

left me with little stamina for these grades. And my knees and ankles were pretty well shot. I was born and raised in the flatlands, I
thought as I puffed along. I needed to get back there and stay
there.

Sounds from above.

I froze. Crouched. Listened. Breezes sounded among the thick
trees around me, but there was definitely noise from up there.
Music.

Not far now.

It was full dark. The moonlight helped some, but it was a devious
trickster, hiding as much as revealing. Ahead I could see an opening, and the trees ended at an artificial clearing. Straight up the
slope — mostly a sleek rock face — I saw the cabin. I was on the
deck side, its posts extending twenty feet or more down to the
earth. Farther up, under the deck, I could make out the concrete
piers that kept the structure from bobsledding down to Dahlon-
ega. Light blazed out lower and upper windows. The music grew:
"Squeeze Box," by the Who.

I hunkered down on my haunches to survey, to plot strategy, and,
oh yeah, to give my aching lungs and knees a break. The cabin's
lower-level doors and windows were clearly visible, but I couldn't
see anyone inside. Due to the angle, I couldn't tell if anyone was on
the deck. Billy & Company had to be home, but who knew where.
The deck rail was deserted, though. And so was the fire pit, off to
the right.

So much for "Kumbaya."

Taking a deep breath, I rose and tore up the rocky slope, running crouched and leaning forward. No cries of alarm issued from
above. I made it to the concrete patio under the deck. Flat solid
ground at last, thank God. I backed up to the cabin wall next to the
door wall and peered in. Pool table, foosball machine, the big flat-
screen TV flickering. No people.

All right.

"Squeeze Box" started over. The door was locked. I applied the
key. Inside, billiard balls were scattered across the green tabletop,
cue sticks leaned from the floor, beer cans lined the edge. From upstairs boomed muffled male voices. Laughter, too. The TV played.
It was a porn video. Jerky, silent, amateur, a close-up of some blond
woman, slowly fellating. After a bit, a glimpse of the man's face.
Billy Suttles. Ah, man . . .

"Forgot my beer!" came a male voice up above. Footsteps thundered down the stairs. I ducked into the bedroom and retreated into a dark corner. From where I hid I could just glimpse Billy's slope-shouldered pal, Bowling-Ball Belly. He grabbed a beer off the pool table, and as he turned for the stair, I saw a camcorder swinging by a strap from his neck.

When he'd thumped back upstairs, I crept out of the bedroom. The voices, laughter, shouting kept rolling from above. "Squeeze Box" started again. Time to see for myself. Picking up a cue stick, I started up the carpeted staircase, treading carefully at the edges to avoid creaking. Several steps up, the staircase turned. I peered around the corner. Up top the door was almost shut. Holding the cue stick in one hand and the stair rail in the other, I headed up some more, one slow step at a time, till I could see through the door crack.

It was the kitchen area. No table. The big brown recliner had been pushed into the brightly lit eating area, next to windows looking out on the deck. On the recliner lay Wendee — at least, I assumed it was her. I could not see her face, just her legs, raised knees, torso, flaccid breasts jouncing. Billy's shaved-headed pal, *#3* ball cap swiveled bill backward, stood tight between her thighs, gripping her knees, rutting her for all he was worth, grunting. Wendee was silent.

"Fuck her, Ricky!" boomed Billy from somewhere. "Fuck that slut."

The Who hammered on. So did Number 3. Wendee shook and wobbled. My mind went stark-white blank. Without thought, without plan, I flung the door back and stepped through, cue stick in both fists. Billy was outside in the hot tub, watching the action through the open windows. Bowling-Ball Belly was to my right, camcorder raised, grinning into the viewfinder at 3 and Wendee, who looked unconscious or nearly so.

Rearing back with the cue stick, I yelled, "Three in the corner!" and swung. The fat end smashed Ricky flush alongside the head, snapping the cue stick clean in half and sending him and his ball cap flying. Ball Belly broke for the door. Spinning, I hurled the busted-off chunk of cue stick. Like a rope from third to first, at which I had always excelled, the shaft flew true, poleaxing him just at the base of the neck, crashing him to the floor.

Wendee lay sprawled and limp on the recliner, arms back, wrists tied with silk scarves to the window handles. Her eyeballs stared out at nothing, puffy lips moving soundlessly. Splashing sounded outside as Billy clambered swiftly out of the hot tub. I ran to the open door to see his naked hairy ass vanish down the stair. "Get back here, asshole!" I shouted, and charged after him. By the time I thundered to the stair bottom, he had disappeared down the slope into the forest blackness. No point in chasing him. Barefoot, naked, with no dough or ID, he wouldn't get far. And I was needed inside.

"Squeeze Box" restarted as I crossed the deck by the humming hot tub. On a small plastic table I saw a wallet, keys, expensive wristwatch, and money clip stuffed thick with folded currency. I didn't even think about it. I stuck the clip into my jeans.

Inside, Wendee shifted and moaned softly. Blood crusted her lower lip, and her arms and ribs looked bruised. I untied her wrists, and she immediately pulled into fetal position. Number 3 lay in the kitchen corner, skinny, naked but for his tank top, head oozing red, out of it. Bowling-Ball Belly, in shorts and tank top, groaned as he climbed the wall painfully to his feet. The camcorder still dangled from his neck. I snapped off the Who and went toward him. "You all right?" I asked, taking his arm.

"You really hurt me, man," he mumbled.

"Come on," I said. "Let's get you to a chair." I wrapped my arm around him, helped him into the kitchen. "Take a deep breath. You'll be okay."

"Ya busted up our weekend," he mumbled as we neared the open basement door.

"Oh, it's your *weekend* I busted up?" With a hard shove I flung him through the doorway out into the open air of the staircase. A quick yelp cut short when he landed on the stairs about halfway down. Hurtling into the wall with a thunderous crash, he ricocheted over to the bottom. Then silence.

"Oops," I said.

Pulling my phone, I went to find a blanket for the girl.

"GHB?" I asked.

"That," Deputy Pike answered, "or something like it. Tox screen'll tell us, maybe."

"Poor girl," Caroleen murmured.

We sat in a spare windowless interview room at a scarred steel table. My formal statement had taken a lot longer than Caroleen's. It was very late and I was beat, but there were things I wanted to know, and the deputy seemed talkative.

Pike, in tans and leather and a thin lined mug very deadpan even for a cop, said, "Yessir, besides this injured gal, quite a score you racked up. Skull fracture on Clinginpeel. The other one, Flemma, got him a broken arm, broken leg, concussion, dislocated shoulder."

I knew where he was headed, and I would not go there if I could help it. "But he's whistling Dixie anyways, huh?" I asked.

Caroleen shot me a look. Pike remained impassive. "Yessir, he's smart enough to know, him that first flips gets the goodies." He shifted. "Told us this Suttles guy set up the whole thing. Met Miz Sakstrup online, romanced her, got her all starry-eyed, then invited her here." Pike's tone got sarcastically precise. "For a romantic getaway weekend."

"At least, that's what *she* thought," I said.

"Right. 'Play-toy Weekend' was what Clinginpeel called it. Him and Suttles and Flemma — they're old high school buddies, always up to some shit — every year they come up here for Final Four, booze, and a doped-up girl to gangbang."

"It's *The Big Chill*," I said. "Updated for the oh-oh decade."

Pike looked blank. "Reckon."

Caroleen, pale and grim, said, "And they've been doing this for years. In my cabin. To all these women." She looked at the deputy, seething. "I hope you throw the book at these bastards. For Wendee, and the other women, too."

"If we find them," Pike said. "They never came forward."

"Prob'ly the videos," I said.

Pike nodded. "Clinginpeel said Suttles picked 'em smart. Married ladies with good reputations, easy to blackmail silent afterward. So unless Suttles decides to tell all, I — 'scuse me."

He pulled out a cell phone and put it to his ear. "Yessir." His deadpan did not change. "All right." Putting his phone away, he said, "They found Suttles over by Fighting Town Creek. Dead."

"Dead," Caroleen echoed.

"How?" I asked.

"Heart blew out," Pike answered. "Best guess right now."

"Huh," I said. "Top-shape guy like him, heart gives out."

"And who'd a thought," Caroleen put in, "he actually had one."

*

Caroleen followed me off her porch to the Fusion. Her jeans and sleeveless green top looked slept in. Dark circles rimmed her eyes. No doubt I looked worse. We'd been with the cops half the night, and what sleep I'd gotten afterward had been fitful.

"Sure you won't stay over?" she asked as I threw my duffel into the car.

"Much obliged," I said, facing her. "But I need to get home."

"Well. All right." Stepping forward impulsively, she took me in her arms, squeezed me tight, surprised me with a quick kiss full on the lips. Stepping back, she said faintly, "Thank you. For all your help. You done good."

"Glad I could do it," I answered. And I meant it. I'd come here for a break, but what I got was, for this point in my life, even better. Some clues to puzzle through, a lady in danger, a moonlit stroll through the woods, and a stick-swinging head-bashing brawl to put out of business some seriously bad guys.

"When you come back to testify," she said, "stay here with me. I mean it."

Ready for that, I said, "Ah, that's sweet. But I'll prob'ly just grab a room."

"Benjy, no. I couldn't let you do that."

"I've imposed on you enough."

"We're family," she said earnestly, cornflower eyes sparkling.

I could still feel her lips on mine. "I'll prob'ly bring my girlfriend next time," I added, with no idea who the hell I meant.

"More'n welcome."

"Rachel, too."

"Love to meet your little gal."

Jingling the car keys, I turned to the door. "Nice of you, though. Thanks." I got in, shut the door, started the engine. Backed the car around and was about to take off when I saw Caroleen coming toward me, making the crank-down signal.

"If you come stay with me," she said, "I'll whomp you up a mess of pecan-crusted catfish and hush puppies, with okra, tomatoes, and turnip greens so tart they'll make the tears roll down your cheeks."

"Sold." I grinned, and drove off.

Room 522 was at the end of the hall on the second floor of the Gilmer County Medical Facility. The far bed was empty; in the near one under a sheet lay a dark-haired woman plugged into a drip, face averted. A guest chair sat at the head of the bed, occupied by a burly sandy-haired mustached man in khakis and polo shirt. At first he didn't realize I was there. Then, startled, he rose. "H'ep you?"

"I'm, uh . . . My name is Ben. And you're —"

"Jim Sakstrup." He neither smiled nor offered a hand.

"Ben Perkins. I was with . . ." Oh hell, how do I put this? When in doubt, lie. "The cabin landlady asked me to stop by."

He just nodded, pale and stricken, lips bloodless. "I just got here. From Spartanburg." He gestured at the chair, his jacket hanging on its back. "Please. Sit."

"Thank you, sir, but I've got a plane. Just wanted to look in."

We stared at the bed in silence. Sakstrup said, "I'm taking her home tomorrow."

"Good."

"Right now she's sedated."

"Prob'ly best."

"Sher'ff said . . ." His voice was drying out. He tried again. "Sher'ff told me . . ."

"It's all right."

"I just don't get it," he said. "I had no idea. How she could be so sad. So angry. How she could just . . . lie to me and the kids, over and over, for months. And end up here. Like this. After going through *that.*"

I didn't have to ask what *that* was. "Gotta be painful."

"World turned upside-down."

"Can't imagine."

Another long silence. Then he said, voice a squeak, "Beg pardon," and quickly left the room.

I stared at Wendee Sakstrup for a while. I had things to say to her, but women often don't hear me, even when conscious. Her roll bag and makeup kit sat on a bench at the foot of the bed. I took the currency from my pocket, started for her bag. Then stopped, thought.

Glancing toward the door, I went to the chair, tucked the money into the jacket pocket, and left.

"This, I take it," Raeanne said in my ear, "was the money you stole from Suttles?"

"Steal, my ass. He didn't need it."

"Well. True. As it turned out. But you couldn't have known that."

"And anyway, I only gave the guy half."

"The rest you kept?"

"Left it with Caroleen."

"That must have pleased her."

"Wouldn't know. I stuck it on her bill spindle when she wasn't looking."

Interstate 575 merged with I-75, thickening up the inbound Atlanta traffic.

Raeanne said, "I do have one bone to pick."

Just one? "Okay."

"You meant the money for Wendee. Instead you gave it to her husband."

"Right."

"To me — as a woman — that suggests you blame Wendee for what happened to her. Because she stepped out on her husband. But *none* of it was her fault. She was purely a victim of some dirty rotten bastards."

"No doubt."

Silence. "Sorry, Ben," she said stubbornly, "but that's what I think. Taking the money was theft. And what you did with it was not justice."

Well, I thought later, neat clean resolutions are nice. But out here in real life, the difference usually gets split. What I did was almost theft. But not quite. And not quite justice either, but it was as close as we were ever likely to get.

ROBERT MCCLURE

My Son

FROM *Thuglit*

I AM A WEEK out of San Quentin when my son pulls to the curb in his Crown Victoria Police Interceptor, an unmarked one that reeks of crack. The odor stings my nose when I lean into the passenger window and say, "Hey, want to come in the house, maybe have a drink?"

"At ten in the morning?" he says, and the way my son looks at me makes him a kid again in my mind: he is ignoring my question about a book he thinks I'd never understand, or he is behind the glass wall of a prison visitation cubicle, gawking like I am a snake on display at the zoo.

What I sorely want to say to him is, What, you would rather us cruise around and get stoned in your pig rig? But I know it would ignite the tension hanging in the air with the crack fumes. So instead I say, "After paying my eight-year debt to society, I am entitled to twenty-four happy hours per day. C'mon, let's get reacquainted before we get going."

His bloodshot eyes burn holes through the windshield.

No, it would take a logging chain and two-ton truck to drag him inside my house. I realize at this moment that my son has a bad feeling about the shitty little bungalow he grew up in, this nostalgic juju that has his head spinning with thoughts of where we started and where we are now, of where we are going to end up.

I toss my car keys in his lap, and I am thinking, *Son, please, do not make our journey more complicated than it is.*

He exits his car and flops behind the wheel of my new Caddy. I tell him to skip the expressway and take the scenic route through the heart of Boyle Heights, Cesar Chavez Avenue, a street called Brooklyn Avenue when I grew up there. I say I want to enjoy the sights — the crazy murals painted on buildings, the street vendors, the new businesses that have sprung up here and there, et cetera, et cetera, et cetera.

He does what I say but does not like it.

I do not care what he likes.

Even after enjoying a week of it at full throttle, freedom still makes me so giddy that nothing much bothers me, even a mute son I have not seen in nine years. The things I notice out the window are a punk boutique, a tattoo joint, and two Chink babes I know are streetwalkers, and I savor the fact I can patronize any of these conveniences at my whim, permission needed from no one.

My son ignores my comments to that effect, seems somehow put off by them, so in a further effort to break the ice, I tell old lard-ass a lie. "Well, uh, you look great, kid. Really great."

He says nothing, and here I was, vainly expecting a return compliment.

For laughs, I slap his thigh, and he jerks as if I had grabbed his dick.

My son, you see, never adjusted to the touch of other human beings. Even refused to let his mother breastfeed him, and would let her hold him just long enough to suck his bottle dry. I picture her in the rocking chair by his crib with her arms crossed, returning my son's stare and saying, "It's unnatural for him to cry every time I hold him. It's too fucking strange to contemplate."

"Well, look at that," I say to him, pointing to my left, "El Parrilla is still open after all these years. Say, how 'bout we pull in and order up some burritos for a late breakfast? You still like steak burritos for breakfast, right?"

He looks at his watch, his anxiety self-evident. His eyes appear ready to pop their sockets, and sweat dots his brow. He knuckles his right eyeball as if to reseat it and cuffs the moisture from his mouth. "We don't have time. Macky'll get pissed if we're late."

I smile. "I will handle Macky. How many times do I have to tell you I will handle him, huh? How many?" I have repeated this fact to him often over the last two days, probably more often than I have ever said any one thing to him.

He looks relieved in a hesitant way; like the only time I ever took him to the doctor, the time I told him the penicillin shot would hurt just a second, then make him feel brand-new.

"I really want to get this over with," he says. "Let's eat after we meet with Macky."

For an instant I forget all about that lump-of-shit Macky, am jubilant to the point of almost wetting my shorts. It is shameful, I know, to get so excited just because my son agreed to eat a simple meal with me. It is nonetheless a heartfelt reaction that in fact makes my heart race, and I actually feel it pound against the two tickets tucked in my breast pocket. I almost ask if he wants to catch the Dodgers game this afternoon, then decide to save the invitation for breakfast.

My smile gets bigger. After all these years, sometimes I actually know when not to push my fucking luck.

Not that my so-called Life of Crime has been an unfortunate one, at least when viewed in strict economic terms. I have hijacked semitrailers chocked with electronics and cigarettes, burglarized mansions and jewelry stores, smuggled drugs, et cetera, et cetera, et cetera, and took only two falls in the process. The falls were hard ones, I admit, that consumed almost a third of my fifty-two years. To me, though, living the Life has always been about taking big risks to achieve big rewards. I got caught two times — so what? I say think positive, consider I got a free pass on the thousand other times I did *not* get caught. Seventeen years, two months, and thirteen days served for a thousand and two criminal acts, all more or less profitable. Not bad, especially when you further consider prison was not totally unbearable for a connected guy like me, and though never what most people would call rich, I always had enough money tucked away to provide for the wife and kid in absentia.

Some say that was my big mistake, throwing away so many hard-earned shekels on people who turned out to be ingrates — a sex-aholic wife and everything-aholic son, two slightly different animals of the same species.

They are right about the wife, to my eternal embarrassment, but women who forget their marriage vows are easily disposed of (to say nothing — repeat, *nothing* — of the so-called friend who induces her to break said vows while you are incarcerated). Sons are different. Whatever indignity he suffers at the hand of his son, a father cannot beat him to within an inch of death, finish him off with a bullet to the head, then reduce his body to sludge in a barrel of nitric acid. A son is the product of his father's labors — or the lack thereof — and for that reason a father's love for his son depends on nothing except that his son is his son.

Believe me when I say these things. These are things I know above all else.

We leave Boyle Heights when we merge on 60 East toward Pomona, are on 605 a few minutes, then take I-10 toward San Bernardino. We are at the West Covina ramp before you know it.

We drive side roads for around ten minutes, then pull into the parking lot.

My son says, "It's a setup. I can feel it."

He parks at the end of a row of luxury cars, and I say, "Nah, this old warehouse has just got you spooked, that's all." I look it over and make some professional observations: "We are, what, over four miles outside town? Christ, you could fight a war out here and never upset a civilian ear. It's a perfect place for a hit, all right."

This is not what he wants to hear.

I recognize this and say right away, "But Macky would've already whacked you if that's what he wanted to do. Relax."

He asks me a question that comes from nowhere, as if it is something that has occupied his mind all along: "Why are you doing this for me? *Why?*"

My son and I are communicating here, making progress, and a small lump rises in my throat. I think a few beats and almost come clean with him, almost reveal all there is to know about the meeting with Macky. I change my mind when I realize I cannot predict his reaction, that he might spoil the dynamics of it all.

"Why else?" I say, and change the subject. "A condition of the sit-down is that we be unarmed. Hand over your weapons."

He unholsters his department-issued Sig Sauer from under his jean jacket, hands it over with no complaints — something of a surprise to me.

I tuck the pistol under the seat, then look him in the eye. "Your throw-down, too. I know you have one."

He pouts, and I hold out my hand and wiggle my fingers. "C'mon, *c'mon* . . ."

He sighs and reaches for his right ankle, unsnaps the peashooter he has strapped there, and palms it to me while looking the other way.

"You got a knife on you, can of Mace, stun gun, any other weapon at all?"

"All I have now is you," he says to the window, and turns to give me that hesitant look of semi-confidence again.

We no sooner set foot on the pavement than a guy walks on the loading dock wearing a beat-up black suit, white shirt, and black tie. I recognize him as Jack Barzi, a mass of muscle with hippy-long and graying hair; everybody called him "Chief" in the old days because he resembled that big injun in the movie *One Flew Over the Cuckoo's Nest.* He has not changed much.

I stroll up to Chief like I am here to buy the place. He is standing a good four feet above me on the dock and looks twenty feet tall. I remove my Ray-Ban Aviators. "Chief? You work for Macky now?"

He nods and twists his mouth around to make it resemble a smile. "Long time, Babe. You ain't changed a bit."

I give him a smile that is genuine. Finally someone recognizes Babe Crucci for the Grade A physical specimen he is, living proof of the adage that age is only a number. My youthful appearance is mostly genetic; the rest of it is attributable to the weights I humped religiously in prison and the food in there I could barely eat enough of to stay alive.

I say to Chief, "Except for the hair, you're hanging in there pretty good yourself." I take out my wallet and dig inside it. "Look, here's my hairdresser's card. Call her, and she'll get rid of that gray for you. My treat."

"You get your hair dyed?" he says, takes the card and says, "I'll be damned," while squinting to examine my hair. He fingers the locks on his shoulder, inspecting them like they are someone else's, and laughs that grunty laugh of his. "Macky says you only been outta the Q a week?"

"Macky speaks the truth."

He digs in his wallet and hands me a card. "This'll connect you to the best call-girl service in L.A. First pop's on me. Just tell 'em I sent ya."

"Good deal," I say, though I am certain I have already found the best call girls in L.A., best in the world even.

Chief looks satisfied before he looks at my son, then his lips snap back to their natural snarl. After a few seconds of this he squats, motions me over with a tug of his head. In a low voice he says, "Babe, listen . . . between you and me. I don't know everything going on here, but I've heard bits and pieces that worry me. Macky pays me — all right? — and I gotta do my job — okay? — so be careful. Don't do nothin' loopy."

"Hey," I say, "you know I do not do loopy things."

"Maybe," he says, with the slightest twinkle in his eye, "but you never been convicted of bein' careful neither."

Chief frisks us, then leads us inside, through an area big enough to store the cargo off an ocean liner that now contains nothing but hundreds of wooden pallets stacked against support beams and concrete walls, into a maze consisting of two stairwells and three hallways. All of it dark and dusty and in need of pest extermination and paint, then into an elevator. We exit the elevator and are walloped with blasts of cleanliness and fluorescent light, walk down a blue-carpeted hallway.

We stop before a metal door and Chief raises an eyebrow at me, no doubt a reminder of the friendly advice he rendered outside. "See ya later," he says. "I haveta go back downstairs."

"Hold down the fort," I say, and give him a wink that I can tell makes him uncomfortable.

I open the door.

Three goons are in the reception area, probably Macky's A Team. They are polluting the atmosphere with wiseguy talk until they see me, then silence grows so thick in the air you can hear the humidity rise.

They sneer and shrug and straighten their jackets and ties.

Before I can ask where Macky is, the fat hump appears at his office door.

"Babe Crucci!" he says, with outstretched arms. "Paisan!"

Paisan, shit. Macky's no more Italian than Sammy Davis Jr. was. He's a fucking mick with a *Godfather* complex, a punk paddy with Pacino pretensions. He has the kind of Irish face Mama always warned you about — dirty red hair, rheumy eyes, and a bloated, splotchy complexion that reminds me of a diseased lung.

I do not usually allow men to hug me — call me homophobic, go ahead, it is still behavior that sends confusing signals on the old cellblock — but circumstances dictate I let Macky do so today.

The Hug is over with, and Macky turns to my son. "So you're Leo."

"Wow," he says, "you figured that out all by yourself?" and starts to light a smoke.

At which point Macky slaps him in the mouth so hard the cigarette ricochets off the wall a good twenty feet away.

Macky steps back and smiles at his bodyguards, who have all pulled their weapons by now.

I prevent my son from doing something stupid by placing my hand on his chest.

Macky turns to me. "Sorry you had to see that, Babe."

I hold out both hands in a conciliatory manner. "You had the right," I say, and part of me is in total agreement, that part of me that wishes I had been around more to properly discipline my son.

The other part of me wants to rip out Macky's heart and bite a chunk from it before his horror-stricken eyes.

It will be that kind of meeting.

Macky closes the office door and sits behind his too-big desk. Me and my son ease into the chairs across from him, and Macky takes a chrome-plated revolver — which is also too big — from the desk drawer and makes a production of assuring it is loaded, unlatching and spinning the cylinder, then flipping it shut. He places it on the desktop, grinning like the cocky asshole he has just confirmed that he is.

"No disrespect intended, Babe, but I was shocked to learn that you are standing up for this pitiful excuse for a son." He looks at him. "A cop. A drug addict. A lousy gambler who don't pay his debts. 'Pathetic' is the best word that comes to mind."

I seethe a few seconds before I say, "He has certain compulsions that he cannot presently control. But — and I say this as objectively as any father can — he also has certain qualities that make him worthy of redemption."

This is a true statement. My son has a good head for academics, especially for math, and has a business administration degree. And he was always as proficient and enthusiastic a street fighter as his father ever was; just ask any of the old neighborhood bullies who don't walk or talk quite right anymore. Better yet, ask any of the so-called criminals who have filed complaints of excessive force against him, and I hear there are quite a few.

Macky looks so bored he is practically yawning, so I take a thick envelope from my breast pocket and toss it over the desk to him. "In any event, this is not about him. It is a matter of honor with me," and I say this because this is the kind of corny goodfella crap I know impresses Macky.

And he is in fact impressed. He sighs after a long few seconds and says, "Well, I certainly understand that," and nods and shrugs as if he would never allow a standup guy like me to dishonor himself. Like he is only accepting the money for my benefit.

He finally picks up the envelope and peeks inside it, thumbs through the bills absent-mindedly like he knows it is all there. He looks up. "I demanded that both of you be here in person so I can make something very clear." He points a fat finger at my son. "The only reason you're not dead or at least seriously fucked up is because I've known your father for years. This is the only pass you get. Ever welsh on another betting tab with one of my guys? I'll have you slaughtered like an Easter lamb — Crucci or no Crucci, cop or no cop. Understood?"

My son barely nods.

Macky looks at me.

I nod.

Macky appears satisfied.

I rise and prepare to say, *We now have no conflicts and no debts between us,* a take on a line from *Godfather III* that I know will make Macky want to hug me again.

But Macky does not stand. Instead he leans back in his chair, picks up the revolver, and rests it on his bloated stomach. "Not yet, Babe. I want to talk about something else."

I sit.

"You need a job?" Macky says.

My son rustles in his seat.

I am not surprised by the question, because I know for a fact my so-called unemployment is the subject of much talk and conjecture on the street. "Why do you ask?" I say.

Macky smiles. "I hear you're not working for Sacci anymore."

"He will not take me back," I say, "because he has problems with him," nudging my head toward my son, "that are similar to the ones I just resolved with you."

This is a true statement.

Macky nods understanding. "You pay him yet?"

"I offered, but he will not return my calls."

This is also a true statement.

He looks disgusted. "Sacci, the prick, never had no sense of justice, no honor . . . Look, you know about Victor Tarasov?" he asks.

"Not much."

This is *not* a true statement.

Macky turns solemn, and his face becomes even more inflamed than usual. "Tarasov's a Russian who's been establishing a growing presence here in L.A. for a couple years now. He's trying to take over my drug and gambling trade. Shit, eliminate me from the face of the fuckin' planet is what he wants to do. I need good men like you to protect my interests. Men who will permanently see to it that Tarasov will no longer present a competitive threat."

He winks, as if a wink is necessary for me to understand the underlying meaning of the latter comment.

I pause as if I am thinking it over — though what I am really doing is savoring the irony of all this. Then we talk amicably about the proposed salary, the car he will provide, et cetera, et cetera, et cetera. I say, "Sure, on those terms I will help you address this Russian menace."

This is *not* a true statement.

I say further, "I have admired and respected you from afar these many years," which is not true either, "and swear upon the soul of my dead mother that I will be loyal to you till my bones turn to dust." Ditto.

Macky is so clearly moved by this goombah bullshit, the likes of which I have heard uttered only in movies, that his eyes mist up.

He rises from his chair, places the revolver back on the desk, and walks around the desk to give me the Welcome-Aboard Hug. "I've always wanted you in my family. C'mere, you big wop, you're one of us now."

I am very relieved he does not hold out his fucking hand for me to kiss, which would have sent me into such a fit of uncontrolled laughter that it would have spoiled everything.

He gives me the Hug, and I enthusiastically return it.

We separate a few inches and look into each other's eyes. I pat his cheek affectionately. "Macky?"

"Yeah, Babe?"

"Victor Tarasov wanted me to say goodbye to you on his behalf," and I clutch his trachea by sticking three fingers just below his voice box on one side and poking the thumb behind the other side, then squeeze my fingers together and twist with all my might.

To learn how to crush a trachea, surround a fat carrot with, say, two sticks of celery. Wrap a flank steak around the entire concoction. Anchor it in a vise, then hold the top steady with one hand and perform the above procedure with your dominant hand — a forceful squeeze followed by a mighty twist. The carrot should be cleanly broken and the celery reduced to a juicy pulp when you unwrap them. If the latter two events do not occur, do not try to kill someone in this fashion — instead, go to the gym.

Macky's unconscious if not dead already, his face turning reddish blue and streaked by a very pallid white.

At the other end of the spectrum is my son's face, which is drained of all color. He lights the wrong end of a cigarette and takes a deep drag before his eyes go wide at the flaming tip. He nonetheless takes another drag, then stares at me and moves his mouth soundlessly, looking like a big fish that needs to jump back in the lake for a dose of oxygen.

I have my son's rapt attention.

So I allow the weight of Macky's body to lower itself to its knees. I halt its descent, step behind it, cup the chin in the palm of my left hand, and grab a hunk of hair with my right. In a rapid counterclockwise motion, I twist the head.

The neck snaps.

My son flinches.

Try as I might, I have never figured out the right combination of inanimate materials that realistically simulate the sensation of snapping a human neck. You can, of course, practice on stray dogs that shit in your yard; the bigger they are, the better. But if you are a kid, I do not recommend you do this to the pet German shepherd you name Adolf who bites you one too many times. Your parents will ask far too many questions.

I ease the carcass to the floor.

My son is relatively composed now, has lit the business end of a fresh smoke, and is gazing wistfully upon the scene.

"Did I really just see what I think I just saw?"

"No, so forget about it."

He smiles. "How much did Tarasov pay you to do that?"

"Kid, I am *flush.*"

His expression now is one that can only be described as "avaricious."

I continue: "Um, sorry I didn't warn you in advance, but —"

He waves me off. "I might've ruined it." Then his expression mutates to one of concern, and he nods at the door. "Hey, how are we, you know, gonna get out of here alive?"

"Oh, *them,*" I say. "They will be no problem." Then I tell him my very straightforward plan: I surprise the bodyguards outside with Macky's pistol, and he ties them up with the pull cords from the window blinds.

"What about the gorilla downstairs?"

"Chief?"

"Yeah."

"I will tell him what happened, then offer him a job with me and Tarasov. Me and Chief are friends, plus he needs work now. He will be no . . ."

He is pouting.

"What now?" I say.

"Why not offer me a job? I — I don't think I can be a cop much longer . . . even if I wanted to."

The way my son looks at me makes him a kid again in my mind, like the times he asked to go to baseball games with me and I ignored him and breezed out the door.

I retrieve the revolver from the desktop, to say nothing of the fat envelope of cash next to it. I move to the door with my son in tow. I conceal the gun behind my back and grip the doorknob. I hesitate and whisper to him, "All right, we can talk over breakfast about you working with me and Tarasov."

He nods in a satisfied manner. "Man, am I ever hungry. Steak burritos, right?"

"At El Parrilla," I say, and start to turn the knob. Before I do, though, I cannot help but ask, "Hey, after breakfast, you want to go to the Dodgers game with me?"

I know, *I know,* I was supposed to wait till breakfast to ask him that. But the thing is, now I have little doubt what his answer will be.

ALICE MUNRO

Free Radicals

FROM *The New Yorker*

AT FIRST people kept phoning, to make sure that Nita was not too depressed, not too lonely, not eating too little or drinking too much. (She had been such a diligent wine drinker that many forgot that she was now forbidden to drink at all.) She held them off, without sounding nobly grief-stricken or unnaturally cheerful or absent-minded or confused. She said that she didn't need groceries; she was working through what she had on hand. She had enough of her prescription pills and enough stamps for her thank-you notes.

Her closer friends probably suspected the truth — that she was not bothering to eat much and that she threw out any sympathy note she happened to get. She had not even informed the people who lived at a distance, to elicit such notes. Not Rich's ex-wife in Arizona or his semi-estranged brother in Nova Scotia, though those two might have understood, perhaps better than the people near at hand, why she had proceeded with the nonfuneral as she had done.

Rich had told her that he was going to the village, to the hardware store. It was around ten o'clock in the morning, and he had just started to paint the railing of the deck. That is, he'd been scraping it to prepare for the painting, and the old scraper had come apart in his hand.

She hadn't had time to wonder about his being late. He'd died bent over the sidewalk sign that stood in front of the hardware store offering a discount on lawnmowers. He hadn't even managed to get into the store. He'd been eighty-one years old and in fine health, aside from some deafness in his right ear. His doctor had checked him over only the week before. Nita was to learn that the recent checkup, the clean bill of health, cropped up in a surprising number of the sudden-death stories that she was now presented with. "You'd almost think that such visits ought to be avoided," she'd said.

She should have spoken like this only to her close and fellow badmouthing friends, Virgie and Carol, women around her own age, which was sixty-two. Her younger friends found this sort of talk unseemly and evasive. At first they had crowded in on Nita. They had not actually spoken of the grieving process, but she had been afraid that at any moment they might start.

As soon as she got on with the arrangements, of course, all but the tried and true had fallen away. The cheapest box, into the ground immediately, no ceremony of any kind. The undertaker had suggested that this might be against the law, but she and Rich had had their facts straight. They'd got their information almost a year before, when the diagnosis of her cancer became final.

"How was I to know he'd steal my thunder?" she'd said.

People had not expected a traditional service, but they had looked forward to some kind of contemporary affair. Celebrating the life. Playing his favorite music, holding hands together, telling stories that praised Rich while touching humorously on his quirks and forgivable faults.

The sort of thing that Rich had said made him puke.

So it was dealt with privately, and soon the stir, the widespread warmth that had surrounded Nita, melted away, though some people, she supposed, were likely still saying that they were concerned about her. Virgie and Carol didn't say that. They said only that she was a selfish bloody bitch if she was thinking of conking out now, any sooner than was necessary. They would come around, they said, and revive her with Grey Goose.

She assured them that she wasn't, though she could see a certain logic to the idea.

Thanks to the radiation last spring, her cancer was at present in remission — whatever that actually meant. It did not mean gone. Not for good, anyway. Her liver was the main theater of operations, and as long as she stuck to nibbles it did not complain. It would only have depressed her friends to remind them that she couldn't have wine, let alone vodka.

*

Rich died in June. Now here it is midsummer. She gets out of bed early and washes herself and dresses in anything that comes to hand. But she does dress and wash, and she brushes her teeth and combs her hair, which has grown back decently, gray around her face and dark at the back, the way it was before. She puts on lipstick and pencils her eyebrows, which are now very scanty, and out of her lifelong respect for a narrow waist and moderate hips, she checks on the achievements she has made in that direction, though she knows that the proper word for all parts of her now might be "scrawny."

She sits in her usual ample armchair, with piles of books and unopened magazines around her. She sips cautiously from the mug of weak herbal tea that is now her substitute for coffee. At one time she thought that she could not live without coffee, but it turned out that it was really just the large warm mug she wanted in her hands, that was the aid to thought or whatever it was she practiced through the procession of hours, or of days.

This was Rich's house. He'd bought it when he was with his first wife, Bett. It had been intended as a weekend place, closed up in the winter. Two tiny bedrooms, a lean-to kitchen, half a mile from the village. But soon Rich had begun working on it, learning carpentry, building a wing for two new bedrooms and a bathroom and another wing for his study, turning the original house into an open-plan living room, dining room, kitchen. Bett had become interested; she'd claimed in the beginning not to understand why he'd bought such a dump, but practical improvements always engaged her, and she bought matching carpenter's aprons. She'd needed something to become involved in, having finished and published the cookbook that had occupied her for several years. They'd had no children.

And at the same time that Bett had been busy telling people that she'd found her role in life as a carpenter's helper and that it had brought her and Rich much closer, Rich had been falling in love with Nita. She'd worked in the registrar's office of the university where he taught medieval literature. The first time they'd made love was amid the shavings and sawn wood of what was to become the house's central room, with its arched ceiling, on a weekend when Bett had stayed in the city. Nita had left her sunglasses behind — not on purpose, though Bett, who never forgot anything,

could not believe that. The usual ruckus followed, trite and painful, and ended with Bett going off to California, then Arizona, Nita
quitting her job at the suggestion of the registrar, and Rich missing
out on becoming dean of arts. He took early retirement, sold the
city house. Nita did not inherit the smaller carpenter's apron, but
she read her books cheerfully in the midst of construction and disorder, made rudimentary dinners on a hot plate, and went for long
exploratory walks, coming back with ragged bouquets of tiger lilies
and wild carrot, which she stuffed into empty paint cans. Later,
when she and Rich had settled down, she felt somewhat embarrassed to think how readily she had played the younger woman,
the happy home-wrecker, the lissome, laughing, tripping ingénue.
She was really a rather serious, physically awkward, self-conscious
woman, who could recite not just the kings but the queens of England and knew the Thirty Years' War backward, but was shy about
dancing in front of people and would never learn, as Bett had, to
get up on a stepladder.

The house had a row of cedars on one side and a railway em-
bankment on the other. The railway traffic had never amounted to
much, and by now there were only a couple of trains a month.
Weeds were lavish between the tracks. One time, when she was on
the verge of menopause, Nita had teased Rich into making love up
there — not on the ties, of course, but on the narrow grass verge
beside them — and they had climbed down inordinately pleased
with themselves.

She thought carefully, every morning when she first took her
seat, of the places where Rich was not. He was not in the smaller
bathroom, where his shaving things still were, along with the prescription pills for various troublesome but not serious ail-
ments which he'd refused to throw out. Nor was he in the bedroom, which she had just tidied and left. Not in the larger
bathroom, which he had entered only to take tub baths. Or in the
kitchen, which had become mostly his domain in the last year. He
was of course not out on the half-scraped deck, ready to peer jok-
ingly in the window — through which she might, in earlier days,
have pretended to be alarmed at the sight of a peeping Tom.

Or in the study. That was where, of all places, his absence had to
be most often verified. At first she had found it necessary to go
to the door and open it and stand there, surveying the piles of pa-

per, the moribund computer, the overflowing files, the books lying open or face-down, as well as crowded on the shelves. Now she could manage just by picturing these things.

One of these days she would have to enter the room. She thought of it as invading. She would have to invade her dead husband's mind. This was one possibility that she had never considered. Rich had seemed to her such a tower of efficiency and competence, so vigorous and firm a presence that she had always believed, quite unreasonably, that he would survive her. Then, in the last year, this had become not a foolish belief at all but in both their minds, she thought, a certainty.

She would deal with the cellar first. It really was a cellar, not a basement. Planks made walkways over the dirt floor, and the small high windows were hung with dirty cobwebs. There was nothing down there that she ever needed. Just Rich's half-filled paint tins, boards of various lengths, tools that were either usable or ready to be discarded. She had opened the door and gone down the steps just once since Rich had died, to see that no lights had been left on and to assure herself that the fuse switches were there, with labels written beside them to tell her which controlled what. When she came up, she had bolted the door as usual, on the kitchen side. Rich used to laugh about that habit of hers, asking what she thought might get in through the stone walls and elf-sized windows to menace them.

Nevertheless, the cellar would be easier to start on; it would be a hundred times easier than the study.

She did make up the bed and tidy her own little messes in the kitchen or the bathroom, but in general the impulse to take on any wholesale sweep of housecleaning was beyond her. She could barely throw out a twisted paper clip or a fridge magnet that had lost its attraction, let alone the dish of Irish coins that she and Rich had brought home from a trip fifteen years ago. Everything seemed to have acquired its own peculiar heft and strangeness.

Carol or Virgie phoned every day, usually toward suppertime, when they must have thought her solitude was least bearable. She told them that she was okay; she would come out of her lair soon. She just needed this time to think and read. And eat and sleep.

It was true, too, except for the part about reading. She sat in her chair surrounded by her books without opening one of them. She had always been such a reader — that was one reason, Rich had said, that she was the right woman for him; she could sit and read and let him alone — but now she couldn't stick to it for even half a page.

She hadn't been just a once-through reader, either. *The Brothers Karamazov, The Mill on the Floss, The Wings of the Dove, The Magic Mountain,* over and over. She would pick one up, planning to read that one special passage, and find herself unable to stop until the whole thing was redigested. She read modern fiction, too. Always fiction. She hated to hear the word "escape" used about fiction. She once might have argued, not just playfully, that it was real life that was the escape. But real life had become too important to argue about.

And now, most strangely, all that was gone. Not just with Rich's death but with her own immersion in illness. She had thought that the change was temporary and the magic of reading would reappear once she was off certain drugs and exhausting treatments.

But apparently not.

Sometimes she tried to explain why, to an imaginary inquisitor.

"I got too busy.".

"So everybody says. Doing what?"

"Too busy paying attention."

"To what?"

"I mean thinking."

"What about?"

"Never mind."

One morning, after sitting for a while, she decided that it was a very hot day. She should get up and turn on the fans. Or she could, with more environmental responsibility, try opening the front and back doors and letting the breeze, if there was any, blow through the house.

She unlocked the front door first. And even before she had allowed half an inch of morning light to show itself, she was aware of a dark stripe cutting that light off.

There was a young man standing outside the screen door, which was hooked.

"Didn't mean to startle you," he said. "I was looking for a doorbell or something. I gave a little knock on the frame here, but I guess you didn't hear me."

"Sorry," she said.

"I'm supposed to look at your fuse box. If you could tell me where it is."

She stepped aside to let him in. She took a moment to remember.

"Yes. In the cellar," she said. "I'll turn the light on. You'll see it."

He shut the door behind him and bent to take off his shoes.

"That's all right," she said. "It's not as if it's raining."

"Might as well, though. I make it a habit. Could leave you dust tracks insteada mud."

She went into the kitchen, not able to sit down again until he left the house.

She opened the cellar door for him as he came up the steps.

"Okay?" she said. "You found it okay?"

"Fine."

She was leading him toward the front door, then realized that there were no footsteps behind her. She turned and saw him still standing in the kitchen.

"You don't happen to have anything you could fix up for me to eat, do you?"

There was a change in his voice — a crack in it, a rising pitch that made her think of a television comedian doing a rural whine. Under the kitchen skylight, she saw that he wasn't as young as she'd thought. When she'd opened the door, she had been aware only of a skinny body, the face dark against the morning glare. The body, as she saw it now, was certainly skinny but more wasted than boyish, affecting a genial slouch. His face was long and rubbery, with prominent light blue eyes. A jokey look, but a persistence, too, as if he generally got his way.

"See, I happen to be a diabetic," he said. "I don't know if you know any diabetics, but the fact is when you get hungry you got to eat. Otherwise your system goes all weird. I shoulda ate before I came in here, but I let myself get in a hurry. You mind if I sit down?"

He was already sitting down at the kitchen table.

"You got any coffee?"

"I have tea. Herbal tea, if you'd like that."

"Sure. Sure."

She measured tea into a strainer, plugged in the kettle, and opened the refrigerator.

"I don't have much on hand," she said. "I have some eggs. Sometimes I scramble an egg and put ketchup on it. Would you like that? I have some English muffins I could toast."

"English, Irish, Yukoranian, I don't care."

She cracked a couple of eggs into the pan, broke up the yolks, and stirred them with a cooking fork, then sliced a muffin and put it into the toaster. She got a plate from the cupboard, set it down in front of him. Then a knife and fork from the cutlery drawer.

"Pretty plate," he said, holding it up as if to see his face in it. Just as she turned her attention back to the eggs, she heard it smash on the floor.

"Oh, mercy me," he said in a new voice, a squeaky and definitely nasty voice. "Look what I gone and done."

"It's all right," she said, knowing now that nothing was.

"Musta slipped through my fingers."

She got down another plate, set it on the counter until she was ready to put the toasted muffin halves and the eggs smeared with ketchup on top of it.

He had stooped down, meanwhile, to gather up the pieces of broken china. He held up one piece that had broken so that it had a sharp point to it. As she set his meal down on the table, he scraped the point lightly down his bare forearm. Tiny beads of blood appeared, at first separate, then joining to form a string.

"It's okay," he said. "It's just a joke. I know how to do it for a joke. If I'd've wanted to be serious, we wouldn't've needed no ketchup, eh?"

There were still some pieces on the floor that he had missed. She turned away, thinking to get the broom, which was in a closet near the back door. He caught her arm in a flash.

"You sit down. You sit right here while I'm eating," he said. He lifted the bloodied arm to show it to her again. Then he made a sandwich out of the muffin and the eggs and ate it in a very few bites. He chewed with his mouth open. The kettle was boiling.

"Tea bag in the cup?" he said.

"Yes. It's loose tea, actually."

"Don't you move. I don't want you near that kettle, do I?"

He poured boiling water through the strainer into the cup.

"Looks like hay. Is that all you got?"

"I'm sorry. Yes."

"Don't go on saying you're sorry. If it's all you got, it's all you got. You never did think I come here to look at the fuse box, did you?"

"Well, yes," Nita said. "I did."

"You don't now. You scared?"

She chose to consider this not as a taunt but as a serious question.

"I don't know. I'm more startled than scared, I guess. I don't know."

"One thing. One thing you don't need to be scared of. I'm not going to rape you."

"I hardly thought so."

"You can't never be too sure." He took a sip of the tea and made a face. "Just because you're an old lady. There's all kinds out there — they'll do it to anything. Babies or dogs and cats or old ladies. Old men. They're not fussy. Well, I am. I'm not interested in getting it any way but normal and with some nice lady I like and what likes me. So rest assured."

Nita said, "Thank you for telling me."

He shrugged, but seemed pleased with himself.

"That your car out front?"

"My husband's car."

"Husband? Where's he?"

"He's dead. I don't drive. I meant to sell it, but I haven't yet."

What a fool, what a fool she was to tell him that.

"Two thousand four?"

"I think so. Yes."

"For a second I thought you were going to try and trick me with the husband stuff. Wouldn't've worked, though. I can smell it if a woman's on her own. I know it the minute I walk in a house. Minute she opens the door. Instinct. So it runs okay? You know the last time he drove it?"

"The seventeenth of June. The day he died."

"Got any gas in it?"

"I would think so."

"Nice if he filled it up right before. You got the keys?"

"Not on me. I know where they are."

"Okay." He pushed his chair back, hitting one of the pieces of china. He stood up, shook his head in some kind of surprise, sat down again.

"I'm wiped. Gotta sit a minute. I thought it'd be better when I'd ate. I was just making that up about being a diabetic."

She shifted in her chair and he jumped.

"You stay where you are. I'm not that wiped I couldn't grab you. It's just that I walked all night."

"I was only going to get the keys."

"You wait till I say. I walked the railway track. Never seen a train. I walked all the way to here and never seen a train."

"There's hardly ever a train."

"Yeah. Good. I went down in the ditch going around some of them half-assed little towns. Then it come daylight and I was still okay, except where it crossed the road and I took a run for it. Then I looked down here and seen the house and the car, and I said to myself, 'That's it.' I coulda took my old man's car, but I got some brains left in my head."

She knew that he wanted her to ask what he had done. She was also sure that the less she knew, the better it would be for her.

Then, for the first time since he had entered the house, she thought of her cancer. She thought of how it freed her, put her out of danger.

"What are you smiling about?"

"I don't know. Was I smiling?"

"I guess you like listening to stories. Want me to tell you a story?"

"I'd rather you'd leave."

"I will leave. First I'll tell you a story."

He put his hand in a back pocket. "Here. Want to see a picture? Here."

It was a photograph of three people, taken in a living room with closed floral curtains as a backdrop. An old man — not really old, maybe in his sixties — and a woman of about the same age were sitting on a couch. A very large younger woman was sitting in a wheelchair drawn up close to one end of the couch and a little in front of it. The old man was heavy and gray-haired, with eyes narrowed and mouth slightly open, as if he were asthmatic, but he was smiling as well as he could. The old woman was much smaller, with dyed brown hair and lipstick. She was wearing what used to be called a peasant blouse, with little red bows at the wrists and neck. She smiled determinedly, even a bit frantically, her lips stretched over perhaps bad teeth.

But it was the younger woman who monopolized the picture. Distinct and monstrous in a bright muumuu, her dark hair done up in a row of little curls along her forehead, cheeks sloping into her neck. And, in spite of all that bulge of flesh, an expression of some satisfaction and cunning.

"That's my mother and that's my dad. And that's my sister, Madelaine. In the wheelchair. She was born funny. Nothing no doctor or anybody could do for her. And ate like a pig. There was bad blood between her and me since ever I remember. She was five years older than me, and she just set out to torment me. Throwing anything at me she could get her hands on and knocking me down and trying to run over me with her fuckin' wheelchair. Pardon my French."

"It must have been hard for you. And for your parents."

"Huh. They just rolled over and took it. They went to this church, see, and this preacher told them she was a gift from God. They took her with them to church and she'd fuckin' howl like a fuckin' cat in the backyard and they'd say, 'Oh, she's tryin' to make music, oh, God fuckin' bless her.' Excuse me again.

"So I never bothered much with sticking around home, you know. I went and got my own life. That's all right, I says, I'm not hanging around for this crap. I got my own life. I got work. I nearly always got work. I never sat around on my ass, drunk on government money. On my rear end, I mean. I never asked my old man for a penny. I'd get up and tar a roof in the ninety-degree heat, or I'd mop the floors in some stinkin' old restaurant or go greasemonkey for some rotten cheatin' garage. I'd do it. But I wasn't always up for taking their shit, so I wasn't lasting too long. That shit that people are always handing people like me, and I couldn't take it. I come from a decent home. My dad worked till he got too sick — he worked on the buses. I wasn't brought up to take shit. Okay, though — never mind that. What my parents always told me was 'The house is yours. The house is all paid up and it's in good shape and it's yours.' That's what they told me. 'We know you had a hard time here when you were young, and if you hadn't had such a hard time you coulda got an education, so we want to make it up to you how we can.' Then not long ago I'm talking to my dad on the phone and he says, 'Of course, you understand the deal.' So I'm, 'What deal?' He says, 'It's only a deal if you sign the papers that you will take care of your sister as long as she lives. It's only your home if it's her home, too,' he says.

"Jesus. I never heard that before. I never heard that was the deal before. I always thought the deal was that when they died she'd go into a home. And it wasn't going to be my home.

"So I told my old man that wasn't the way I understood it, and he says, 'It's all sewed up for you to sign, and if you don't want to sign it you don't have to. If you do sign it, your Aunt Rennie will be around to keep an eye on you, so when we're gone you see you stick to the arrangements.' Yeah, my Aunt Rennie. She's my mom's youngest sister, and she is one prize bitch. Anyway, he says, 'Your Aunt Rennie will be keeping an eye on you,' and suddenly I just switched. I said, 'Well, I guess that's the way it is, and I guess it is only fair. Okay. Okay. Is it all right if I come over and eat dinner with you this Sunday?' 'Sure,' he says. 'Glad you have come to look at it the right way. You always fire off too quick,' he says. 'At your age you ought to have some sense.' 'Funny you should say that,' I says to myself.

"So over I go, and Mom has cooked chicken. Nice smell when I first go into the house. Then I get the smell of Madelaine, just her same old awful smell. I don't know what it is, but even if Mom washes her every day, it's there. But I acted very nice. I said, 'This is an occasion. I should take a picture.' I told them I had this wonderful new camera that developed right away and they could see the picture. 'Right off the bat, you can see yourself — what do you think of that?' And I got them all sitting in the front room just the way I showed you. Mom, she says, 'Hurry up. I have to get back in my kitchen.' 'Do it in no time,' I says. So I take their picture, and she says, 'Come on, now, let's see how we look,' and I say, 'Hang on, just be patient, it'll only take a minute.' And while they're waiting to see how they look, I take out my nice little gun and *bin-bang-bam* I shoot the works of them.

"Then I took another picture, and I went out to the kitchen and ate up some of the chicken and didn't look at them no more. I kind of had expected Aunt Rennie to be there, but Mom said she had some church thing. I would've shot her, too, just as easy.

"So lookie here. Before and after."

The man's head had fallen sideways, the woman's backward. Their expressions were blown away. The sister had fallen forward, so there was no face to be seen, just her great flowery swathed knees and dark hair with its elaborate and outdated coiffure.

"I coulda just sat there feelin' good for a week. I felt so relaxed. But I didn't stay past dark. I made sure I was all cleaned up and I finished off the chicken and I knew I better get out. I was prepared for Aunt Rennie walkin' in, but I got out of the mood I'd been in, and I knew I'd have to work myself up to do her. I just didn't feel like it no more. One thing, my stomach was so full. It was a big chicken, and I ate it all instead of packin' it with me, because I was scared the dogs would smell it and cut up a fuss when I went by the back lanes like I figured to do. I thought that chicken inside of me would do me for a week. Yet look how hungry I was when I got to you."

He glanced around the kitchen. "I don't suppose you got anything to drink here, do you? That tea was awful."

"There might be some wine," she said. "I don't know — I don't drink anymore."

"You AA?"

"No. It just doesn't agree with me."

She got up and found that her legs were shaking. Of course.

"I fixed up the phone line before I come in here," he said. "Just thought you ought to know."

Would he get careless and more easygoing as he drank, or meaner and wilder? How could she tell? She found the wine without having to leave the kitchen. She and Rich used to drink red wine every day in reasonable quantities because it was supposed to be good for your heart. Or bad for something that was not good for your heart. In her fright and confusion, she was not able to think what that was called.

Because she *was* frightened. Certainly. Her cancer was not going to be any help to her at the present moment, none at all. The fact that she was going to die within a year refused to cancel out the fact that she might die now.

He said, "Hey, this is the good stuff. No screw top. Haven't you got no corkscrew?"

She moved toward a drawer, but he jumped up and put her aside, not too roughly.

"Uh-uh, I get it. You stay away from this drawer. Oh my, lots of good stuff in here."

He put the knives on the seat of his chair, where she would never be able to grab them, and used the corkscrew. She did not fail to see what a wicked instrument it could be in his hands, but there was not the least possibility that she herself would ever be able to use it.

"I'm just getting up for glasses," she said, but he said no.

"No glass," he said. "You got any plastic?"

"No."

"Cups, then. I can see you."

She set down two cups and said, "Just a very little for me."

"And me," he said, businesslike. "I gotta drive." But he filled his cup to the brim. "I don't want no cop stickin' his head in to see how I am."

"Free radicals," she said.

"What's that supposed to mean?"

"It's something about red wine. It either destroys them because they're bad or builds them up because they're good — I can't remember."

She drank a sip of the wine, and it didn't make her feel sick, as she had expected. He drank, still standing. She said, "Watch for those knives when you sit down."

"Don't start kidding with me."

He gathered the knives and put them back in the drawer and sat.

"You think I'm dumb? You think I'm nervous?"

She took a big chance. She said, "I just think you haven't ever done anything like this before."

"Course I haven't. You think I'm a murderer? Yeah, I killed them, but I'm not a murderer."

"There's a difference," she said.

"You bet."

"I know what it's like. I know what it's like to get rid of somebody who has injured you."

"Yeah?"

"I have done the same thing you did."

"You never." He pushed back his chair but did not stand.

"Don't believe me if you don't want to," she said. "But I did it."

"Hell, you did. How'd you do it, then?"

"Poison."

"What are you talkin' about? You make them drink some of that fuckin' tea or what?"

"It wasn't a *them* — it was a *her.* There's nothing wrong with the tea. It's supposed to prolong your life."

"Don't want my life prolonged if it means drinkin' junk like that. They can find out poison in a body when it's dead, anyway."

"I'm not sure that's true of vegetable poisons. Anyway, nobody would have thought to look. She was one of those girls who had rheumatic fever as a child and coasted along on it, couldn't play sports or do anything much, always having to sit down and have a rest. Her dying was not any big surprise."

"What she ever done to you?"

"She was the girl my husband was in love with. He was going to leave me and marry her. He had told me. I'd done everything for him. He and I were working on this house together. He was everything I had. We hadn't had any children, because he didn't want them. I learned carpentry and I was frightened to get up on ladders, but I did it. He was my whole life. And he was going to kick me out for this useless whiner who worked in the registrar's office. Everything we'd worked for was going to go to her. Was that fair?"

"How would a person get poison?"

"I didn't have to get it. It was right in the back garden. Here. There was a rhubarb patch from years back. There's a perfectly adequate poison in the veins of rhubarb leaves. Not the stalks — the stalks are what we eat, they're fine — but the thin little red veins in the big rhubarb leaves, they're poisonous. I knew about this, but I didn't know exactly how much it would take to be effective, so what I did was more in the nature of an experiment. Various things were lucky for me. First, my husband was away at a symposium in Minneapolis. He might have taken her along, of course, but it was summer holidays, and she had to keep the office going. Another thing, though — she might not have been absolutely on her own. There might have been another person around. And she might have been suspicious of me. I had to assume that she didn't know I knew. She had come to dinner at my house; we were friendly. I had to count on my husband's being the kind of person who puts everything off, who would tell me to see how I took it but not yet tell her that he had done so. So then you say, Why get rid of her? He might still have been thinking of staying with me? No. And he would have kept her on somehow. And even if he didn't, our life had been poisoned by her. She'd poisoned my life, so I had to poison hers."

"I baked two tarts. One had the poison in it and one didn't. I drove down to the university and got two cups of coffee and went to her office. There was nobody there but her. I told her I'd had to come into town, and as I was passing the campus I'd seen this nice little bakery that my husband was always talking about, so I dropped in and bought a couple of tarts and two cups of coffee. I'd been thinking of her all alone when the rest of them got to go on their holidays, and of me all alone, with my husband in Minneapolis. She was sweet and grateful. She said that it was very boring for her at the office, and the cafeteria was closed, so she had to go over to the science building for coffee and they put hydrochloric acid in it. Ha-ha. So we had our little party."

"I hate rhubarb," he said. "It wouldn't have worked with me."

"It did with her. I had to take a chance that it would work fast, before she realized what was wrong and had her stomach pumped. But not so fast that she would associate it with me. I had to be out of the way, and so I was. The building was deserted, and as far as I know to this day nobody saw me arrive or leave. Of course, I knew some back ways."

"You think you're smart. You got away scot-free."

"But so have you."

"What I done wasn't so underhanded as what you done."

"It was necessary to you."

"You bet it was."

"Mine was necessary to me. I kept my marriage. He came to see that she wouldn't have been good for him anyway. She'd have got sick on him, almost certainly. She was just the type. She'd have been nothing but a burden to him. He saw that."

"You better not have put nothing in them eggs," he said. "You did, you'll be sorry."

"Of course I didn't. It's not something you'd go around doing regularly. I don't actually know anything about poison. It was just by chance that I had that one little piece of information."

He stood up so suddenly that he knocked over his chair. She noticed that there was not much wine left in the bottle.

"I need the keys to the car."

She couldn't think for a moment.

"Keys to the car. Where'd you put them?"

It could happen. As soon as she gave him the keys, it could happen. Would it help to tell him that she was dying of cancer? How stupid. It wouldn't help at all. Death in the future would not keep her from talking today.

"Nobody knows what I've told you," she said. "You are the only person I've told."

A fat lot of good that might do. The whole advantage she had presented to him had probably gone right over his head.

"Nobody knows *yet,*" he said, and she thought, Thank God. He's on the right track. He does realize. Does he realize?

Thank God, maybe.

"The keys are in the blue teapot."

"Where? What the fuck blue teapot?"

"At the end of the counter — the lid got broken, so we used it to just throw things in —"

"Shut up. Shut up or I'll shut you up for good." He tried to stick his fist in the blue teapot, but it would not go in. "Fuck, fuck, fuck!" he cried, and he turned the teapot over and banged it on the counter, so that not only did the car keys and house keys and various coins and a wad of old Canadian Tire money fall out on the floor but pieces of blue pottery hit the boards.

"With the red string on them," she said faintly.

He kicked things about for a moment before he picked up the proper keys.

"So what are you going to say about the car?" he said. "You sold it to a stranger. Right?"

The import of this did not come to her for a moment. When it did, the room quivered. *Going to say.* "Thank you," she said, but her mouth was so dry that she was not sure any sound came out.

It must have, though, for he said, "Don't thank me yet. I got a good memory. Good long memory. You make that stranger look nothin' like me. You don't want them goin' into graveyards diggin' up dead bodies. You just remember, a word outta you and there'll be a word outta me."

She kept looking down. Not stirring or speaking, just looking at the mess on the floor.

Gone. The door closed. Still she didn't move. She wanted to lock the door, but she couldn't move. She heard the engine start, then die. What now? He was so jumpy, he'd do everything wrong. Then again, starting, starting, turning over. The tires on the gravel. She walked trembling to the phone and found that he had told the truth: it was dead.

Beside the phone was one of their many bookcases. This one held mostly old books, books that had not been opened for years. There was *The Proud Tower.* Albert Speer. Rich's books.

A Celebration of Familiar Fruits and Vegetables: Hearty and Elegant Dishes and Fresh Surprises, assembled, tested, and created by Bett Underhill.

Once Rich had got the kitchen finished, Nita had made the mistake for a while of trying to cook like Bett. For a rather short while, because it turned out that Rich hadn't wanted to be reminded of all that fuss, and she herself hadn't had enough patience for so much chopping and simmering. But she had learned a few things that surprised her. Such as the poisonous aspects of certain familiar and generally benign plants.

She should write to Bett.

Dear Bett, Rich is dead, and I have saved my life by becoming you.

But what would Bett care that her life had been saved? There was only one person really worth telling.

Rich. Rich. Now she knew what it was to miss him. Like having the air sucked out of the sky.

She told herself that she could walk down to the village. There was a police office in the back of the Township Hall.

She should get a cell phone.

But she was so shaken, so deeply tired, that she could hardly stir a foot. She had first of all to rest.

She was wakened by a knock on her still unlocked door. It was a policeman, not the one from the village but one of the provincial traffic police. He asked if she knew where her car was.

She looked at the patch of gravel where it had been parked.

"It's gone," she said. "It was over there."

"You didn't know it was stolen? When did you last look out and see it?"

"It must have been last night."

"The keys were left in it?"

"I suppose they must have been."

"I have to tell you it's been in a bad accident. A one-car accident just this side of Wallenstein. The driver rolled it down into the cul-

vert and totaled it. And that's not all. He's wanted for a triple murder. That's the latest we heard, anyway. Murder in Mitchellston.
You were lucky you didn't run into him."

"Was he hurt?"

"Killed. Instantly. Serves him right."

There followed a kindly stern lecture. Leaving keys in the car.
Woman living alone. These days you never know.

Never know.

JOYCE CAROL OATES

Dear Husband

FROM *Conjunctions*

DEAR HUSBAND,

Let no man cast asunder what God hath brought together is my belief. And so I have faith that you will not abandon me in my hour of need. Dear husband, you will forgive me and you will pray for me as you alone will know the truth of what has happened in this house, in the early hours 6:10 A.M. to 6:50 A.M. as you alone have the right to condemn me. For it was my failure as a wife and the mother of your children that is my true crime. I am confessing this crime only to you, dear husband, for it is you I have wronged. Our children were to be beautiful souls in the eyes of God. You led our prayers: Heavenly Father, we will be perfect in your eyes. And in the eyes of Jesus Christ. "With men it is impossible but not with God: for with God all things are possible." Our firstborn son named for you, dear husband, was most beloved of you, I think. Though you were careful not to say so. For a father must love all his children equally, as a mother must. Loell Jr. was meant to be perfect. And Loell Jr. was a very happy baby. That he would not be a "fast learner" like some in your family was hurtful to him, for children can be cruel, but he did not cry overmuch in his crib. It is true your mother fretted over him for her grandson did not "thrive" as Mother McKeon would say. Loell Jr. had such warm brown eyes! — a sparkle in his eyes though he came late to speech and could not seem to hear words spoken to him unless loudly, and you were facing him. It was God's wish to cause our firstborn to be as he was. And then God sent us twin daughters: Rosalyn and Rosanna. Bright, lively girls with white-blond hair so much prettier than their mother's hair, which has grown darker — "dirty blond" — with each year. The twins were closest to Mommy's heart, when they were not misbehaving. And little Paul, with his daddy's sharp eyes and wavy hair, and little Dolores Ann: Dolly-Ann, our "sudden gift" from God, born within a year of your second son. All of my life here in Meridian City has been our family, dear husband. You said, I will make a home for us. Like a city on a hill our family will be, shining in the sun for all to behold. You are praised as a draftsman and the plans you work with, blueprints out of a computer, I can't comprehend. It is like a foreign language to me, which you can so easily speak. Though in high school I took algebra, geometry, trigonometry, one of the few girls in Meridian High in Mr. Ryce's class, I did not do badly. Each semester my name was on the honor roll and I was president of Hi-Y in senior year and a guard on the girls' basketball team and at the Christian Youth Conference in Atlanta, I was a delegate in my senior year. You would not remember, for you were three years older than "Lauri Lynn Mueller" and a popular boy on the football team, yearbook staff, studying mechanical engineering, and one of those to receive scholarships at Georgia Polytech. It was unbelievable to me that Loell McKeon would wish to date me, still less to marry me, I must pinch myself to believe it! Dear husband, this letter I will be leaving for you on the kitchen table, where I have cleared a space. My handwriting is poor, I know. My hand is shaky, I must steady it as I write. I will dial 911 when it is time. Within the hour, I think. On the counter, there are three knives. Who has placed them there so shiny sharp, I am not certain. The longest is the carving knife, which has been so clumsy in my hand, you would take it from me to carve our roasts. I have swallowed five OxyContin tablets you did not know that I had saved out of my prescription, and there are twelve more I am to swallow when God so instructs me, it is time. I am so grateful, each step has been urged on me, by God. "No step of our lives is without God." Upstairs, the children are peaceful at last. They have been placed on our bed in the exact order of their age for it is this order in which God sent them to us. There is Loell Jr., and there is Rosalyn, and there is Rosanna, and there is Paul, and there is Dolly-Ann, and you would believe those children are beautiful children, so peaceful! Dear husband, when the "bad feelings" first began, even before I went to that doctor you believed to be Pakistani, or Indian, from

the health plan, I would have a dream while awake and my eyes
staring open driving out on the highway and my hands would turn
the wheel of the car to the right — quick! — quick as a lightning
flash! — before any of the children could perceive it, we would
crash into the concrete wall at the overpass and all would be over
in an explosion of flame. This dream was so searing, dear husband, my eyes have burned with it. It is the purest of all flame, all
is cleansed within it both the wickedness and the goodness of hu-
mankind in that flame annihilated for as Reverend Hewett has
preached to us out of the pulpit, *Unto every one that hath shall be*
given, and he shall have abundance: but from him that hath not shall be
taken away even that which he hath. This was long ago it seems when
Rosalyn and Rosanna were still in car seats in the back, and Loell Jr.
was buckled in beside me, fretting and kicking. A later time, when
Paulie was in back with the twins, it was the station wagon I was driving, on Route 19 South, and the children were fretting as usual, for
a kind of devil would come into them when Mommy was behind
the wheel and anxious in traffic, little Paulie would shriek to torment me, his cries were sharp like an ice pick in my brain! Mother
McKeon said — she did not mean to be harsh but was kindly in her
speech — Can't you control these children, Lauri Lynn? It should
not be that hard, you are their mother. Your mother looks at me
with such disappointment, I do not blame her, of course. Your
mother has a right to expect so much better of Loell McKeon's
wife, all of the family has a right to expect this for you are their
shining son. Now in her face there is disappointment like a creased
glove someone has crushed in his hand. Mother McKeon had no
difficulty raising her three children. You, and Benjamin, and Emily
May. You are perfect, God has blessed you. To some, it is given.
From others, it is taken away. Why this is, Reverend Hewett has said,
is a mystery we must not question. At Thanksgiving, I was very anxious. You said, Why on earth are you hiding away in the kitchen
washing dishes before the meal is concluded, why do you behave so
rudely, what is wrong with you? — you were on the honor roll at
school, you won the *Meridian Times* essay prize, $300 and publica-
tion in the paper — "Why Good Citizenship Is Our Responsibility
in a Democracy." Little Dolly-Ann had diarrhea and the twins could
not be seated together for their giggling and squabbling and Loell
Jr. ate so fast, with his head lowered, and was so messy, and Paulie

sulked, wanting to play his videos, and shoved at me saying, Go away, Mommy, I don't love you, Mommy. The children eat so fast, and are so messy, Mother McKeon crinkled her nose saying, You'd think these children are starving, and nobody taught them table manners, look at the messes they make. It is sweet things that make them so excitable, out of control. Always at family meals there are many sweet things. Even squash, and cranberry sauce, your mother laces with sugar. Dear husband, I have tried to keep them bathed. It is hard to fight them sometimes, for they kick and splash in the bath knowing how fearful I am the floor will get wet, and the tile will warp, and water will drip down through the dining room ceiling. I have tried to keep this house clean. You would laugh at me, your angry laugh like silk tearing, dear husband, but it is so, that I have tried. When the police come into this house this morning, I am ashamed to think what they will see. Of the houses on Fox Run Lane, you would not believe that 37 is the house of shame, for from the street it looks like all the others. Of all the "colonials" in New Meridian Estates, you would not believe that this is the house of shame. The bathrooms are not clean. The toilets cannot be kept clean. Beneath the cellar steps, there is something so shameful, I could not bring myself to reveal it to you. You have been so disgusted, dear husband, and I know that you are right. I know that it is not what you expected of this marriage, and what was promised to you. And you are working such long hours, and you are away more often in Atlanta. I know that I am the mother, and I am the wife. I do not need anyone to help me. Mother McKeon is right, it is a dangerous idea to bring strangers into our homes, to carry away stories of us. Such wrong stories as are told of Loell Jr. at his school, that he bites his own fingers and arms, it is in frustration with the other children teasing him. Yet, as a baby, his eyes were so happy and unclouded, your mother said what a blessed baby, look at those eyes. For in Loell Jr.'s eyes, your mother perceived your eyes, dear husband. None of this is your fault, dear husband. At Christmastime you bought me an excellent vacuum cleaner to replace the old. It is a fine machine. I have seen it advertised on TV. It is a heavier machine than the other, which is needed in this house. It is difficult to drag up the stairs, I am ashamed of what the police officers will discover. The boys' rooms are not clean. The boys' bed-clothes are stained. There is a harsh smell of the baby's diapers and of bleach. The twins' hair cannot be kept free of snarls. They push at my hands, they whimper and kick, when I try to comb their hair. And so many dirtied clothes, socks and sneakers, and towels. Worse yet are certain things that have been hidden. I am so ashamed of what will be revealed to you, after I am gone. It was my fault, to provoke you to say such things. I know that such terrible words would never erupt from your mouth, dear husband, except for me. And never would you strike a woman. My jaw still hurts but it is a good hurt. A waking-up hurt. You said, Lauri Lynn, what the hell do you do all day long, look at this house. You have nothing to do but take care of the children and this house and look at this house, Lauri Lynn. You are a failure as a mother as you are a failure as a wife, Lauri Lynn. Tricked me into marrying you, pretending to be someone you are not. You were right to say such things, dear husband. Many times I have said them to myself. In a weak moment, when little Paulie was just born, I asked you could the Morse girl drop by after school to help me sometimes, I would pay her out of my household money. I was not begging from the neighbors, dear husband! I was not telling "sob stories" as you have accused. I did take counsel with Reverend Hewett, as you know. Reverend Hewett was kindly and patient saying God will not send us any burdens greater than we can bear, that is God's promise to mankind. I began to cry, I said I am a failed mother. I am a failed wife. My children are not good children, Reverend. My children are flawed and broken like dolls, like the dolls and toys they break, the stuffed animals they have torn. I am so tired, Reverend Hewett. It was held against me that at Sunday services I slept. I could not keep my eyes open, and I slept. Our church is the most beautiful of all churches in New Meridian, we are very proud of our church. It is a vision of heaven in our Church of the Risen Christ, which is only three years old, like an ark it is built with its prow rising. Two thousand worshippers can gather in our church and sing praises to the Lord, it is like a single voice so strong you can believe it would rise to heaven to be heard. In such joyous sound, Lauri Lynn was but a tiny bubble and what sorrow there is in a tiny bubble is of no consequence. I am the Way, the Truth, and the Life so Jesus has promised but Jesus was disgusted with Lauri Lynn, you could not blame him. If I could sleep, I would be happy again. I do not deserve to be happy ever again, I know. It is for this reason, I think, that this morning at last I acted, as God has instructed. For now what is done is done. For now it cannot be undone. Mommy! Rosanna cried but I did not heed her, for the strength of God flowed through my limbs. When we were first married, dear husband, I weighed 126 pounds but after the babies, these past few years my weight has been 160, I am so heavy, my thighs are so heavy, the veins are blue and broken in my flesh like lard and my breasts are loose sagging sacs, you would not believe that I am twenty-eight years old, which is not old. I stand in front of the mirror gripping my breasts in my hands and I am so ashamed, yet there is a fascination in it, what I have become. For I am not now Lauri Lynn who was a plain girl but known for her smiles, to make others feel welcome. And in some snapshots, I am almost pretty. Where that girl has gone, I do not know. Truly she was not a "trick" to beguile you, dear husband! You will say, Lauri Lynn will abide in hell. But Lauri Lynn is not here, the children scarcely knew her. In the 7-Eleven if there are teenaged boys outside, I am ashamed to walk past. These boys jeering and mocking as boys had done with my friend Nola, who weighed 150 pounds when we were girls. Look at the cow, look at the fat cow, look at the udders on that cow, moo-cow, moo-cow, moooo-cow like hyenas the boys laughed, for nothing is so funny to them as a female who is not attractive. We must not pay attention to such crude remarks, and yet. And yet in your eyes, dear husband, I see that scorn. It is the scorn of the male, it cannot be contested. In the mirror, in my own eyes, I see it. In Jesus's eyes, I see it. I am a bad mother, and now all the world will know. It is time, all the world should know. It was very hard to force them, dear husband. Like you they are not patient with me any longer, they have smelled the weakness in me. In animals, weakness must be hidden. For a weak animal will be destroyed by its own kind. There is a logic to this. I began with Loell Jr. for he was the oldest, and the biggest. Loell Jr. I had to chase for he seemed to know what Mommy wished to do, to make things right again. Loell Jr. is named for you, he is your firstborn son though he has been a disappointment to you, I know. For Loell Jr. cannot comprehend arithmetic, the numerals "fly" in his head he says. He fought me, I was surprised. When I chased him in the upstairs hallway he ran screaming and squealing like one of our games except when I caught him he didn't giggle — I didn't tickle him, the "spider tickle" he used to love — he fought me, and bit my fingers, but I was too strong for him, and carried him back to the bathroom and to the tub where the water was just warm the way the children like it, and now there is so much water on the floor, it is leaking through the floor and through the dining room ceiling, you will be so disgusted. Some parts of what happened, I don't remember. I remember laying Loell Jr. on our bed, his pajamas so wet, the bedspread became wet. Next was Rosanna, for she had wakened, and Rosalyn was still sleeping. (This was very early, dear husband. At the Days Inn in Atlanta, you would still be asleep.) Jesus said to me, It is true that you are a bad mother but there is a way: "If thine eye offend thee, pluck it out." There is a way to be forgiven, and cleansed. Dear husband, I wish that the toilet was not so stained but the stain is in the porcelain and cannot be scrubbed out. And the tub, I have scoured with cleanser so many times tearful and in a fury but the stains will not come out. Even steel wool would not clean it, please forgive me. After Loell Jr. the others were wakening and God instructed me, Lauri Lynn! You must act now. A feeling of flames ran through the upstairs hall, I could see this flame like heat waves in the summer and from these flames, which were the flames of God, I drew strength. From these flames, I understood what was ordained. For he who hath not, from him shall be taken away even that which he hath, I had not understood until now is God's mercy, and God's pity. It is not God's punishment for God is a spirit, who does not punish. So swiftly this truth ran through me, I cried aloud in joy. The little ones believed it was their bath time. And the promise of bath time in the morning is breakfast, and if they do not misbehave, they can have their favorite cereal, which is Count Chocula, which is covered in chocolate. It was so very early — not yet dawn! The house is quiet before the start of the long day. The children must be scrubbed if they have soiled themselves in the night and they must be readied for school except for Paulie and the baby and then there is the return from school, noise and excitement, it is a very long day like a corridor in a great motel where you cannot see the end of it, for the lighting is poor, and the rooms are strangely numbered. Mommy is so tired! Which of those doors in the corridor is Mommy's door is not certain. For the day has no end. My sister said, chiding, You look so tired, Lauri Lynn, you should see a doctor. I was furious with her poking her nose in our business, I said, I am not tired! I will not break down and cry. I will not be ridiculed, or pitied. I will not be laughed at. I am not a TV woman, to spill her guts to strangers, to reveal such shameful secrets, to receive applause. I have done a good job, I think, to hide from them. From the McKeons especially. But it is too hard, I am so tired, one by one I drowned them in the tub, it was not so very different from bathing them, for always they kicked, and splashed, and whimpered, and whined, and made such ugly faces. Some parts of what God instructed me, I can recall, but others are faded already now, like a dream that is so powerful when you are asleep, you would wish to keep it, but when your eyes open, already it begins to fade. It was a hard task but needed to be accomplished for the children had not turned out right, that is the simple fact. As at birth, some babies are not right, malformed, or their hearts are too small, or their brains, or the baby itself is too small, and God does not mean for such babies to survive, in his infinite wisdom. These children, who did not show their deformities to the eye, except sometimes Loell Jr., when he twisted his mouth as he did, and made that bellowing sound. I am a bad mother, I confess this. For a long time I did not wish to acknowledge this fact, in my pride. But the flames cleanse us of all pride. Even Reverend Hewett would not know, for in his heart he is a proud man, that pride is but a burden, and when it is taken from you, what joy enters your heart! In your eyes, dear husband, I hope that this is restitution. I hope that this is a good way of beginning again for you. The baby did not suffer, I promise. Like the others Dolly-Ann thrashed and kicked with surprising strength for a five-month infant but could not fight her mother as the others tried to do, and beneath the water little Dolly-Ann could not scream. How many times you have pressed your hands over your ears, dear husband: Why does that baby scream so? Why is it our baby that screams? It is a cleansing now. God has instructed me, and Jesus Christ has guided my hand. As I am a bad mother I will be punished by the laws of man, I will be strapped into the chair of infamy, and flames will leap from my head, but I will not be punished by God for God has forgiven me. Dear husband, you will be called at work, in Atlanta. You will be asked to return home. In heaven, the children will be at peace. They will no longer be dirty, and squabbling, but they will be perfect as they were meant to be. Always you will know from this day forward, your beloved children are with God, and are perfect in his bosom.

There will be strangers in this house, which has been a house of pride too long. To the police officers who are men like yourself you will say with your angry laugh, there is not a clean glass in this house, if one of the police officers requests a glass of water. And the broken toys on the floor. Ugly Robo-Boy that Mommy could not fix, for the battery did not fit right, that provoked Paulie to scream, It won't walk! It won't walk! Mommy, I hate you! The twins I have wrapped in their new plaid coats, to lay on the bed. I brushed out their snarled hair like halos around their heads. The others are in their pajamas, which are wet, and I have hidden their faces with a sheet. These are not beautiful children, I am afraid. For their mother was not a beautiful woman. My big girl, you called me. My breasts filled to bursting with milk, you held in your two hands in wonder. My big-busty girl, you moaned making love to me, lying on top of me and a sob in your throat, your weight was heavy upon me, often I could not breathe, and your breath was sour in my face sometimes, a smell as of something coppery, I hid such thoughts from you of course. Now you are released from our wedding vows, dear husband. In the place where I am going, I will not have children. If I had been strong enough, the fire would consume me. But the fire has burned down now, I am very tired, it is all that I can do to swallow these pills, and take up the carving knife, at the kitchen sink. You will find another woman to honor and to cherish and to bear your children and they will be beautiful as you deserve, and they will be perfect. Lastly, dear husband, I beg you to forgive me for the heavy casserole dish hidden beneath the cellar stairs, that is badly scorched and disgusting for not even steel wool could scrape away the burned macaroni and cheese, now in cold water it has been soaking since Thanksgiving. I could not hide it in the trash to dispose of for it is a gift from your mother, it is CorningWare and expensive and might yet be scoured clean and made usable again, by another's hand.

Your loving wife,
Lauri Lynn

NIC PIZZOLATTO

Wanted Man

FROM *The Oxford American*

1.

IN THE VILLAGE of LaTourse that exists south between Port Salvador and Travis City in Louisiana, where decades ago the pine for-
ests had been stripped and unable to regrow and the refineries
now employed half of their original numbers, most of the eight
hundred or so residents weren't aware of the Prater estate, and
many who were, when asked, often just hung their faces and shook
their heads back and forth in a pitying gesture, and some less sympathetic people curled their nostrils as if smelling something ran-
cid. The place was out where the old Chenault Air Base used to be,
a few acres of empty grassland south of the runway now overgrown
and cracked with weeds, on the side of Lake Quelqueshue opposite
the refineries, which at night reflect into the water the image of a
future metropolis built of metal and fire. Once there'd been a family, but the old man, Burris Prater, lived there now with only his
youngest son, Wesley, who had been home for two months and still
found himself missing vaguely the order and security and care of
the hospital. Meals had been regimented, arrows painted on the
floor told you where to walk, and people had asked how he was
doing.

That morning a shotgun severed his dreams. Wes Prater startled
awake at the sound of firearms, the crash still echoing beyond the
transparent yellow drapes. Another boom; it careened in his ears,
blasted him into memories, and he saw TJ out in the field at dawn,
how he must have knelt and rested on the barrel as if praying to

it. He never liked sleeping on the top part of the bunk bed but couldn't bring himself to fill the groove his older brother had worn in the bottom mattress.

Wes jumped down from the bed and pulled on a pair of jeans. His father sat on the porch, in a folding lawn chair, facing the broad sea of cord grass around their house. The old man fit three more shells into the pump-action. Sweet-smelling smoke drifted from the breech, and it was as though the smell reminded Wes of a memory he no longer possessed. His father's hair had gone thin and a sandy, metallic color, his face pressed inward and spattered with dark freckles. He wore a tattered pink terry-cloth robe that had belonged to his wife, and Wes recalled his mother wearing that robe while smoking a cigarette above a pan of eggs and back bacon. Beside his father's bare, veiny feet, shotgun shells were scattered around a half-empty bottle of Dickel. Two garbage bags filled with High Life cans slumped against the corner of the porch, near the weathered blue oxygen tank and its plastic mask. The old man kept his Dickel in a locked cabinet, the key hidden on him.

"They's something out there." His father used the shotgun to point into the vast fields of khaki grass while using his other hand to pull the pink robe shut over his chest. "Not sure what. A coyote. A bobcat. I could just glimpse it." He raised his glass off the porch and tipped it to his receded lips. "It's brown. Light brown."

"Pop . . ." The ends of the yellow ribbon tied around a live oak were frayed and stringy. A flaccid American flag drooped from a pole jutting out the single gable above the porch. Paint on the house had faded, cracked, and peeled so that the small A-frame seemed to wear bark, and over Wes's left shoulder a deserted gray barn leaned westward as though trying to hear something. "We don't have nothing for a coyote anyway. It's not like we got chickens or something."

The old man's boxy head darted up. "What's that supposed to mean? That's a shot at me, isn't it?" He laid the shotgun across his knees and cinched the robe around his neck.

"No," said Wes. "I was just —"

His father raised the gun and resumed scanning the field, which went unchanged, the color of dulled brass and spreading out from their home as though it had leaked or bled in every direction. The grass seemed cooked of all character by the sun, and it gave the house a quality of being adrift, a skiff unmoored in a piss-colored sea. The moon was still visible, like a cloud lathed in the morning sky. Beside the oak in the small dirt yard three signs leaned more or less in line. A breeze wobbled the one that read POWER OF PRIDE. A blast rang and Wes leaped back, heat and gritty residue of the gunshot crashing over his side. The old man ejected the smoking shell.

"I didn't see anything."

"Well, I did."

Wes turned and looked through the front door toward the back of the living room, where the gun rack was visible. He could identify which gun was missing, his brother's Remington lying across the lap of the pink robe. His father raised his glass and drained it, smacked. Wes said, "You're using . . . ?"

His father bristled, waited. "Am I using what?" He lifted the gun to his shoulder.

"Nothing."

"You gone to the store today, or what? I need sausages and there's hardly any beer."

Wes nodded, and beneath the gunpowder a stale, sharp scent like ammonia stung his eyes. The chair his father sat in had canvas straps crisscrossing an aluminum frame, and beneath it a shiny puddle glistened on the porch. He stepped in front of his father and saw the lap of the pink robe was soaking wet. "Dag, Pop. Again?"

The old man scowled at his crotch, and both hands clutched the gun. "Shut up. Get out the way. They's something out there."

Wes went inside and got dressed and heard the gun a few more times, each blast making him feel sickly and timid. He shaved and watched a string of blood pulled down from his throat. He was thinking a lot about TJ this morning. TJ in the desert, liberating Kuwait City. TJ back home, tattooed and telling stories about a Mexican girl, some kind of witch who'd married him in some kind of ceremony. TJ flinching a finger and turning his head to red mist in the useless plain of dry grass outside the window. Walking out the yard, Wes mimicked a karate kick and knocked over the sign that read IN GOD WE TRUST. His father called from the porch, "Pussy."

The F-150 had not been new when his father bought it thirteen years before. It bounced and jostled over the deep ruts that ran in front their house. The drive to the nearest grocery store took him about three miles north, and at first there had been the urge to just keep driving, but a destination eluded him. A girl named Clara worked the cash register at Cormier's Grocery, and he sensed that she could be a destination, sensed, like a man falling past a line of rope, that she might fill some nagging imperative. The store had one of the short old signs whose letters could be replaced to spell different messages, a light-bulb arrow above the words pointing toward the road. Today it read AM I Y BROTHERS KEEPER? YES I M. The oyster shells of the parking lot crackled like fire under the truck's bald tires.

He'd talked to Clara before. She and the woman who owned the store both believed he'd been in Iraq. He'd told Clara he just got back from the war; a sergeant. Her lips were thin and pink, and she had a pointed face covered in blond freckles, blond hair like a sunlit lake, and from that sunny field her green eyes seemed to fly outward, or one of them did. Her left eye was lazy or perhaps glass, and it wandered discreetly to one corner, as if trying to watch her shoulder.

She was working, but there was a long line, and so he didn't get to talk to her much when he bought ten cans of Vienna sausage, two loaves of Wonder Bread, mayonnaise, milk, toilet paper, and a High Life suitcase of thirty-six cans, and it was okay, because when she smiled at him, he lost a significant amount of his speech facility anyway. Absently, he handed her a ten and in a kind of daze hustled out the door.

On the way home he turned onto Big Plain Drive, toward town, and popped a beer. He'd start off thinking about Clara, but then his thoughts would move to memories of the day the refinery exploded. He kept seeing his sister, Anneise, rise up out the field, appearing in the middle of the grass with Barret Wagner, his brother's friend. Loose grass stuck in Anneise's hair, and across Lake Quelqueshue a cluster of orange flames bloomed from the metal haze of the petroleum refineries; another boom made the ground quiver, and birds erupted from the trees fencing the shoreline. On the far side of the water, sections of the air had become heaving red blobs, spitting into the lake. The heat was intense, air greasy and particulate, dimpled by gas fumes and heat. His pop and Wagner had run to the stable to secure the horses. One of them had kicked the stall and had broken its leg, and its owner would sue for negligence. After that, his father wouldn't board any more horses and the last occasion for work vanished from the farm. Wes and his sister stayed out there watching the eruptions and listening to the wailing sirens. Later on, his father explained to them what had happened, that twelve men had died, but those facts never stole away the beauty of the roiling fire or the sensation, unique and unexpected, that something had happened. Something had busted open the quiet hours of sunlight. He remembered the dry yellow grass that caked his sister's back and the grass stains on her kneecaps.

Back then it had felt like life was not just one thing; it could be other things. Then one day it felt the exact opposite; life was one thing and one thing only, a wait.

Anneise had left home with Barret Wagner when she was seventeen and Wes was thirteen. They hadn't heard from her in a couple years, and their father wouldn't speak about her. Wes drank three beers while driving a small circle around the village square and the football field and the old pine mill and the Indian casino just outside the town limits. He imagined that when Clara was his girlfriend, he'd learn the truth about her eye.

When he returned home about an hour later, the green Dodge Shadow parked in the yard cut his reverie with a foreboding, sinking sensation. Clara was inside the house. She was sitting in the living room, talking to his father, and she wore a look of dim horror.

"Ho!" his father coughed. "The war hero returns!" He laughed and brought his oxygen mask up to his face. Clara was standing now.

"I came by 'cause you didn't give me enough cash. It was nineteen and you gave me a ten. I told Miss Marie I'd just come by and get it. I thought you'd be back."

"No," he said, and set the beer and groceries down.

"I want to hear some war stories!" his father called, then sucked at the mask. He twisted the spigot and the tank hissed.

"Um," said Wes.

Clara started to move past him, shy and hurried, tucking a strand of hair back. She was at the door now, and he said, "You want that cash?"

"Oh. Yeah. All right. It was, um, you only gave me ten. So."

"I want to hear some war stories!"

"Shut up!"

"Or . . . I could just . . . get it later," she said, opening the door. "Whatever. I mean."

"Okay. Wait." His smile felt so awkward it was excruciating, and he could see his father grinning out the corner of his eye as he pulled two crumpled fives from his pocket. She took them and tried to smile, but even her good eye avoided him, and she scrambled to her Dodge, started it as if fleeing a crime.

Wes stood in the doorway. A blob of spittle nestled in the corner of his father's crooked smile. He said, "You ought to be ashamed of yourself. To steal your brother's legacy."

"I got a *uniform*. I *was* in army."

The slit mouth, like a wound in his face, opened and cackled. "You wasn't in no *Iraq*. Less than two months. A washout's what they said. Crazy."

Wes looked out the door to the long fields, the yard signs, the dust cloud disintegrating above the road.

His father counted on one hand. "Mental instability. Panic attacks. Anxiety disorder. Dys-phas-ia." Wes's fists clenched, and the dust from Clara's car wafted over the road like a ghostly scarf. His father went on. "You can't fake stuff like that with them. They'd of caught you. That means you're bat-shit crazy."

A hot tide coursed through Wes's face. "I wonder why your whole family ran away," he said. "I wonder why Ma and Anneise left."

His father raised the bottle of Dickel. "The one should of left's still here."

"Everybody's tired of you."

His father lit a cigarette. "You oughta be ashamed. A *sergeant?*"

"Ma hated you. So did Anneise. TJ —"

"Oh, that's *my* fault, I guess. Blame me, you goddamn coward."

Wes marched into the old man's face. "What're you good for except pissing yourself?" Flakes of spit landed on his mottled cheeks, and it seemed to please the old man, his eyes flaring with the only vitality they knew.

"What about you? Telling some little girl you're a big war hero. Pretending you your brother."

Wes grabbed the flaps of the robe and jerked his father up. "You didn't have to say nothing!"

"Oh, big man!" His father coughed. "Even as a kid. Sitting out there in the fields. Talking to rocks. You crazy sumbitch."

"Ma didn't think you were much of a man, huh?"

His father swung the nearly empty bottle of Dickel and clipped Wes's cheek, sent him reeling back. "That's it, you pussy. Come back over here and find out what it's about."

Wes snatched the bottle from his father. Emptied it into his mouth while his father groped in the air for it. "Section 8ed! Go talk to your rocks!"

Wes lifted the bottle by the neck as if to bring it down.

"Go ahead, big man!" his father barked, neck outstretched, snarling.

"You let her run off! With Wagner! And you didn't even try to stop it!"

His father lost some of the rigidity in his neck, shook his head. "I hated that boy. Bastard. I hated him."

Wes's arm lowered. "Yeah. Me too."

"Don't talk about your brother, though."

Wes dropped the bottle on the floor and walked to the east window, looked out at the field of high, dead grass. TJ's tattoos were acquired in Mexico, after he was discharged. They were strange, convoluted Indian signs that sleeved both his arms. Black and interlocking, a maze of tribal signature. Wes imagined the markings jerked back, the blast, a red burst in the dawn light.

"It's not Section 8," Wesley said. "It was called AR 635-200."

"Get me another bottle. It's unlocked."

"You remember TJ talking about that girl that tattooed him in Mexico? A priestess?"

"No."

"No. 'Cause he never talked to you. 'You're better off talking to those rocks, Wes.' That's what he said."

"Get me another bottle." Finally his father hoisted himself off the couch with trembling arms. Returned with a new bottle of Dickel.

"You find that bobcat?"

"I didn't say for sure it was a bobcat." The old man settled back on the couch. "They's something out there, though."

Wes turned back to the window, his reflection imposed on the morbid field that was just then rustled by a wind. He heard the sound of his father's gulping, the smacking of his lips. *He aims to die,* Wes thought, and heard his father chuckle. Then Wes muttered, "It should have been you."

"Say again?"

"It should have been you out there. With a gun."

Another chuckle. "It should have been *you*."

"Saved everybody the trouble of having to leave."

"You ever think I wanted her to leave? That ever cross your dumb little mind?"

He still faced the window. Their land was without fences, yet a border seemed definitely construed, limitations drawn of psychic, historical materials. He heard the match strike and smelled the sulfur and then the tobacco of his father's Pall Mall.

"You know, you ain't mine," the old man said.

A pause, and Wesley knew his father was choosing his next words. He'd heard rumors. Anneise had told him something about their mother once, out on the lake. They'd been skinny-dipping when Wes was ten, and he'd been afraid to leave the water because of his erection.

"Nope," his father said. "You couldn't of been. You wasn't mine and she didn't even take you with her. What's that say?"

"Who?"

"Who what?"

"Who was it?"

His father shrugged. "Who knows. You mother was a whore."

The news didn't unmoor Wes at all. He'd always felt held outside his own history, his family's, and in the consolations of rock and grass his loneliness had accommodated itself to a secret, imaginary reality. So he'd already inhabited this bastard status beyond any verification.

Burris Prater must have had a shot of guilt, because he spoke in a meager tone toward Wes's back. "It wasn't your fault, though. I told myself. I kept you here 'cause it wasn't your fault. It was hers. I raised you like my own."

Wes stared into the field. He'd left high school when he was fifteen, after Anneise ran off and after his mother had long ago left to follow a man who traveled with a revival. Three years then where he dug irrigation ditches in the sun. Sat outside with his favorite stones, watching the refineries across the water. Then army and the hospital. He moved away from the window and looked without expression at the slumped, freckled body under its robe.

"I'm just drunk," the old man muttered. Wes moved past him. "Where you going? They's a Rangers game later on." Wes didn't answer. He closed the front door behind him.

Grazed by sharp, bending blades, Wes cut through the grass and walked to the lake. The refineries resembled a pipe organ, and nothing had lived in the lake for many years except a black and purplish layer of algae. He sat on the moist shore with a beer, crossed his legs.

Time, as in his childhood, could smear here like liquid in a sluice, the beat of moments passed by making observations, watching things. Grass, stone, water, cloud. Each observance demarked time and gave him possession of it, became something he inhabited. Sun and sunset, light-dappled water. He could fold time here and have it pass without feelings, turn hours into a moment, feel the stone, and disappear while the daylight crushed down, thick as wax.

Mosquitoes and the overwhelming urge to piss woke him from his trance. A couple hours had passed. He walked inside and found his father sprawled across the floor, the oxygen tank upended and two empty bottles of Dickel beside his body. Wes continued past the body to the bathroom, relieved himself, and sometime during that process he realized the old man was dead.

He walked back in the room and stared at the body. A pool of dark vomit spread under its face, but none of the liquor looked spilled, and so he concluded that his father had emptied both bottles into himself within the space of a few hours. *He meant to die,* Wes thought, *from the moment he woke up this morning.*

It was a little like the day the refineries had exploded.

2.

They buried his father in a cemetery overlooking the Gulf of Mexico. Exactly five people gathered under a green tarp that held a sea-colored light beneath it, the way a cloud holds a rain shower. Odor of dead fish. Wesley had the sense they were all standing in an emptied aquarium. The young priest affected an air of liturgical drama, punctuated his phrases with jerky dips and twists of his head. His altar boy kept gazing off at the gulf, and two cemetery workers looked bored as they watched the simple pine box lower into its hole.

Wesley still thought of him as his father, because he had no one else to picture in the role. Burris Prater had no middle name, and all Wes knew of his paternal grandparents were snippets the old man had always used in an accusatory self-defense. "My daddy made shoes and he left us when I was five. I had two sisters, and my mother couldn't work because she was sick. When she died I went to work at the plants." He'd married late in life to a younger woman and bought farmland, but the land couldn't produce crops because of pollution that had seeped across the lake and into the ground water. If he'd had a vision then, it had turned on him, twisted itself inside-out.

He had his father's truck and what was left of the subsidies, but three weeks later he was still in the house.

The key to the liquor cabinet sat on the mantel and a few empty bottles dotted the shelves. Wes stood at the center of the living room, trying to pitch peanuts into the mouth of one of the bottles and clutching TJ's shotgun in the other hand. On each chair and the sofa sat a large white rock, five of them altogether, surrounding him. He'd scrubbed each one clean and selected its placement carefully.

The front door burst open like a starter's pistol, and he whipped around, heard footsteps in the foyer.

The girl at the room's threshold was lean and tan, in short cut-offs and a white tank top. Her hair was tangled and pulled on top of her head. Taut and pleasing, she removed a pair of sunglasses and surveyed the room with a somewhat appalled expression, staring at his rocks.

"Jesus, Wes," said Anneise. "What's going on here?"

"Um."

"Why're you dressed like that?"

He started trying to button the top of his military fatigues, but his fingers fumbled, and the gun kept slipping out his grasp. Stunned and exhaustingly drunk, unsure if her appearance was even real, he only said, "I was in the army."

He realized he'd always felt, if you wait long enough in one spot, everything could come to you.

It was almost fall and the windows were open. She came out the shower in a long, faded purple T-shirt that just covered her panties. She curled her legs on the couch and drank coffee he'd made.

"Dead. Jesus. That's so weird it happens now. Right before I come home."

"Yeah," said Wes. He sat on the chair across the room, his fingers gripping his knees.

"Isn't that weird? God. I bet I had a premonition, and that's why I came home."

"Yeah." He nodded and glanced around, as if expecting some-one to burst out a closet. A bluish oval of bruise was stamped on her outer thigh. He asked her about where-all she'd been and what-all she'd been doing.

"Oh God, Wes. How could I start to tell you?"

"Well, you were still with Barret?"

"Barret's in trouble. Barret's gone now. But you should tell me about the army. Tell me about that, Wes. Did you go to Fallujah?"

"No," he said. Her face was strewn with gossamer fractures around the eyes, and the center of her chest looked like it had been sunburned too many times. The skin was finely wrinkled and bunched like crepe paper, reddened, not flushed. "But I was some places. A sergeant. There were gunfights."

"God. Barret had a gun. Let me tell you how *brave* he was when he had a gun. God. Wes, I been to Georgia, Florida, Alabama, and Texas. I was in Crawford, Wes. I saw the president. He lives there. If I'd known you were in the army, I'd of tried to tell him. I finally made it here on a bus from Corpus Christi. Wes, I was walking and — do you remember Jimmy Dupres? Did you know him? He was at our high school. He's a deputy now. I was walking and he pulled up, and he saw it was me. He recognized me. He's a nice guy. He gave me a ride out here in his cruiser. We were on the Parish Road and he turned the lights on for me. They gave him a siren, and he has a gun, too."

"All right."

"What're you so nervous for, Wes? You look like somebody's sneaking up on you."

"No I don't. I don't know. I'm excited to see you."

"You're all grown now. Look at you." She uncoiled her legs and stood, walked to the kitchen to refill her mug. He could see the crescent edges of red panties from behind and looked away.

He stood and started pacing and was by the window when she came back in and sat down. "Isn't that aces, Wes? That Jimmy

Dupres recognized me? He remembered me from high school. He told me he remembered a class I was in."

Out the window the fields undulated, had a character of striving. "I just don't get it now. What're you back for?"

She shrugged and looked down into her coffee. He regretted the question, and he suddenly felt he had to be careful with his questions, that this new situation was too fragile and could be broken by their stories. "You want a drink?" That perked her up.

They sat drinking their father's bourbon the rest of the night. He told her about the remaining farm subsidies. She seemed slightly confused about what he'd been doing here, or what he was planning to do, and he was just as confused by her accounts. Anneise told circular stories that never closed the loop but spiraled off into different anecdotes, and an incidental description could set off an entirely new narrative, and she would forget the original story she was telling. She put on some music, an old record by the Oak Ridge Boys.

She talked about a group of people who lived in a close grouping of beach shacks owned by an old wealthy guy whose band played every night to the commune; he seemed to have some attachment to the sixties, though he was a little too young to have seen any of it. She talked about Atlanta and Birmingham and the Dinosaur Diamond Prehistoric Highway between Colorado and Utah, because she remembered Wes had liked dinosaurs. Wes understood that she remembered things about him that were no longer true. He'd taken all the rocks outside while she was in the shower, and she hadn't brought them up again. He felt she might, though.

She didn't want to talk about TJ at all, and only said, "God, it was rough on me when I heard that. I had a wild few months. Rough living." He asked her what had happened to Barret Wagner.

Barret had been with a motorcycle club for the last couple years, and he was attempting forays into stolen cars and drugs. "Long story short, he got in trouble with some people, I think. He had to take off, and people were looking for him. I went back to Apollo Village in Corpus, that's what the beach place was called. And after a while I kind of started to realize that I had to forget about Barret, and I was like, Anneise, what *are* you doing, *girl?* Everybody was naked in the shack, and Felan, that was his name, was playing these drums, and I said, Okay, maybe four years of this is enough. How

many parties do you need to go to? And I don't know, maybe I
sensed something, maybe I could feel something. Do you believe in
telepathy? Have you heard of that? I met some people in New Orleans that did. They were kind of silly people. But maybe I did know
something out in Corpus, like something had happened, and I just
felt it was time to come back home for a bit, to see it, and then I get
here and he died. Wes, do you think I could *feel* that he died?"

"Maybe. Sure." He cracked open another bottle of Dickel while a
cigarette shook in his lips. A bag of ice sat in a bucket on the coffee
table, along with an empty can of Vienna sausage filled with butts
that now and then he'd take to the kitchen and empty in the garbage. She smoked more than him.

"I bet that's what it was. I bet I felt him die," she said, and he
knew that from now on this would be the mystic heart of a story she
would tell people.

"He told me something before he died."

"What?"

"He said I wasn't his."

"Oh." She lifted her glass and her eyes were hooded, lazy.
"Course you weren't. I might not be either."

He swallowed and paced along the shelf where his father kept a
bent antique bugle from the Civil War. "You ever heard from her?"

"No," Anneise said. "Don't know and don't care. Hey." She held
her hand out to him and he took it. She used his grip to raise off
the couch and stepped into his arms to dance to the song. "We got
the house, at least." She felt heavy in his arms. Close up, he could
see more wrinkles and sun spots along the edges of her face. She
brushed his cheek and laughed and they spun once to the music
and Wes fell into the couch. She laughed at him and then said she
was going to bed.

"All worn out. I'll see you tomorrow. I want to drive into town."

He waved her goodnight and sank into the couch with his drink
on his stomach. The room blurred and rocked. The needle hit the
end of the record, and it kept spinning with a clicking sound like a
metronome.

A week unwound into strange domesticity. Anneise now believed
she was psychic and had taken to asking Wes questions like "Were
you just thinking of a dog? Were you just thinking about Pop?" She
said, "Think of a color. Any color. I'll tell you what it is."

She guessed and he shook his head. "Red."

She looked at him with pity, as if he'd forgotten his alphabet. "No, Wes. Green. *Green.*"

Wes bought their groceries at a Kroger's in town, as he now avoided Cormier's. They ate in front the television, usually around six, when a local station showed reruns of *Cheers.* After they finished their bowls of canned pasta, Anneise took his with hers, as if to clean up, but just left both bowls on a shelf next to the dented bugle, then sat back down with her legs tucked. She leaned on one elbow against the couch's back, her head cocked and held by her hand. There was a browsy, lazy light below her half-dropped eyelids. "Wes?" she said. "Come here, Wes." She patted the cushion.

He stood and sat down beside her, and she turned her head a little, shifted her legs beneath her.

"Whyn't you have a girlfriend?"

He didn't answer.

"It's okay, Wes. Do they make you nervous?"

She bent to lift her beer off the coffee table and her neckline expanded and he could see down to the tips of her breasts beneath the shirt. She sat up and licked foam off her lip. "It's okay," she said. "I just wanted to know."

"No. Not really. They don't."

"So whyn't you have a girlfriend? You're a cute enough guy."

"I don't meet anyone." He shrugged, feeling shrunken, pathetic. "Where do you *meet* them? *How* do you meet them?"

She squinted at him and pondered his words. "I'd think of trying to get into school if I was you. Say McDeere or something. They got some kind of program you could get to, I bet."

He shrugged. "How do I do *that,* though? See, Anneise . . ." His voice shook, and he felt suddenly on the verge of tears. "I can't do *anything*. I don't know *how* to do *anything*."

"Oh. Wes, come here." She leaned forward and hugged him, lifted his face with one hand, stroking the back of his head. "We'll just have to teach you. Okay?"

Her green eyes absorbed his vision, and he had the sense of being tugged gently into them.

A booming from the doorway shook through the walls. His heart skipped a beat, more than one. Someone hammering on the front door with a mallet, maybe. *Boomboomboomboom.*

"Who?" Anneise said. But it didn't matter. There was such urgency in the knocking he knew the only way to get it to stop was to answer the door. He opened it slightly, ready to leap away. The door slammed open and a large, hairy man in a leather vest and filthy blue jeans burst into the foyer. Without turning around, he slammed the door behind him, his head whipping from side to side and causing the matted hair at his ears to flap. Wes was sitting on the floor. The man looked down at him and one thick eyebrow raised, the eye red and shaking. It moved to Anneise.

"Baby, by God. Baby baby baby. The whole time, baby, I was only like a couple days behind you. I'd hear 'She just went so-and-so,' or 'She was here last week,' or 'Said she was going home,' and when I heard that one, I thought, Well, maybe now she'll stay put long enough for me to catch up, and baby, here you are. Whoo." Barret Wagner again looked down at Wes and lent him a hand in rising.

"God. Damn. Sorry to bust in that way. I don't like being in the open too long. It sure feels vulnerable standing under that porch light. Which one are you again? It's Wesley, right? Old Wesley. Weird Wes. Wussley. Wuss. Hey, man. Hey. Goddamn." He shook Wes's hand and with his other stroked the chin of his dark beard. Mud and small debris cluttered its hairs.

The flesh of his arms was tumorous with muscle and bluish tattoos, each a different badly drawn picture, not like TJ's tattoos, which were a system of similar markings rather than individual designs. Wes looked over one of the hairy, spherical shoulders and saw Anneise rushing off the couch, her arms outstretched and her eyes glazed with the look of unquenchable loving fever he'd once seen in people at a revival.

"Oh God, Barret. Did I know you were coming? I think I might of known it. I think I might of *felt* it."

Wagner took a long bath that first night, refilling the tub with hot water each time it turned tepid and having Anneise bring him beers and stay in there, and when she came out, the front of her lavender T-shirt was soaking wet. He'd settled those guys that were after him, he said. That was old news, and as it turned out nothing, really. But there was still paper on him; he was a wanted man. It would be good for him to stay there awhile before deciding on his next move.

The next day Wagner had Wes go to the grocery store and buy

some provisions, including a number of seeds: tomato and water-melon and cabbage, also rosemary, basil, mint, thyme. He came home to the sounds of hooting from the back bedroom, a thump and squeak keeping erratic time against floor and wall. Wes left the groceries in the foyer and walked back outside to sit at the lake with the rocks.

The day after that, Anneise was up early and tilling rows to plant the seeds. Barret stood at the back door, his shirt off, nappy hair tugged into a ponytail. He was shockingly old, his face brazened and crusty, lumps of scar interrupting his thick black eyebrows. His skin was coarse and unevenly colored, his throat and arms the same fine texture of crepe paper Wes'd seen on Anneise's chest, but the torso pale and furred with swaths of coarse black hair. He nodded to Anneise in the small field of dirt spreading into the backyard. She was shoving a tiller back and forth like it was a mop.

"Meant to talk at you a bit," Wagner said.

"Why do you want to plant that stuff?" Wes asked. He'd just real-ized that the time it took to grow things from seed seemed to indi-cate on Wagner's part an intent to remain here, in his house and on his father's land.

"She's the kind needs something to do. That's one thing I always keep in mind about Anneise. She needs something to do. She's a sweet person, and she's got a lot of love to give, but you got to give her projects, things she can sink her teeth into. Or else she can be-come confused and do who knows what. She just gets bored too easy. That's one of the reasons we always got along: we both have complex minds. But I know how to handle her. She told me y'all just been sitting around ever' day. Drinking and listening to music and whatnot. So I figured I'd get her to start a garden. I know how to handle her. Give her a project. The girl's mind needs to be occu-pied, or she's like to get up to anything. There's always going to be a special sort of relationship a girl has to the man who first gutted her fish. You understand what I'm saying? I first shucked your sis-ter's clam, she was fifteen, and that's what she knows. I'm natural to her, like her hair, or like her fingernails." Anneise looked up at them both and waved, wiped her brow, and went back to shoving the tiller to and fro. Her hair was pulled up in a ponytail, and she wore a loose, flowered sundress. Wes's jaw was clenching so tightly he heard a molar crack.

Wagner crushed his beer can and let it drop at his feet. "Okay. Why I called you out here. One. I knowed you weren't in no army. It was TJ. I remember hearing that when I heard about him shooting himself. I seen your papers in the desk in there. Said you couldn't be in the army. Something wrong with your head. Anyway, just so you know. Anneise don't know right now, but I do, just so you know. Two. We're going to need to be splitting those subsidies from now on. Three ways. Two parts to us and one to you. You know they ain't yours anyway. You didn't do nothing to earn them, and if the taxman or whoever finds out your daddy's gone, you're going to lose them anyway. Three. You're welcome to stay on here if you want, but sometimes a man decides it's time to stop wandering and put down some roots. I think that finding Anneise here and it being where we come from and with the house empty, your dad dying I mean, it seems pretty right to me that I should marry her and fill her with some babies. You don't like any of that, I understand, but keep it to yourself. I tolerate you, Wes. That's it. And don't think of turning her against me, because it can't happen. Like I said, the holes in both your sister's body and heart are molded around my gristle-missile, and she will forever after follow me wherever after that I may lead." He spit on the ground and scratched his stomach, turned his face up to the sun. "Anyways. I wanted to be clear about all that."

3.

Wesley stood slightly behind Deputy Jimmy Dupres, between two of the five police cars whose flashing lights surrounded his house. Dupres talked into a megaphone.

"You need to come on out now, Barret! Keeping the girl a hostage isn't doing anybody no good!" He looked over his shoulder, still holding the megaphone outstretched. "You said they's guns in there, yeah?"

"Yeah. We got shotguns. I'm telling you. He's plain crazy."

From the house they heard Wagner shout, "She's not a hostage!"

"Well, let her go then, Barret! This ain't have nothing to do with her!"

The house was silent, and the other deputies, five of them, had their pistols drawn, fingers squirming around the handles. Dupres was tall, broad-shouldered in his crisp tan uniform, but he had an unfortunately recessive chin, and rather than a jaw line, his face more or less just narrowed into his neck, giving it the appearance of something squeezed out his shoulders. He looked around at his fellow officers, all wearing sunglasses and clearly uncomfortable with just standing there. Three of the cars were stationed in the cord grass, and two others were in the front. They'd ridden over Anneise's newly planted garden and crushed the three signs his father had kept out front.

"Hey," said Wes, "what's the warrant for, exactly?"

"One in Texas is for narco trafficking and assault. One in Oklahoma's for indecent exposure and destruction of property. Didn't get the whole story on that one. Something about lawn furniture."

The front door of the house opened and the deputies all raised their guns, hammers clicked, but it was only Anneise, her arms lifted and hands up. She wore high denim shorts and a red halter, and one of the deputies whistled. Her head turned back and forth, taking it all in, and she smiled sheepishly to the officers as she walked with delicate steps toward Dupres, keeping her arms up the whole time.

"Hey, Jimmy," she said.

He nodded to her and said, "You can put your arms down, hon. He alone in there now?"

"Well, yeah. Hey, Wes. But he's worried. He wanted to know if there's something y'all could work out or something. He sent me to negotiate, like."

"We're not going to be doing any of that, I think," said the deputy, and he touched her elbow and guided her to the rear of the formation.

"Oh," she said. "Well, what's going to happen?"

"Look, Anneise, you got to be honest with yourself about a few things here." Still holding her elbow, he turned her gently toward him and frowned sympathetically. "You got mixed up with a bad man, hon. It ain't your fault, really. I remember him a little. He's always been trouble, and your pop prob'ly should of kept him from you, but that didn't happen. He's a bad man and a wanted man. As a sworn officer of the law, it is my duty to bring him to justice." As he said the last part, Dupres's face tilted up and off into the distance, and if he'd had a jaw, it would have been a noble, soldierly pose.

"Oh," said Anneise. She glanced at Wes. Deputy Dupres had set the megaphone on the car hood, and he grabbed her shoulders and squared her toward him.

He spoke in a halting kind of cadence. "I'm sorry you had to be witness to all this, Anneise. I'd have liked to spare you from it. It's a sour side of justice when it has to touch the innocent. But I am bound by duty. Can you understand that, Anneise?" He braced her shoulders and drew her closer to him.

"Okay," she said.

"Be glad your brother gave us the tip. This way we're able to come in, get him out your life. You still got time to start over." He touched her face. "Best to think of him as already gone."

"Wait. Wes?" She turned suddenly to her brother, her face crinkled in anger. "Wes gave you a tip? You ratted on Barret, Wes?"

Wes shrugged and took a step back. "Well, look —"

Anneise ran over and started hitting Wes on the shoulders, back and forth, crying, "How could you, Wes? He *loved* you. Like a *brother!* Damn you, Wesley!" Dupres pulled her off, and she turned into his chest, burying her face there while he patted her back.

"Mind," the deputy said, "I never have had much respect for the type to sell out somebody, specially someone's practically family. There's a cowardice there I find hard to abide. A hardheartedness. But besides what this tells us about your brother's character, I am still duty-bound to the law."

Anneise hugged the deputy and lifted her wet face to gaze up at him. "I *knew* something like this would happen. I *felt* it."

A gunshot crashed and everyone ducked and crouched, Deputy Dupres throwing Anneise to the ground and wrapping around her like a parka. In the echo of the shot, one of the deputies called, "That's me, sir!"

Without rising off Anneise, Dupres called over his shoulder, "What? What was that?"

The deputy called from the side of the house. "Thought I saw something, sir. Out in this field. Looked like a big cat or something."

"Jesus Christ. Holster your weapon. No, wait. Don't. But you're an asshole, Kilpatrick!"

"Yessir," the deputy replied.

"Hey!" they all heard, muffled, from the house. "What's going on out there?"

Dupres finally rose off Wes's sister and helped her to her feet. "It'll be all right, Anneise." He stepped back from her and wiped her cheek. "But right now we've got an armed and dangerous fugitive barricaded in your house, and it's my duty to bring him in."

Anneise sniffled and held on to the deputy's hand, staring up at his mirrored sunglasses and chinless beard stubble. "I could feel that all of this was going to happen, Jimmy. I can sense things."

Wagner called from the house again. "I'm not going to jail!"

"All right, boys," said Dupres. "You heard him." He lifted the megaphone and called, "Have it your way, Barret!" Adjusting his glasses, he held up his hands to shoo Wes and Anneise backward. "Keep back, y'all. All right, boys. Swarm."

The deputies rushed the house, five of them scattering around the front and back. One kicked open the front door, ducked aside, and the rest invaded the foyer. They heard someone shout, and then an eruption of gunfire filled the white A-frame, the windows blinking with muzzle flashes. At the front and back doors, they poured all their bullets into the house. Dupres watched while clutching Anneise to his chest, telling her, "Shh. Don't look, hon."

Wes stood alone, smelling the pungent smoke that wafted outward from the house and spilled over the grass and the cars. When he turned, Anneise was clutching Dupres, and she said, "I always *knew* I'd have a broken heart."

They'd made a terrible mess of Barret, as if he'd exploded, and Wes was the one who scraped and scrubbed the blood and meat off the walls and ceiling, threw out the rug, and on his hands and knees scoured the living room floor with steel wool and powdered cleaner that bleached and roughened the floorboards. The cops had dug out the bullets, but the holes still riddled the walls. Anneise couldn't stay there after what happened. One of the deputies had gathered her things and brought them outside to her, and before the ambulance arrived to gather Barret's remains, she had already left for Jimmy Dupres's trailer, which he said she was welcome to use as long as needs be.

Two weeks later the house had been cleaned except for a few tiny dark spots, which he'd now and then see that he'd missed, the ragged bullet holes. The Dickel was gone.

He took his pop's old lawn chair out into the cord grass, dragging it along behind him while holding TJ's old shotgun over one shoulder.

He sat down in the chair, the rough grass taller than his head now. It was midmorning, the sun still low, and a light breeze tickled his skin, the frame creaking at his weight. He stood the shotgun up and held the stock with his feet on the ground. He'd received a letter yesterday. His sister was going to contest ownership of the house. She said that she and Jimmy Dupres would need to move in after their wedding.

The grass rustled like parchment, like seeds in the husks of a kind of marsh plant whose name he couldn't recall. Each stalk of grass had a bright, burning spot at its tip, like comets. Grackles chattered from the trees, unseen, a little hysterical. He thought of TJ in his tattoos. Did he see the sun come up? Had his brother watched for the sunrise, letting it act as a kind of signal?

He leaned forward and pulled the gun toward him till his chin rested on the barrel. Reaching down, his thumb hooked the trigger. The sun's angle changed, and suddenly the stalks became like candles holding flames that were each growing more intense and bright, and it seemed he was surrounded by fire. He knew he had to do it, if it was going to get done. Shut his eyes and pressed down on the trigger, flinched and yelped at the same time. The trigger didn't budge, and he had to press the safety off.

Trembling, he moved to deactivate the catch, and when he glanced up, the creature was staring at him through a break in the grass ahead. It was near, maybe eight feet away.

Tawny, the colors of wheat and dust and wood smoke in evening, its face like an arrowhead, the nose flat and pinkish gray, the bobcat took a step out, toward him, its feet falling softly as ash, not making a sound. Its eyes were two bronze coins, utterly without pity or regard, only staring coldly, almost without interest, but observing still. Wes's breath caught and his fingers trembled. Smoothly as he could, Wes lifted the gun and leaned the barrel forward until aiming at the creature. The cat began to circle him slowly, each of its movements an implication of coiled power and restrained speed. He let the gun follow, the chair groaning. He turned around in the chair when the cat was behind him, and it continued circling, the eyes flat and nearly daring him, he felt. His breath stuttered in his ears, and he could taste the sweat now soaking his face.

The cat completed a circle and returned in front of him. The creature studied him, then turned and sauntered slowly back into the brightening grass, crackling the dried stalks, until its colors blended and faded into the color of the field and he could see it no more. A noise thundered from the north field, and Wes ran out the grass, looked across the lake as bursts of fire crowned the top of the refineries, and a thick black smoke rose up, wobbling and crooked, with a slanting flow that trailed across the hot blue sky. Thin streamers of fire arced down and sizzled to steam in the water. A searing wind blew across his face and bent the high stalks.

Turning back, he saw to the road, where now a plume of dust rose above it, a rooster tail of dirt kicked up by an approaching car. A vehicle was coming toward the house. Another explosion, and the heat washed over him; he could see the orange and yellow snapping, hear the sirens, and as the dark smoke fled into the sky and the dust advanced on the road, he felt himself there in both streams, both coming and going, staying and leaving all at once.

GARRY CRAIG POWELL

Kamila and the King of Kandy

MALSIRI HAD BEEN on his feet so long that the plinking of
the piano was turning into the tinkling of the lobby fountain
and the tingling in his back. A trained masseur, he knew which
muscles were seizing up — deltoids, calves, and quadriceps — and
stretched as much as was seemly for a man in his position. His promotion two weeks ago had come as a surprise: all the other manag-
ers in the Al Maghreb Hotel were Westerners or Arabs. He felt
smart in his black suit, if also a trifle comical, as he performed shallow knee bends. Maintaining his dignity was essential, of course. At
home in Sri Lanka, his wife and daughters depended on him, and
he never forgot it.

Yet for all his stretching, Malsiri couldn't help tensing up when
he saw the white girl lurching through the date palms, her bare feet
flapping soundlessly on the red marble floor, her hair clumped like
flax. She wore a cream miniskirt and a misbuttoned blouse that
looked torn. As she passed the coffee shop, Emirati men in *dishdashas* stared. She was no older than his eldest, Yosodhara. He had
often seen her talking to older white men with florid faces and Ha-
waiian shirts and Arabs in business suits. Usually she smoldered or
smiled; today her eyes were shuttered. Even so, she was walking
with a purpose. She glanced at Angie and Edna but had obviously
picked him out. Her arms and neck were bruised and scratched,
Malsiri saw as she came closer, and she wasn't wearing a brassiere.
Something red spotted her skirt — nail polish or blood? But her
karma would not unsettle him: he would stay serene.

She sagged over the black marble counter. Her breasts reposed
on it like plastic bags of milk. She raised her head and pushed her-

self back. Two of her fingernails were broken; one was bleeding. "Call the police," she said in English, with an accent like a Russian in a James Bond film.

Her eyes were as blue as tropical fish yet seemed not to see him; or rather, they detected his presence but looked through him as if he were a shadow. She reeked of scent, alcohol and cigarettes, and a cocktail of other smells, glandular and primal. Twenty-five years of massaging naked people had given him a sensitive nose.

"Miss — Madam," he corrected himself, masking his distaste. If he was not mistaken, he smelled burning. "I hope we can avoid —"

"The police," she said, eyes brimming. Like him, she was controlling herself. Again he was reminded of Yosodhara and wished he could comfort her.

"It's better to keep the police out of things in the UAE. Why don't you tell me what is the problem?"

"Room 424," she said, rolling her R's. "Three Arabs. Drunk."

"This is bad," Malsiri said in his soft baritone. His voice had become as soothing as a saxophone over the years, as he rubbed clenched muscles with sandalwood, cedar oil, and myrrh, while tapes of chimes, streams, waterfalls, windblown leaves, and songbirds played in the background. "But in a hotel like this, the police usually have blind eyes to such things. Who are these Arabs?"

"Locals."

He couldn't recall having seen her with locals; she seemed a cut above that kind of customer. So much the worse, if true. "You are sure?"

Her upper lip curled. "They speak Arabic. They have *dishdashas* and sandals. Beards. Two of them wear *ghutras* on their heads. One, a baseball cap."

"A baseball cap?"

"Backwards."

Malsiri shook his head. "Very bad."

Her surprise came through her hollow tone. "The *baseball cap* is bad?"

"No," he said, though it was — Emirati youths who wore baseball caps backward were invariably troublesome. Many had "studied" in America, where it seemed they learned nothing but bad English and worse manners. "No, I mean it is bad that they are locals. You are Russian?"

"Polish."

"Ah." Poland was near Sweden, where he had taken courses. Those were cold countries; people had to run like machines there. Love, it had seemed to him in Sweden, was in the process of being abolished. It was each person for himself. Malsiri was acutely and constantly aware of the racial hierarchy in the Gulf. Whites were above Asians and Africans but below locals, who were God's favorites. He thought aloud. "A Polish girl — lady. And they are men, Emiratis."

"You are saying the police will not believe me?"

"You must understand: the police in the UAE are most of them Moroccans. Some Sudanese, some Yemenis. Only the officers are Emiratis. It is not a question of who they believe. They are afraid. The Emiratis have the *wasta*."

Malsiri could generally mute the background music, but now it intruded, the tuneless plinking giving way to a melodramatic swell that reminded him of scores in black-and-white American movies. It echoed horribly amid the marble columns and palm trees of the foyer. The pianist was a Pole, he recalled. Her name began like his, Mal-something. She was a pretty blonde in her thirties with a Yemeni lover. Rich, no doubt.

"They pay me for sex," her tattered compatriot proclaimed.

Malsiri had learned not to show emotion when clients, facedown on the massage table, revealed their shameful secrets. Angie and Edna were listening, slyly glancing at her, at him, and at one another. The Filipinas were a mystery to him, deferential, eager to please, childish in size and manner, and yet seductive — in spite of himself, Malsiri lusted for them sometimes — and also, if he was not mistaken, cool and calculating. He was sure they despised this girl. But he was a Buddhist, and all living creatures deserved his compassion. He looked at the courtesan, as he thought of her in the Victorian English he had learned at school, until her expression softened.

"Miss," he began, and this time did not correct himself, "if you are . . . if this is your profession, the police will say you are the guilty — you are guilty, too, at least. You understand? I can make a complaint only if you stay and give your name."

She gave him a defiant look. "No problem."

Imagining how badly they must have hurt or humiliated her, he wanted to whip the Arabs. Thank goodness his daughters would have college educations — Yosodhara was already doing her B.A.

in public relations in Colombo. In their brick bungalow in the sacred city of Kandy, they had air conditioning, a Sony TV, a satellite dish, a computer. On his biennial vacations, neighbors joked that he was the King of Kandy, and indeed, according to family legend, his great-grandfather had been an illegitimate son of the nineteenth-century monarch. "The police will take you," he said, the possible consequences playing out like a Sinhalese melodrama. "And you will go to prison." Malsiri saw himself being fired and returning in ignominy to Sri Lanka. The Tigers would bomb Kandy again, and this time they would destroy his house. If his daughters survived, they would have to marry beneath them, take jobs as secretaries — even come to the Gulf to work as housemaids. He pictured his wife in the loony bin. "It is better you forget this."

"I don't mind if I go to prison, if they go also."

Her eyes were so blue that he thought of the ocean and recalled the time his parents had taken him to visit a fisherman, a distant kinsman. Malsiri had been so proud when his "uncle" let him steer the wooden boat. But then the men cast lines over the stern and hooked two kingfish, fierce warriors in armor, which were left to thrash in a tin bowl. Soon they weakened and lay with sides heaving, gills flapping, and mouths agape, astonished at what had happened to them. When would his father throw them back? He didn't dare ask. At length he put the question to his mother, who said the fisherman would eat them later. He begged her to save them. When she didn't respond, he whispered that he would throw them into the sea. His mother gave him a menacing glare. In the end he had watched helplessly as the creatures suffocated, and this, he had realized, was what it meant to be a man: you must be cruel and hard. His mother praised him afterward for not crying. But even then Malsiri knew that it was only cowardice that kept him from flipping the fish into the ocean. Afterward he must have repressed the memory, for he did not think about it for years. It was much later before it troubled him again — only when he was grown did he begin to ask himself what a man truly was.

After his brief trance faded, the courtesan was looking at him with Yosodhara's trustful eyes.

"I do not know what they did do," he said, satisfied that she could see him now, that he was no longer just a faceless flunky to her, "but adultery is a serious crime in the UAE." He told her what was supposed to happen. Their names and photos would be published in the newspapers. They would go to prison and be flogged. And this might actually happen — if the Emiratis were from poor families with no *wasta*. But how could he say anything so tactless? How could he warn her that they would probably get off scot-free, because they were men and locals and she was nothing but a foreign whore? Yet to him, she was a child needing reassurance that justice would prevail. What was the right thing to do?

He could still have Mahesh escort her out. That was what he *should* do, in her interest and his. It was what the GM would expect of him, too. He took a deep breath, settled into himself, pictured the oblong lake in Kandy and the Temple of the Tooth with its seated gilded Buddha; he muttered a Pali mantra from the Dhammapada, and the chakra at the top of his skull opened, buzzing and crackling. Should he be kind or tell the truth? What sort of man was he? His Buddha-nature would decide.

She heard the wheezing and panting of a dog having nightmares, but of course there were no dogs in five-star hotels in the Gulf. It was her own breathing.

"What is your good name, madam?" asked the man — *Malsiri,* according to the black tag with white letters on his lapel. He had brandy-brown eyes and a receding hairline and was as glossy as the furniture in her parents' flat in Krakow.

She didn't say Sonya, which she'd been calling herself since she'd seduced the Englishman in Lord Jim's, with a gaucheness that was incredible to her now. *Kamila,* she said, her real name sounding sonorous and regal to her after so long. He wrote it down with a fat fountain pen like her grandfather's, which spoke to her of fireside folktales in the Tatra Mountains. He asked more questions. Was she sure she was doing the right thing? She had better wait until she was no longer so upset. Kamila told him she didn't care what happened to her, as long as the pigs were punished.

It was impossible to explain why she was willing to go to prison. She had no desire to relive all she had been through since arriving in Dubai — resigning from her hotel job after the Egyptian GM had almost raped her, working illegally in nightclubs for a while, then slipping into prostitution when she could no longer pay her way at Andrzej's. She didn't admit that she couldn't face telling her parents what she had become. She didn't try to depict the images of home that appeared in her mind with the sudden sadness of a diminished chord: the ashen apartment blocks in the suburbs, five stories high and kilometers long, where Poles roosted like battery hens; the cellulose factory of Nowa Huta that made the medieval city smell as if it were rotting; and Auschwitz-Birkenau, which clung to Krakow's skirts like a festering sore, out of sight but never out of mind. Why mention the squandering of her talent — who would believe that theater critics had once praised her roles in Chekhov and Ibsen? And was there any point in declaring that she was finished, that she could not turn another trick, not one, even with the shy, affable middle-aged men Andrzej did his best to pick out for her from the colleges and Internet City? She was aware that she wasn't being rational. Nevertheless, she knew what she was doing, she assured the man in the black suit, who nodded like her father. But it was too late for sympathy, compassion, or even love, to save her. She was Hedda Gabler. Only self-annihilation could satisfy her now.

"Hurry, please," she begged. "They will leave."

Malgosia, a fellow Pole whom Kamila knew, was pounding out "Penny Lane," a cheerful song with wistful undertones, even in her heavy-handed delivery. An Omani was checking in, some dignitary with a silver belt and curved *khanjar* — Kamila had an impulse to snatch it, run to room 424, and stab and slash and cover herself with gore. Maybe if she went to jail she could expiate her shame, like Lord Jim on his island. She knew what women's prisons in the Emirates were like: in Al Ain she had visited one of Andrzej's Somali girls, who had been sentenced to seven years for "adultery" when she had a baby. Kamila thought she might be able to comfort the despairing maids from the Philippines, Sri Lanka, and Indonesia who had become pregnant after being raped by their masters; she could teach their children to read, make up plays for them to perform. A blood vessel above her right eye pulsed as if fit to burst. She yearned for extinction, but maybe she could do some good first.

"Call the police." She put on her Clytemnestra face and cast all her imperiousness into her voice. She had been renowned for her withering looks. *Your eyes lacerate like broken glass,* the great Kieslowski had once told her.

"Tell me what happened first," Malsiri said. "How did you get away?"

Musabbah, the ringleader, had gone to the bathroom, and the

one with the Hard Rock Cafe cap had passed out. The last of the trio, a skinny boy wearing kohl and mascara, she kneed in the balls, making him yelp like a puppy, and then she jabbed her claws into his eyes. Leaving her shoes and purse where they'd fallen, she dashed into the corridor, wadding her panties to stanch the blood, and dressed in a frenzy, lest one of them dragged her back in. No time to comb her hair, wipe her face, rinse her mouth. In the elevator a woman in a sari pretended not to see her. Her stomach heaved. She told Malsiri this but wouldn't tell what they had done, she decided.

"But why did you agree to go to with three men?"

The fountain burbled, hissed, and foamed. The Omani with the dagger had gone, and the receptionists stole glances at her. Piano notes sprayed over a scene that came back in stroboscopic flashes. *I knew it was wrong to trust him.* In the coffee shop, the three *shabob* had sat beside her. Musabbah, a short, muscular man who boasted that he could lift a baby camel with one hand, had invited her to drink Scotch and watch a porno film — *Very excited,* he said. There were three rules in this game, Andrzej had taught her. *Rule number one: never accept a client unless I'm there to protect you.* The Somali girls had seconded him. Andrzej was not like some pimps, who did business with men they knew to be violent. *Rule number two: no locals, however much they offer.* Andrzej had been known to break this rule when he was short on blow, but only with the Somalis, not his principal asset. The going rate was a hundred dirhams a trick, just under thirty dollars, but as a natural blonde, Kamila could charge wealthy businessmen five hundred or even more. *Come,* Musabbah said, *we give you thousand. We,* she noted. *Rule number three:* never, never, never *take more than one at a time.* But the sirens were singing more seductively each day. A hair dryer in the bath, they chanted. Pills. Poison. Stuff the exhaust pipes of a client's car. Slip into the amniotic waters of the creek.

Or this? "One thousand each?" she asked hopefully.

Musabbah and his friends grinned at each other. *"Inshallah."*

She would be able to fly to Warsaw and pay her train fare to Krakow.

"What do you want me to do?"

The Emiratis sniggered like schoolboys.

"Everything," said the pretty boy with the Hard Rock Dubai cap. He had a fluffy beard, pimples, and candid eyes.

The skinny one with eyeliner sneered.

"Everything, no," Musabbah said. "What you like. You say."

Kamila sipped her cappuccino and sized him up. He gave her a disarming grin, all crooked teeth and flaring eyes. Something about him, and the skinny one, made her queasy. For some reason she thought of the Tartar hordes who had overrun Krakow in the fourteenth century. She was changing her mind when she heard the opening chords of a Chopin prelude. In spite of Malgosia's clumsy rendition, a wave of homesickness swept over her.

"All right, I suck your dicks," Kamila said, not without revulsion, however often she had used such terms. "You understand?"

Musabbah and the Hard Rock Cafe had to explain to Eyeliner.

Oral sex gave her a measure of control; at least she wouldn't be pinned beneath the weight of a man, and if one of them tried anything, he was in a vulnerable position. One of the Somalis claimed she had bitten off a Chinaman's cock when he had pinched her nipples. "Only sucking," she said, to make it clear. "No fucking."

"You are poet," Musabbah joked.

She ignored him. "Agreed?"

"Agree."

Three in the room, though, spelled danger. "One at a time," she said.

"*Shu?*"

"Not all together," she explained. "First you, then you, then him." The Chopin cascaded around her, bright as a waterfall or shattering glass, sharp, piercing.

Musabbah raised his eyebrows. "We not hurt you. I swear. We Muslim."

One last time she repeated her terms, and the boys nodded.

"*Yallah,*" she said, standing. She preferred Arabic when she was playing Sonya.

"What happened?" Malsiri asked her point-blank.

She found herself telling him most of it. They drank Johnnie Walker and for a few minutes didn't touch her. They put on the video, and she saw a woman sucking off a donkey and a man pissing in a woman's mouth. She wanted to run, but one of them was standing by the door. The other two touched themselves, pawed her. She asked them to turn the movie off, but they laughed. The room had gold velvet curtains, like a theater. She made a break for it, but Musabbah caught her and slammed her against the wall, hurled her down on the bed. They roared. She didn't tell Malsiri about the black horse rearing over her, a beast of fire, striking her down, smothering her. The Arabs' movements were synchronized. The Hard Rock and Eyeliner held her down and splayed her legs, while Musabbah stubbed cigarettes on her inner thighs and Arab pop music drowned her screams. His eyes were those of the stuffed stoat in her grandfather's cabin in Zakopane. *Help me, Jesus.* It all ran together and backward. The Hard Rock pulled up the skirt of his *dishdasha,* unwrapped his loincloth, and straddled her face. He was limp. He slapped her face, screamed at her to suck. She opened her mouth. Maybe they would stop hurting her if she was submissive. The Tartars had raped in packs, swarming like rodents over women, using every orifice in their victims' bodies and opening more with their knives. God couldn't exist. When the pimple-faced savage pissed in her mouth, it knocked the breath out of her, and she sputtered and choked. She couldn't bring herself to relate this, but she told Malsiri what the thin one had done to her with the whiskey bottle. She forced herself to go on. They had turned her over on her stomach and done what she never allowed clients to do. Fucked her up the ass. *Twice.* "And the bastards didn't even pay me," she ended.

Malsiri shut his eyes. "I am sorry," he said, compressing his lips. His voice almost broke. "I understand that you want to punish them. But if I call the police, you will go to prison. It will be better for you to leave."

"I know what will happen to me. I want them to lock me away. I want them to take these animals off the streets. Please."

Malsiri gazed into her eyes longer than her boyfriend Jacek had ever done. She felt no awkwardness, but rather a stillness that reminded her of taking communion or cocaine. She gazed back, unafraid and unashamed. For the first time in months, someone saw her as a human being. This stranger was looking into her soul, accepting her — *loving* her — as Jesus once had. Malgosia thumped the keys as if she were angry and bored, which she surely was, but Kamila no longer felt agitated. "I am certain," she said.

And yet Malsiri still seemed unsure. What was he thinking?

How could he save her? He'd explained that she would go to prison. He was about to ask Mahesh to lead her away when he realized that she would take it as a betrayal. A pang of longing overwhelmed him. If only he could see Yosodhara now; if he could just spend a single hour with his family in Kandy.

"If they have *wasta*, they may go free," he said.

Her eyes were blue, clear, cold. *I'll take that chance*, they told him plainly.

He was strong enough to accept his dharma. But what about his family? What about Yosodhara? His daughter was too plain and dark-skinned to attract suitors, although she was clever and the purest, sweetest person he had ever known. As he wavered, her presence touched him, flickering like a candle, bathing him in mysterious light. Like Kamila, she didn't speak, or need to. From the look in her eyes, steadfast and selfless, he knew he had to honor this poor girl's confidence in him. Yosodhara would be disappointed if he put himself or even his family first.

"Call the police," he told Angie, without taking his eyes off Kamila.

"Sir?"

"Call the police."

The Filipina sidled over to him. "Maybe we should speak first with the GM, sir," she said in her little-girl voice.

"All right. Call him."

"In this moment he is with the sheikh."

He frowned. "I'm not going to wait. Call the police."

"The GM will be angry with us, sir."

"I will take responsibility."

"Sir."

As Angie turned away and picked up the phone, Kamila thanked Malsiri with her eyes. Near collapse though she was, and knowing the police would humiliate her and prison might be the end of her, aware that she had made a mess of her life — yet she would demand justice, no matter what the cost. Her communion with this stranger had given her the strength to endure. She had stood up and would stay on her feet or go down fighting. Only when the gray uniforms and black boots pressed around her did she feel herself swooning, just as a messy mazurka blurred into a jerky polka.

How could a Pole butcher Chopin like that?

RANDY ROHN

The Man Who Fell in Love with the Stump of a Tree

FROM *Loch Raven Review*

THE STRANGEST MAN in the world came to town about a year
ago. People don't come to this town. They leave. At one time, it
had been a pretty good town. But no more. It had once been a nice
little bedroom community for a huge auto plant in nearby Ander-
son, Indiana. But, the plant closed years ago, and our town started
closing down, too. About the only people who stayed were older
folks who didn't see any other options that made a lot of sense.
There were a handful of people scattered throughout younger age
groups that didn't have any other options, period. And me. I found
another better-paying job in another state but turned it down.
Then I stopped looking.

I stayed here because I couldn't think of anywhere else I'd rather
be. I had a job. I felt comfortable with the people I knew, even if
most of them were older than me. I liked my home. I liked my bar. I
liked the diner in town a lot. I ate there every day. I couldn't imagine having lunch anywhere else. I couldn't imagine living in another home or going to another bar or doing anything else on Friday nights than attending local high school football games and
basketball games. That was pretty much my problem, I guess. I
wasn't one for imagining things. What-ifs made me feel uncomfortable.

My town, Tivoli, Indiana, wasn't near anything worthwhile. It
wasn't on the way to anywhere worth going to. It didn't have anything worth seeing. It was just a town with half the businesses shut-

tered up, a few old-man bars, a truly spectacular diner, a library
that no one used, two gas stations, an old doctor, an older dentist,
and a drunken lawyer. It had an abandoned stock car track south of
town. An abandoned glass factory also south of town. Some abandoned car lots. Abandoned churches and lumberyards here and
there. Abandoned hope everywhere.

In a small town you run across some strange folks. When I was
growing up, when things were good and the future was fine, some
off-the-wall folks here and there were part of everyday life. We
didn't think much about them. My kindergarten teacher was an
old maid who had once gone to bed for twenty years because her
fiancé left her standing at the altar. There were four or five farmers
who got together in a pole barn outside of town and smoked bella-
donna every Saturday night. One of the town dentists — we had
two at the time — used to have a bucket by his dental chair for dis-
carding extracted teeth. His cure for any dental problem was to
pull a tooth or two. And he only emptied the bucketful of teeth
when it started overflowing, about once every year and a half.

He was the one who stayed.

When a town starts going sour, as Tivoli did, people get even
stranger. More people talk to themselves. The graffiti painted on
the schoolhouse makes less sense. A church that worships UFOs is
founded.

So, in a town of strange, you had to really zigzag outside the lines
to be called that. And Ringo Wink Pitchwinger was, as everyone
who met him agreed, one of the strangest acts in our dying circus
of a town.

He looked strange. He dressed strange. He talked strange. He had
a strange name, for cryin' out loud. He made it even stranger by
the way he introduced himself.

"I'm Ringo Wink," he would say in his voice that jumped around
from high-pitched to low-pitched like a nervous adolescent on
speed. "But you can call me Wink, winky-wink-wink," he would say
while winking his loopy left eye.

Behind his back people called him Winky Walleye.

He was moderately tall, about six feet two, and very, very skinny
except for a round little potbelly that looked like he had swallowed
a playground kickball. He had one blue eye and that crazy brown

eye. His skin was a delicate shade of Elmer's Glue-All with a cellu-
lose-sponge complexion that spoke of teenage years squeezing zits.
His hair was saddle brown and stringy with a bald spot that was a
thick stripe down the center of his scalp, for a reverse-Mohawk effect. He had Dave Letterman gap in his front teeth. He smiled all
the time.

His clothes were clean but silly. No natural fibers were to be
found anywhere in his wardrobe. He usually wore sky-blue, too-
short, Sansabelt slacks, short-sleeved shirts in Starburst candy colors of some shiny material that was so thin you could see the wife-
beater undershirt underneath, neon-colored socks with two stripes
at the top, and PF Flyers tennis shoes, black with pencil-eraser-col-
ored soles.

Women found him creepy. Children found him scary. Men
found him full of it, but funny. I found him at Annie's Diner. Or
rather, he found me.

I was having Dixie's Diablo mixed meat hash with poached eggs.
It was one of the diner's specialties and my favorite. I was at the
point where the spices, peppers, and whatever else mixed into it
that elevated regular mixed meat hash to Diablo were beginning to
make my scalp tingle and forehead pop tiny beads of sweat.

He walked in and sat down.

Annie's wasn't one of those places you just walked in. Everything
about it screamed old grease and bad food. The windows facing the
street were buggy on the outside and smeary on the inside. Scotch-
taped on them were all sorts of Xeroxed flyers in various shades of
white, dirty white, and sun-faded colors. If anyone wanted to tape
something up, they could. Annie never took anything down. Never.
I know there was a missing-cat flyer from 1988.

Against one wall were booths with cracked vinyl seats and dirty-
yellow foam rubber trying to escape. When Annie and her sister,
Dixie, felt unusually energetic, they slapped some duct tape over
the cracks. The wall beside the booths was decorated with anything
anyone wanted to tack up, also. There were old insurance calen-
dars, football schedules from junior high and high school, business
cards from real estate people, and tri-fold brochures hawking who
knows what.

When Wink sat down, Annie walked over and gave him a menu
featuring mainly breakfast food, served all day, a few soups, and

many chilies, from Chili Blanco, made with chicken and white corn, to Cincinnati Chili, served on top of spaghetti. The grease may have been old, but the food was good.

"Need some coffee, honey?" Annie asked. Strangers were called "honey," and regulars were called "sugar" if unmarried, "darlin'" if married.

Wink did his Ringo Wink, winky-wink-wink bit.

Annie smiled and asked him again about the coffee.

"I like my coffee like I like my women, black and full-bodied," he said.

Annie stopped smiling and snorted. The only other time I had heard her snort was when the county health inspector came around and told her the hanging light bulb above the grill wasn't up to code and needed to be encased in something so it wouldn't shatter and get glass in the food.

"If it ever shatters and glass gets in the food, we'll throw the food away," she said. But he wasn't convinced, so she eventually bolted it to the wall and put a screen-wire cage around it. After Wink described his coffee preference, he proceeded to tell no one in particular but everyone in the place some unfunny, corny, yet borderline offensive jokes. No one even laughed politely, which was unusual considering most of the people were of the age that compelled polite laughter for anyone trying their hand at humor, especially strangers.

He cleared out Annie's in a hurry.

I stuck around because his bad jokes and silly banter amused me.

In fact, I kind of stuck around most of the afternoon because I didn't have anything better to do.

"What do you see in that jerk?" people in town would ask me.

"Well, for one thing I enjoy his BS. He makes me laugh. And deep down I think he's a nice guy."

I couldn't have been more wrong.

"I just don't like him," Annie told me one of the few times I was hanging out at the diner without him.

"I also think I've seen him before. I just can't figure out where," she said.

Another old coot sitting in the diner, Gifford Brown, told me practically the same thing.

"He's been around here before," Gifford said. "I'm sure of it."

Gifford looks to me like he's had some chromosome damage. People in town say he's "touched in the head." He usually doesn't talk much, and when he does say something, it usually has nothing to do with what anyone else is talking about and rarely has much to do with reality. So it was rather odd that he said something not odd.

However, I asked Wink about what they said, and he said he'd never even been in the state of Indiana before.

Wink and I usually met at the diner, and I'd have my Diablo hash and poached eggs or mile-high meatloaf, and he'd have a cup of coffee and a plate of crinkle-cut fries.

Annie didn't say much to us when we were together.

The few times I came in alone she had plenty to say.

"You're a pretty nice guy. That Wink clown is going to get you in trouble," she'd say.

There were whispers in town that we were a gay couple. We weren't. I wasn't.

After spending some time at the diner, I would go back to work and meet him at the Tic-Tock Bar afterward. We'd drink boilermakers until closing and tell stories and joke around. The guys in the bar eventually accepted him and grew to appreciate his silly stories, bad jokes, and drunken banter.

Then he fell in love with a stump.

One Friday night he wanted me to take a drive out in the country instead of taking him home to the apartment he rented above the old five-and-dime, which was now a consignment shop.

"Where are we going?" I asked.

"Just drive," he said.

So I drove up and down gravel roads west of town, turning left or right when he told me. We drove until a little past four, and finally he asked me to take him home.

The next night, after the bar closed, we did the same thing. Sunday, after I went to church, we drove around again, only this time we were sober. Finally, around midnight, he asked me to stop. We were on the county line road next to the abandoned Rutherford farm. I pulled the car over to the side of the road.

He got out of the car. He walked around, squinting at the fields.

"Turn in here," he said.

"There's nowhere to turn."

"C'mon, do the old Winkmeister a favor and turn in," he begged.

I didn't much like the idea. Even though there wasn't a fence, I was afraid of getting stuck. However, there did seem to be an old lane running into the heart of the farm, although it was overgrown with weeds. So I turned in and drove for about a hundred yards, until the vegetation seemed to be fighting back a little too much.

"Satisfied?" I asked.

"You ain't got what it takes to satisfy the Winkman," he said.

The car made its usual clicks and pops of a heated engine cooling down.

"Let's get out," he said.

"Wink, I'm tired, let's head back."

"C'mon, let's get out and take a walk. The Winkster doesn't ask for much."

"The hell you don't. For the past three days we've been driving around all over the damn county."

"I'll give you some money for gas."

"Whatever. Anyway, I'm tired and want to go home."

"Please? Pretty please with titties on top?" That's the kind of politically incorrect stuff Wink said. You'd laugh and feel guilty at the same time.

"Oh, all right," I said.

"Jeez, you're a pain in the butt," I added, just to keep the grumble going.

So we started walking farther back from the road. It was hard going because the land had little knots and holes in it, and there were rocks and old cans and stuff to trip you up. We crossed a dry creek bed and walked up a bit of a hill. At the top of the hill we turned left and made our way through an overgrown mess of trees, burs, and thorny things. I followed Wink silently, because he seemed to know where we was going.

Finally, we came to a clearing.

"Isn't it beautiful?" he asked.

"What?" I said. I could barely see anything in the darkness.

"This area. This tree."

"What tree?"

"This tree," he said, pointing.

"Wink, that isn't a tree."

"It was a tree."

"It isn't now."

"But it was. It was once a beautiful walnut tree. Full of life. A strong, hard tree."

I chuckled, because Wink never talked like that. Those words sounded funny coming from him. But he wasn't kidding. In fact, I wasn't sure, because there wasn't much light, but I could've sworn I saw a tear at the corner of Wink's eye.

"Let's sit awhile," he said as he sat on the stump.

It was about four feet across and rose up off the ground about a foot.

So we sat. I didn't think this would be a good time to talk, so I didn't. Wink didn't. I could hear a train rumbling in the distance and some wildlife sounds I couldn't identify, except for the crickets.

Finally, after about fifteen minutes, Ringo sighed dramatically.

"Are you ready to go?" he asked.

"Yeah, I guess."

It seemed like a good time to bring up something.

"You know, Wink, I Googled you the other day," I said.

"I must've been pretty damn drunk, 'cuz I sure as hell don't remember it," he said. "Was it good for you?"

"No, I'm serious."

"I have no idea what you're talking about."

"What don't you understand?"

"This word 'Google.'"

"You don't know what Google is?" I asked.

"No friggin' clue. Sounds dirty, though."

I didn't believe him. I thought I had seen a laptop at his place one time when I dropped him off and had to walk him upstairs. He also seemed pretty current in his thinking. He would know Google. But I let it drop.

"Anyway, I looked you up on the computer, the Internet."

"What did it say about me?"

"Nothing."

"Nothing?"

"You don't exist. Your name doesn't exist. There's no such thing as a name Pitchwinger. There's not even one in the New York phone directory."

"Yet I do exist, don't I?"

"Yes, you do."

"See, computers don't know everything."

"I guess not." I was too tired to argue.

Later, on the way home, he said, "Maybe Pitchwinger is my stage name."

"You were onstage?"

"I'm always onstage, my friend," he said.

"Tell me how the play turns out," I said.

"Probably not happily," he replied.

That was the last time I ever broached the subject.

Wink disappeared after that. I didn't see him the next day. Or the next. And the days turned into weeks. I wondered if he had left town, although I never checked his apartment. Annie, at the diner, seemed a bit nicer to me, although she never mentioned him. In fact, no one ever mentioned the lack of Wink.

It was as if my little town could only accept so much strange. Wink was just a little too much. The town wanted to slowly die with what little dignity it had left. Wink wanted to paint it in clown face and dress it in slap shoes and throw cream pies until the very end. Wink had left no mark. He had affected no one. To me, his so-called best friend, his departure seemed neither bad nor good. It just was. His memory was a vapor. It had substance and then was gone. I remembered he looked strange, but I couldn't remember his face. I didn't miss him. On the other hand, I wasn't glad he was gone. My life was neither richer nor poorer for having known him.

The odd routine of Tivoli, Indiana, quickly reverted to what it was before Wink.

Seven and a half weeks passed.

It was half past noon in Annie's Diner.

I was battling the demons of the Diablo hash yet again. Gifford was talking nonsense to no one. The drunken lawyer was nursing a hangover.

The door to the diner opened. One of the old-timers stopped in midsentence a harangue about Paris Hilton. Annie tensed. Gifford stopped talking.

"Hey, buddy boy, how's your hammer hanging?" Wink asked before the door had even slammed shut.

Thus began the subtle change that was life in Tivoli with Wink. Annie got a little grouchier. The old coots left Hollywood behind and gossiped about Wink instead. Gifford's gibberish revolved around knowing Wink.

Wink and I began again our nightly drinking. I didn't realize how much I missed his profanity-stained humor until I was around him. It was comfortable and kept the mood light. Once in a while, I even laughed.

However, the complexion of the nights took on a different hue from before. If Wink got too drunk, he would insist we visit the stump. I really didn't like going out to the stump. But I didn't dislike it enough to make a fuss about it. So about three nights a week, sometimes four, we ended up sitting on the stump and staring at stars.

Wink's mood would change when we were at the stump. The innuendos and schoolyard jokes would stop. His drunken slur would become almost romantic.

One time he said to me, "I love this place."

"What, Tivoli?" I asked.

"No, here, right here."

"This tree stump."

"You guessed 'er, Chester."

"You love this tree stump."

"Yep."

"You're not right."

"Never claimed I was. Don't you like it out here?"

"Wink, I'm not quite as fond of it as you are. In fact, there are many places I like a whole lot better," I said.

"Well, you just don't know much about what's important in life."

I couldn't think of an answer, so I didn't say anything. But for the life of me, I couldn't figure out what was important about a tree stump.

Most of the nights when Wink and I ended up at the stump, I could tell what was going to happen pretty early. Wink would order two shots with his beer, and that was my clue to slow way down, because I was going to be doing some driving. In fact, I would pace myself with glasses of water and stick to beer, skipping the bourbon.

One night, however, I'm ashamed to say that I didn't pace myself very well. And in our drunk-logic, we figured it was a good idea if we stopped off at a package store and got a bottle of Wild Turkey to pass around.

I had this feeling that the night sounds were somehow a little different around the stump. But maybe it was just the liquor.

We sat with our backs against the stump and passed the pint

bottle back and forth. We were about three quarters of the way through the bottle when a man stepped out from the shadows of the woods.

I couldn't see him very well in the darkness, but he appeared to have a shaved head and was wearing dark clothing.

He walked briskly, purposefully, and in a straight line to within three feet of Wink, staring straight at him the entire time. I noticed the man was holding something in his right hand, down by his side. He didn't once even look at me.

"Greg Day?" he asked.

"How did you find me?" Wink asked.

"You are Greg Day, aren't you?" the man asked.

"No, his name is . . ." I didn't finish because Wink nodded yes and the man raised his gun and blew Wink's head off. He fired two more shots into Wink's chest. He turned his back on me and calmly walked back into the shadows. I had blood and bits of Wink all over me.

At first the county sheriff thought I was involved somehow. Or at least that's the way it seemed. He questioned me on and off for twelve hours. Finally, even though he thought my description of the shooter was "lame," he let me go.

A day later a team from the FBI showed up. They questioned me, too, but only for an hour. They seemed to believe I had nothing to do with Wink's death. It was almost as if they didn't care.

On that very same day, they found the remains of the first child. They eventually found twelve others. Eleven of them were girls between the ages of five and eleven and had gone missing during a five-year span that ended thirteen years ago. One was a young girl buried two months ago, sometime during the period when Wink went missing. All of them had been tortured and molested. All of them were from within a ten-mile radius of Tivoli, but none from the town itself. I heard that there were other children's graveyards in other cities in the Midwest that the authorities attributed to Wink.

I never did find out who the stranger was who had finished off Wink. Maybe it was a rogue FBI agent. Maybe it was the father or brother of one of the girls killed. Maybe it was some sort of bounty hunter.

In a small town, even one that was a little peculiar like Tivoli, there are lines you shouldn't cross. My friendship with Wink crossed it. I heard the whispers and the gossip and the innuendos. People were polite to me, but there was a certain brittleness whenever they talked to me. Most people thought that somehow I was involved in the last child's death. There was nothing else to explain why Wink and I were together so much.

I always realized I didn't have much of a future in Tivoli. Now, I knew I didn't have much of a present, either.

It was time to leave.

KRISTINE KATHRYN RUSCH

G-Men

FROM *Sideways in Crime*

There's something addicting about a secret.
— J. Edgar Hoover

THE SQUALID LITTLE ALLEY smelled of piss. Detective Seamus
O'Reilly tugged his overcoat closed and wished he'd worn boots.
He could feel the chill of his metal flashlight through the worn
glove on his right hand.

Two beat cops stood in front of the bodies, and the coroner
crouched over them. His assistant was already setting up the gur-
neys, body bags draped over his arm. The coroner's van had
blocked the alley's entrance, only a few yards away.

O'Reilly's partner, Joseph McKinnon, followed him. McKinnon
had trained his own flashlight on the fire escapes above, uninten-
tionally alerting any residents to the police presence.

But they probably already knew. Shootings in this part of the city
were common. The neighborhood teetered between swank and
corrupt. Far enough from Central Park for degenerates and muggers to use the alleys as corridors, and, conversely, close enough for
new money to want to live with a peek of the city's most famous expanse of green.

The coroner, Thomas Brunner, had set up two expensive, bat-
tery-operated lights on garbage can lids placed on top of the dirty
ice, one at the top of the bodies, the other near the feet. O'Reilly
crouched so he wouldn't create any more shadows.

"What've we got?" he asked.

"Dunno yet." Brunner was using his gloved hands to part the

hair on the back of the nearest corpse's skull. "It could be one of those nights."

O'Reilly had worked with Brunner for eighteen years now, since they both got back from the war, and he hated it when Brunner said it could be one of those nights. That meant the corpses would stack up, which was usually a summer thing, but almost never happened in the middle of winter.

"Why?" O'Reilly asked. "What else we got?"

"Some colored limo driver shot two blocks from here." Brunner was still parting the hair. It took O'Reilly a minute to realize it was matted with blood. "And two white guys pulled out of their cars and shot about four blocks from that."

O'Reilly felt a shiver run through him that had nothing to do with the cold. "You think the shootings are related?"

"Dunno," Brunner said. "But I think it's odd, don't you? Five dead in the space of an hour, all in a six-block radius."

O'Reilly closed his eyes for a moment. Two white guys pulled out of their cars, one Negro driver of a limo, and now two white guys in an alley. Maybe they were related, maybe they weren't.

He opened his eyes, then wished he hadn't. Brunner had his finger inside a bullet hole, a quick way to judge caliber.

"Same type of bullet," Brunner said.

"You handled the other shootings?"

"I was on scene with the driver when some fag called this one in."

O'Reilly looked at Brunner. Eighteen years, and he still wasn't used to the man's casual bigotry.

"How did you know the guy was queer?" O'Reilly asked. "You talk to him?"

"Didn't have to." Brunner nodded toward the building in front of them. "Weekly party for degenerates in the penthouse apartment every Thursday night. Thought you knew."

O'Reilly looked up. Now he understood why McKinnon had been shining his flashlight at the upper-story windows. McKinnon had worked Vice before he got promoted to Homicide.

"Why would I know?" O'Reilly said.

McKinnon was the one who answered. "Because of the standing orders."

"I'm not playing twenty questions," O'Reilly said. "I don't know about a party in this building, and I don't know about standing orders."

"The standing orders are," McKinnon said, as if he were an elementary-school teacher, "not to bust it, no matter what kind of lead you got. You see someone go in, you forget about it. You see someone come out, you avert your eyes. You complain, you get moved to a different shift, maybe a different precinct."

"Jesus." O'Reilly was too far below to see if there was any movement against the glass in the penthouse suite. But whoever lived there — whoever partied there — had learned to shut off the lights before the cops arrived.

"Shot in the back of the head," Brunner said before O'Reilly could process all of the information. "That's just damn strange."

O'Reilly looked at the corpses — really looked at them — for the first time. Two men, both rather heavyset. Their faces were gone, probably splattered all over the walls. Gloved hands, nice shoes, one of them wearing a white scarf that caught the light.

Brunner had to search for the wound in the back of the head, which made that the entry point. The exit wounds had destroyed the faces.

O'Reilly looked behind him. No door on that building, but there was one on the building where the party was held. If they'd been exiting the building and were surprised by a queer basher or a mugger, they'd've been shot in the front, not the back.

"How many times were they shot?" O'Reilly asked.

"Looks like just the once. Large caliber, close range. I'd say it was a purposeful headshot, designed to do maximum damage." Brunner felt the back of the closest corpse. "There doesn't seem to be anything on the torso."

"They still got their wallets?" McKinnon asked.

"Haven't checked yet." Brunner reached into the back pants pocket of the corpse he'd been searching and clearly found nothing. So he grabbed the front of the overcoat and reached inside.

He removed a long thin wallet — old-fashioned, the kind made for the larger bills of forty years before. Hand-tailored, beautifully made.

These men weren't hurting for money.

Brunner handed the wallet to O'Reilly, who opened it. And stopped when he saw the badge inside. His mouth went dry.

"We got a feebee," he said, his voice sounding strangled.

"What?" McKinnon asked.

"FBI," Brunner said dryly. McKinnon had only moved to Homicide the year before. Vice rarely had to deal with FBI. Homicide did only on sensational cases. O'Reilly could count on one hand the number of times he'd spoken to agents in the New York bureau.

"Not just any feebee, either," O'Reilly said. "The associate director. Clyde A. Tolson."

McKinnon whistled. "Who's the other guy?"

This time O'Reilly did the search. The other corpse, the heavier of the two, also smelled faintly of perfume. This man had kept his wallet in the inner pocket of his suit coat, just like his companion had.

O'Reilly opened the wallet. Another badge, just like he expected. But he didn't expect the bulldog face glaring at him from the wallet's interior.

Nor had he expected the name.

"Jesus, Mary, and Joseph," he said.

"What've we got?" McKinnon asked.

O'Reilly handed him the wallet, opened to the slim paper identification.

"The director of the FBI," he said, his voice shaking. "Public Hero Number One. J. Edgar Hoover."

Francis Xavier Bryce — Frank to his friends, what few of them he still had left — had just dropped off to sleep when the phone rang. He cursed, caught himself, apologized to Mary, and then remembered she wasn't there.

The phone rang again and he fumbled for the light, knocking over the highball glass he'd used to mix his mom's recipe for sleepless nights: hot milk, butter, and honey. It turned out that at the tender age of thirty-six, hot milk and butter laced with honey wasn't a recipe for sleep; it was a recipe for heartburn.

And for a smelly carpet if he didn't clean the mess up.

He found the phone before he found the light.

"What?" he snapped.

"You live near Central Park, right?" A voice he didn't recognize, but one that was clearly official, asked the question without a hello or an introduction.

"More or less." Bryce rarely talked about his apartment. His parents had left it to him, and as his wife was fond of sniping, it was too fancy for a junior G-man.

The voice rattled off an address. "How far is that from you?"

"About five minutes." If he didn't clean up the mess on the floor. If he spent thirty seconds pulling on the clothes he'd piled onto the chair beside the bed.

"Get there. Now. We got a situation."

"What about my partner?" Bryce's partner lived in Queens.

"You'll have backup. You just have to get to the scene. The moment you get there, you shut it down."

"Um." Bryce hated sounding uncertain, but he had no choice. "First, sir, I need to know who I'm talking to. Then I need to know what I'll find."

"You'll find a double homicide. And you're talking to Eugene Hart, the special agent in charge. I shouldn't have to identify myself to you."

Now that he had, Bryce recognized Hart's voice. "Sorry, sir. It's just procedure."

"Fuck procedure. Take over that scene. *Now.*"

"Yes, sir," Bryce said, but he was talking into an empty phone line. He hung up, hands shaking, wishing he had some Bromo Seltzer.

He'd just come off a long, messy investigation of another agent. Walter Cain had been about to get married when he remembered he had to inform the Bureau of that fact and, as per regulation, get his bride vetted before walking down the aisle.

Bryce had been the one to investigate the future Mrs. Cain and had been the one to find out about her rather seamy past — two Vice convictions under a different name and one hospitalization after a rather messy backstreet abortion. Turned out Cain knew about his future wife's past, but the Bureau hadn't liked it.

And two nights ago Bryce had to be the one to tell Cain that he couldn't marry his now reformed, somewhat religious beloved. The soon-to-be Mrs. Cain had taken the news hard. She had gone to Bellevue this afternoon after slashing her wrists.

And Bryce had been the one to tell Cain what his former fiancée had done. Just a few hours ago.

Sometimes Bryce hated this job.

Despite his orders, he went into the bathroom, soaked one of Mary's precious company towels in water, and dropped the thing on the spilled milk. Then he pulled on his clothes and finger-combed his hair.

He was a mess — certainly not the perfect representative of the

Bureau. His white shirt was stained with marinade from that night's take-out, and his tie wouldn't keep a crisp knot. The crease had long since left his trousers, and his shoes hadn't been shined in weeks. Still, he grabbed his black overcoat, hoping it would hide everything.

He let himself out of the apartment before he remembered the required and much hated hat, went back inside, grabbed the hat as well as his gun and his identification. Jesus, he was tired. He hadn't slept since Mary walked out. Mary, who had been vetted by the FBI and who had passed with flying colors. Mary, who had turned out to be more of a liability than any former hooker ever could have been.

And now, because of her, he was heading toward something big, and he was one tenth as sharp as usual.

All he could hope for was that the SAC had overreacted. And he had a hunch — a two-in-the-morning, get-your-ass-over-there-now hunch — that the SAC hadn't overreacted at all.

Attorney General Robert F. Kennedy sat in his favorite chair near the fire in his library. The house was quiet even though his wife and eight children were asleep upstairs. Outside, the rolling landscape was covered in a light dusting of snow — rare for McLean, Virginia, even at this time of year.

He held a book in his left hand, his finger marking the spot. The Greeks had comforted him in the few months since Jack died, but lately Kennedy had discovered Camus.

He had been about to copy a passage into his notebook when the phone rang. At first he sighed, feeling all of the exhaustion that had weighed on him since the assassination. He didn't want to answer the phone. He didn't want to be bothered — not now, not ever again.

But this was the direct line from the White House, and if he didn't answer it, someone else in the house would.

He set the Camus book face-down on his chair and crossed to the desk before the third ring. He answered with a curt "Yes?"

"Attorney General Kennedy, sir?" The voice on the other end sounded urgent. The voice sounded familiar to him, even though he couldn't place it.

"Yes?"

"This is Special Agent John Haskell. You asked me to contact you, sir, if I heard anything important about Director Hoover, no matter what the time."

Kennedy leaned against the desk. He had made that request back when his brother had been president, back when Kennedy had been the first attorney general since the 1920s who actually demanded accountability from Hoover.

Since Lyndon Johnson had taken over the presidency, accountability had gone by the wayside. These days Hoover rarely returned Kennedy's phone calls.

"Yes, I did tell you that," Kennedy said, resisting the urge to add, *But I don't care about that old man any longer.*

"Sir, there are rumors — credible ones — that Director Hoover has died in New York."

Kennedy froze. For a moment he flashed back to that unseasonably warm afternoon when he'd sat just outside with the federal attorney for New York City, Robert Morgenthau, and the chief of Morgenthau's criminal division, Silvio Mollo, talking about prosecuting various organized crime figures.

Kennedy could still remember the glint of the sunlight on the swimming pool, the taste of the tuna-fish sandwich Ethel had brought him, the way the men — despite their topic — had seemed lighthearted.

Then the phone rang, and J. Edgar Hoover was on the line. Kennedy almost didn't take the call, but he did, and Hoover's cold voice said, *I have news for you. The president's been shot.*

Kennedy had always disliked Hoover, but since that day, that awful day in the bright sunshine, he had hated that fat bastard. Not once — not in that call, not in the subsequent calls — did Hoover express condolences or show a shred of human concern.

"Credible rumors?" Kennedy repeated, knowing he probably sounded as cold as Hoover had three months ago and not caring. He'd chosen Haskell as his liaison precisely because the man didn't like Hoover either. Kennedy had needed someone inside Hoover's hierarchy, unbeknownst to Hoover, which was difficult since Hoover kept his hand in everything. Haskell was one of the few who fit the bill.

"Yes, sir, quite credible."

"Then why haven't I received official contact?"

"I'm not even sure the president knows, sir."

Kennedy leaned against the desk. "Why not, if the rumors are credible?"

"Um, because, sir, um, it seems Associate Director Tolson was also shot, and um, they were, um, in a rather suspect area."

Kennedy closed his eyes. All of Washington knew that Tolson was the closest thing Hoover had to a wife. The two old men had been lifelong companions. Even though they didn't live together, they had every meal together. Tolson had been Hoover's hatchet man until the last year or so, when Tolson's health hadn't permitted it.

Then a word Haskell used sank in. "You said shot."

"Yes, sir."

"Is Tolson dead too, then?"

"And three other people in the neighborhood," Haskell said.

"My God." Kennedy ran a hand over his face. "But they think this is personal?"

"Yes, sir."

"Because of the location of the shooting?"

"Yes, sir. It seems there was an exclusive gathering in a nearby building. You know the type, sir."

Kennedy didn't know the type — at least, not through personal experience. But he'd heard of places like that, where the rich, famous, and deviant could spend time with each other and do whatever it was they liked to do in something approaching privacy.

"So," he said, "the Bureau's trying to figure out how to cover this up."

"Or at least contain it, sir."

Without Hoover or Tolson, no one in the Bureau was gong to know what to do.

Kennedy's hand started to shake. "What about the files?"

"Files, sir?"

"Hoover's confidential files. Has anyone secured them?"

"Not yet, sir. But I'm sure someone has called Miss Gandy."

Helen Gandy was Hoover's longtime secretary. She had been his right hand as long as Tolson had operated that hatchet.

"So procedure's being followed," Kennedy said, then frowned. If procedure were being followed, shouldn't the acting head of the Bureau be calling him?

"No, sir. But the Director put some private instructions in place should he be killed or incapacitated. Private emergency instruc-

tions. And those involve letting Miss Gandy know before anyone
else."

Even me, Kennedy thought. *Hoover's nominal boss.* "She's not there
yet, right?"

"No, sir."

"Do you know where those files are?" Kennedy asked, trying not
to let desperation into his voice.

"I've made it my business to know, sir." There was a pause, and
then Haskell lowered his voice. "They're in Miss Gandy's office,
sir."

Not Hoover's, like everyone thought. For the first time in
months, Kennedy felt a glimmer of hope. "Secure those files."

"Sir?"

"Do whatever it takes. I want them out of there, and I want someone to secure Hoover's house, too. I'm acting on the orders of
the president. If anyone tells you that they are doing the same,
they're mistaken. The president made his wishes clear on this
point. He often said that if anything happens to that old queer" —
and here Kennedy deliberately used LBJ's favorite phrase for Hoover — "then we need those files before they can get into the wrong
hands."

"I'm on it, sir."

"I can't stress to you the importance of this," Kennedy said. In
fact, he couldn't talk about the importance at all. Those files could
ruin his brother's legacy. The secrets in there could bring down
Kennedy, too, and his entire family.

"And if the rumors about the Director's death are wrong, sir?"

Kennedy felt a shiver of fear. "Are they?"

"I seriously doubt it."

"Then let me worry about that."

And about what LBJ would do when he found out. Because the
president upon whose orders Kennedy acted wasn't the current
one. Kennedy was following the orders of the only man he believed
should be president at the moment.

His brother Jack.

The scene wasn't hard to find; a coroner's van blocked the entrance to the alley. Bryce walked quickly, already cold, his heartburn worse than it had been when he had gone to bed.

The neighborhood was in transition. An urban renewal project had knocked down some wonderful turn-of-the-century buildings that had become eyesores. But so far the buildings that had replaced them were the worst kind of modern — all planes and angles and white with few windows.

In the buildings closest to the park, the lights worked and the streets looked safe. But here, on a side street not far from the construction, the city's shady side showed. The dirty snow was piled against the curb, the streets were dark, and nothing seemed inhabited except that alley with the coroner's van blocking the entrance.

The coroner's van and at least one unmarked car. No press, which surprised him. He shoved his gloved hands in the pockets of his overcoat, even though it was against FBI dress code, and slipped between the van and the wall of a grimy brick building.

The alley smelled of old urine and fresh blood. Two beat cops blocked his way until he showed identification. Then, like people usually did, they parted as if he could burn them.

The bodies had fallen side by side in the center of the alley. They looked posed, with their arms up, their legs in classic P position — one leg bent, the other straight. They looked like they could fit perfectly on the dead-body diagrams the FBI used to put out in the 1930s. He wondered if they had fallen like this or if this had been the result of the coroner's tampering.

The coroner had messed with other parts of the crime scene — if, indeed, he had been the one who put the garbage can lids on the ice and set battery-powered lamps on them. The warmth of the lamps was melting the ice and sending runnels of water into a nearby grate.

"I hope to hell someone thought to photograph the scene before you melted it," he said.

The coroner and the two cops who had been crouching beside the bodies stood up guiltily. The coroner looked at the garbage can lids and closed his eyes. Then he took a deep breath, opened them, and snapped his fingers at the assistant who was waiting beside a gurney.

"Camera," he said.

"That's Crime Scene's —" the assistant began, then saw everyone looking at him. He glanced at the van. "Never mind."

He walked behind the bodies, further disturbing the scene. Bryce's mouth thinned in irritation. The cops who stood were in plain clothes.

"Detectives," Bryce said, holding his identification, "Special Agent Frank Bryce of the FBI. I've been told to secure this scene. More of my people will be here shortly."

He hoped that last statement was true. He had no idea who was coming or when they would arrive.

"Good," said the younger detective, a tall man with broad shoulders and an all-American jaw. "The sooner we get out of here, the better."

Bryce had never gotten that reaction from a detective before. Usually the detectives were territorial, always reminding him that this was New York City and that the scene belonged to them.

The other detective, older, face grizzled by time and work, held out his gloved hand. "Forgive my partner's rudeness. I'm Seamus O'Reilly. He's Joseph McKinnon, and we'll help you in any way we can."

"I appreciate it," Bryce said, taking O'Reilly's hand and shaking it. "I guess the first thing you can do is tell me what we've got."

"A hell of a mess, that's for sure," said McKinnon. "You'll understand when . . ."

His voice trailed off as his partner took out two long old-fashioned wallets and handed them to Bryce.

Bryce took them, feeling confused. Then he opened the first, saw the familiar badge, and felt his breath catch. Two FBI agents, in this alley? Shot side by side? He looked up, saw the darkened windows.

There used to be rumors about this neighborhood. Some exclusive private sex parties used to be held here, and his old partner had always wanted to visit one just to see if it was a hotbed of communists like some of the agents had claimed. Bryce had begged off. He was an investigator, not a voyeur.

The two detectives were staring at him, as if they expected more from him. He still had the wallet open in his hand. If the dead men were New York agents, he would know them. He hated solving the deaths of people he knew.

But he steeled himself, looked at the identification, and felt the blood leave his face. His skin grew cold, and for a moment he felt lightheaded.

"No," he said.

The detectives still stared at him.

He swallowed. "Have you done a visual ID?"

Hoover was recognizable. His picture was on everything. Sometimes Bryce thought Hoover was more famous than the president — any president. He'd certainly been in power longer.

"Faces are gone," O'Reilly said.

"Exit wounds," the coroner added from beside the bodies. His assistant had returned and was taking pictures, the flash showing just how much melt had happened since the coroner arrived.

"Shot in the back of the head?" Bryce blinked. He was tired and his brain was working slowly, but something about the shots didn't match with the body positions.

"If they came out that door," O'Reilly said as he indicated a dark metal door almost hidden in the side of the brick building, "then the shooters had to be waiting beside it."

"Your crime scene people haven't arrived yet, I take it?" Bryce asked.

"No," the coroner said. "They think it's a fag kill. They'll get here when they get here."

Bryce clenched his left fist and had to remind himself to let the fingers loose.

O'Reilly saw the reaction. "Sorry about that," he said, shooting a glare at the coroner. "I'm sure the Director was here on business."

Funny business. But Bryce didn't say that. The rumors about Hoover had been around since Bryce joined the FBI, just after the war. Hoover quashed them, like he quashed any criticism, but it seemed like the criticism got made, no matter what.

Bryce opened the other wallet, but he already had a guess as to who was beside Hoover, and his guess turned out to be right.

"You want to tell me why your crime scene people believe this is a homosexual killing?" Bryce asked, trying not to let what Mary called his FBI tone into his voice. If Hoover was still alive and this was some kind of plant, Hoover would want to crush the source of this assumption. Bryce would make sure that the source was worth pursuing before going any further.

"Neighborhood, mostly," McKinnon said. "There're a couple of bars, mostly high-end. You have to know someone to get in. Then there's the party, held every week upstairs. Some of the most important men in the city show up at it, or so they used to say in Vice when they told us to stay away."

Bryce nodded, letting it go at that.

"We need your crime scene people here ASAP, and a lot more cops so that we can protect what's left of this scene, in case these men turn out to be who their identification says they are. You search the bodies to see if this was the only identification on them?"

O'Reilly started. He clearly hadn't thought of that. Probably had been too shocked by the first wallets that he found.

The younger detective had already gone back to the bodies. The coroner put out a hand and did the searching himself.

"You think this was a plant?" O'Reilly asked.

"I don't know what to think," Bryce said. "I'm not here to think. I'm here to make sure everything goes smoothly."

And to make sure the case goes to the FBI. Those words hung unspoken between the two of them. Not that O'Reilly objected, and now Bryce could understand why. This case would be a political nightmare, and no good detective wanted to be in the middle of it.

"How come there's no press?" Bryce asked O'Reilly. "You manage to get rid of them somehow?"

"Fag kill," the coroner said.

Bryce was getting tired of those words. His fist had clenched again, and he had to work at unclenching it.

"Ignore him," O'Reilly said softly. "He's an asshole and the best coroner in the city."

"I heard that," the coroner said affably. "There's no other identification on either of them."

O'Reilly's shoulders slumped, as if he'd been hoping for a different outcome. Bryce should have been hoping as well, but he hadn't been. He had known that Hoover was in town. The entire New York bureau knew, since Hoover always took it over when he arrived — breezing in, giving instructions, making sure everything was just the way he wanted it.

"Before this gets too complicated," O'Reilly said, "you want to see the other bodies?"

"Other bodies?" Bryce felt numb. He could use some caffeine now, but Hoover had ordered agents not to drink coffee on the job. Getting coffee now felt almost disrespectful.

"We got three more." O'Reilly took a deep breath. "And just before you arrived, I got word that they're agents, too."

*

Special Agent John Haskell had just installed six of his best agents outside the Director's suite of offices when a small woman showed up, key clutched in her gloved right hand. Helen Gandy, the Director's secretary, looked up at Haskell with the coldest stare he'd ever seen outside of the Director's.

"May I go into my office, Agent Haskell?" Her voice was just as cold. She didn't look upset, and if he hadn't known that she never stayed past five unless directed by Hoover himself, Haskell would have thought she was coming back from a prolonged work break.

"I'm sorry, ma'am," he said. "No one is allowed inside. President's orders."

"Really?" God, that voice was chilling. He remembered the first time he'd heard it, when he'd been brought to this suite of offices as a brand-new agent, after getting his "Meet the Boss" training before his introduction to the Director. She'd frightened him more than Hoover had.

"Yes, ma'am. The president says no one can enter."

"Surely he didn't mean me."

Surely he did. But Haskell bit the comment back. "I'm sorry, ma'am."

"I have a few personal items that I'd like to get, if you don't mind. And the Director instructed me that in the case of . . ." And for the first time she paused. Her voice didn't break, nor did she clear her throat. But she seemed to need a moment to gather herself. "In case of emergency, I was to remove some of his personal items as well."

"If you could tell me what they are, ma'am, I'll get them."

Her eyes narrowed. "The Director doesn't like others to touch his possessions."

"I'm sorry, ma'am," he said gently. "But I don't think that matters any longer."

Any other woman would have broken down. After all, she had worked for the old man for forty-five years, side by side, every day. Never marrying, not because they had a relationship — Helen Gandy, more than anyone, probably knew the truth behind the Director's relationship with the associate director — but because for Helen Gandy, just as for the Director himself, the FBI was her entire life.

"It matters," she said. "Now if you'll excuse me . . ."

She tried to wriggle past him. She was wiry and stronger than he expected. He had to put out an arm to block her.

"Ma'am," he said in the gentlest tone he could summon, "the president's orders supersede the Director's."

How often had he wanted to say that over the years? How often had he wanted to remind everyone in the Bureau that the president led the free world, not J. Edgar Hoover?

"In this instance," she snapped, "they do not."

"Ma'am, I'd hate to have some agents restrain you." Although he wasn't sure about that. She had never been nice to him or to anyone he knew. She'd always been sharp or rude. "You're distraught."

"I am not." She clipped each word.

"You are because I say you are, ma'am."

She raised her chin. For a moment he thought she hadn't understood. But she finally did.

The balance of power had shifted. At the moment it was on his side.

"Do I have to call the president, then, to get my personal effects?" she asked.

But they both knew she wasn't talking about her personal things. And the president was smart enough to know that as well. As hungry to get those files as the attorney general had seemed despite his eastern reserve, the president would be utterly ravenous. He wouldn't let some old skirt, as he'd been known to call Miss Gandy, get in his way.

"Go ahead," Haskell said. "Feel free to use the phone in the office across the hall."

She glared at him, then turned on one foot and marched down the corridor. But she didn't head toward a phone — at least, not one he could see.

He wondered who she would call. The president wouldn't listen. The attorney general had issued the order in the president's name. Maybe she would contact one of Hoover's assistant directors, the four or five men that Hoover had in his pocket.

Haskell had been waiting for them. But word still hadn't spread through the Bureau. The only reason he knew was because he'd received a call from the SAC of the New York office. New York hated the Director, mostly because the old man went there so often and harassed them.

Someone had probably figured out that there was a crisis from the moment that Haskell had brought his people in to secure the Director's suite. But no one would know that the Director was dead until Miss Gandy made the calls or until someone in the Bureau started along the chain of command — the one designated in the book Hoover had written all those years ago.

Haskell crossed his arms. Sometimes he wished he hadn't let the AG know how he felt about the Director. Sometimes he wished he were still a humble assistant, the man who had joined the FBI because he wanted to be a top cop like his hero, J. Edgar Hoover.

A man who, it turned out, had never made a real arrest or fired a gun or even understood investigation.

There was a lot to admire about the Director — no matter what you said, he'd built a hell of an agency almost from scratch — but he wasn't the man his press made him out to be.

And that was the source of Haskell's disillusionment. He'd wanted to be a top cop. Instead he snooped into homes and businesses and sometimes even investigated fairly blameless people, looking for a mistake in their past.

Since he'd been transferred to FBI HQ, he hadn't done any real investigating at all. His arrests had slowed, his cases dwindled.

And he'd found himself investigating his boss, trying to find out where the legend ended and the man began. Once he realized that the old man was just a bureaucrat who had learned where all the bodies were buried and used that to make everyone bow to his bidding, Haskell was ripe for the undercover work the AG had asked him to do.

Only now he wasn't undercover anymore. Now he was standing in the open before the Director's cache of secrets, on the president's orders, hoping that no one would call his bluff.

As O'Reilly led him to the limousine, Bryce surreptitiously checked his watch. He'd already been on scene for half an hour and no backup had arrived. If he was supposed to secure everything and chase off the NYPD, he'd need some manpower.

But for now he wanted to see the extent of the problem. The night had gotten colder, and this street was even darker than the street he'd walked down. All of the streetlights were out. The only light came from some porch bulbs above a few entrances. He could barely make out the limousine at the end of the block, and then only because he could see the shadowy forms of the two beat cops standing at the scene, their squad cars parking the limo in.

As he got closer, he recognized the shape of the limo. It was thicker than most limos and rode lower to the ground because it was encased in an extra frame, making it bulletproof. Supposedly the glass would all be bulletproof as well.

"You said the driver was shot inside the limo?" Bryce asked.

"That's what they told me," O'Reilly said. "I wasn't called to this scene. We were brought in because of the two men in the alley. Even then we were called late."

Bryce nodded. He remembered the coroner's bigotry. "Is that standard procedure for cases involving minorities?"

O'Reilly gave him a sideways glance. Bryce couldn't read O'Reilly's expression in the dark.

"We're overtaxed," O'Reilly said after a moment. "Some cases don't get the kind of treatment they deserve."

"Limo drivers," Bryce said.

"If he'd been killed in the parking garage under the Plaza, maybe," O'Reilly said. "But not because of who he was. Because of where he was."

Bryce nodded. He knew how the world worked. He didn't like it. He spoke up against it too many times, which was why he was on shaky ground at the Bureau.

Then his already upset stomach clenched. Maybe he wasn't going to get backup. Maybe they'd put him on his own here to claim he'd botched the investigation, so that they would be able to cover it up.

He couldn't concentrate on that now. What he had to do was take good notes, make the best case he could, and keep a copy of every damn thing — maybe in more than one place.

"You were called in because of the possibility that the men in the alley could be important," Bryce said.

"That's my guess," O'Reilly said.

"What about the others down the block? Has anyone taken those cases?"

"Probably not," O'Reilly said. "Those bars, you know. It's department policy. The coroner checks bodies in the suspect area, and decides, based on, um, evidence of . . . um, activity . . . whether or not to bring in detectives."

Bryce frowned. He almost asked what the coroner was checking for when he figured out that it was evidence on the body itself, evidence not of the crime but of certain kinds of sex acts. If that evidence was present, apparently no one thought it worthwhile to investigate the crime.

"You'd think the city would revise that," Bryce said. "A lot of people live dual lives — productive and interesting people."

"Yeah," O'Reilly said. "You'd think. Especially after tonight."

Bryce grinned. He was liking this grizzled cop more and more.

O'Reilly spoke to the beat cops, then motioned Bryce to the limo. As Bryce approached, O'Reilly trained his flashlight on the driver's side.

The window wasn't broken like Bryce had expected. It had been rolled down.

"You got here one James Crawford," said one of the beat cops. "He got identification says he's a feebee, but I ain't never heard of no colored feebee."

"There's only four," Bryce said dryly. And they all worked for Hoover as his personal housekeepers or drivers. "Can I see that identification?"

The beat cop handed him a wallet that matched the ones on Tolson and Hoover. Inside was a badge and identification for James Crawford, as well as family photographs. Neither Tolson nor Hoover had had any photographs in their wallets.

Bryce motioned O'Reilly to move a little closer to the body. The head was tilted toward the window. The right side of the skull was gone, the hair glistening with drying blood. With one gloved finger, Bryce pushed the head upright. A single entrance wound above the left ear had caused the damage.

"Brunner says the shots are the same caliber," O'Reilly said.

It took Bryce a moment to realize that Brunner was the coroner.

Bryce carefully searched Crawford but didn't find the man's weapon. Nor could he find a holster or any way to carry a weapon.

"It looks like he wasn't carrying a weapon," Bryce said.

"Neither were the two in the alley," O'Reilly said, and Bryce appreciated his caution in not identifying the other two corpses. "You'd think they would have been."

Bryce shook his head. "They were known for not carrying weapons. But you'd think their driver would have one."

"Maybe they had protection," O'Reilly said.

And Bryce's mouth went dry. Of course they did. The office always joked about who would get HooverWatch on each trip. He'd had to do it a few times.

Agents on HooverWatch followed strict rules, like everything else with Hoover. Remain close enough to see the men entering and exiting an area, stop any suspicious characters, and yet somehow remain inconspicuous.

"You said there were two others shot?"

"Yeah. A block or so from here." O'Reilly waved a hand vaguely down the street.

"Pulled out of one car or two?"

"Not my case," O'Reilly said.

"Two," said the beat cop. "Black sedans. Could barely see them on this cruddy street."

HooverWatch. Bryce swallowed hard, kept that bile back. Of course. He probably knew the men who were shot.

"Let's look," he said. "You two, make sure the coroner's man photographs this scene before he leaves."

"Yessir," said the second beat cop. He hadn't spoken before.

"And don't let anyone near this scene unless I give the okay," Bryce said.

"How come this guy's in charge?" the talkative beat cop asked O'Reilly.

O'Reilly grinned. "Because he's a feebee."

"I'm sorry," the beat cop said automatically, turning to Bryce. "I didn't know, sir."

"Feebee" was an insult — or at least some in the Bureau thought so. Bryce didn't mind it. Any more than he minded when some rookie said "Sack" when he meant "Ess-Ay-Cee." Shorthand worked, sometimes better than people wanted it to.

"Point me in the right direction," he said to the talkative cop.

The cop nodded south. "One block down, sir. You can't miss it. We got guys on those scenes, too, but we weren't so sure it was important. You know. We coulda missed stuff."

In other words, they hadn't buttoned up the scene immediately. They'd waited for the coroner to make his verdict, and he probably hadn't, not with the three new corpses nearby.

Bryce took one last look at James Crawford. The man had rolled down his window, despite the cold, and in a bad section of town.

He leaned forward. Underneath the faint scent of cordite and mingled with the thicker smell of blood was the smell of a cigar.

He took the flashlight from O'Reilly and trained it on the dirty snow against the curb. It had been trampled by everyone coming to this crime scene.

He crouched and poked just a little, finding three fairly fresh cigarette butts.

As he stood, he said to the beat cops, "When the scene-of-the-crime guys get here, make sure they take everything from the curb."

O'Reilly was watching him. The beat cops were frowning, but they nodded.

Bryce handed O'Reilly back his flashlight and headed down the street.

"You think he was smoking and tossing the butts out the window?" O'Reilly asked.

"Either that," Bryce said, "or he rolled his window down to talk to someone. And if someone was pointing a gun at him, he wouldn't have done it. This vehicle was armored. He had a better chance starting it up and driving away than he did cooperating."

"If he wasn't smoking," O'Reilly said, "he knew his killer."

"Yeah," Bryce said. And he was pretty sure that was going to make his job a whole hell of a lot harder.

Kennedy took the elevator up to the fifth floor of the Justice Department. He probably should have stayed home, but he simply couldn't. He needed to get into those files, and he needed to do so before anyone else.

As he strode into the corridor he shared with the director of the FBI, he saw Helen Gandy hurry in the other direction. She looked like she had just come from the beauty salon. He had never seen her look anything less than completely put together, but he was surprised by her perfect appearance on this night, after the news that her longtime boss was dead.

Kennedy tugged at the overcoat he'd put on over his favorite sweater. He hadn't taken the time to change or even comb his hair. He probably looked as tousled as he had in the days after Jack died.

Although, for the first time in three months, he felt like he had a purpose. He didn't know how long this feeling would last or how long he wanted it to. But this death had given him an odd kind of hope that control was coming back into his world.

Haskell stood in front of the Director's office suite, arms crossed. The Director's suite was just down the corridor from the attorney general's offices. It felt odd to go toward Hoover's domain instead of his own.

Haskell looked relieved when he saw Kennedy.

"Was that the dragon lady I just saw?" Kennedy asked.

"She wanted to get some personal effects from her office," Haskell said.

"Did you let her?"

"You said the orders were to secure it, so I have."

"Excellent." Kennedy glanced in both directions and saw no one. "Make sure your staff continues to protect the doors. I'm going inside."

"Sir?" Haskell raised his eyebrows.

"This may not be the right place," Kennedy said. "I'm worried that he moved everything to his house."

The lie came easily. Kennedy would have heard if Hoover had moved files to his own home. But Haskell didn't know that.

Haskell moved away from the door. It was unlocked. Two more agents stood inside, guarding the interior doors.

"Give me a minute, please, gentlemen," Kennedy said.

The men nodded and went outside.

Kennedy stopped and took a deep breath. He had been in Miss Gandy's office countless times, but he had never really looked at it. He'd always been staring at the door to Hoover's inner sanctum, waiting for it to open and the old man to come out.

That office was interesting. In the antechamber, Hoover had memorabilia and photographs from his major cases. He even had the plaster-of-Paris death mask of John Dillinger on display. It was a ghastly thing, which made Kennedy think of the way that English kings used to keep severed heads on the entrance to London Bridge to warn traitors of their potential fate.

But this office had always looked like a waiting room to him. Nothing very special. The woman behind the desk was the focal point. Jack had been the one who nicknamed her the dragon lady and had even called her that to her face once, only with his trademark grin, so infectious that she hadn't made a sound or a grimace in protest.

Of course, she hadn't smiled back, either.

Her desk was clear except for a blotter, a telephone, and a jar of pens. A typewriter sat on a credenza with paper stacked beside it.

But it wasn't the desk that interested him the most. It was the floor-to-ceiling filing cabinets and storage bins. He walked to them. Instead of the typical system — marked by letters of the alphabet — this one had numbers that were clearly part of a code.

He pulled open the nearest drawer and found row after row of accordion files, each with its own number, and manila folders with the first number set followed by another. He cursed softly under his breath.

Of course the old dog wouldn't file his confidentials by name. He'd use a secret code. The old man liked nothing more than his secrets.

Still, Kennedy opened half a dozen drawers just to see if the system continued throughout. And it wasn't until he got to a bin near the corner of the desk that he found a file labeled *Obscene*.

His hand shook as he pulled it out. Jack, for all his brilliance, had been sexually insatiable. Back when their brother Joe was still alive and no one ever thought Jack would be running for president, Jack had had an affair with a Danish émigré named Inga Arvad. Inga Binga, as Jack used to call her, was married to a man with ties to Hitler. She'd even met and liked der Führer, and had said so in print.

She'd been the target of FBI surveillance as a possible spy, and during that surveillance who should turn up in her bed but a young naval lieutenant whose father had once been ambassador to England. The Ambassador, as he preferred to be called even by his sons, found out about the affair, told Jack in no uncertain terms to end it, and then made sure he did by getting him assigned to a PT boat in the Pacific, as far from Inga Binga as possible.

Kennedy had always suspected that Hoover had leaked the information to the Ambassador, but he hadn't known for certain until Jack became president, when Hoover told them. Hoover had been surveilling all of the Kennedy children at the Ambassador's request. He'd given Kennedy a list of scandalous items as a sample and hoped that would control the president and his brother.

It might have controlled Jack, but Hoover hadn't known Kennedy very well. Kennedy had told Hoover that if any of this information made it into the press, then other things would appear in print as well, things like the strange FBI budget items for payments covering Hoover's visits to the track or the fact that Hoover made some interesting friends, mobster friends, when he was vacationing in Palm Beach.

It wasn't quite a Mexican standoff — Jack was really afraid of the old man — but it gave Kennedy more power than any attorney general had had over Hoover since the beginnings of the Roosevelt administration.

But now Kennedy needed those files, and he had a hunch Hoover would label them obscene.

Kennedy opened the file and was shocked to see Richard Nixon's name on the sheets inside. Kennedy thumbed through quickly, not caring what dirt they'd found on that loser. Nixon couldn't win an election after his defeat in 1960. He'd even told the press after he lost a California race that they wouldn't have him to kick around anymore.

Yet Hoover had kept the files, just to be safe.

That old bastard really and truly had known where all the bodies were buried. And it wouldn't be easy to find them.

Kennedy took a deep breath. He stood, shoved his hands in his pockets, and surveyed the walls of files. It would take days to search each folder. He didn't have days. He probably didn't have hours.

But he was Hoover's immediate supervisor, whether the old man had recognized it or not. Hoover answered to him. Which meant that the files belonged to the Justice Department, of which the FBI was only one small part.

He glanced at his watch. No one pounded on the door. He probably had until dawn before someone tried to stop him. If he was really lucky, no one would think of the files until midmorning.

He went to the door and beckoned Haskell inside.

"We're taking the files to my office," he said.

"All of them, sir?"

"All of them. These first, then whatever is in Hoover's office, and then any other confidential files you can find."

Haskell looked up the wall as if he couldn't believe the command. "That'll take some time, sir."

"Not if you get a lot of people to help."

"Sir, I thought you wanted to keep this secret."

He did. But it wouldn't remain secret for long. So he had to control when the information got out — just like he had to control the information itself.

"Get this done as quickly as possible," he said.

Haskell nodded and turned the doorknob, but Kennedy stopped him before he went out.

"These are filed by code," he said. "Do you know where the key is?"

"I was told that Miss Gandy had the keys to everything from codes to offices," Haskell said.

Kennedy felt a shiver run through him. Knowing Hoover, he would have made sure he had the key to the attorney general's office as well.

"Do you have any idea where she might have kept the code keys?" Kennedy asked.

"No," Haskell said. "I wasn't part of the need-to-know group. I already knew too much."

Kennedy nodded. He appreciated how much Haskell knew. It had gotten him this far.

"On your way out," Kennedy said, "call building maintenance and have them change all the locks in my office."

"Yes, sir." Haskell kept his hand on the doorknob. "Are you sure you want to do this, sir? Couldn't you just change the locks here? Wouldn't that secure everything for the president?"

"Everyone in Washington wants these files," Kennedy said. "They're going to come to this office suite. They won't think of mine."

"Until they heard that you moved everything."

Kennedy nodded. "And then they'll know how futile their quest really is."

The final crime scene was a mess. The bodies were already gone — probably inside the coroner's van that blocked the alley a few blocks back. It had taken Bryce nearly a half an hour to find someone who knew what the scene had looked like when the police had first arrived.

That someone was Officer Ralph Voight. He was tall and trim, with a pristine uniform despite the fact that he'd been on duty all night.

O'Reilly was the one who convinced him to talk with Bryce. Voight was the first to show the traditional animosity between the

NYPD and the FBI, but that was because Voight didn't know who had died only a few blocks away.

Bryce had Voight walk him through the crime scene. The buildings on this street were boarded up and the lights burned out. Broken glass littered the sidewalk — and it hadn't come from this particular crime. Rusted beer cans, half buried in the ice piles, cluttered each stoop like passed-out drunks.

"Okay," Voight said, using his flashlight as a pointer, "we come up on these two cars first."

The two sedans were parked against the curb, one behind the other. The sedans were too nice for the neighborhood — new, black, without a dent. Bryce recognized them as FBI issue — he had access to a sedan like that himself when he needed it.

He patted his pocket, was disgusted to realize he'd left his notebook at the apartment, and turned to O'Reilly. "You got paper? I need those plates."

O'Reilly nodded. He pulled out a notebook and wrote down the plate numbers.

"They just looked wrong," Voight was saying. "So we stopped, figuring maybe someone needed assistance."

He pointed the flashlight across the street. The squad had stopped directly across from the two cars.

"That's when we seen the first body."

He walked them to the middle of the street. This part of the city hadn't been plowed regularly, and a layer of ice had built over the pavement. A large pool of blood had melted through that ice, leaving its edges reddish black and revealing the pavement below.

"The guy was face-down, hands out like he'd tried to catch himself."

"Face gone?" Bryce asked, thinking maybe it was a headshot like the others.

"No. Turns out he was shot in the back."

Bryce glanced at O'Reilly, whose lips had thinned. This one was different. Because it was the first? Or because it was unrelated?

"We pull our weapons, scan to see if we see anyone else, which we don't. The door's open on the first sedan, but we didn't see anyone in the dome light. And we didn't see anyone obvious on the street, but it's really dark here, and the flashlights don't reach far." Voight turned his light toward the block with the parked limousine, but neither the car nor the sidewalk was visible from this distance.

"So we go to the cars, careful now, and find the other body right there."

He flashed his light on the curb beside the door to the first sedan.

"This one's on his back and the door is open. We figure he was getting out when he got plugged. Then the other guy — maybe he was outside his car trying to help this guy with I don't know what, some car trouble or something, then his buddy gets hit, so he runs for cover across the street and gets nailed. End of story."

"Did you check to see if the cars start?" O'Reilly asked. Bryce nodded; that was going to be his next question as well.

"I'm not supposed to touch the scene, sir," Voight said with some resentment. "We secured the area, figured everything was okay, then called it in."

"Did you hear the other shots?"

"No," Voight said. "I know we got three more up there, and you'd think I'd've heard the shooting if something happened, but I didn't. And as you can tell, it's damn quiet around here at night."

Bryce could tell. He didn't like the silence in the middle of the city. Neighborhoods that got quiet like this so close to dawn were usually among the worst. The early morning maintenance workers and the delivery drivers stayed away whenever they could.

He peered in the sedan, then pulled the door open. The interior light went on, and there was blood all over the front seat and steering wheel. There were Styrofoam coffee cups on both sides of the little rise between the seats. And the keys were in the ignition. Like all Bureau issue, the car was an automatic.

Carefully, so that he wouldn't disturb anything important in the scene, he turned the key. The sedan purred to life, sounding well tuned, just like it was supposed to.

"Check to see if there are other problems," Bryce said to O'Reilly. "A flat, maybe."

Although Bryce knew there wouldn't be one. He shut off the ignition.

"You didn't see the interior light when you pulled up?" he asked Voight.

"Yeah, but it was dim," Voight said. "That's why I figured there was car problems. I figured they left the lights on so they could see."

Bryce nodded. He understood the assumption. He backed out of the sedan, then walked around it, shining his own flashlight at the hole in the ice and then back at the first sedan.

Directly across.

He walked to the second sedan. Its interior was clean — no Styrofoam cups, no wadded-up food containers, no notebooks. Not even some tools hastily pulled to help the other drivers in need.

He let out a small sigh. He finally figured out what was bothering him.

"You find weapons on the two men?" he asked Voight.

"Yes, sir."

"Holstered?"

"The guy by the car. The other one had his in his right hand. We figured we just happened on the scene or someone would have taken the weapon."

Or not. People tended to hide for a while after shots were fired, particularly if they had nothing to do with the shootings but might get blamed anyway.

Bryce tried to open the passenger door on the second sedan, but it was locked. He walked around to the driver's door. Locked as well.

"No one looked inside this car?"

"No, sir. We figured crime scene would do it."

"But they haven't been here yet?" Bryce asked.

"It's the neighborhood, sir. Right there" — Voight aimed his flashlight at stairs heading down to a lower level — "is one of those men-only clubs, you know? The kind that you go to when you're . . . you know . . . looking for other men."

Bryce felt a flash of irritation. He'd been running into this all night. "Okay. What I'm hearing in a sideways way from every representative of the NYPD on this scene is that crimes in this neighborhood don't get investigated."

Voight sputtered. "They get investigated —"

"They get investigated," O'Reilly said, "enough to tell the families they probably want to back off. You heard Brunner. That's what most in the department call it. The rest of us, we call them lifestyle kills. And we get in trouble if we waste too many resources on them."

"Lovely," Bryce said dryly. His philosophy, which had gotten him in trouble with the Bureau more than once, was that all crimes deserved investigation, no matter how distasteful you found the victims. Which was why he kept getting moved, from communists to reviewing wiretaps to digging dirt on other agents.

And that was probably why he was here. He was expendable.

"Did you find car keys on either of the victims?" Bryce asked.

"No, sir," Voight said. "And I helped the coroner when he first arrived."

"Then start looking. See if they got dropped in the struggle."

Although Bryce doubted they had.

"I got something to jimmy the lock in my car," O'Reilly said.

Bryce nodded. Then he stood back, surveying the whole thing. He didn't like how he was thinking. It was making his heartburn grow worse.

But it was the only thing that made sense.

Agents worked HooverWatch in pairs. There were two dead agents and two cars. If the second sedan was backup, there should have been four agents and two cars.

But it didn't look that way. It looked like someone had pulled up behind the HooverWatch vehicle and got out, carefully locking the door.

Then he went to the door of the HooverWatch car. The driver had got out to talk to him, and the new guy shot him.

At that point, the second HooverWatch agent was an easy target. He scrambled out of the car, grabbed his own weapon, and headed across the street — maybe shooting as he went. The shooter got him and then casually walked up the street to the limo, which he had to know was there even though he couldn't see it.

As he approached the limo, the limo driver lowered his window. He would have recognized the approaching man and thought he was going to report on the danger.

Instead the man shot him, then went to lie in wait for Hoover and Tolson.

Bryce shivered. It would have happened very fast, and long before the beat cops showed up.

The guy in the street had time to bleed out. The limo driver couldn't warn his boss. And the beat cops hadn't heard the shots in the alley, which they would have on such a quiet night.

O'Reilly brought the jimmy, shoved it into the space between the

window and the lock, and flipped the lock up with a single movement. Then he opened the door.

No keys in the ignition.

Bryce flipped open the glove box. Nothing inside but the vehicle
registration. Which, as he expected, identified it as an FBI vehicle.

The shooter had planned to come back. He'd planned to drive
away in this car. But he got delayed. And by the time he got here,
the two beat cops were on scene. He couldn't get his car.

He had to improvise. So he probably walked away or took the
subway, hoping the cops would think the extra car belonged to one
of the victims.

And that was his mistake.

"How come you guys were here in the middle of the night?"
Bryce asked Voight.

Voight swallowed. It was the first sign of nervousness he'd shown.
"This is part of our beat."

"But?" Bryce asked.

Voight looked away. "We're supposed to go up Central Park
West."

"And you don't."

"Yeah, we do. Just not every time."

"Because?"

"Because I figure, you know, when the bars let out, we could, you
know, let our presence be known."

"Prevent a lifestyle kill."

"Yes, sir."

"And you care about this because . . . ?"

"Everyone should," Voight snapped. "Serve and protect, right,
sir?"

Voight was touchy. He thought Bryce was accusing him of protecting the lifestyle because he lived it.

"Does your partner like this drive?" Bryce asked.

"He complains, sir, but he lets me do it."

"Have you stopped any crimes?"

"Broken up a few fights," Voight said.

"But not something like this."

"No, sir."

"You don't patrol every night, do you, Voight?"

"No, sir. We get different regions different nights."

"Do you think our killer would have thought that this street was unprotected?"

"It usually is, sir."

O'Reilly was frowning, but not at Voight. At Bryce. "You think this was planned?" O'Reilly asked.

Bryce didn't answer. This was a Bureau matter, and he wasn't sure how the Bureau would handle it.

But he did think the killing was planned. And he had a hunch it would be easy to solve because of the abandoned sedan.

And that abandoned sedan bothered him more than he wanted to admit. Because the presence of that sedan meant only one thing: that the person who had shot all five FBI agents was — almost without a doubt — an FBI agent himself.

Kennedy looked at the bins and the filing cabinets stacked around his office and allowed himself one moment to feel overwhelmed. People ribbed him about the office; he had taken the reception area and made it his rather than use the standard-size office in the back.

As a result, his office was as long as a football field, with stunning windows along the walls. The watercolors painted by his children had been covered by the cabinets. His furniture was pushed aside to make room for the bins, and for the first time this space felt small.

He put his hands on his hips and wondered how to begin.

Since six agents began moving the filing cabinets across the corridor more than an hour ago, Kennedy had received five phone calls from LBJ's chief of staff. Kennedy hadn't taken one of them. The last had been a direct order to come to the Oval Office.

Kennedy ignored it.

He also ignored the ringing telephone — the White House line — and the messages his own assistant (called in after a short night's sleep) had been bringing to him.

Helen Gandy stood in the corridor, arms crossed, her purse hanging off her wrist, and watching with deep disapproval. Haskell was trying to find out if there were remaining files and where they were. But Kennedy had found the one thing he was looking for: the key.

It was in a large, innocuous index file box inside the lowest drawer of Helen Gandy's desk. Kennedy had brought it into his office and was thumbing through it, hoping to understand it before he got interrupted again.

A man from building maintenance had changed the lock on the door leading into the interior offices and was working on the main doors now that the files were all inside. Kennedy figured he'd have his own office secure by seven A.M.

Then he heard a rustling in the hallway, a lot of startled "Mr. President, sir!" followed by official "Make way for the president," and instinctively he turned toward the door. The maintenance man was leaning out of it, the doorknob loose in his hand.

"Where the fuck is that bastard?" Lyndon Baines Johnson's voice echoed from the corridor. "Doesn't anyone in this building have balls enough to tell him that he works for me?"

Even though the question was rhetorical, someone tried to answer. Kennedy heard something about "your orders, sir."

"Horseshit!" Then LBJ stood in the doorway. Two Secret Service agents flanked him. He motioned with one hand at the maintenance man. "I suggest you get out."

The man didn't have to be told twice. He scurried away, still carrying the doorknob. LBJ came inside alone, pushed the door closed, then grimaced as it popped back open. He grabbed a chair and set it in front of the door, then glared at Kennedy.

The glare was effective in that hangdog face, despite LBJ's attire. He wore a plaid silk pajama top stuffed into a pair of suit pants, finished with dress shoes and no socks. His hair — what remained of it — hadn't been Brylcreemed down as usual and stood up on the sides and the back.

"I get a phone call from some weasel underling of that old cocksucker, informing me that he's dead and you're stealing from his tomb. I try to contact you, find out that you are indeed removing files from the Director's office and that you won't take my calls. Now, I should've sent one of my boys over here, but I figured they're still walking on tiptoe around you because you're in fucking mourning, and this don't require tiptoe. Especially since you got to be wondering about now what the hell you did to deserve all of this."

"Deserve what?" Kennedy had expected LBJ's anger, but he hadn't expected it so soon. He also hadn't expected it here, in his office, instead of in the Oval Office a day or so later.

"Well, there's only two things that tie J. Edgar and your brother.

The first is that someone was gunning for them and succeeded. The second is that they went after the mob on your bidding. There's a lot of shit running around here that says your brother's shooting was a mob hit, and I know personally that J. Edgar was doing his best to make it seem like that Oswald character acted alone. But now Edgar is dead and Jack is dead and the only tie they have is the way they kowtowed to your stupid prosecution of the men that got your brother elected."

Kennedy felt lightheaded. He hadn't even thought that the deaths of his brother and J. Edgar were connected. But LBJ had a point. Maybe there was a conspiracy to kill government officials. Maybe the mob was showing its power. He'd had warning.

Hell, he'd had suspicions. He hadn't let himself look at any of the evidence in his brother's assassination, not after he secured the body and prevented a disastrous autopsy in Texas. If those doctors at Parkland had done their job, they would've seen just how advanced Jack's Addison's disease was. The best-kept secret of the Kennedy administration — an administration full of secrets — was how close Jack was to incapacitation and death.

Kennedy clutched the file box. But LBJ knew that. He knew a lot of the secrets — had even promised to keep a few of them. And he wanted the files as badly as Kennedy did.

There had to be a lot in here on LBJ, too. Not just the women, which was something he had in common with Jack, but other things, from his days in Congress.

"From what I heard," Kennedy said, making certain his voice was calm even though he wasn't, "all they know is someone shot Hoover. Did you get more details than that? Something that mentions organized crime in particular?"

"I'm sure it'll come out," LBJ said.

"You're sure that saying such things would upset me," Kennedy said. "You're after the files."

"Damn straight," LBJ said. "I'm the head of this government. Those files are mine."

"You're the head of this government for another year. Next January someone'll take the oath of office and it might not be you. Do you really want to claim these in the name of the presidency? Because you might be handing them over to Goldwater come January."

LBJ blanched.

Someone knocked on the door and startled both men. Kennedy frowned. He couldn't think of anyone who would have enough nerve to interrupt him when he was getting shouted at by LBJ. But someone had.

LBJ pulled the door open. Helen Gandy stood there.

"You boys can be heard in the hallway," she said, sweeping in as if the leader of the free world weren't holding the door for her. "And it's embarrassing. It was precisely this kind of thing the Director hoped to avoid."

Then she nodded at LBJ. Kennedy watched her. The dragon lady. Jack, as usual, had been right with his gibes. Only the dragon lady would walk in here as if she were the most important person in the room.

"Mr. President," she said, "these files are the Director's personal business. He wanted me to take care of them and get them out of the office, where they do not belong."

"Personal files, Miss Gandy?" LBJ asked. "These are his secret files."

"If they were secret, Mr. President, then you wouldn't be here. Mr. Hoover kept his secrets."

Mr. Hoover used his secrets, Kennedy thought but didn't say.

"These are just his confidential files," Miss Gandy was saying. "Let me take care of them, and they won't be here to tempt anyone. That's what the Director wanted."

"These are government property," LBJ said, with a sly look at Kennedy. For the first time, Kennedy realized his Goldwater argument had gotten through. "They belong here. I do thank you for your time and concern, though, ma'am."

Then he gave her a courtly little bow, put his hand on the small of her back, and propelled her out of the room.

Despite himself, Kennedy was impressed. He'd never seen anyone handle the dragon lady that efficiently before.

LBJ grabbed one of the cabinets and slid it in front of the door he had just closed. Kennedy had forgotten how strong the man was. He had invited Kennedy down to his Texas ranch before the election, trying to find out what Kennedy was made of, and instead Kennedy had realized just what LBJ was made of — strength, not bluster, brains *and* brawn.

He'd do well to remember that.

"All right," LBJ said as he turned around. "Here's what I'm gonna offer. You can have your family's files. You can watch while we search for them, and you can have everything. Just give me the rest."

Kennedy raised his eyebrows. He hadn't felt this alive since November. "No."

"I can fire your ass in five minutes, put someone else in this fancy office, and then you can't do a goddamn thing," LBJ said. "I'm being kind."

"There's historical precedent for a cabinet member barricading himself in his office after he got fired," Kennedy said. "Seems to me it happened to a previous president named Johnson. While I'm barricaded in, I'll just go through the files and find out everything I need to know."

LBJ crossed his arms.

It was a standoff, and neither of them had a good play. They only had a guess as to what was in those files — not just theirs, but all of the others as well. They did know that whatever was in those files had given Hoover enough power to last in the office for more than forty years.

The files had brought down presidents. They could bring down congressmen, Supreme Court justices, and maybe even the current president. In that way, Helen Gandy was right.

The best solution was to destroy everything.

Only Kennedy wouldn't. Just like he knew LBJ wouldn't. There was too much history here, too much knowledge.

And too much power.

"These are our files," Kennedy said after a moment, although the word "our" galled him, "yours and mine. Right now we control them."

LBJ nodded, almost imperceptibly. "What do you want?"

What did he want? To be left alone? To have his family left alone? At midnight he might have said that. But now his old self was reasserting itself. He felt like the man who had gone after the corrupt leaders of the Teamsters, not the man who had accidentally gotten his brother murdered.

Besides, there might be things in that file that could head off other problems in the future. Other murders. Other manipulations.

He needed a bulletproof position. LBJ was right: the attorney general could be fired. But there was one position, constitutionally, that the president couldn't touch.

"I want to be your vice president," Kennedy said. "And in 1972, when you can't run again, I want your endorsement. I want you to back me for the nomination."

LBJ swallowed hard. Color suffused his face, and for a moment Kennedy thought he was going to shout again.

But he didn't.

Instead he said, "And what happens if we don't win?"

"We move these to a location of our choosing. And we do it with trusted associates. We get this stuff out of here."

LBJ glanced at the door. He was clearly thinking of what Helen Gandy had said, how it was better to be rid of all of this than it was to have it corrupting the office, endangering everyone.

But if LBJ and Kennedy controlled the entire cache, they also controlled their own files. LBJ could destroy his, and Kennedy could preserve his family's legacy.

If it weren't for the fact that LBJ hated him almost as much as Kennedy hated LBJ, the decision would be easy.

"You'd trust me to a gentleman's agreement?" LBJ asked, not disguising the sarcasm in his tone. He knew Kennedy thought he was too uncouth to ever be considered a gentleman.

"You know where your interests lie. Just like I do," Kennedy said. "If we don't let Miss Gandy have the files, then this is the only choice."

LBJ sighed. "I hoped to be rid of the Kennedys by inauguration day."

"And what if I planned to run against you?" Kennedy asked, even though he knew he wouldn't. Already the party stalwarts had been approaching him about a 1964 presidential bid, and he had put them off. He had been too shaky, too emotionally fragile.

He didn't feel fragile now.

LBJ didn't answer that question. Instead he said, "You can be an incautious asshole. Why should I trust you?"

"Because I saved Jack's ass more times than you can count," Kennedy said. "I'm saving yours, too."

"How do you figure?" LBJ asked.

"Your fear of those files brought you to me, Mr. President." Kennedy put an emphasis on the title, which he usually avoided using around LBJ. "If I barricade myself in here, I'll have the keys to the kingdom and no qualms about letting the information free when I go free. If you work with me, your secrets remain just secrets."

"You're a son of a bitch, you know that?" LBJ asked.

Kennedy nodded. "The hell of it is you are, too, or you wouldn't've brought up Jack's death before we knew what really happened to Hoover. So let's control the presidency for the next sixteen years. By then the information in these files will probably be worthless."

LBJ stared at him. It took Kennedy a minute to realize that although he'd won the argument, he wouldn't get an agreement from LBJ, not if Kennedy didn't make the first move.

Kennedy held out his hand. "Deal?"

LBJ stared at Kennedy's extended hand for a long moment before taking it in his own big clammy one.

"You goddamn son of a bitch," LBJ said. "You've got a deal."

It took Bryce only one phone call. The guy who ran the motor pool told him who had checked out the sedan without asking why Bryce want to know. And Bryce, as he leaned in the cold telephone booth half a block from the first crime scene, instantly understood what had happened and why.

The agent who had checked out the sedan was Walter Cain. He should've been on extended leave. Bryce had recommended it after he had told Cain that his ex-fiancée had tried to commit suicide. On getting the news, Cain had just had that look, that blank, my-life-is-over look.

And it had scared Bryce. Scared him enough that he asked for Cain to be put on indefinite leave. How long ago had that been? Less than twelve hours.

More than enough time to get rid of the morals police — the one man who made all the rules at the FBI. The man who had no morals himself.

J. Edgar Hoover.

Bryce had spent the past week studying Cain's file. Cain had had HooverWatch off and on throughout the past year. Cain knew the procedure, and he knew how to thwart it.

He'd killed five agents.

Because no one would listen to Bryce about that vacant look in Cain's eye.

Bryce let himself out of the phone booth. He walked back to the coroner's van. If he didn't have backup by now, he'd call for some all over again. They couldn't leave him hanging on this. They had to let him know, if nothing else, what to do with the Director's body.

But he needn't've worried. When he got back to the alley, he saw five more sedans, all FBI issue. And as he stepped into the alley proper, the first person he saw was his boss, crouching over Hoover's corpse.

"I thought I told you to secure the scene," said the SAC for the district of New York, Eugene Hart. "In fact, I ordered you to do it."

"The scene extends over six blocks. I'm just one guy," Bryce said.

Hart walked over to him. He looked tired.

"I need to speak to you," Bryce said. He walked Hart back to the two sedans, explained what he'd learned, and watched Hart's face.

The man flinched, then, to Bryce's surprise, put his hand on Bryce's shoulder. "It's good work."

Bryce didn't thank him. He was worried that Hart hadn't asked any questions. "I'd heard Cain bitch more than once about Hoover setting the moral values for the office. And with what happened this week —"

"I know." Hart squeezed his shoulder. "We'll take care of it."

Bryce turned so quickly that he made Hart lose his grip. "You're going to cover it up."

Hart closed his eyes.

"You weren't hanging me out to dry. You were trying to figure out how to handle this. Son of a bitch. And you're going to let Cain walk."

"He won't walk," Hart said. "He'll just . . . be guilty of something else."

"You can't cover this up. It's too important. So soon after President Kennedy —"

"That's precisely why we're going to handle it," Hart said. "We don't want a panic."

"And you don't want anyone to know where Hoover and Tolson were found. What're you going to say? That they died of natural causes in their beds? Their *separate* beds?"

"It's not your concern," Hart said. "You've done well for us. You'll be rewarded."

"If I keep my mouth shut."

Hart sighed. He didn't seem to have the energy to glare. "I don't honestly care. I'm glad to have the old man gone. But I'm not in charge of this. We've got orders now, and everything'll get taken care of at a much higher level than either you or me. You should be grateful for that."

Bryce supposed he should be. It took the political pressure off him. It also took the personal pressure off.

But he couldn't help feeling that if someone had listened to him before, if someone had paid attention, then none of this would have happened.

No one cared that an FBI agent was going to marry a former prostitute. If the Bureau knew, and it did, then not even the KGB could use that as blackmail.

It was all about appearances. It would always be about appearances. Hoover had designed a damn booklet about appearances, and it hadn't stopped him from getting shot in a back alley after a party he would never admit to attending.

Hoover had been so worried about people using secrets against each other, he hadn't even realized how his own secrets could be used against him.

Bryce looked at Hart. They were both tired. It had been a long night. And it would be an even longer few weeks for Hart. Bryce would get some don't-tell promotion, and he'd stay there for as long as he had to. He had to make sure that Cain got prosecuted for something, that he paid for five deaths.

Then Bryce would resign.

He didn't need the Bureau, any more than he had needed Mary, his own preapproved wife. Maybe he'd talk to O'Reilly, see if he could put in a good word with the NYPD. At least the NYPD occasionally investigated cases.

If they happened in the right neighborhood.

To the right people.

Bryce shoved his hands in his pockets and walked back to his apartment. Hart didn't try to stop him. They both knew Bryce's work on this case was done. He wouldn't even have to write a report.

In fact, he didn't dare write a report, didn't dare put any of this on paper, where someone else might discover it. The wrong someone. Someone who didn't care about handling and the proper information.

Someone who would use that information to his own benefit.
Like the Director had.
For more than forty-five years.
   Bryce shook the thought off. It wasn't his concern. He no longer had concerns. Except getting a good night's sleep.
   And somehow he knew that he wouldn't get one of those for a long, long time.

JONATHAN TEL

Bola de la Fortuna

FROM *The Yale Review*

IT WAS NOT THE CASE that Kent's decision to pull off the highway and eat a tamale at a rest stop outside of Raton, New Mexico, on the morning of 17 July 1985 was what ruined his life, except in the sense that all our lives are ruined. This was the deal: late on the sixteenth there was a load to pick up in Las Cruces, and it didn't have to be dropped off in Colorado Springs till the following afternoon. He was an independent subcontractor, driving an Iveco semitrailer that belonged to a company based in Denver called Integrated Vattings; what was in the back of the semi he didn't know or care.

Now, Kent had a girlfriend who was not a girlfriend, who lived in a trailer near Bernalillo. If he timed it right, he could spend the night with her, get up early, and cruise into the Springs on schedule, then pick up another load for the return journey, stopping off with her again the following night. He'd been driving the route for years; he could practically do it in his sleep. Her name was Dionne.

To begin with, everything went according to plan. He left Las Cruces after the rush hour, slipped smoothly past Truth or Consequences, and had only a minor delay in Albuquerque. He arrived at Dionne's before midnight. Her sons were Zee, who was four, and Lallo, who was one and three quarters. (Their real names were Ze'ev and Laszlo, but nobody ever called them that.) Kent whispered hello to the sleeping boys and climbed into Dionne's bed.

He had an alarm clock with a buzzer that woke him without waking Dionne at 5:30 A.M. He liked being here well enough — even though Dionne was not really his girlfriend, and her sons were not his sons. They had an arrangement; in her closet he kept a change of clothing, pajamas, socks, and sneakers. His toothbrush and shampoo and shaving kit were in her bathroom. But in the closet there was also a change of clothing belonging to some other man, and that man's toothbrush and shampoo and razor were also in the bathroom.

That other man — Kent didn't know his name or a damn thing about him. He didn't want to know. Just about the only thing Kent couldn't help noticing was that the other man wore brown shoes. Kent never wore brown shoes. Many years ago somebody had told Kent that only insurance salesmen and fairies wear brown shoes; Kent didn't believe it, but he didn't wear brown shoes either. The brown shoes were worn down on the outer side of the heel and were one size smaller, but wider, than his own.

That morning, bleary-eyed, fumbling in the semidark, Kent thrust the other man's toothbrush into his own mouth. As soon it was in there, rubbing away at his teeth, he knew something was wrong. The brush was the wrong shape, somehow both too hard and too soft, and tasted of brown shoes. Kent spat. He washed his mouth out very thoroughly.

Then, with a mouth not quite his own, he kissed his not-quite-sleeping not-quite-girlfriend (she kissed back very sweetly but didn't stir from her half-dream), whispered bye-bye to the sleeping boys, and headed out into the world. The sun was huge and red on the horizon, and birds were singing. Frost on the sagebrush. It was the kind of day that would become hot later. He climbed into the cab of the truck.

That evening the truck was parked outside her trailer again, and inside Kent and Dionne were making love quietly, so as not to disturb the boys. Suddenly they heard a small cracking noise like a twig breaking, and then a clamor of footsteps. Kent looked through the window. The trailer was surrounded by half a dozen men wearing black jumpsuits with the word "POLICE" on back and front. The police ran into the bedroom and grabbed Kent from the bed, punching him on the chin and in the testicles, and handcuffed him. Meanwhile, Dionne had pulled the sheet up to her neck to cover her nakedness and was screaming. All Kent could think to say was, "It's not me! It's the other man!" while at the same time he noticed that the interesting thing about Dionne was that her face, screaming, looked just like it did when she had an orgasm. A police officer, mustached, pushed his face very close to hers. "Is he holding you and the children hostage?" She kept on screaming. The police officer asked, "Do you know this man?"

Kent was about as law-abiding as most people. He'd grown up in Española. His ancestors had been in New Mexico before it became part of the United States. His mother tongue was the New Mexico dialect of Spanish; his generation was the first to use English among themselves, to differentiate themselves from the wetbacks. There were Mexican children in his class at high school, who were called Latinos. He and his friends called themselves Hispanics. There were more Hispanics than Latinos, so the Hispanic gang always beat up the Latino gang. As a teen he'd been taken in by the police a few times, nothing serious, let off with warnings. Then when he was seventeen a friend of his stole a Dodge Shadow and let Kent drive it. The Shadow was involved in a collision (not Kent's fault, exactly), and when the police searched it, they found ecstasy in the glove compartment. Maybe the pills belonged to his friend, or maybe to whoever the car had been stolen from, or maybe the police planted them. Kent plea-bargained it down to a count of possession and was given ninety days. It scared him off. That was seven years ago, and he'd never been charged with anything since.

He was taken to operational headquarters in Albuquerque. The detective in charge of the case, Ruíz, yelled, "Where were you this morning at twelve forty-five?"

Kent wasn't sure where he'd been at that precise time. "I was on the road."

"No, you weren't! We know where you were!"

As best as Kent could work out, he must have been well south of the state line, heading toward Taos. But he didn't understand why the cop was calling 12:45 "morning." Surely it was already afternoon?

"Did you stop on the way?"

Well, yes. Though that had been a little earlier. He'd parked the truck near Raton. It was one of those places where people are supposed to relax and eat their food, with a bench and a sign showing a table under a tree, also a word of advice from Smokey the Bear. He'd walked about five minutes farther through the woods, into a *rincón,* to get some peace and quiet, and sat down on the earth. He ate a chicken tamale and drank a Dr Pepper and smoked a joint. Then he came back to the truck and continued his drive south.

What had happened (he deduced the story from the accusations of the detective) was that approximately one hour after he'd finished his lunch, less than half a mile away, a woman named Darathea Mondragon had been raped and murdered by a person or persons unknown. All that could be said about Mondragon was that she was eighteen, from Texas, and had last been heard of the previous day in El Paso. She was believed to be hitching north; she'd told a friend she was aiming for a Rainbow Gathering near Boulder. The body was left by the road fifty yards from the rest stop. It was found by a vacationing family from Washington state. The police scoured the terrain and soon discovered the remains of Kent's lunch. His fingerprints were on the Dr Pepper.

Ruíz trusted his hunch. He *knew* Kent was the one. When you've been at this as long as he had, you acquire an intuition. Anyway, who else could it be? There were no further clues, no other potential suspects to consider. Ruíz could smell Kent's guilt just looking at the printout of his priors. Pity no witness had come forward, no forensic evidence pinned Kent to the crime. So the detective, along with his deputy, Lazaroff, set about getting the man to confess.

Ruíz grabbed the handcuffed man's shoulders, shook him. "Motherfucker! *Jota!* I'm gonna cut off your balls personally!" Then Lazaroff said in a quiet voice, "Why don't we just get it over with? You can tell us how you did it." When that line didn't work, Ruíz shouted, "Your friend confessed already! Diane told us everything we want to know!" Lazaroff took out pen and notepad; "Now let's begin your confession from the top." Kent muttered, "Her name's *Dionne.*" Ruíz went, *"What?"* "It's not important," Kent said.

They told him he'd be locked up as long as they fucking wanted and he wasn't ever going to get out. They left him alone an hour, then came back for another go. Lazaroff said, "That girl was a total slut, wasn't she? Tight jeans. Hitchhiking. She was begging for it." Ruíz said, "I know her sort. She lets you do everything you always dreamed of." Lazaroff said, "You'll get a shorter sentence if you confess." Ruíz said, "The forensics prove it was you, your stinking cum all over the stinking bitch!"

It continued like this for two days. The light was permanently on in his cell — a round fluorescent fixture, like a halo, secured behind metal bars on the ceiling. Often the detectives took turns interrogating him, so that Kent got hardly any sleep. They took him through the details of the crime, reconstructing it in a kind of gestured, indicative act, with Lazaroff playing the role of the victim and Ruíz the perpetrator. They showed him what they said he did, what he must have done, in exquisite detail, so he'd know precisely what to say when he finally did get around to confessing.

So convincing were the detectives that Kent began to half believe in his own guilt. He couldn't understand his motive, though. It made no sense. He was not a violent man and had never seriously desired to rape or murder anyone. Yet these detectives were knowledgeable, experienced, sure of themselves; and if they were confident he'd done it, who was he to deny it? The only thing holding him back from confessing — and it seemed a very small thing — was that he knew he was innocent. It struck him as remarkable that he had *not* carried out the crime — as if there were a million parallel universes in which he was a rapist and murderer, and by an amazing coincidence he found himself in the unique universe where that fundamental element of his life story was missing. He felt in himself the emotions that he guessed an actual murderer would feel under the circumstances. Defiance, remorse, crazy glee, a frantic desire to go back in time and undo what cannot be undone. Something like when you come out of a movie sad as hell, and it was a figure on the screen the tragedy happened to. Forty-eight hours later, he still had not confessed. The nearest he came to it was saying, "You can't prove a thing." Ruíz grinned; in his book, this counted as a full confession, though it wouldn't stand up in court.

Kent was released. He stayed in Albuquerque, in a motel off Airport Road. He got drunk on Jose Cuervo and waited to be arrested again. Which happened a day later. This time the FBI was involved; they were trying to link him to a serial killing in Colorado. He was interviewed briefly — just a couple of hours. Then he was passed back to Ruíz and Lazaroff. Then released again.

The pattern repeated itself over the next several weeks. Kent was brought in for questioning and released; he lost count of how many times. The detectives kept asking him the same questions, though he had nothing new to add. Once they locked him in a cell with another prisoner, who was in for dealing crystal meth. The other prisoner asked Kent about his crime, and Kent understood that the meth dealer was supposed to be the snitch and felt sorry for him, but still he did not confess.

Integrated Vattings blacklisted him, of course. And Dionne wrote him a letter stating that she wanted nothing to do with him. She wrote that she'd burned all his things, and she was crying at the thought of what he might have done to Lallo and Zee.

He couldn't stay at the motel indefinitely. He could no longer afford the apartment he had in Denver. He called around among his friends and acquaintances trying to find a place, but the news had gotten around. Eventually a high school acquaintance, Pete, who was now born again and living near Madrid, said maybe. Kent warned Pete he'd have to give the address to the police, and there was a good chance they'd come knocking. A pause. Then Pete said, "Say, tell me what you did again." "Nothing." "What do they *say* you did?" "They say I raped and strangled a girl." A longer pause. "There are no girls here. I guess you can come and keep me company."

The two men shared the house. Kent slept on the couch in the living room. The couch gave him a backache, so he slept on the floor instead. On Sundays they went to a Pentecostal church. The pastor called on the congregation to let Jesus in. Everyone lifted their hands on high, as if waving goodbye or surrendering, and they sang a hymn. Pete spoke in tongues, while Kent stared at the ground.

This arrangement lasted the better part of a year. Sometimes Kent got a temporary job, hauling or warehouse work; then he helped with the rent. In bad times, Pete shrugged: "Pay me when you can." There was no question of Kent's looking for a permanent, better-paying job now, since every couple of months or so he'd be taken to Albuquerque for interrogation. The way it worked was that he was handcuffed and put in a police car and driven down there; he was let go in downtown Albuquerque, and he had to find his own way back. He depended on the Greyhound schedules. Usually he managed to make the 7:05 P.M. to Santa Fe. Then he would loiter around the terminal alongside German tourists wearing turquoise bracelets and troupes of cheerful Japanese backpackers till Pete could come by and pick him up. The day after Christmas, Kent drank half a bottle of Taos Moonshine and somehow broke the electrical connection to Pete's tree; it wouldn't ever light up again. Pete kicked him out and said he'd pray for him.

After that, Kent lived in some other places briefly, staying with acquaintances and acquaintances of acquaintances in northern New Mexico and southern Colorado. As a last resort, he unrolled his sleeping bag on the floor of his great-aunt Marta's. She lived in Española, in the house where she'd been born. She was hard of hearing and her mind wandered. Often she addressed him as "Federico," though there was nobody of that name in the family. By the fall of 1987 Kent still had no proper home or job; the detectives had stopped interrogating him, but the thought that they might do so at any moment hung over him.

What stopped him from going under completely was Alcoholics Anonymous. He went to a meeting in Santa Fe, near where the railroad tracks meet Second Street. "My name is Kent, and I'm an alcoholic." He wasn't exactly sure he *was* an alcoholic, but that was not the main thing. Now at last he was in a place where people freely confess, sometimes boast about, their sins; even if he had been a rapist and murderer, he thought, it would not have been so dreadful here. Also the meeting was a common area — a plaza, a *zócalo* — where different kinds of New Mexicans meet on fairly equal terms: Hispanics, Anglos, Indians, even Latinos are acceptable, poor, and getting by, and rich. He fitted in as well as anyone. AAers don't use the word "God" on its own; instead they talk of "God as we understand him" or a "higher power" — which was as much as Kent could buy. He didn't tell the group about his recent problems (though some of them knew) but about his childhood. He'd never thought of himself as particularly interesting — like most people he'd grown up with, he'd been drinking and taking drugs since he was about ten — but these intimate strangers, perched on a circle of stackable plastic chairs in a church hall, found his story touching and gripping, unique yet curiously similar to their own. Listeners nodded and sighed and grunted sympathetically as he spoke. Often somebody squeezed his hand or arm; from time to time he was hugged. Then it would be the next person's turn to become the hero of their shared myth. Many of the alcoholics, as they related the suffering they'd brought on themselves and their loved ones, broke down in tears. Once the drama would have seemed inordinate — grown men don't behave like this — but now he thought these ones had a clue as to the real nature of the world. In practical terms, AA connections helped him find work. He got a succession of seasonal jobs that paid quite well, landscaping and forestry. Then an Anglo realtor with a thirst for single malts hooked him up with a widow who was retired in Oahu but still kept a house in Ranchos de Taos. In return for guarding it and maintaining the grounds, Kent got to stay there rent-free. In this home, furnished by a couple he had never met, adorned with memories and photographs of the widow, her deceased husband, and their children and grandchildren, he lived as peaceably as could reasonably be wished for.

In February 1988 Kent was interrogated again. What had happened was that Ruíz had taken early retirement. His replacement, Slichter, had been headhunted from Flagstaff. First thing Slichter did was to leaf through the old CUNC files (Case Uncleared Not Closed) looking for quick arrests and convictions. Slichter tried much the same line of questioning as Ruíz and Lazaroff. Kent still did not confess. In disgust Slichter threw a *Reader's Digest* at his head and accused him of wasting his time.

Slichter left under a cloud; the next detective, Canella, had a go at breaking down Kent in March 1990. Canella tried a different tactic. "Listen, we're all men here. We all have our needs, our urges. I'm not blaming you for anything. I just want to get this thing over with, as I'm sure you do. So let's get together and reach an agreement, huh? In both our interests. So tell me your best offer. Hmm, how about you accept the rape, and I let you off the homicide, huh? Or how about we forget the rape, and I raise you a homicide third degree? Seven years in jail max; you'll be out on parole before you have time to decorate your cell." Canella held out his right hand, as if to shake on the deal.

Another interrogation took place in 1992, and again in 1994. Each time it was a new detective, eager to close a case that seemed so straightforward, so almost concluded, but for the little matter of getting the criminal to confess. Each time was like the previous times, with subtle variations. Each time Kent took a deep breath and responded, "Yes, I drove along that road. Yes, I parked my truck. Yes, I got out and walked into the woods. No, I did not rape and murder Darathea Mondragon."

Meanwhile, Kent kept attending Alcoholics Anonymous; what-

ever happened, he'd never miss his Thursdays. He committed himself to going through the twelve steps — slowly, pacing himself;
he couldn't imagine how he'd deal with it when he reached the
eighth, in which you write a list of the people you've harmed and
make amends to all of them. He had various jobs, lasting anywhere
from one day to six months. He had girlfriends, too, who lasted no
longer. Tamara . . . Cynthia . . . Annie . . . Laverne . . . Grace . . .
Sooner or later, the girlfriend would find out. A rumor would wind
its way to her, and Kent was not up to lying. The worst was with
Laverne. A *lengua larga* dropped off an unsigned letter at the candle factory where she worked. That night Laverne invited him
round to her *casita* and showed him the letter — a scrawl in non-
joined-up letters, purple ink on blue paper — and panted in his
ear, "Tie me up, Kent! Hit me! Do whatever you want!" Horrified,
he fled and never saw her again.

Did he confess his guilt? Just once.

In October 1995 Kent was sitting in a booth in a diner he often
went to, Hector's House of Enchiladas, which is to the south of the
plaza in Española, less than a block from where Great-Aunt Marta
had lived before she was taken to the hospital. That month he
was working in Pojoaque, delivering firewood and pumpkins and
breeze blocks to the pueblo; he had come to Hector's during his
lunch break, and he ordered a bowl of the green chili.

A woman — at first she looked elderly, but on second glance she
was about his own age — asked if she could sit opposite. He nodded and gestured at the seat. A red shawl was tied over the top of
her head. She was short, with dark wrinkles on either side of her
mouth, an Indian-looking face. She spoke to him in Spanish — not
the dialect of New Mexico though, an accent he did not recognize.
She asked if he wanted to know his future. He stirred his chili and
did not answer. Then she asked if he wanted to know his past.

"I know my past already," he said.

"Sometimes we forget."

"Uh, well. Got to go."

He rose and left money on the table for Hector and walked out
back to his Toyota pickup. As he was about to get in, he saw that
Red Shawl had followed him.

"Maybe you can drop me along the way? I live only five minutes
from here."

He could think of no polite way of refusing.

She sat beside him. Kent fastened his seatbelt, as he always did. She left hers open, trusting the driver or fate. She gave directions, after a fashion; she was saying, "One block more . . . One block more . . . ," but wherever she was aiming at kept receding into the distance. He knew she wanted something from him, but he did not know what. He knew it was more than a simple lift home. He did not think it was sex. He couldn't believe she meant to rob him, either. Most days, going to and from work, he passed the state penitentiary — the razor wire and the guard towers and the blazing security lamps. DANGER! DO NOT PICK UP HITCHHIKERS. And here he was doing it. She was the first hitchhiker he'd picked up since . . . well, since he could remember.

The house was on the other side of Española. It was small. The door was not locked. They went inside, and there was no heating; his breath plumed in the air, and he sat down on a blue-painted wooden chair. There was another such chair for herself, facing him, and between them an old wooden packing crate served as a table. Plastered walls; holy pictures were tacked up: Saint Joseph, Saint Sebastian, *Nuestra Señora de Guadalupe,* the Sacred Heart. One entire wall was covered with a kind of wallpaper that was actually a reproduction of a landscape — mountains, trees, a waterfall — similar to but definitely not the landscape around here, maybe Europe, maybe somewhere like Switzerland. She produced a greasy pack of cards, invited him to cut it, shuffled, and dealt face-down on the crate. He guessed she was a hustler of sorts; he waited for the suggestion that they play for real money. She turned the cards over. This was not the usual pack: it was a tarot. She looked at the cards and shook her head. "You have much trouble in your life."

He was becoming impatient. He was sure she said this to everyone. Sooner or later she would tell him he was destined to meet a beautiful woman and find wealth and health and happiness, and then she would ask him to pay up. He was on to that game. He swore inwardly: whatever happened, he would give her nothing. He would not go even halfway toward meeting her.

She set the pack aside. She opened the side of the packing crate and took out what she called *bola de la fortuna.* She said the English for it — the first English words she'd spoken in his presence — "crystal ball." She settled it on top of the crate.

To Kent, it did not look crystal at all. More like plastic. The thing was about the size of a regulation baseball or a little bigger. He turned his head away — looked at anything *but* the ball — the flaking paint on the ceiling, the bare floorboards, Switzerland . . .

Finally he gave up and gazed into the crystal ball. She was gazing into it also. The only sound was the sound of human breathing, as both of them entered the murky clarity.

Here is the woman. Her name is María de Guadalupe. Some call her Guadalupe, and some call her Pia for short, but most know her simply as María. (She has an Indian name, too, but this must not be told, lest the hearer have power over her.) She was born in the village of Chamula in the state of Chiapas; jungle surrounded her. At the age of eighteen she left Chiapas for the first time; she traveled to the border and crossed into America. To her the land looked the same on both sides — desert and desert — but she was conscious that a vast difference existed. She had heard stories of coyotes who rob and rape the travelers they purport to help; she had heard of immigrants dying of thirst in the desert. She had not known in advance whether she would ever see America. But here she was. Arizona. Somebody whose name she never found out pushed her inside a white van and drove her direct to Albuquerque, where her cousin lived.

It was the cousin who had paid for the journey. As agreed, Guadalupe worked as a maid for her cousin for five years, until she had paid off the debt. Then she became free. She moved to Española and began her own life.

By the time she met Kent, she had been independent for eight years. She had a business card printed with her name followed by *Bruja y Curandera* (Witch and Healer). It was true she was a healer; it was not altogether true she was a witch, but when you are in America, you have to make a living how you can. Her craft as a *curandera* she had learned from her mother. These were her skills: She could pass a hen's egg over a woman with monthly pains and transfer the pain into the egg; then the egg is cracked, and the pain goes away. There is a kind of tea which cures headaches about half of the time. For a baby with croup, you fill the room with steam from a kettle and burn frankincense and say a prayer in Tzotzil; this always works, though the cure may take several months. For arthritis, tie a red thread around the aching limb and burn an ear of corn; this doesn't completely stop the pain but makes it not so bad. When somebody suffers from *susto* — for example, when they get wet and unhappy and stand in a cold wind, and so their soul wanders — do the thing with the hen's egg; also it helps to paint a cross with coffee on their forehead. This is a disease the physicians cannot help with at all: only a *curandera* can treat it.

And was she a *bruja*? When she was a girl, she wondered if she might be. Her mother didn't have the talent, but her grandmother had; maybe it had skipped a generation. Her mother told her, "Wait and see. It may come to you." She waited, and she was still waiting.

Listen and I will tell you the strangest thing ever to happen to María de Guadalupe. It was a month after her arrival in the United States. She was living in a suburb of Albuquerque, and over the horizon the Hot Air Balloon Festival was taking place. You should know that the festival takes place every year and is the largest such gathering in the world. The balloons are launched at dawn, for only then are the thermals reliable. Guadalupe woke up early and cooked herself a dish of *atole*. She had duties to carry out; she would have to set the house in order and prepare her cousin's breakfast before waking her. It so happened that one balloon, caught by a freak gust, was blown off course. The pilot opened a vent to release hot air and made an emergency landing. Guadalupe drew the curtains and saw a colossal red-and-gold balloon on the driveway; also there was a basket with three people in it. She opened the door and greeted these arrivals, two men and a woman. "*Buenos días*," she said to them. "Good morning," they answered her. Then the propane heater roared and spurted flame. The fabric of the balloon expanded, becoming taut and rounded, pregnant, and slowly the thing lifted off the driveway. For what seemed like a minute the three gringos were hovering, their waists at the height of her head. They rose higher and higher still, till they were no larger than a seed, and drifted beyond the horizon. And she had not foretold this! She had had no foreknowledge of it whatsoever! It was then she knew for certain she was not a *bruja*.

However, this is America, where you must give the customers what they want. She tried to avoid misrepresenting her abilities. People asked her for spells to make them wealthy and to find them true love. She declared, "If I knew of such a spell, wouldn't I use it on myself?" When her clients insisted, she offered them only the kind of prepackaged spells you can buy anywhere. As for the crystal ball . . . Ah, who's to say? Everybody can see into the future sometimes.

We are drawn back to the room where the *curandera* and the trucker were facing one another. In a quiet voice, deeper and more gradual than her usual one, she began to speak. "I see grass. I see trees. I see sagebrush. I see a woman, a young woman, lying on the ground . . . Her clothes are torn. Does this mean anything to you?"

"Yes," he said.

"I see a tamale, wrapped in tinfoil. I see a marijuana cigarette. I see a can of Dr Pepper."

"Yes."

"I see you. You are standing over the woman."

"Yes."

"I see her twisting, struggling, crying out . . ."

"Yes."

"Her neck is broken. She is dead."

"Yes."

"Tell me what you did to her."

Kent thought back to that day in July 1985. He remembered how careful he had been to obey Smokey the Bear: "Only You Can Prevent Forest Fires." He had made sure his roach was no longer glowing and had crumbled the warm ash between finger and thumb before letting it fall among the dry undergrowth. He thought, If I had *not* decided to park my Iveco and walk out a little way and eat my food and smoke my joint and drink my soda, then the world would have been different. Only a little different, but enough. *Darathea Mondragon waits by the road in El Paso with her thumb out — one minute earlier, or one minute later — and a different person offers a lift, and so she travels without any hassle all the way through to Boulder, Colorado.* "It's my fault," he said.

"It's all your fault," the *bruja* echoed.

"Madre de Dios," he said. "I never touched her."

"But you are the man, no?"

"Oh, the poor girl, oh, the poor girl," and he was weeping.

Then the bathroom door swung open and two broad-shouldered, red-faced detectives burst out. They were the ones who had pressured María de Guadalupe, threatening to have her deported as an illegal, and had orchestrated the episode. They shouted at him in English as they knocked him to the ground. Meanwhile the fortuneteller — her eyes screwed up but without tears — said, "I'm sorry, so sorry, please forgive me," to the man who was being hauled out of her house like a sack of garbage. When she was alone again, she took off her red shawl and threw it over the crystal ball, the way you cover a birdcage to make the bird stop singing.

That was the last time the police tried to pin the crime on him. Still, he never knew for certain. Any day they might return and try once again. He was employed more often than not and was frugal with his money, and by the time the widow passed away and her heirs sold the house he had been living in, he had saved up enough to put down a deposit on a place of his own in Ojo Caliente. This happened in the summer of 1999. At about the same time he found himself a steady girlfriend. Karin was originally from Utah, Irish ancestry with some Navajo, and she worked as a chambermaid at a hotel in Angelfire. They met at an AA Memorial Day party. Straight out on meeting her, he knew she was special, and he confessed to her his history. He had never been so open before. Silence; then she asked him, "How long ago was it?" He said his problems had begun in 1985. She said thoughtfully, "Long enough." He added that he was innocent. She said, "Yeah. And that, too." Besides, she had issues of her own — "Me and bulimia; where do I begin?" — along with their shared alcoholism, of course. Each reckoned the other was as good a person as they had any right to expect.

It was Karin who got him a regular job, working as a landscaper and general laborer at a spa attached to her hotel. The work was tough, especially in winter — when cleaning out a pool, he'd get drenched, then frozen — but it paid quite well and came with benefits and occasional tips. You have to do what you can. With their two salaries, they were getting by better than most.

In April 2000 he turned forty. The rule was that during the half-hour after the spa was officially shut to the clients, the employees were permitted to soak in one of the Jacuzzis: a perk of the job. In practice, the Latino employees — semilegals from Mexico and El Salvador — never took advantage of this offer, being in a hurry to get back to wherever they lived or to work at a second job, but Kent and Karin quite often did. They passed the word around that it was his birthday, and on that night a dozen employees were relaxing in the tub, mostly Hispanics with a background similar to Kent's own, also a couple of lesbians with college degrees who, like him, did the heavy laboring work; he didn't understand people nowadays and had accepted the futility of trying. The Jacuzzi was in an outdoor area, prettily landscaped. The coworkers were acquaintances rather than friends. Collectively they lolled, teased by jets of water, looking up at the stars and the almost-full moon, from time to time reaching out to grab a Coke or a bag of Doritos or those herbal teas that are served gratis to clients. Kent turned up a few minutes late for his own party, because there'd been a problem with a hinge on the lid of one of the dumpsters and wildlife was getting in: he fixed it with a bit of wire. In the locker room he stripped off his Carhartt's and his *uniones* and stepped into the shower; then he changed into trunks and joined the others. He reflected that there were worse ways to spend a fortieth birthday. The spa clients (a mixture of locals and tourists) were well-to-do, in some cases superrich, and he'd often overheard them grumbling about *their* problems. The fact is that of the boys he'd grown up around, nearly half were dead or in jail. By contrast, he was alive, free, healthy. In his dreams he'd have a beautiful wife and be a father (sex with Karin wasn't up to much, and she wasn't ever going to have children), but you have to count your blessings and take it day by day is what they teach in AA. She clambered out and came back with a couple of sparklers. The two of them stood in the hot water waving the sparklers about — if you move them quickly enough, they seem to make continuous shapes, circles or figure eights or letters — until the things burned out.

Kent was called on one last time by the authorities. This happened on 4 December 2001. Hard to believe a case could be made against him after so long, but Detective Henderson (despite his name, three-quarters Hispanic) had a degree in penology from UNM and wanted to prove the value of modern methods of police work. In contrast to the previous occasions, Henderson did not handcuff the suspect, nor did he shout at him, nor did he even ask many questions. Rather, he put on latex gloves and requested Kent to open his mouth. Then Henderson slid a swab over the inside of

Kent's cheek (an intimate, faintly tickling sensation) and put the used swab carefully inside a labeled evidence pouch. Then: "This will hurt a little." But it didn't hurt, or rather to such a minuscule degree that the word scarcely applied. A single hair was pulled from Kent's scalp. He was balding anyhow, and here comes the law, removing one of his surviving strands! Years in the future he remembered this moment. The act and the pain of it magnified in his memory, until it nearly blocked out the nonmemory of what he had not done on 17 July 1985. Kent bowed his head while Henderson (a short man) stood on tiptoe, the better to reach forward and select a perfect hair. At that instant a tiny but intense ache was born in Kent's scalp and entered his brain and his bloodstream and spread throughout his entire being. This hair, too, was placed in a separate evidence pouch.

Henderson never contacted Kent again. However, a week later Kent happened to be lying on the couch at home, eating a Banquet microwaved dinner and watching the local TV news, when he heard the anchor declare — just a short piece, after the serious story from Afghanistan and before the humorous spot about a woman in Peñasco whose name really is Mary Christmas and every year she gets prank calls from teenagers who find her name in the phone book and go, "Merry Christmas!" and giggle; the interviewer asked why she didn't have her full name removed from the book, and she answered that she'd married Mr. Christmas for richer and poorer, in sickness and in health, and she wasn't going to chicken out of it — that an old murder case had been solved. Laboratory tests proved conclusively that a semen sample found on the body of Darathea Mondragon had DNA corresponding with that of a convicted rapist currently serving ninety-nine years in the state penitentiary at Los Lunas; that man had confessed.

It was shortly after six o'clock. The TV news is broadcast every hour. Kent knew that if he waited until seven o'clock, he would hear the same story. Then again at eight, and at nine . . . until at some point whoever was in charge decided it was no longer sufficiently important, and they'd broadcast something else instead.

Where was Karin? Probably she was in the bedroom, lying down with her eyes shut, coping with one of her headaches. Kent thought to tell her, but the idea of doing so seemed a colossal effort. Instead he crept out through the screen door and climbed into his faithful

Toyota. The key turned in the ignition; he gunned it — down the hill, heading for Highway 285 and the road to Española.

María de Guadalupe was at home, preparing cures and setting out spells for the following day's work. A painstaking series of tasks that she took pleasure in and during which her mind floated freely. As was her custom in the evenings, she had on her best outfit: high heels, flesh-colored stockings, a pink dress, a red *huipil* with an embroidered crisscross pattern at the bodice; her hair was in two bunches, with a rose fixed in it. The radio was tuned to a Latino station — *norteña* songs about men who live among horses and cattle, men who are passionately, unrequitedly in love . . .

Lightning before thunder — she had a vision of the man storming in *before* she felt the wind from the slammed-open door and the footsteps just outside and the noise of the pickup approaching and its engine cutting out. A silent plea for guidance from Our Lady. Here he was now, that intruder, clothes rumpled, jaw sagging, unshaven. She recognized him; since their last meeting, she had met him many times in her dreams. She smelled the tequila on his breath. He thrust both open palms toward her, as if, she thought, to break her like a piñata, but instead his arms swerved and flapped in an attempt at a greeting. This much he understood: there was no one else who might have an answer for him. He drew back, puzzled and abashed at his own emotion.

They kept their distance, neither knowing what was supposed to happen next. She was on the only chair; he walked slowly toward her, his head hanging. She gazed into his opaque skull. "Forgive me . . ," she said, or prompted. He knelt. He looked up at her, his eyes damp. Now it was her turn to hold him, reaching to stroke his wispy hair, and she patted him between the shoulders the way you burp a disconsolate baby. The man's head came to rest on the fortuneteller's lap, and at last he fell asleep.

VU TRAN

This or Any Desert

FROM *Las Vegas Noir*

SIX MONTHS AGO, before all this, I drove into Las Vegas on a hot August twilight. My first time in the city. From the highway, I could see the Strip in the far distance, but also a lone dark cloud above it, flushed on a bed of light, glowing alien and purplish in the sky. My tired pulpy brain at the time, I thought the cloud was a UFO or something and nearly hit the truck ahead of me. Fifteen minutes later, at a gas station, I was told about the beam of light from atop that pyramid casino and how you can even see the beam from space, given no clouds were in the way. My disappointment surprised me.

The drive from Oakland had taken me almost a full day, so I checked into the Motel 6 near Chinatown and fell asleep with my shoes on and my gun still strapped to my ankle. I slept stupid for nine hours straight and woke up at six in the morning, my mouth and nostrils so dry it felt like someone had shoveled dirt over me in the night. The sun had not yet come out, but it was already one hundred degrees outside. Not a cloud in the sky.

After taking a long cold shower, I walked to the front office. The clerk — Chinese, probably — was slurping his breakfast behind the counter and ignored me. I thought about flashing him my badge, but instead I brandished three days' stay in advance, cash, which made him set down his chopsticks easily enough. He said nothing and hardly looked at me before handing me a receipt and walking back to his noodles or whatever the hell he was eating. When I asked him where I could get some eggs, he mumbled something in broken English, his mouth stuffed, glistening. In my younger days, I would have slapped him for his rudeness, just so I could. But I'd learned after Suzy left me to control my temper.

I did see a *pho* shop across the street and hoped they made it like she used to — the beef not too fatty, the soup not too sweet. Turned out theirs was even better, which didn't surprise me, but it reminded me of something her best friend — a Vietnamese girl named Happy, of all things — once told me four years ago when she was over at the house for Sunday *pho*. Suzy had been mad at me that morning for nodding off at church, as I often did, since my patrols didn't end until midnight, and though she knew I'd only converted for her and had never really taken churchgoing seriously, she chewed me out all the way home, and with more venom than usual. So when she stepped outside to smoke after lunch, I asked Happy, "What's bugging her lately?" Happy knew her better than anyone. She had been Suzy's bridesmaid, and they talked on the phone every day in a mix of English and Vietnamese I never did understand — but she just shrugged at my question. I chuckled and said, "Only me, huh? I bet she tells you every bad thing about me." But again she shrugged and said, very innocently, "She don't talk about you much, Bob." I'd long figured this much was true, but it burned to hear it acknowledged so casually. Suzy and I had been married ten years at the time. She'd leave me two years later.

At the *pho* shop, I stared out into the parking lot and watched a stout, middle-aged Asian man climb into a red BMW. It could have been him, but on his driver's license, Suzy's new husband had broader cheeks and more stubborn eyes and also sported a thin, sly mustache. DPS did list a silver Porsche and a brand-new red BMW under his name — Sonny Nguyen. The master files at Vegas Metro confirmed that he was my age, that he owned a posh restaurant in town, that he once shot at a guy for insulting him — aggravated assault, no time done. It was Happy who told me he was a gambler, fully equipped, apparently, with a gambler's temper and a gambler's penchant for taking risks with little sense of the reward. Something in that reminded me of myself.

In my twenty-five years on the Oakland force, I'd shot at people several times, in the arm, in the fleshy part of the thigh, mostly in response to them shooting at me; I had punched a hooker for biting my hand, choked out a belligerent Bible salesman, wrestled thugs twice my size and half my age; I once had to watch a five-year-old boy bleed to death after I nightsticked his mother, who had stabbed him, coked up out of her mind; and three or six times other officers have had to pull me off a scrotbag who'd gotten on my bad side. But never, not even once, had I come close to killing anyone.

I walked down Spring Mountain Road and quickly regretted not taking my car. Vegas, outside of the Strip, is not a place for walkers, especially in this brutal heat. I'd pictured a Chinatown similar to Oakland's or San Francisco's, but the Vegas Chinatown was nothing more than a bloated strip mall — three or four blocks of it painted red and yellow, and pagodafied, a theme park like the rest of the city. Nearly every establishment was a restaurant, and the one I was looking for was called Fuji West. I found it easily enough in one of those strip malls — nestled, with its dark templelike entrance, between an Oriental art gallery and a two-story pet store. It was not set to open for another hour.

Hardly surprising that a Vietnamese would own a sushi joint — Happy's uncle owned a cowboy clothing store in Oakland. What did startle me was the seven-foot, white-aproned Mexican sweeping the patio, though you might as well have called it swinging a broom. He gazed down at me blankly when I asked for Sonny. He didn't look dumb, just bored.

"The owner," I repeated. "Is he here?"

"His name's no Sonny."

"Well, can I speak to him, whatever his name is?"

The Mexican, for whatever reason, handed me his broom and disappeared behind the two giant mahogany doors. A minute later a young Vietnamese man — late twenties probably, brightly groomed, dressed in a splendidly tailored charcoal suit and a precise pink tie — appeared in his place. He smiled at me, shook my hand. He relieved me of the broom and leaned it against one of the two wooden pillars that flanked the patio.

"How may I help you, sir?" He spoke with a slight accent, his tone as formal as if he'd ironed it. He held his hands behind his back.

"I'd like to see Sonny."

"I am sorry, but no one by that name works here. Perhaps you are mistaken? There are many sushi restaurants around here. If you like, I can direct you."

"I was told he owns this restaurant."

"Then you *are* mistaken. I am the owner." He spoke like it was a happy mistake, but his eyes had strayed twice from mine: once to the parking lot, once to my waist.

"I'm not mistaken," I replied, and looked at him hard to see if he would flinch.

He did not. I was a head taller than him, my arms twice the size of his, but all I felt in his presence was my age. Even his hesitation seemed assured. He said, "I am not sure what I can do for you, sir."

"How about this. I'll come back in two hours for some sushi and tea. And then, for dessert, all I'd like is a word or two with Mr. Nguyen. Please tell him that."

I turned to go, but then felt a movement toward me. The young man was no longer smiling. There was no meanness in his face, but his words had become chiseled.

"Your name is Robert, isn't it?" he declared. When I didn't answer, he leaned in closer.

"You should not be here. If you do not understand why I am saying this, then please understand my seriousness. Go back to your city and try to be happy."

That last thing somehow moved me. It was like he had patted my shoulder. I suddenly realized how handsome he was — how, if he wanted to, he could've modeled magazine ads for cologne or expensive sunglasses. For a moment I might have doubted that he was dangerous at all. He nodded at me, a succinct little bow, then grabbed the broom and walked back through the heavy mahogany doors of the restaurant.

I felt tired again. *Pho* always made me sleepy. I walked back to the hotel and in my room stripped down to my boxers and cranked up the AC before falling back into bed.

People my age get certain *feelings* all the time, even if intuition had never been our strong suit in youth, and my inkling about this Sonny guy was that he was the type of restaurant owner who, if he came by at all, would only do so at night. My second inkling was that his dapper guard dog stayed on duty from open to close and that he was just itching for the chance to eat me alive. I had a long night ahead of me. Before shutting my eyes, I decided to put my badge away, deep in the recesses of my suitcase. I would not need it.

*

When Suzy left me two years ago, it was easy at first. No children. Few possessions to split up. And no one we knew really cared: her family all still lived in Vietnam, my parents were long dead, and in our thirteen years together, I'd never gotten to know her Asian friends, and the only things my cop buddies knew about her was her name and her temper. She gave me the news after Sunday dinner. I was sitting at the dining table, and she approached me from the kitchen, her mouth still swollen, and said, "I'm leaving tomorrow, and I'm taking my clothes. You can have everything else." Then she carried away my empty plate, and I heard it shatter in the sink.

The first time I met her I knew she was fearless. My partner and I were responding to a robbery at the flower shop where she worked. She'd been in America for a year. Her English was bad. When we arrived, she stood at the door with a baseball bat in one hand and pruning shears in the other. Before I could step out of the patrol car, she erupted in an angry, torrid description of what had happened. I barely understood a word — something about a gun and ruined roses — but I did know I liked her. The petite sprightly body. Her lips, her cheekbones, full and bold. Eyes that made me think of firecrackers. We found the perp two miles away, limping and bleeding from a stab wound in his thigh. The pruning shears had done it. Suzy and I married four months later.

Her real name was Hong, which meant "rose" in Vietnamese, but it sounded a bit piggish the way Americans pronounced it, so I suggested the name of my first girlfriend in high school, and *this* she did give me, even though her friends still called her Hong.

Our first few years were happy. She took over the flower shop, and I'd stop by every afternoon during my patrol to check in on her. We had a third of the week together, and we spent it trying out every restaurant in Chinatown, going to the movies (she loved horror flicks), and walking the waterfront since the smell and the waves reminded her of Vietnam. At first I didn't mind losing myself in her world: the Vietnamese church, the crosses in every room, the food, the sappy ballads on the stereo, all her friends who (with the exception of Happy) barely spoke a lick of English, even the morbid altar in the corner of the living room with the gruesome crucifix and the candles and pictures of dead grandparents and uncles and aunts. That was all fine, because being with her was like

discovering a new, unexpected person in myself. But after two years
of this, I finally noticed that she had no interest in discovering me:
my job, my friends, my love for baseball, my craving for a burger or
spaghetti now and then, the fact that until her I had not thought of
Vietnam since 1973, when my unit just barely missed deployment.
Vietnam was suddenly everything again . . . until she made it mean
nothing. The least she could do was share her stories from the
homeland, like how poor she'd grown up, or what cruel assholes
the communists were, or how her uncle or father or neighbor had
gone to a concentration camp and was tortured or starved, or *something;* but she'd only say her life back there was *difficult* and *lonely,*
and she'd only speak of it with this kind of vague mysteriousness,
like she was teaching me her language, like I'd never get it anyway.
So I got nothing.

When we made love, she'd whimper, a childlike thing a lot of
Asian women do, only her whimper sounded more like a wounded
animal's, so that eventually it was just another way of making me
feel like a stranger in her presence. An intruder.

I suppose our marriage became a typical one: petty arguments,
silent treatments, no sex for months, both of us spending our free
time more with friends than with each other. And still we kept at it,
God knows why, until I came to believe, in an accepting kind of way,
that she was both naive and practical about love, that she'd only
ever loved me because I was a cop, because that was supposed to
mean that I'd never hurt her.

The night I hit her was a rainy night. I'd just come home from a
shooting in West Oakland, where a guy had tried robbing someone's seventy-year-old grandmother and, when she fought back,
shot her in the head. I was too spent to care about tracking mud on
Suzy's spotless kitchen floor or to listen to her when she saw the
mess and began yelling at me. Couldn't she understand that brains
on a sidewalk is a world worse than mud on a tile floor? Shouldn't
she, coming from where she came from, appreciate something like
that? I told her to fuck off — which I rarely throw at anyone. She
glared at me, and then she started with something she'd been doing for the last few years every time we argued: she began speaking
in Vietnamese. Not loudly or irrationally, like she was venting her
anger at me, but calmly and deliberately, as if I actually understood
her, as if she were daring me to understand her, flaunting all the

nasty things she could be saying to me and knowing full well that it could have been fucking gibberish for all I knew and that I could do nothing of the sort to her. I usually just ignored her or walked away. But this time, after a minute of staring her down as she delivered whatever the hell she was saying, I backhanded her across the face as hard as I could. It shut her up, sent her bumping into a dining chair.

I had never before raised my hand to her. I'd arrested men who'd done worse to their girlfriends and wives, and I always remembered how pathetic and weak those guys looked when I confronted them. But when I felt the sting in my fingernails, saw the blood curling down Suzy's busted lip and her just standing there in a kind of angry stubborn silence, I hit her again. She yelped this time, holding that side of her face and still staring at me, though now with a look of recognition that told me she'd never been as tough as I thought, which somehow annoyed me more. Would I have stopped if she had hit me back, as I'd expected? Her nose began bleeding. Her eyes teared up. But her hand fell from her face and she stood her ground. So I hit her a third time. She stumbled back a few steps, covering her mouth with one hand and steadying herself on the dining table with the other, until she finally went down on one knee, her head bowed, like she was about to vomit. She spat blood two or three times. As I walked upstairs, I heard the TV from the living room and the rain pummeling the gutters outside and then the kitchen faucet running, and everything had the sound of finality to it.

In the divorce, she was true to her word, and I was left with a house full of eggshell paintings and crucifixes and rattan furniture. Months later, someone told me she had moved to Vegas. I sold the house and everything in it and tried my best to forget I had ever married anyone. I also went on a strict diet of hamburgers and spaghetti.

But then a month ago I bumped into Happy at the grocery store. To my shock, instead of ignoring me or telling me off, she treated me like an old friend. She had always lived up to her name in that way, and actually she looked a lot like Suzy, a taller and more carefree version of her — and, in truth, a version I'd always been attracted to. I asked her out to dinner that night. Afterward we went home together. We drank wine and went to bed, and it wasn't until we finished that I realized my other reason for doing all this. With her blissfully drunk and more talkative than ever, I finally asked about Suzy. She told me everything: how Suzy had become a card dealer in Vegas and met up with this rich, cocky Vietnamese poker player who owned a fancy restaurant and a big house and apparently had some shady dealings in town, and how they got married and she quit her job, and how everything had been good for more than a year.

"Until he begin losing," Happy declared soberly, sitting back on the headboard. She said nothing more, and I had to tell her several times to get on with it. She glanced at me impatiently, like I should already know. "He hit her," she said. "She hit him back, but he very strong and he drink a lot. Last month, he throw her down the stairs and broke her arm. I saw her two week ago with a sling, her cheek purple. But he too rich for her to leave. And he always say he need her, he need her."

I stood from the bed, a bit tipsy. I knocked the lamp off the nightstand.

Happy flinched. After a moment she said, "Why you still love her?" There was no envy or bitterness in her voice. She was simply curious.

"Who said I did?"

She checked me with her eyes as though I didn't understand my own emotions.

I tried to soften my voice, but it still came out in a growl: "Is it just the money? What — is he handsome?"

"Not really. But you not either." She patted my arm and laughed.

"You know what? I'm gonna go to Vegas and I'm gonna find this fucker. And then I'm gonna hit him a little bit before I break his arm."

This time she laughed hard, covering her mouth and looking at me with drunken pity.

"You such a silly, stupid man," she said.

I returned to Fuji West at 7:30 that evening, just as the sun was setting. I drove this time. The parking lot was half full, mostly fancy cars, and I immediately spotted the silver Porsche in the back row. Sure enough, those were the tags. I rechecked the five-shot in my ankle holster. My hands felt bruised from the hot, dry air.

Inside, the restaurant was cool and dark and very Zen. Piano music drifted along the ceiling beams overhead. Booth tables with high wooden seats, lighted by small suspended lanterns, lined the walls like confessionals. Candlelit tables filled in the space between the booths and the circular sushi bar, which stood in the center of the restaurant like an island, manned by three sushi chefs in white who with their hats resembled sailors. Flanking the bar were two enormous aquariums, filled with exotic-looking fish that were staring out calmly at the twenty or so patrons in the restaurant, most of whom easily outdressed me.

I asked for a table near the bar and ordered a Japanese beer and told the hostess I was waiting for a friend. I'd barely wet my lips before Sonny's young Doberman appeared and sat himself across from me, just as casually as if I'd invited him.

He was now dressed in a black pinstripe suit, set off by another beautiful pink tie, looking very ready to be anyone's best man. He waved at a waitress, who swiftly brought him a bottle of Perrier and a glass with a straw. Pouring the Perrier into the glass, he said to me, "So you did not like my advice." His voice was gentle but humorless.

"I appreciate the wisdom — but my business with Sonny is important."

"I know it is," he said, nodding agreeably. "Except my father has no business with *you*." He sipped his Perrier with the straw like a child. In the aquarium directly behind him, a long brown eel swam slowly through his head.

"Your father, huh? Well I guess that makes some sense." I downed half my beer, wiped my mouth with two fingers. "So how do you know who I am?"

"Your friend Happy is also a friend of mine. She visits here often. She came to me last week and told me what you have been planning to do. She told me for your sake. She likes you, Mr. Robert, and she knows you can be a foolish man. She did not tell Suzy, of course, or my father. So only I know that you are here. And that, Mr. Robert, is a good thing."

"Because your father is a dangerous man?"

He eyed me sternly, drawing together his dark handsome eyebrows. "Because my father does not have my patience."

A waiter came by and whispered something into his ear, and

Sonny Jr. looked to the front doors, where two large parties of customers had just appeared. He stood from the table and gestured at
the hostess, who walked quickly over to our table, and he gave her
and the waiter rapid orders in Vietnamese. He glanced at me, a bit
distractedly, then turned again to them and went on with his instructions. He watched them walk away and continued watching as
they saw to the parties. His father might have been a poker-playing
gangster or maybe a gangster-playing poker player, but I was getting the feeling that Junior was nothing more than what he appeared: the young manager of a restaurant.

He appeared to sigh and finally turned back to me, adjusting his
tie, his face once again as calm as the fish. "You are a police officer,
so I should not show you this. But I know you are here with other,
less official concerns, however silly they might be. Please come with
me then."

"And where are we going?"

"As I said, you are the police officer here. It should be me who is
nervous."

I offered him a smile, which he did not return. I stood and followed him to the kitchen.

We passed two private tatami rooms, each being prepared by the
staff for the new parties. Foolishly or not, the presence of so many
people eased my mind a bit.

The kitchen was staffed by Mexicans and Asians, all in white
uniforms. No one paid us any attention as we walked to the back,
toward a door marked *Office*. Junior unlocked it, and once we
stepped inside, he relocked it and approached a huge, life-size oil
painting of a geisha walking up a dark flight of stairs. There was a
clock on the wall beside it, which he set to midnight, then he
turned the minute hand three revolutions clockwise and two revolutions counterclockwise. The painting slowly swung open from
the wall like a door, revealing a passageway and a dark descending
staircase. He walked down and without looking back at me said, "It
will close again in five seconds."

We reached a long dim hallway and passed six closed doors, each
with a keypad over the knob. At the end we stopped at a door that
was set much farther away from the others. He punched a series of
numbers on the keypad and something clicked. He pushed the
door open completely before walking inside.

I heard soft Oriental music. The room glowed bluish and shim-
mered. It was no more than a thousand square feet but felt cav-
ernous, with walls of glass surrounding us, behind them water and
fish. I had entered a gigantic aquarium. Each wall showed the
flushed faces of four separate tanks, framed in quadrants like enormous television monitors, their blue waters filled with stingrays and
sharks and what appeared to be piranha and other odd-looking
fish, all swimming around beds of coral and white gravel. Against
the brick wall behind me were three aisles of smaller aquariums,
with smaller fish, stacked on two rows of iron shelves. On a large
Oriental rug in the center of the room stood a black leather couch,
two dolphin chairs, and a glass coffee table.

Sonny Jr. walked to the table and took a cigarette from the pack
lying there, lit it, and approached the tank of stingrays. I felt a
movement behind me and turned to see, at last, the seven-foot
Mexican standing in the hall just outside the doorway, his forehead
out of view. God knows where he'd come from. His white apron
looked like an oversized bib, and he still wore that heavy, dull-eyed
Frankenstein expression. Junior spoke Vietnamese to him, and he
stepped inside the room, bowing to do so, and closed the door. So
that was at least three languages the Mexican understood.

"Is Dad making an appearance, too?" I asked.

"He is not here, Mr. Robert," Junior replied calmly, and ashed
into an ashtray he held in his other hand — yet another annoyingly
formal mannerism. He gestured at the entire room and said, "But I
have brought you to meet his fish. These are all illegal, you see.
And all very expensive. This one here" — and he pointed at a foot-
long fish with a huge chin and an elongated, undulating body —
"is a silver Asian *arowana*, also called a dragonfish, as you can see
why. Our clients will pay over ten thousand dollars for one."

"I can sell you my car for half that."

He turned his back to me, ignoring the comment, and continued. "We installed a couch and a stereo because my father likes to
come here and relax. The fish, the lights, and the music give him
peace. For all his flaws, he is a man who values peace."

I took a step toward him and heard the Mexican shuffle his feet
behind me. I spoke to Junior's back: "I've met your fish. Why else
have you brought me here?"

He turned around and expelled smoke through his nostrils,

dragonlike. "I have brought you here to tell you a story." He licked his lips and brushed ash from his breast. "You see, my father appreciates these fish because they are beautiful and bring him a lot of money. But he also appreciates them because they remind him of home — they *bring* home to him. It is the irony, you see, that is valuable: a tiny tropical ocean here in the middle of the desert; all these fish swimming beneath sand. The casinos in this city sell you a similar kind of irony, but what we have here is genuine and real, because it also keeps us who we are."

"*Who you are?* No irony, you think, in you and your father owning a Japanese restaurant?"

"Shut up, Mr. Robert, and listen." He put out his cigarette and walked over to take a seat in one of the dolphin chairs. He unbuttoned his jacket and crossed his legs elegantly. He offered me the face of a boy but sounded like an old man. "More than twenty years ago, my parents and I escaped Vietnam by boat. Two hundred people in a little fishing boat made for no more than twenty, headed for Malaysia. On our second night at sea we hit a terrible storm, and my mother fell overboard. It was too dark and stormy for anyone to see her or hear her cry out, and the waters were too rough to save her anyway. She drowned. I was seven at the time. I will not bore you with a tragedy. I will only say that her death hardened my father, made him more fearless than he already was.

"In any case, after sixteen days, our boat finally made it to the refugee camp in Malaysia, on the island of Pulau Bidong. The first day my father and I were there, the ruffians in the camp made themselves known and threatened us. My father was once in a gang back in Vietnam, so he was not afraid. He ignored them. A week later one of them stole my rice ration. The thief slapped me across the face, pushed me to the ground, ripped the sack out of my hand. To scare me even more, he grabbed my wrist and ran a knife across it, barely cutting the skin. I ran to my father, bawling, and he shut me up with a slap of his own."

Junior stared at his hands for a moment, like he was studying his nails. Then he went on.

"He took me by the arm and dragged me to the part of the camp where the ruffians hung out. He made me stand under a palm tree and ordered me to watch him. There were many people there, minding their business. A few shacks away, the man who had attacked me was kneeling and playing dice with two friends. On a tree stump nearby, someone butchering an animal had left his bloody cleaver, and my father grabbed it and marched up behind the man and kicked him hard in the back of the head. The man fell forward and his two friends pounced at my father, but he was already brandishing the cleaver at them. They backed off. My father then grabbed the man by the back of his shirt and dragged him to the tree stump. In one swift motion, never once hesitating, he placed the man's hand on the stump and threw down the cleaver and hacked off his hand at the wrist.

"Blood spurted and the man screamed. I do not remember how horrified the people around me looked, but I remember hearing a few women shriek. My father dropped the cleaver, bent down, and muttered something in the man's ear as he writhed on the ground, moaning and clasping his bloody forearm to his chest. His severed hand still lay on the tree stump. My father wiped his own hand on his pants and held mine as we walked back to our shack. We stayed in that camp for two more months before we came to the States, and those ruffians never once bothered us again."

Sonny Jr. stood from the chair and walked over again to the stingrays. He took out a handkerchief and wiped the glass where his finger had pointed at the *arowana*. He turned to me thoughtfully.

"I still occasionally have dreams about that afternoon. But I have not told you this story so that you will pity me, or anyone, for that matter. I have told you so that you will understand what kind of man my father is — and in a way respect it. Think of this conversation — this situation — as an exchange of trust. Remember that I have brought you, a police officer, here to see my father's illegal business. I am trusting that you will forget your plans in this city, go home, and not say a word of what you have seen. In exchange, since I have made this rather foolish gesture for you, you will trust that I am trying to help you, and you will do all those things. A man of your sentiments should appreciate the sincerity of this offer."

I watched him neatly fold his handkerchief and place it back in the breast pocket of his suit. His logic was giving me a headache. I walked over to the couch and sat down, facing him. I hadn't smoked since Suzy left me — another part of my detox plan, since smoking together was one of the few things we never stopped doing. But now I took a cigarette from the pack and lit up. It was my turn to talk.

"Why do you want so badly to help me?" I said. "Why do you care what happens to me? Is it really *me* you're protecting? Or is it your father? Because somehow I feel he's no longer — maybe never was — the hard man you say he is. And I'm guessing maybe you made up that dramatic little story just to scare me. But even if it's true, I've dealt with scarier people. Now why you've chosen to show me all this fish stuff is still a mystery to me — though I'd wager you just like getting off on your own smarts and impressing people. You've either read too many books or listened to people who've read too many books. Either way, it's not my fault that I can't understand half the things you say. But what I do understand is this . . ." I leaned forward on the couch and looked at him squarely. "Your father is a thug. Not only that, he's an asshole, and a coward, too. He threw a woman down the stairs and broke her arm. Who knows what else he did, could have done, or might do in the future, but men like him only have the guts to do that to a woman. And the fact that you haven't blinked yet tells me all of this is true. You're a smart boy, and you seem to be a good enough son to want to protect him. That's fine. It's even admirable. But my business with him has nothing to do with you. So fuck off."

I stood up and walked around the table and stopped a few yards from him. I took a long drag off my cigarette and then flicked it at his feet. "I have police buddies who know exactly where I am and who your father is, and if I don't say hi to them next week, they'll know where to come find me. And they all hate sushi."

He was glaring at me. From behind him, the stingrays swam languidly around his thin, stiff figure like a flock of vultures.

His eyes looked past me and he nodded his head, and before I could turn around I felt the Mexican's enormous arms wrap around my chest, hugging me so tightly I could hardly breathe. I soon felt a fumbling at my ankle holster and then saw Sonny Jr. with my five-shot, which he deposited in his jacket pocket. He said something in Vietnamese, and the Mexican pushed me down to the floor, forcing me flat onto my stomach. With his knee digging into my lower back, he twisted one of my arms behind my shoulder and held my other arm to the floor before my flattened face. I could do nothing but grunt beneath him, a doll in his hands, the tile floor numbing my cheek.

I looked up, and Sonny Jr. had taken off his jacket. From his pant pocket he now pulled out a switchblade, which he opened. The

Mexican wrenched my extended forearm so that my wrist was exposed. Sonny Jr. knelt and planted his shoe on my palm. Then he steadied the blade across my wrist.

"Wait!" I gasped. I struggled but could hardly budge under the Mexican, his boulder of a knee still lodged in my lower back.

Sonny Jr. slowly, gently, dragged the blade. I could feel its icy sharpness slice the surface of my skin. The pain was no more than an itch, but waiting for it had made me clench my jaw so tightly that it now ached. Sonny Jr. lifted his shoe. A thread of blood appeared across my wrist.

"You and I," Junior murmured casually, "now share something." He wiped the blade with two fingers, closed it, and returned it to his pocket. He stood and I could no longer see his face, but his voice came out bitter and hard, like he was shaking his head at me: "I know exactly who you are, Mr. Robert. The minute you arrived at our door, I knew. You are a man who has nothing to lose. But that does not make you brave, it only makes you naive. Happy told me you were a silly, stupid man. What were you going to do — kill my father? Break his arm? Yell at him? Everything I have told you is true, and I meant every sentiment. And yet you are too sentimental to listen. You want to come here and be a hero and save your former wife from a bad man. You want to know how he has hurt her, and why. But in the end, the only thing you *really* want is to know why she would leave you for slapping her and then stay with a man who threw her down a flight of stairs and broke her arm."

His shoes reappeared before my eyes, a foot from my nose. He was now speaking directly over my head like he was ready to spit on it. "You see, we keep most of these fish separated not because they will eat each other — though that is true — but because they like it this way. Just like *we* like it this way. Why do you think, when you walk into any casino in this city, that nearly every dealer is Asian and nearly every Asian dealer is Vietnamese? Because we enjoy cards and colorful chips? *No.* Because we flock to each other. We flock to where there are many of us, so that we will belong. It is a very simple reality, Mr. Robert. A primal reality."

He bent down, speaking closer now to my ear.

"What made you think she ever belonged to you, or, more importantly, that *you* ever belonged with her? America, Mr. Robert, is not the melting pot you Americans like to say or think it is. Things get stirred, yes, but like oil and vinegar they eventually separate and settle, and the like things always go back to each other. They have made new friends, perhaps even fucked them, but in their heart they will always wander back to where they belong. Love has absolutely nothing to do with it."

He sighed dramatically and stood back up.

"That is enough. I am tired of speeches." With this, he lifted his shoe and stomped on my hand with the heel.

I screamed out and he let me. The Mexican dismounted me then. After a long writhing moment, I forced myself to sit up. I was holding my injured hand like a dead bird. I couldn't tell if anything was broken, but my knuckles and fingers felt hot with numbing pain, right alongside the ache in my shoulder where the Mexican had twisted and held my arm.

Junior now stood before the tank of piranhas, in his jacket again and with his hands in his pockets. As if ordering a child, he said to me, "If I ever see you again, I will do much worse. You will now go with Menendez here, and he will take you back outside. Remember, you have seen nothing here. If necessary, I will hurt my new mother at your expense. I like her, but not that much."

He handed Menendez my gun, and Menendez led me out of the room by the arm, almost gently.

Junior's voice followed me out: "Go home, Mr. Robert, and try to be happy."

I let the Mexican drag me to another door, which revealed another staircase, which ascended into another office, which opened out into what looked like the pet store next door to the restaurant. Everything was dark, save for the shifting shadows of birds in their cages, dogs and rodents in their pens. We passed aquariums with goldfish and droning water pumps. Something squawked irritably in the putrid darkness.

I was released outside into a rainy, windy night. It was like stepping into another part of the country, far from the desert, near the ocean perhaps. I must have looked at Menendez with shock, because he said to me, in a gruff but pleasant voice, "Monsoon season." He handed me my five-shot, closed the door, and I saw his giant shadow fade back into the darkness of the store.

I drove down Highway 15, toward California. My right hand was wrapped tightly in a handkerchief. I could move my fingers but didn't want to. It was ten o'clock, an hour after I had left Fuji West, and the rain had not yet stopped. On my way out of town, I saw three car accidents, one of which appeared deadly — a Toyota on its side, a truck with no front door, no windshield, a body beneath wet tarp. I had worked so many of these scenes in my time, and yet that evening they spooked me — chilled me. Rain must fall like an ice storm upon this town.

I kept thinking of the night I hit Suzy. But soon I was remembering another rainy night, many years ago, when I came home from work all drenched and tired and she made me strip down to my underwear and sat me at the dining table with a bowl of hot chicken porridge. As I ate the porridge, she stood close behind my chair and hummed one of her sad Vietnamese ballads and dried my hair with a towel. I remember, between spoonfuls, trying to hum along with her.

Sonny Jr.'s parting words flashed through my mind. What did he know about other people's happiness?

I took the very next exit and turned around and began driving in the direction of their house. I had wanted all along to avoid this — I knew she might be there. It took me half an hour to find it. By the time I turned into the neighborhood, the street curbs were overflowing with ankle-deep water and I could feel my tires slicing through the currents.

Their house, like many of the others, was a two-story stucco job with a manicured rock garden and several giant palm trees out front. It looked big and warm. All the windows were dark. A red BMW sat in the circular driveway behind the brown Toyota Camry I'd bought Suzy eight years ago. God knows why she was still driving it with what he could buy her now.

I parked by the neighbor's curb and approached the side of the house, beneath the palm trees that swayed and thrashed in the wind. The rain was coming down even harder now, blinding sheets of it, and I was drenched within seconds. On their patio I saw the same kind of potted cacti that stood on our porch years ago, except the pots were much nicer. And also, there in front of me, like I was staring at the front door of our old house, was a silver cross hanging beneath the peephole.

The rain soothed my injured hand. I unwrapped the wet handkerchief and tossed it on the driveway. I tried to make a fist and realized I could, though the ache was still there, and also some of the numbness. I rang the doorbell and stood there waiting, shivering. I didn't know who I wanted to answer the door, but when the porch light turned on and he finally opened it, I understood what I wanted to do.

He looked exactly as he did on his driver's license but was shorter than I expected, shorter than both Suzy and his son. He was wearing a white T-shirt and blue pajama bottoms, his arms tan and muscular, his face a mixture of sleepiness, curiosity, and annoyance. "Yes?" he muttered.

I noticed the tattoo of a cross on his neck. I raised my gun at his face. He snapped his head back but then froze. He was looking at me, not the gun. There was a stubborn quality in his expression, like he'd had a gun in his face before, like he didn't want to be afraid but couldn't help it either.

"Open the door and then put up your hands," I ordered calmly.

He did as I said, slowly, withdrawing into the foyer of the house, then into the edge of the living room as I followed him inside, leaving some distance between us. I kept the front door half open, then turned on a small lamp by the couch and caught the familiar scent of shrimp paste in the air.

Their house was furnished with all the fancy stuff required of a wealthy, middle-aged couple, but what caught my eye was the large aquarium against the wall, the tall wooden crucifix above the fireplace, and the vases everywhere filled with fresh flowers. Daffodils, pink tulips, Oriental lilies, chrysanthemums — I had become used to all of them over the years.

The rain was pummeling the roof above us — a steady, violent drone. I watched him watch me and imagined what I must have looked like to him: a pale bald stranger with a gun, still pointed squarely at his face, standing there in his dark living room in drenched clothes, dripping water onto his wife's pristine carpet. She used to yell at me for merely walking on the carpet in my shoes.

"You take what you want," he said in a loud whisper. "I not gonna stop you. My wallet right there." He nodded at the table beside me, where his wallet lay by the telephone and some car keys. Behind the phone stood a photo of him and Suzy on a beach. "Take my car, too," he added. "Just go."

I picked up the phone, listened for the dial tone, and then placed it face up on the table. "Anyone else here in the house?"

"No," he said immediately.

"No? Your wife — where's she?"

I could see him about to shake his head, like he was ready to deny having a wife, but then he realized he had all but pointed out the photo.

"She not here. She sleep at her mother house tonight. Just me here."

"Then why are there two cars in the driveway?"

"What do that matter? I tell you it just me here tonight." He sounded irritated now, but his eyes were still wide and wary.

"So if I make you take me into the bedroom, I won't find anyone in there?"

He didn't say anything at first. He glanced toward the dark hallway to my left and then returned his scowl back on me. "I told you," he growled, but then lowered his voice. He didn't want to wake her. "Take my car. My wallet. Take anything you want and go."

"I tell you what," I said. "I'm gonna let *you* go. Walk out the door. Call for help if you want. You're free to leave."

"What?" He lowered his hands a bit.

"Go."

"What wrong with you?"

"I'm giving you a chance to leave without me shooting your face in. If no one's here, then you have nothing to worry about."

He just glowered at me. Then his hands fell. "Who are you?" he said in a thick voice. "What you want?"

I took a step closer to him, and he slowly put up his hands again without adjusting his glare on me.

"Last chance," I said.

"I not going anywhere."

I could still see fear in his eyes, but there was an angry calm in his demeanor now, in the flimsy way he held up his hands like I was an annoying child with a toy gun. I decided to believe everything his son had told me, and it filled me with both disappointment and relief, and then suddenly a heavy decisive sadness, like I no longer recognized that shrimp paste smell in the air or any of the outlandish flowers in this strange house — like a stone door had just closed on the last fifteen years of my life.

I edged closer, but he did not budge. When my gun was finally within a foot of his face, I said, "Okay then," and struck him across the cheek with it. He staggered back and threw up a hand to shield himself.

I backed away. With his hand on his cheek, he watched me move toward the front door. I glanced at the hallway, at the doors in the darkness, wondering which room was their bedroom, which room she might be sleeping in, which door she might be standing behind right now, cupping her ear to the wood, holding her breath. I took a last look back at Sonny. His cheek was bleeding, his eyes dark and wide. How many more times would he save her like tonight?

I turned and ran out into the rain, stumbling across the gushing lawn, through the surging water in the street, toward my car. My engine roared to life. As I drove frantically past the house, I glimpsed Sonny standing on their front porch with his arms at his side, watching me speed away. I could have sworn I saw a darker, slimmer figure looming behind him.

I drove like a maniac for a few miles, cars honking at me as I passed them one by one. Then I slowed down. I turned on the radio. I reentered the highway. My body felt cool, and the rain was soothing on the roof of the car. I turned off the radio and let the droning rain fill my ears. The night was like a tunnel. I drove a steady clip down the highway, promising myself that I would never again return to this or any desert.

Contributors' Notes

N. J. (Noreen) Ayres is the author of three forensics-based crime novels that predate the CSI television phenomenon. For twenty years she wrote and edited complex technical manuals for engineering companies and defense contractors. She now develops reports for lead reclamation at private and police shooting ranges and, with her longtime partner, rescues feral cats in northeast Pennsylvania.

▪ Two haunting locations stirred the writing of "Rust." If I were braver and not so blond, I'd have responded to their beckoning on foot. Instead I went by imagination. One site is a curving stretch of railroad tracks hooded by trees, beside an orderly graveyard. Bearded men emerge from there to head for food or short-lived shelter in a nearby Wal-Mart. Who are these men? How did they come to be there? The other is the massive skeleton of the once ringing Bethlehem Steel Works. Even from a distance it echoes, if only in wind-whispers.

Until last month, as I write this, I had a brother who for years lived in an abandoned Texaco station. Days from death, he assured me he'd had a good life. Another brother resides in a remote desert hovel piled so high with boxes that navigation is a challenge.

The disenfranchised. The lonely road. High goals pillaged by human failings. These are themes often running in my work. We are fascinated by what we fear.

Tom Bissell was born in Escanaba, Michigan, in 1974. He is the author of *Chasing the Sea*, a travel narrative; *Speak, Commentary* (with Jeff Alexander), a work of satire; *God Lives in St. Petersburg*, a story collection; and *The Father of All Things*, a hybrid work of history and memoir. In 2006 he was awarded the Rome Prize, and his work has appeared in many magazines, including

Harper's, The Virginia Quarterly Review, McSweeney's, Granta, and *The New Yorker.* He is currently working on a book about the tombs of the twelve apostles and another, shorter book about video games. "My Interview with the Avenger" marks his sixth appearance in the Best American Series.

▪ I wrote this story at the invitation of my dear friend Owen King, who, with John McNally, had the intriguing idea to convince a bunch of so-called literary writers to attempt stories about superheroes. (The anthology that resulted is called *Who Can Save Us Now?* I entreat all to purchase it.) After trying and failing to come up with a superpower that was neither derivative nor ludicrous, I somewhat defeatedly settled on a story about a plain old good-fashioned vigilante, an idea that rapidly grew on me. One of the fun things about this story was trying to think through the actual, real-world ramifications of a man embarking on an Avenger-like mission, not to mention getting to read through the World Superhero Registry, which, no fooling, really exists. While my story may strain credulity from time to time, it is my hope that the line never quite snaps. I can't honestly say that I intended to write a mystery, but I'm delighted it was read as such, because that's what, technically, it is.

Alafair Burke is the author of five critically acclaimed crime novels, most recently *Angel's Tip.* She is a distinguished graduate of Stanford Law School, a former prosecutor, and a professor and vice dean of faculty research at Hofstra Law School. Her sixth novel, *212,* will be published in early 2010.

▪ The story of Jenny and Greg Sutton is a story not only about what love can bring us to do to protect our partners but also about gendered reactions to violence. I called it "Winning" because it was inspired by an anecdote that a friend told to the feminist legal scholar Martha Mahoney, which Mahoney uses to illustrate how men and women differ in their perceptions of control. Her friend once told a man in a bar that if she were attacked and managed to run away safely, she would consider herself the winner of the encounter. The man resisted her characterization of the win, arguing that flight from an attack was a defeat, not a victory.

Greg Sutton is a man who loves his wife, so he does what he believes a loving husband should do to avenge his wife's victimization (and defeat). But when Jenny ultimately chooses to take care of Greg while she's still learning to care for herself, we see that she is the one with real strength. As she sits in her assailant's home and remembers what she underwent to survive that night, we understand why she perceives herself as the winner, the one in control. And with the final sentence of the story, we wonder whether Mahoney's friend and the man at the bar might both have been right about human responses to violence.

"Winning" is the first and only short story I have written and may prove to be evidence that I'm incapable of leaving a character behind. To my surprise, in the months since I finished writing "Winning," I often find myself thinking about Jenny Sutton.

James Lee Burke was born in 1936 in Houston, Texas, and grew up on the Texas-Louisiana coast. He attended Southwestern Louisiana Institute (now the University of Louisiana at Lafayette) and later the University of Missouri at Columbia, where he received a B.A. and an M.A. in English literature.

Over the years he has published twenty-seven novels and two short story collections. The stories have appeared in *Atlantic Monthly, Southern Review, Antioch Review, Kenyon Review, New Stories from the South, The Best American Short Stories,* and *The Best American Mystery Stories.* His novels *Heaven's Prisoners* and *Two for Texas* were adapted as motion pictures.

Burke's work has received two Edgar Awards for best novel of the year, and the Mystery Writers of America honored Burke as its grand master in 2009. He is a Bread Loaf fellow and a Guggenheim fellow and has been the recipient of an NEA grant. He and his wife of forty-nine years, Pearl Burke, have four children and divide their time between Missoula, Montana, and New Iberia, Louisiana.

▪ "Big Midnight Special" is less a story about prisons and criminality than it is about the presence of the egalitarian rebel and artist in the midst of mediocrity. Dave Robicheaux, another person whose point of view I often share, asks the rhetorical question "Have you ever seen a mob rush across town to do a good deed?" My experience in life has been that people in groups, particularly when they start marching in lockstep, slamming boot soles down on the cobblestones, are to be avoided at all costs.

Arlen, the narrator of the story, is not only an iconoclast but one of those at whom God has arbitrarily pointed his finger and said "You!" Talent is not acquired or earned; it is given. Anyone who has ever taught a creative writing class will be the first to tell us his or her best students were usually the most unlikely ones to have the enormous gift that obviously has been bestowed on them.

This story is also about oppression, the nature of collective fear, and the institutionalization of cruelty. The bones in the Mississippi levee at Angola Prison, the electric chair in the Red Hat House, the placing of inmates in cast-iron sweatboxes and on the top of anthills are not the creations of a writer's pen. Years ago I knew black religious people who would not sing the blues because they thought it was the devil's music. But their objection was not because they thought the music was evil. They believed the subject was, and the subject was the cruelty and violence and despair that often characterized their lives.

I'm real proud of this story. I think it is the best one I have written.

Ron Carlson is the author of ten books of fiction, most recently the novels *The Signal* and *Five Skies*. His book on writing short fiction is *Ron Carlson Writes a Story*. He teaches at the University of California, Irvine.

▪ I've played baseball all my life, and I've written a few stories that use it as a world. In my first at-bat in Little League, I was knocked out by a side-arm fastball, and therefore for fifty years I've been awake to that danger in the sport. Every time a batter steps into the box, it wakes my empathy. I've seen players hit by pitches, and I read the sad account of Roy Chapman, the only major leaguer ever killed by a pitch. I also look for moments that cross the line, when the game becomes real, and I wrote "Beanball," which was originally titled "Chin Music," real slowly, and I saw that it would differ from most of my stories by being a kind of small novel. There were many surprises in the writing, none greater than when Driscoll uses his pistol.

Michael Connelly is a former journalist and the author of the number-one bestsellers *The Brass Verdict* and *The Lincoln Lawyer,* the best-selling series of Harry Bosch novels, and the best-selling novels *Chasing the Dime, Void Moon, Blood Work,* and *The Poet. Crime Beat,* a collection of his journalism, was also a *New York Times* bestseller. His twentieth novel, *The Scarecrow,* was published in spring 2009 — Jack McEvoy, the hero of *The Poet,* is back in this terrifying new thriller. Connelly spends his time in California and Florida.

▪ I used this short story as sort of a training exercise for an upcoming novel. Harry Bosch has a young daughter who lives far away from him. She is hinted at in several of the novels but is not a realized character. My plan is to write a novel in which Harry's relationship with her is fully explored. To get ready for this, I wanted to write a story in which Harry would follow a case that tapped into his feelings and thoughts on fatherhood. And this is it.

David Corbett is the author of three critically acclaimed novels: *The Devil's Redhead, Done for a Dime* (a New York Times Notable Book), and *Blood of Paradise,* which was nominated for numerous awards, including the Edgar, and was named both one of the top ten mysteries and thrillers of 2007 by the *Washington Post* and a San Francisco Chronicle Notable Book. His fourth novel, *Do They Know I'm Running?,* is due in early 2010. His short fiction has appeared in numerous anthologies, and he contributed a chapter to the world's first serial audio thriller, *The Chopin Manuscript,* winner of the Audie Award for Best Audio Book of 2008, and has contributed a chapter to its follow-up, *The Copper Bracelet.* For more, go to www.davidcorbett.com.

▪ The source material for "Pretty Little Parasite" arose from two cases in

Las Vegas I worked on as a private investigator. The cop, on whom Jimmy is loosely based, was the subject of our scrutiny, since he had set up our client. One of the things one learned quickly in that world was how many undercover narcs had addictive personalities, if not full-blown addictions, and how badly that skewed their judgment. At the same time, as one of my sources on Las Vegas Metro assured me, this guy was a standup cop. The woman on whom Sam is based was honestly one of the sweetest people I ever interviewed, though I found her judgment a little, shall we say, off-kilter as well. She'd righted that by the time we met, and things turned out for her and her daughter much better than they do for Sam, but it could easily have been otherwise. For there's a corollary to the motto Las Vegas champions so proudly — "What Happens in Vegas Stays in Vegas" — that being, "Unless It Ends Up in the Desert."

M.M.M. Hayes comes from a ranching family in the mountains of northeastern Nevada, has lived in the Middle East, Europe, Mexico, and New York, and currently resides in both Chicago and Nevada. Hayes's stories have been anthologized in *Best New Stories from the South, Best of the West, 2Plus2: An International Anthology,* and other collections. She has received screenwriting fellowships, a Katherine Anne Porter Prize from *Nimrod,* and other fiction awards. Her most recent fiction appears in the *Kenyon Review* and *War, Literature & the Arts* and is upcoming in *Stand Magazine.* Hayes is a former editor and publisher and currently a senior contributing editor of *StoryQuarterly.*

▪ For those who ask, I disclaim any autobiographical basis for this story and haven't killed anyone to date, although the setting comes from a land where I have deep roots. The story began with a random comment by an aunt about an itinerant ranch hand. I'd also done research on meth dealing across the Great Basin and later read a police report about a wild night and fire set by two teenagers in Elko. It all figured in, and I woke up one morning in the right mood to explore the mind of a Quentin Ghlee.

Chuck Hogan's crime novels include *The Standoff, The Killing Moon, Prince of Thieves,* which was awarded the Hammett Prize, and *Sugar Bandits.* He is also the author of *The Blood Artists* and, with Guillermo del Toro, *The Strain.*

▪ *"Guy learns he is grilling a burger that will be killer's last meal."*

There it is right there. I can see the entire story in that one-line note, jotted down in January 2004. All that remained was a reason to commit time to writing it.

Then, in June 2007, Janet Hutchings, editor of *Ellery Queen's Mystery Magazine,* commissioned me to inaugurate the return of the "Black Mask" department to the magazine. This was no mere assignment as far as I was concerned, but in fact a tremendous personal and professional honor, for my story was to run alongside a reprint of Dashiell Hammett's "Bodies Piled Up," originally published in *Black Mask Magazine* in December 1923. Seeing my name on the cover alongside the great Hammett's, as well as being associated with the legendary hard-boiled pulp magazine — all within the pages of the only remaining publication directly linked to that golden, grubby era of crime fiction — stands as the coolest highlight of my career to date.

Although best known for his true crime books, notably the Edgar-nominated *Six Against the Rock*, about Alcatraz, and *Zebra*, also nominated, which examined the infamous San Francisco murders of the early 1970s, **Clark Howard** has developed a great following for his short stories, five of which have been nominated for Edgar Awards; one, "Horn Man," was picked as the best of the year for 1980. He has also won the Derringer Award and in 2009 was voted the Golden Derringer for Lifetime Achievement in the mystery genre. Other nominations have been for Shamus and Spur awards, and five times he has been named as the favorite for the Ellery Queen Mystery Magazine Reader's Choice Award.

▪ My late wife, Judith, and I were in Cebu City in the Philippines some twenty years ago, visiting a showroom of the Jared Company, which was a government-approved outlet for the manufacture of controlled fossil-stone products. We ordered a large coffee table, three end tables, and two tall casual tables five feet long. They were built and shipped to us by sea, arriving four months later.

Following Cebu, we returned to Manila, and it was there, while visiting a Catholic hospital, that we first saw the garbage heap that was to grow, year by year, into Smoky Mountain. "The government has promised to clean it up," our host, the mother superior, told us. The government never did.

Years later, when I became involved in the Smile Train, an organization that provides free cleft palate and harelip surgeries to impoverished children in the Philippines (and many other places), I was shocked to learn what that garbage heap had grown into. All of the memories came together in my mind — the fossil stone, children with deformed mouths, lips, and noses, the shame of Smoky Mountain — and the story "Manila Burning" was born.

Rob Kantner (www.robkantner.com) has authored many long and short works of fiction and nonfiction. He lives with his wife, Deanna, on their Michigan horse farm. This is his second appearance in the *Best American Mystery Stories* series.

• I grew up in north Georgia and have always loved the mountains. Deanna and I go there often. "Down Home Blues," like many stories, emerged from the sick spot in my head that's always evaluating seemingly mundane real-life situations for their potential for evil.

Robert McClure read pulp fiction as an adolescent when he should have been studying schoolbooks but ultimately cracked down enough to obtain a B.A. in criminology from Murray State University. A 1991 graduate of the University of Louisville School of Law, he is now an attorney and writer who lives and works in Louisville, Kentucky, with his wife, Kathie, daughter, Courtney, and son, Nick. His stories have appeared in *Hardboiled, Thuglit,* and *Plots with Guns,* and his first one, "Harlan's Salvation," published in *MudRock Stories & Tales,* was included in the "Other Distinguished Stories" category of *The Best American Mystery Stories 2005.* He is currently hard at work on a novel and can be reached at mcmac3607@insightbb.com.

• For some reason — maybe Father's Day was the impetus, but I'm not sure — I wanted to write a father-son story, and I ended up with "My Son." When writing the story, there was a point where I feared it would end badly for Babe and Leo, and I'm glad it didn't. They'll be back (God bless 'em), so don't think you've seen the last of them. Many thanks are in order: to Francis Coppola and his staff for providing so many of us with Zoetrope.com, the Virtual Studio, as fine a place as any to hone the fiction-writing craft; to Sue O'Neill, my supportive friend and reader who works for chocolates and is worthy of infinitely more; to Gerald Tyrell, who encouraged me very early in my writing life and continues to do so; to Big Daddy, Lady D, and the rest of the gang at *Thuglit;* and to Otto Penzler and Jeffery Deaver for honoring "My Son," and me, in this truly special way. Finally, thanks to Kathie, my lover, my partner, my friend — always.

Alice Munro grew up in Wingham, Ontario, and attended the University of Western Ontario. She has published twelve collections of stories — *Dance of the Happy Shades; Something I've Been Meaning to Tell You; The Beggar Maid; The Moons of Jupiter; The Progress of Love; Friend of My Youth; Open Secrets; The Love of a Good Woman; Hateship, Friendship, Courtship, Loveship, Marriage; Runaway; The View from Castle Rock;* and a volume of *Selected Stories* — as well as a novel, *Lives of Girls and Women.* During her distinguished career she has been the recipient of many awards and prizes, including three of Canada's Governor General's Literary Awards and two of its Giller Prizes, the Rea Award for the Short Story, the Lannan Literary Award, England's W. H. Smith Book Award, the United States' National Book Critics Circle Award, and the Edward MacDowell Medal in literature. Her stories have appeared in *The New Yorker, Atlantic Monthly, Paris Review,* and other publications, and her collections have been translated into thirteen languages. Alice Munro divides her time between Clinton, Ontario, near Lake Huron, and Comox, British Columbia.

Joyce Carol Oates, whose stories have appeared in previous editions of *The Best American Mystery Stories*, is the author most recently of the short story collection *Dear Husband* and the suspense novel *A Fair Maiden*. She is a recipient of the National Book Award for her novel *them* and more recently the Prix Femina for her novel *The Falls*, as well as the 2009 Medal of Honor for Literature from the National Arts Club.

▪ The voice of "Dear Husband" — disembodied, slow, stunned, as if the speaker has been struck a blow to the head, yet oddly and incongruously "girlish" and "naive" — came to me after I had read about the Andrea Yates tragedy in Texas some years ago.

In our imaginations, we "speak" to ourselves — often, as if to justify ourselves — in a continuous monologue. This is the very voice of the soul, discernible to others only through a medium of art. The speaker of "Dear Husband" is not the historic or biographical Andrea Yates but a young Southern woman who shares Yates's compulsive attachment to her identity as a Christian wife and mother and would be incapable of comprehending any other identity. Her hurt, resentment, rage, and sheer physical exhaustion in the likelihood of what is called postpartum depression are shunted from her, in denial — she seems to have no sense of herself as a victim of her husband's and her mother-in-law's manipulation of her. Like many mothers who kill their children, she is killing herself, she thinks — killing the "bad" in her that has so disappointed others. There is intended an elliptical sort of black, bleak humor at the very conclusion of the story, with which any housewife might identify.

Nic Pizzolatto was born in New Orleans and raised on Louisiana's Gulf Coast. In recent years his stories have appeared in *The Atlantic Monthly, Oxford American, Missouri Review,* and several other journals. His work has been a finalist for the National Magazine Award in Fiction, among other prizes. A collection of his stories, *Between Here and the Yellow Sea,* was published in 2006 and named by *Poets & Writers* magazine as one of the top five fiction debuts of the year. His first novel, *Galveston,* will be published in early 2010.

▪ A few years ago I came up with the setting for this story, and a tangled family history to go with it. My energies were directed elsewhere at the time, though, so the material sat on the shelf until I went back to it early last year. It must have been gestating in my subconscious, because when I returned to the subject, the story wrote itself fairly quickly. Thanks to Marc

Smirnoff for providing the title and, not incidentally, putting the story in a great magazine.

Garry Craig Powell grew up in England and spent eight years in the United Arab Emirates. He teaches creative writing at the University of Central Arkansas and has been awarded fellowships by the Arkansas Arts Council and the Writers' Colony at Dairy Hollow. His short stories have appeared in *McSweeney's, Nimrod, New Orleans Review,* and other magazines. He is completing a novel, *The Gulf,* set in the UAE. For more information, see www.garrycraigpowell.com.

▪ A few years ago I wrote a story for *Talking River* about a Polish actress who had gone to the Emirates to work in a hotel, then lost her job and slid into prostitution, and for some reason I kept remembering her, so when I heard a supposedly true tale about a Chinese prostitute in a Dubai hotel demanding that the manager call the police, she came to mind, and I wrote the new story about her. Her predicament intrigued me. How cruel, I wondered, would clients' behavior have to be for a prostitute to risk a near-certain prison sentence in order to get her revenge on them? The more I thought about it, the more I realized that the hotel manager, particularly if he were a junior one, would also be in a tough spot. So I came up with Malsiri, the kind Sri Lankan front desk manager, who is torn because he's worried that his boss may demote him if he does as Kamila asks, and feels protective toward her because she reminds him of his own daughter. (Malsiri was based on a wonderful serene masseur I knew when I lived in the UAE.) For some time, inspired by Richard Yates, I'd wanted to write a story from a dual point of view, and I knew at once that this was the right perspective for this one.

Randy Rohn is an internationally recognized, award-winning advertising creative director. He has worked in three of the larger Chicago agencies and is now executive creative director at Keller Crescent Advertising, well known as one of the most creative Midwest agencies outside of Chicago. He grew up in a small town not unlike Tivoli. He graduated from Northwestern University with a B.A. in radio/TV/film and a master's in journalism. Like other advertising creatives, such as James Patterson, Clive Cussler, Marshall Karp, and Chris Grabenstein, he hopes eventually to transition into fiction writing full-time. So far his short stories have appeared in *Out of the Gutter* and the *Loch Raven Review,* in *Your Darkest Dreamspell,* an anthology, and in a dozen or so e-zines.

▪ Because of my background, I have an intense affection for the people, the culture, and the atmosphere of small-town America. Besides growing up in a small town, many times when traveling I will pull off the main highway and, if a town looks interesting, just park the car and spend the day talking to people, hanging out at the local restaurants and visiting the few shops and stores that aren't boarded up. I wanted to bring to life the colorful characters and places in most small towns. Some of the characters in my story are based on people I knew growing up, and some of them are based on people I've met in other small towns. A few, of course, are totally the product of my imagination but certainly *could* have been part of small-town life. This story is about a small town that is fading away, as many of them are in the Midwest. It has been interesting for me to watch this happen, because I was part of what was probably the first generation, at least in my town, to leave town right after high school with little inclination to return, unless visiting relatives. In every small town, when someone new moves in, it changes the texture of everyday life — sometimes not in good ways. Perhaps even in malevolent ways. I put a little twist on the idea with the mystery of whether the newcomer was really a newcomer or some evil that was finding its way back.

Kristine Kathryn Rusch has published novels in the mystery, science fiction, fantasy, and romance genres under a variety of names. Her Smokey Dalton mystery novels, written under the name Kris Nelscott, have received accolades worldwide. Under both names (Rusch and Nelscott), she has received Edgar nominations. Under the Rusch name, she has won the Ellery Queen Mystery Magazine Reader's Choice Award twice, the most recent time for "The Secret Lives of Cats," published in 2008. Her Retrieval Artist series, published as science fiction, are really science fiction mystery novels. The most recent, *Duplicate Effort,* appeared in February.

▪ When Lou Anders asked me to contribute a story to his alternate history mystery anthology, I happily said yes. I have written historical mysteries and alternate history science fiction novels, so I'm comfortable working in both genres.

Then I went about writing the story. I looked up several possible scenarios and got overwhelmed by the amount of research I needed. My husband, the writer Dean Wesley Smith, suggested I choose something set in the 1960s. I protested, saying that the sixties belong to my Kris Nelscott pen name, and I wasn't about to do a Smokey Dalton alternate history. But Dean kept at me, and he finally said, "What if something happens to J. Edgar Hoover in 1968?"

I stopped, thought, and realized that 1968 was too complicated to deal with. But what happens if Hoover died in early 1964, a few months after JFK? And suddenly I was off and running, researching Hoover, Bobby Kennedy, and those dark months after the first Kennedy assassination.

The story is doing well. I've expanded it into a novel, which I just started to market. The story itself will also appear in *The Year's Best Science Fiction,* edited by Gardner Dozois, which is, I think, the first time the same story has been chosen for a science fiction year's best and a mystery year's best.

I'm glad the story worked, since mystery short stories are always a balancing act and alternate history stories are a different kind of balancing act. I felt like one of those plate spinners as I wrote it — and I'm pleased that none of the plates crashed.

Jonathan Tel's collection of stories set in contemporary China, *The Beijing of Possibilities,* was published in June 2009. He is writing a screenplay based on the story in this anthology.

▪ I read an article in a regional newspaper in China about a man who for decades was suspected of a murder but never convicted and was at last cleared.

I used to live in Taos and hitched regularly to Santa Fe and Albuquerque. Often I got rides from truckers, most of them Hispanic, many of them alcoholics. So I invented Kent and conceived how he might be falsely accused. Also I've traveled in Chiapas and met witches there. Let the destiny of such a witch intersect with my hero's. I wrote the story rapidly, but for a long time I couldn't find an ending. After many revisions, the ending appeared.

Vu Tran's stories have appeared in *The O. Henry Prize Stories, The Southern Review, Glimmer Train Stories, Fence,* and many other publications. Vu Tran was born in Saigon, Vietnam, and raised in Oklahoma. He currently teaches literature and creative writing at the University of Nevada, Las Vegas, and is finishing his first novel.

▪ Las Vegas is an ideal backdrop for noir fiction. And not merely because of all the nefarious and salacious stuff that everyone knows (or at least hears) about. In a place where most people hail from somewhere else and constantly come and go, or have no idea where they're headed next, where there's a constant dynamic between the surface and the substance of things, constant even once you go beyond the Strip — in a place like this, ambiguity suffuses everyone's story. This is what I mean by *noir.* Shadows and vagaries. And for the same reason, Las Vegas is also a great backdrop for the immigrant story. Who, after all, proceeds with more ambiguity than a stranger who arrives in a strange land and must make a life among other strangers? Who has — and withholds — more stories? I suppose that Robert's dilemma in "This or Any Desert" is that the woman he believed he loved, believed was *his,* had always been an inaccessible stranger, and everything he does in the story is in part a way of denying that.

Other Distinguished Mystery Stories of 2008

ALLEN, PRESTON L.
  Crip. *Las Vegas Noir*, ed. Jarret Keene and Todd James Pierce (Akashic)
APPEL, JACOB M.
  Ad Valorem. *Subtropics*, Spring/Summer

BOLAND, JOHN C.
  Sargasso Sea. *Alfred Hitchcock's Mystery Magazine*, September
BORN, JAMES
  The Drought. *Blue Religion*, ed. Michael Connelly (Back Bay)
BUDEWITZ, LESLIE
  Snow Angels. *Thuglit*, April/May
BUENTELLO, JOHN
  A Certain Recollection. *Blue Religion*, ed. Michael Connelly (Back Bay)

CURRAN, COLLEEN
  The Dearborns Aren't Home. *Glimmer Train Stories*, Summer

FARRINGTON, ANTHONY
  Railway Killers. *Indiana Review*, Winter

GISCHLER, VICTOR
  Kill Posse. *Hardcore Hardboiled*, ed. Todd Robinson (Kensington)
GLASS, LESLIE
  The Herald. *Blue Religion*, ed. Michael Connelly (Back Bay)
GOLDBERG, TOD
  Mitzvah. *Las Vegas Noir*, ed. Jarret Keene and Todd James Pierce (Akashic)

HAGENSTON, BECKY
  Midnight, Licorice, Shadow. *Crazyhorse*, Fall

HILL, DIXON
A Thin Bright Line. *Ellery Queen's Mystery Magazine,* December

KOSMATKA, TED
The Art of Alchemy. *Fantasy & Science Fiction,* June

MACKER, TEDDY
The Wild Rubicon. *Antioch Review,* Summer
MORAN, TERRIE FARLEY
When a Bright Star Fades. *Hardluck Stories,* ed. Ed Gorman and David
Zeltserman
MURRAY, CHRISTINE
Can't Buy Me Love. *Toronto Noir,* ed. Janine Armin and Nathaniel G. Moore
(Akashic)

NADZAM, BONNIE
No Story. *Storyglossia,* May
NIX, SHELLEY
Monkey. *Hayden's Ferry Review,* Spring/Summer

PHILLIPS, SCOTT
Babs. *Las Vegas Noir,* ed. Jarret Keene and Todd James Pierce (Akashic)

RASH, RON
Into the Gorge. *Southern Review,* Autumn

SELLYN, NATHAN
The Emancipation of Christine Alpert. *Toronto Noir,* ed. Janine Armin and
Nathaniel G. Moore (Akashic)
SHEPARD, JIM
Classical Scenes of Farewell. *McSweeney's,* no. 27
SMITH, R. T.
Rose-Handled Pistol. *Louisiana Literature,* Spring/Summer

VINCENT, BEV
Rule Number One. *Blue Religion,* ed. Michael Connelly (Back Bay)

WHITE, HAL
Murder at the Fall Festival. *The Mysteries of Reverend Dean,* by Hal White
(Lighthouse)
WILLIAMS, TIM L.
Exposure. *Ellery Queen's Mystery Magazine,* April/May
WOODRELL, DANIEL
Night Stand. *Esquire,* June